PRAISE FOR

"Susan Stoker knows what women want. A hot hero who needs to save a damsel in distress . . . even if she can save herself!"

—CD Reiss, *New York Times* bestselling author

"Irresistible characters and seat-of-the-pants action will keep you glued to the pages."

—Elle James, *New York Times* bestselling author

"Susan does romantic suspense right! Edge of my seat + smokin' hot = read ALL of her books! Now."

—Carly Phillips, *New York Times* bestselling author

"Susan Stoker writes the perfect book boyfriends!"

—Laurann Dohner, *New York Times* bestselling author

"These books should come with a warning label. Once you start, you can't stop until you've read them all."

—Sharon Hamilton, *New York Times* bestselling author

"Susan Stoker never disappoints. She delivers alpha males with heart and heroines with moxie."

—Jana Aston, *New York Times* bestselling author

"Susan Stoker gives me everything I need in romance: heat, humor, intensity, and the perfect HEA."

—Carrie Ann Ryan, *New York Times* bestselling author

"Susan Stoker packs one heck of a punch!"

—Lainey Reese, *USA Today* bestselling author

DEFENDING RAVEN

DISCOVER OTHER TITLES BY SUSAN STOKER

Mountain Mercenaries Series

Defending Allye
Defending Chloe
Defending Morgan
Defending Harlow
Defending Everly
Defending Zara
Defending Raven

Silverstone Series

Trusting Skylar (December 2020)
Trusting Taylor (TBA)
Trusting Molly (TBA)
Trusting Cassidy (TBA)

Ace Security Series

Claiming Grace
Claiming Alexis
Claiming Bailey
Claiming Felicity
Claiming Sarah

Delta Force Heroes

Rescuing Rayne
Rescuing Aimee (novella)
Rescuing Emily
Rescuing Harley

Marrying Emily

Rescuing Kassie

Rescuing Bryn

Rescuing Casey

Rescuing Sadie (novella)

Rescuing Wendy

Rescuing Mary

Rescuing Macie (novella)

Delta Team Two Series

Shielding Gillian

Shielding Kinley (August 2020)

Shielding Aspen (October 2020)

Shielding Riley (January 2021)

Shielding Devyn (TBA)

Shielding Ember (TBA)

Shielding Sierra (TBA)

Badge of Honor: Texas Heroes Series

Justice for Mackenzie

Justice for Mickie

Justice for Corrie

Justice for Laine (novella)

Shelter for Elizabeth

Justice for Boone

Shelter for Adeline

Shelter for Sophie

Justice for Erin

Justice for Milena

Shelter for Blythe

Justice for Hope
Shelter for Quinn
Shelter for Koren
Shelter for Penelope

SEAL of Protection Series

Protecting Caroline
Protecting Alabama
Protecting Alabama's Kids (novella)
Protecting Fiona
Marrying Caroline (novella)
Protecting Summer
Protecting Cheyenne
Protecting Jessyka
Protecting Julie (novella)
Protecting Melody
Protecting the Future
Protecting Kiera (novella)
Protecting Dakota

SEAL of Protection: Legacy Series

Securing Caite
Securing Sidney
Securing Piper
Securing Zoey
Securing Avery
Securing Kalee (September 2020)
Securing Jane (February 2021)

Beyond Reality Series

Outback Hearts

Flaming Hearts

Frozen Hearts

Stand-Alone Novels

The Guardian Mist

A Princess for Cale

A Moment in Time (a short-story collection)

Lambert's Lady

Writing as Annie George

Stepbrother Virgin (erotic novella)

DEFENDING RAVEN

Mountain Mercenaries, Book 7

Susan Stoker

This is a work of fiction. Names, characters, organizations, places, events, and incidents are either products of the author's imagination or are used fictitiously.

Published by Montlake, Seattle

www.apub.com

ISBN-13: 9781542018593
ISBN-10: 1542018595

Cover design by Eileen Carey

Cover photography © 2019 Jean Woodfin/JW Photography and Cover

Printed in the United States of America

DEFENDING RAVEN

Chapter One

Dave "Rex" Justice couldn't sit still. He and the six men he'd been working with for a few years, along with Zara Layne, were on a private plane on their way to Lima, Peru.

No one had said much since boarding, probably still in shock from learning that the man who they knew as the bartender at The Pit was in reality the leader of the Mountain Mercenaries. The tension in the plane was thick as any he could remember, and his team had definitely been in tense situations in the past. Dave knew he should probably say something to lighten the mood, but he could think about only one thing. His wife.

He'd found her after ten agonizingly long years.

Well, *he* hadn't found her. Ironic, considering the amount of money, time, and effort he'd spent looking for her.

"Why don't you sit down, Dave," Gray suggested.

Dave ignored him. He couldn't sit. Couldn't eat, couldn't sleep. Knowing he was so close to seeing his wife again made him unable to do anything besides pace the short aisle in agitation.

What if she'd disappeared in the few months since Zara had last seen her?

What if he'd come this close, only to lose her again?

The thought was repugnant and unacceptable.

"I think it's time you told us the entire story about Rex and the Mountain Mercenaries," Black said.

Dave turned to look at the men he'd recruited and hired, and sighed. Black was right, they deserved some answers. Lord knew he'd been too stressed to do more than grunt in response since they'd refused to let him come down to Peru by himself.

He sat on the very edge of one of the leather chairs in the plane and faced the men he thought of as brothers. To them, however, he'd simply been Dave, the bartender. They hadn't suspected he could be the elusive "Rex," their handler and boss. He'd been able to keep eyes and ears on them because they spent a lot of time in The Pit, the bar he'd owned for years.

Ever since they'd each found a woman to love and cherish, however, they'd been spending less and less time in the bar, and he knew things were changing.

Yes. They'd earned some answers. But after Zara, Meat's fiancée, had recognized his Raven from a picture posted behind the bar, Dave hadn't been able to think about anything other than getting to his wife.

Sighing again, he ran a hand through his dark-brown hair. He wasn't sure exactly where to start. The last decade had been one crushing disappointment after another when it came to the search for Raven, and to be this close now was literally about to drive him crazy.

"As you're now aware, I'm the man you used to know as Rex," he finally said. His southern accent was more pronounced, probably because he hadn't gotten much more than two hours of sleep in the last twenty-four. He'd been busy arranging for a flight to Peru and running through different scenarios as to how the reunion with his long-lost wife might go.

"After my wife disappeared, law enforcement officials in Las Vegas did what they could to find her, but their time and abilities were limited. After her case went cold, I began learning as much as I could about the sex-trafficking industry. I scoured the internet and quickly learned exactly how depraved mankind could be. In the process of looking for my wife, however, I stumbled across other missing women . . . and children. But I didn't have any way of helping them. All I could do was turn over the information to law enforcement in their hometowns and hope they acted on it. It was frustrating and sickening. So I started thinking about the what-ifs . . .

"What if I got a group of men together who could go in and rescue the people I'd found through my research? What if I could return wives, sisters, children, to their families? I know what it would've meant to *me* if someone had found Raven and helped her get back home. Through my research and my rather uncanny ability to find people, I'd already made some good connections in the government and with some other very powerful people. When word got out about what I was doing, how I was successfully tracking down kidnapping victims, I even began to get . . . donations. You wouldn't believe the amount of money that was thrown my way. Relatives of people we've found, organizations who advocate for the missing and abused, all sorts of people and groups were willing to give money to aid the cause.

"Once I realized I needed boots on the ground, and that simply finding people on the computer wasn't good enough, I began looking for men I could trust to go in and rescue the helpless victims I'd found. I researched each and every one of you, and handpicked you because of your military records and your expertise in different areas.

"Black, you're the best negotiator I've ever seen. Meat, you, of course, are a genius with computers. Ro's ability with cars and engines is unparalleled. Gray, your skill at being invisible on missions is legendary, and Ball, you can outdrive just about anyone on the planet. As for Arrow . . . you're just an all-around badass. I needed the best of the best, and you all were it."

"So, you wanted us to find your wife?" Ro asked. "Hell, Rex . . . er . . . Dave, we didn't even *know* about your wife until a year or so ago."

Dave shook his head. "Yes and no. I mean, if I found her, I definitely wanted men I could trust to go and get her, but it was more than that." He shook his head. "I suppose I need to go back to the beginning."

Seven pairs of eyes simply watched Dave intently without interrupting, which he appreciated.

"My wife's name is Margaret. Her family calls her Mags. I thought it was cute and started calling her Magpie. It didn't seem to fit her, though, so I eventually settled on Raven. With her long, black hair and her nickname, it fit. Anyway, ten or so years ago, we went to Las Vegas to celebrate our five-year anniversary. We were more in love than ever, and it had been a while since either of us had taken a break from our jobs. I had bought this bar right before we met, and had been working long hours for years to make it a success. I loved it, and *was* successful, so I wanted to give my wife something special. A trip to remember.

"Raven was an insurance underwriter. We had completely normal and boring lives, so spending a week in Vegas seemed exciting and extravagant. It was on our fourth night there when we decided instead of going to another show, we would check out some of the popular and famous clubs on the strip. We both knew to be careful about our drinks and not to let them out of our sight. I mean, I'm a bartender—I know all about date-rape drugs. We were cautious, but also having a good time. Drinking and enjoying spending time together."

Dave paused and took a deep breath. He hated thinking about that night, about the terror he'd felt. There were so many things he wished he'd done differently, and he'd spent all the years since kicking his own ass for being so careless with his wife's safety.

He continued, knowing he owed it to the men around him.

"It was around two in the morning or so, and we were in a club at one of the casinos. Raven said that she needed to use the restroom. I didn't think anything of it. I kissed her and told her I'd order us a round while she was gone. She turned around and blew me a kiss before disappearing into a crowd of people on the other side of the bar near the restrooms. That was the last time I saw her.

"After about ten minutes, I started to get concerned, as she usually doesn't take so long, so I went looking for her. There was a line to get into the restroom, but none of the women there had seen Raven. I even had one check inside the bathroom, but Raven wasn't there. I figured I'd just missed her and went back to our table. When she didn't return after another couple minutes, I wasn't sure what to do. I called her phone, and it went straight to voice mail. I wondered if she'd gotten sick or something and had gone back to our hotel room.

"Stupidly, I left the bar and walked all the way back to our hotel, but when I got there, she wasn't in the room. I panicked then. I had no idea what to do. I called the police, but they pretty much laughed and said she'd most likely turn up soon. I *knew* something was wrong, but couldn't get anyone to believe me. It was Vegas, after all. The cops just assumed Raven had been drunk, or was maybe even having a wild affair with someone she'd met. It wasn't until two days had passed with absolutely no sign of her that the cops finally took me seriously. But by then, it was too late. Way too fucking late."

Dave took a deep breath to try to get some control over his emotions.

"Did they check the surveillance cameras?" Meat asked.

Dave nodded. "Yeah. She exited the restroom, and a guy came up to her and put his arm around her shoulders. He leaned down and said something to her . . . and she walked out of the hallway, through the crowd, and straight out the door, toward the casino. She didn't call out for me or try to signal anyone in any way."

"So he threatened her," Gray surmised.

"I'm guessing he told her something had happened to me, or that something *would* happen to me if she struggled or brought attention to herself," Dave agreed. His voice lowered. "I was pissed as hell at her for that for quite a while," he admitted. "I know she was probably worried and scared, but look at me." He threw his arms out. "I'm not exactly the kind of guy people mess with."

Dave knew he was intimidating. He was a big man. Very big. His biceps were huge—he worked out a lot, including back then, and took pride in looking scary enough that people thought twice about messing with him. His current beard gave him even more of a wild look. Between his height, his bulk, and his looks, people didn't often fuck with him. His skin was naturally dark, and even though ten years ago he hadn't had the large scar that went down the side of his neck, he'd still been big and mean-looking.

"The police had no leads at all?" Zara asked quietly.

Meat had argued against his fiancée coming with them to Peru, especially because she didn't have very good memories of her time there, but she was adamant. She'd argued that she spoke fluent Spanish, and they'd need her to talk to the residents in the barrio where she'd last seen Mags. If Raven had moved on, Zara could talk to people she knew and hopefully find out where she'd gone. Dave wasn't thrilled about having to put her back into a situation that could bring up painful memories, but he'd never been as close to finding his wife as he was right now, and he'd use whatever assistance he could get if it meant rescuing Raven.

Over the years, various police officers, detectives, and private investigators had suggested that he move on, that his wife was most likely dead, but Dave had refused. It may have been crazy, but he truly felt as if he'd know if she was deceased. Something deep within him would instinctively feel it.

When Gray cleared his throat, Dave remembered that Zara had asked him a question.

"None that actually went anywhere. I have no idea what happened to her. One second she was there, and the next she was gone. Even with all the cameras in Vegas, no one could track where that man took her. He helped her into a four-door sedan, which was waiting at the front of the hotel, but the windows were tinted. The license plates were stolen and were a dead end. The police did their best, but it was no use. She was gone. *Poof.* After a while, they had other cases to solve, and because I didn't even live there, I couldn't keep the kind of pressure on the detectives that I would've liked. Raven was a damn statistic before a year had passed. The cops assumed she was dead and urged me to get on with my life."

Dave snorted. "As if that was possible. Raven was my everything. She was the light to my dark. I didn't realize how much she smoothed out my rough edges until she was gone. I kept The Pit going, simply because if she somehow got away from her captors, she'd know where to go. Where to find me. But after another year passed, I knew she wasn't going to miraculously appear on my doorstep. It was going to be up to me to find her.

"That's when I began to do research. I learned more than I ever wanted to about sex trafficking and exactly how many women and children get caught in its clutches every year. I looked at case studies of women who'd escaped and learned how the operations typically worked. I got in touch with someone via the internet who taught me the ins and outs of hacking and video surveillance. I didn't sleep a lot, and I kept what I was doing a secret from the few friends who hadn't given up on me."

"So, I'm curious," Ball interjected. "You truly don't have *any* military experience?"

Dave shook his head.

"How in the fuck have you been able to talk tactics and weapons, plan missions, and basically make yourself sound like you've spent your entire life in the military?" Arrow asked.

"I told you. I did a lot of research," Dave replied. Seeing the disbelief on everyone's faces, he shrugged slightly. "And this right here is why I never told you who I was."

"You should've," Gray said, the anger easy to hear in his tone.

"Why?" Dave shot back. "So you could turn me down? Think less of me because I wasn't Special Forces? I needed you to trust me. To treat me like a valued member of the team. If you knew I was merely a man desperate to find his wife—and just a bartender, to boot—would any of you have taken the job?"

An awkward silence followed his question.

"Exactly," Dave said more quietly after a moment. "I know what I did was underhanded. But becoming the mysterious and elusive Rex is the only reason the Mountain Mercenaries even exist. I left the dangerous hands-on stuff to you guys, and I dug up all the information you needed in order to be successful. I'm not going to apologize or beg for your forgiveness. We're a damn good team, and just because I wasn't Delta or a SEAL or SAS or any other kind of supersoldier like you guys were doesn't mean I haven't worked my ass off to keep you safe every single time you went on a mission. I've bent over backward to make connections and cultivate valuable relationships. Yes, at first I merely wanted a team to go in and save the women and children I'd found during the hunt for my wife, just so I could sleep at night, but the Mountain Mercenaries quickly became more than that. You guys became my friends, even if you didn't know who I was. I worried about you, and I prayed every time you left that I'd see you again."

"I have to admit, I'm not thrilled with everything you did," Meat said. "But none of us would've gone along with any of the missions if we didn't trust your intel. You're one hell of a leader, despite your lack of training, and I can't speak for everyone else, but I'd trust you with my life, and the life of my woman, any day of the week."

"Same here," Gray admitted. "You've come through time and time again. It's actually pretty fucking amazing that you've learned what you have all on your own."

"Agreed," Ball said. "The fact that you basically learned military tactics from just research and gained as many supporters as you have is a small miracle."

"So . . . now that we know the truth, what's the plan when we get to Peru?" Black asked.

"Especially since you aren't military," Arrow added. "You might be good at planning a mission, but that doesn't exactly translate into being an accurate shot or knowing how to infiltrate an enemy's stronghold."

"I agree. And I need your help more than ever. I can barely hold a thought long enough to come up with a plan. I'd love to just go into the barrio, grab Raven, and get the hell out, but after talking to Zara about the person Raven is now, and knowing what we know about the barrio from the last mission there, I'm not sure that's going to work," Dave said.

"We know the barrio's dangerous as fuck, and we can't go in there being too cocky," Meat said. "That's what got me in trouble last time. I'm thinking we get our asses over there and assess the situation. There's a chance Mags isn't even there anymore."

Dave's fists clenched. Raven had to be there. She *had* to. He couldn't get this close to finding her, only to fail now.

"I don't think she would've left," Zara assured them. "She's pretty entrenched there, with the other women she helps and all."

"Right. Okay, so we go in, check things out in the barrio, and then you can approach your wife," Meat concluded. "If she's nervous about you or not sure she wants to go . . . you're going to have to talk her into it, I guess."

Dave chuckled, but it wasn't in amusement. "Raven's always been pretty hard to convince to do anything she doesn't want to. I mean, I'm hoping she'll be head-over-heels happy to see me, but I'm guessing there's a lot more to her situation than we know."

"Agreed," Gray said. "We'll have your back while you meet with her, and we'll go from there."

"It's not much of a plan," Ro commented.

Dave shrugged. "I'm truly hoping this will be an easy in-and-out thing, but if it's not, we can refine as we go. I've kept Raven's passport up to date using an age-progression picture that an ex-FBI friend made for me. Not exactly legal, but I've got enough people who owe me that it was overlooked. That . . . and I'm sure no one thought I'd ever find Raven and have a chance to actually use it," Dave said.

"We're going as tourists," Ball said. "Thousands of people do it every year. I'm sure no one will scrutinize her passport that closely."

"While we're there, I'd love to see about finding a place to set up a free clinic," Zara threw out. "God knows the people in the barrios could use it. And if anything happens, maybe you guys can use that as a reason as to why we're there. The barrios aren't exactly a typical tourist destination."

"She's got a good point," Meat said, putting his arm around her. "A humanitarian effort as a reason for our visit would probably put a lot of eyes on us, but if push comes to shove, we can throw that out as a secondary reason why we're there."

"Del Rio might be an issue with the clinic, however. He likes to keep people dependent and under his thumb, all while acting like a benevolent leader helping out those less fortunate. Having a free clinic might take away some of the attention that he craves," Zara said.

"Fuck. That guy again?" Black asked.

Zara nodded.

Dave's eyes narrowed. They all knew about Roberto del Rio. He was one of the worst sex traffickers Dave had ever come across. He had no morals, no scruples. They'd learned the last time they were in Peru that he trafficked children as well as women.

A couple months ago, Dave had been more than happy to volunteer the Mountain Mercenaries to go to Peru and assist in a mission to save local children bound for the sex trade in Lima—but everything had gone wrong. Mostly because del Rio didn't want their mission to succeed. He had a lot of influence in the country. Since then, Dave had learned the majority of the police force, locals, and even the military were either under his control or being paid to look the other way.

But honestly, at the moment, Dave was having a hard time caring about anything other than Raven. From what Zara had said, Raven hated del Rio and no longer had anything to do with him, so for now, del Rio wasn't their objective. Finding and rescuing Dave's wife *was*.

Dave leaned forward and said in a somewhat desperate tone, "No offense, Zara—I'm happy to help set up a clinic and bribe whoever we have to, but my main objective on this trip is to go into that barrio, grab my wife, and get the fuck out."

"It probably won't be that easy," Zara told him.

Dave nodded. "I know. Raven and I have been separated longer than we were together. She's been through a kind of hell I can't even begin to understand. But I'm not leaving without her." The last was said a bit harsher than he'd intended, but it didn't matter. He *wouldn't* leave the country without Raven.

"She might not want to leave," Zara said quietly.

Dave ground his teeth together to keep the sharp words that sprang to mind from escaping.

"The Mags I know is as independent as anyone I've ever met," Zara went on. "She's smart and doesn't show a lot of emotion. When she was trying to convince me to tell Meat that I was an American, to share my story and get him to take me back to the States, I asked if she would come with me. I knew about the time she'd spent working for del Rio, but to me, she was a fellow American. She didn't seem all that happy to be here, but when I asked her to come with me, she shook her head and said her life was in Peru."

Zara's words were more painful than anything Dave had ever heard.

He had no idea *why* Raven hadn't jumped at the chance to get back to the States. Back to *him*.

"Is she being held captive there?" he asked.

Zara slowly shook her head. "Not that I know of. But I've always thought something wasn't quite right about her situation. Three days a week, she's gone most of the day and doesn't tell anyone where she goes.

But she always comes back to the barrio before the sun goes down. I haven't seen anyone following her, and she doesn't act like she's being threatened. Well . . . any more than anyone else, that is."

"What do you mean?" Meat asked, putting his hand on his fiancée's knee.

"Just that life as a woman in the barrio, especially one without a husband, isn't exactly a walk in the park. We always had to worry about Ruben or one of his friends stealing what food we'd managed to scavenge, or . . . you know."

Dave saw each and every one of the men frown in anger. Yeah, they knew what Zara meant. She'd already told them all about Ruben Martínez and his friends in the barrio. Zara guessed him to be in his mid-twenties. He thought he was not only God's gift to women, but some sort of untouchable badass. He and his gang harassed everyone in the barrio and didn't hesitate to take what they wanted, using force whenever necessary.

They were also the ones who'd beaten up Meat and Black. Every single one of the Mountain Mercenaries was hoping to have a run-in with the gang, if only for a little payback.

"All I'm saying," Zara continued, "is that out of all the women I got to know, Mags is the only one who never talked about getting out of the barrio. She just seemed to accept her situation. Everyone else dreamed about either finding a husband wealthy enough to have a place to live outside the barrio, or getting back to their families in the countries they were kidnapped from to work for del Rio."

"Raven's life is *not* in Peru," Dave stated. "It's in Colorado, with me."

Seeing the uneasy and pitying looks his friends were giving him, Dave couldn't bear to sit still any longer. He sprang to his feet and resumed his pacing.

He didn't know why Raven hadn't attempted to contact him. He didn't know what she'd been through over the last ten years, although he could guess. But none of that mattered. All that mattered was that she was still the woman he loved with all his heart. Nothing she'd done or been made to do over the years would ever change that.

He had no idea what he'd be up against when he finally set eyes on her again, but he wasn't giving up on his wife, not after all these years.

Impatiently, Dave looked at his watch and swore. It was taking way too long to get there. And every minute that passed was one more minute during which Raven could slip out of his life without a trace. Again. Someone could hurt her, or she could be kidnapped again.

"I'm coming for you, sweetheart," he whispered as he paced. "Just keep hanging on until I can get there."

Chapter Two

Margaret "Mags" Crawford Justice held back a groan as she shifted on the hard-packed dirt in the ramshackle hut she was currently sharing with five other women. They were all at least a decade younger than she was, and she was feeling every day of her forty-two years.

Life certainly hadn't gone the way she'd expected it to, but she had to keep going. One day at a time. It had been her motto for the last ten years.

She sighed in disappointment that she'd be spending all day in the barrio with her friends. It wasn't that she didn't like Gabriella and the others—very much the contrary. It was just that she much preferred Mondays, Wednesdays, and Fridays.

Her stomach was empty, but that wasn't anything unusual. She'd gotten as used to the hunger pains as she had the dirt and filth all around her.

Mags rolled over and stood. It was still dark out, but she hadn't been sleeping well lately. She worried about her friend Zara, who had gone back to the States a few months ago. She worried about Maria and the other women she lived with. She worried about Ruben and his gang of assholes who patrolled the barrio day in and day out. She worried about where they were going to find enough food to eat for the day . . .

And she worried about her husband.

It wasn't often she let herself think about Dave, but for some reason, she hadn't been able to put him out of her mind lately. Probably because Zara had returned to the US.

How Mags wished she could've gone with her.

Once upon a time, she would've done absolutely anything to get back to Colorado, back to Dave. She would've swallowed the deep shame she felt over everything she'd done if only she could see her husband again. To have his arms around her, telling her she was safe and loved.

But too much time had gone by now. Not only was she a completely different person than she used to be, and her husband had probably moved on and remarried, but she simply couldn't leave. Lima was her home now, for better or worse.

Being as quiet as she could, Mags headed behind a piece of metal set up as a crude privacy screen and did her business in a bucket, something that would've disturbed her ten years ago, but now she didn't even think twice about it. They didn't have a lot of food left, and Mags wanted to get to the bakery quickly to have first pick of the day-old bread that was thrown away each morning. The shop was about a mile away, and she needed to get going.

But first she paused to check on the other women, who were still sleeping.

Gabriella had grown up in the barrio. She was the only native Peruvian out of the lot of them. Teresa and Bonita were from Brazil. Carmen said she was Venezuelan, and Maria was from Mexico. They were a ragtag lot, but they shared a bond most people couldn't begin to understand. Except for Gabriella, they'd all been "guests" of del Rio's. They'd been used and abused and tossed out without a second thought when they'd become useless to him. Other than Maria, they'd all learned Spanish after being kidnapped and all spoke with differing accents, but they were able to understand each other without issue.

Teresa's eyes opened, and Mags crouched down by her pallet on the ground. "I'm going to the baker's. I'll be back as soon as I can," she said quietly.

The other woman nodded. "Do you want me to come with you?"

Mags shook her head. "I'll be okay. We do need some water. If you and the others feel up to it, maybe you could make a water run?"

"Okay. We can do that. Mags?"

"Yeah?"

"Do you think Zara is all right?"

Blinking in surprise, Mags nodded. "Yes. Why?"

"I don't know. I had a dream about her."

"Good dream or bad dream?" Mags asked.

"Good," Teresa said quickly.

"Well, maybe that means we'll hear from her soon. She said that when she did get back to America, she'd do what she could to send word once she was settled."

"Hopefully," Teresa said. "Go on, before it gets too late and someone else takes the bread."

Mags smiled and nodded. "Be safe while I'm gone." She stood and, besides running a quick hand through her hair, didn't think twice about her appearance. Her hair was greasy and dirty and tended to get into knots quite easily, but she couldn't bear to cut it. It was far longer than it had been a decade ago, hanging past the middle of her back. She'd broken down and trimmed it a few times, but never too short.

A memory of how Dave used to love to run his fingers through her hair flickered through her mind. He'd always had a lock of it in his hand. Whenever they were sitting next to each other, whether they were alone at home or in a crowded restaurant, he'd put his arm around her and run a strand through his fingers. He'd loved her midnight-black hair, and had nicknamed her Raven because of it.

He'd be shocked to see her hair now. Choppy ends, greasy, covered in dirt, dull and limp.

She used to take such pride in her looks, but now she rarely gave her hair more than a second thought. Only enough to pull it into a ponytail at the nape of her neck to keep it out of her face.

She slipped out of the hut and moved the piece of corrugated metal they used as a door back into place before heading down one of the dusty alleys to the exit of the barrio. Praying she wouldn't run into Ruben or any of his friends, she held her breath . . . and let it out on a loud exhale as she successfully made it to one of the openings in the wall on the south side of the barrio. It was a bit early for any of the bullies who prowled the area to be up and about. They were most likely still sleeping off the effects of the alcohol they'd managed to steal the night before.

Mags tucked her chin into her chest and tried to look as unassuming as possible as she made her way toward the bakery. She was average height for a woman, though when she'd walked next to Dave, she'd felt absolutely tiny.

Cursing under her breath at the way her thoughts kept turning to her husband, Mags took a deep breath. She suspected she'd also been thinking about him lately because of the Americans who had shown up in the barrio a few months ago. Her husband wasn't a military guy, but something about them had reminded her of Dave. Including their loyalty and determination.

Dave was smart. So much smarter than anyone gave him credit for. And successful. At least, he had been a decade ago. He'd bought a run-down building, kept the outside looking mostly the same—according to the pictures he'd shown her when they met—and spruced up the inside of the bar, making it comfortable and homey, not so fancy that people in the working-class neighborhood would feel intimidated stopping in for a beer after work. He'd been protective of his patrons, insisting on walking single women to their cars and kicking out anyone who dared give another customer a hard time.

Neither of them had a lot of friends back then, but they didn't need them, not when they had each other. Memories of them just vegging on their couch, watching television and eating takeout, were painful enough that she did her best to push *all* memories of her husband to the back of her mind.

Dave was in her past. There was no room for him in her present . . . not that he'd want anything to do with her now.

She arrived at the alley behind the bakery just in time. She watched as one of the employees slammed the lid of the trash can behind the store and headed back inside. Mags hurried over to the trash and opened the lid. The smell of rotten food and curdled milk was overwhelming, but she was used to it. There wasn't much today, but Mags pulled out the plastic bag she always carried around, just in case, and filled it with stale bread. There was also a cinnamon roll, and after brushing off some coffee grounds, Mags knew Gabriella would be thrilled with it.

Knowing she needed to get going, she quietly shut the lid of the trash can and turned around to head back to the barrio.

But she stopped in her tracks.

Standing behind her was a small boy, probably around eight or so. His cheeks were so gaunt he looked like a stiff breeze would blow him over. She'd never seen him before, and her heart immediately went out to him. She wished she could just ignore him and go on her way, but Mags knew she couldn't.

"Hello," she said in Spanish.

He didn't respond and, in fact, took a step away from her.

"Are you here looking for food?"

He nodded once.

Knowing she'd taken most of the edible bread out of the trash can already, Mags knelt on the ground, pulled one of the long loaves out of her bag, and held it out. "Here. Take this."

When the boy didn't come forward, she said, "It's okay. I'm not going to hurt you. Have you got a family somewhere?"

He gave her another small nod.

"I bet they're hungry, too, huh?"

He nodded again.

"Right, so come on, take this bread before someone else comes along and decides to take it for himself."

With that, the boy moved so fast, Mags almost didn't see him. One second she was holding the bread out, and the next it was under his shirt and he was backing away from her once more. She couldn't help but be impressed.

"Advice . . . get here a little earlier on Mondays, Wednesdays, and Fridays, and you'll have the trash can all to yourself and you can get a lot more. I'm here on Tuesdays and Thursdays and sometimes the weekends. We'll share the bounty. Okay?"

She knew the boy didn't have to agree with her, but he nodded again anyway, then turned and ran out of the alley.

Sighing, Mags stood. The boy's brown hair had been messy, and his face was covered in dirt, like many of the people who lived in the barrios, and she couldn't help but imagine what he might've looked like a few years ago. Before he'd lost his innocence completely. Before life in the barrios had changed him.

She didn't have to think too hard; she easily guessed what he may have looked like. How the excitement of a new day might've shone in his eyes, how he probably took great pleasure in the smallest things.

But children had to grow up quickly in the barrios, and it was heart wrenching and sad.

Knowing she couldn't linger, lest others came by and simply took by force the bread she and her friends so badly needed, Mags took a deep breath and headed back the way she had come.

By the time she got back to the barrio, the sun was up. People were out and about, and while she knew most of them, the locals tended to keep to themselves. Mostly out of self-preservation.

When she turned a corner to head to the hut she shared with the others, Mags froze.

Teresa, Gabriella, Bonita, Carmen, and Maria were all standing outside, with Ruben and Marcus watching over them.

Cursing under her breath, Mags hurried toward them.

She wasn't exactly scared of Ruben's gang, but she wasn't an idiot either. She'd seen them take down two of the Americans quite easily, and if they could do that to them, they could seriously hurt or kill her and her friends.

"What's going on?" she asked with as much bravado as she could muster.

"Thanks for breakfast!" Marcus exclaimed as he tried to wrench the plastic bag out of her hand.

Mags held on, refusing to let go. But Ruben walked over and, calmly and without hesitation, hit her in the face.

Her head went flying backward, and she fell onto her tailbone in the dirt.

"What we want, we take," Ruben snarled. "You want to keep living here, you gotta pay your dues."

Mags held a hand to her face and stayed on the ground, glaring up at him. God, she hated this place. Hated everything about it.

Fortuno, Eberto, and Alfonso walked out of the women's hut carrying a pot Carmen had found the other day, a large jug of water that one of the women had probably just lugged back, and two plastic bags full of other odds and ends the women had worked hard to scavenge.

"Looks like you girls have been holding out on us," Eberto sneered. "We're not too happy. If I were you, I'd do what I can to make it up to us. Gabriella, how 'bout it? I'm sure spending a little one-on-one time with Ruben would go a long way toward softening him up. Maybe he'd even let you keep some of the things you've so painstakingly collected. Your place is looking a bit sparse."

Mags bit her tongue to keep herself from telling Eberto what an asshole he was, and declaring Ruben wouldn't put a finger on Gabriella as long as she was alive and kicking. It was no secret the leader of the group of punks wanted the younger woman.

Maria helped Mags stand up, and they all glared at the laughing men as they sauntered down the alley toward their next target.

"Are you all right?" Bonita asked.

"Let me see," Carmen ordered, pulling at the hand Mags used to cover her cheek.

"I'm fine," Mags told them. "It's nothing I haven't experienced before. Come on, let's go see what the damage is."

They all filed inside the hut, and Mags wanted to rage at the destruction that met her gaze.

Alfonso and the others had thrown everything everywhere. The pallets they slept on had been sliced with knives, likely to make sure they hadn't hidden anything valuable inside the thin material. They'd left the things that were already broken and not worth taking, like a few cracked mugs and plates and some tattered clothing.

It had been a while since their hut had been searched and plundered, but Mags was tired of it. So fucking tired.

And now they were all hungry as well. All she wanted to do was sit in the dirt and cry.

Life wasn't fair. But she didn't have the time or energy to sit around and wallow. If they were going to eat, they had to get to work.

Mags had a second to be grateful the "ambulance" they used—actually, a bicycle with a small trailer attached—was hidden in a nearby alley, disguised among the trash that had built up and never been removed by the city officials. Marcus and the others would surely have stolen that from them as well.

"I'll take the bicycle and head to the dump," Mags informed her friends. "See what I can scavenge."

"I'll come too," Gabriella declared.

"Me and Bonita will see if we can find a corner to beg from," Carmen said.

"And I'll clean up in here," Maria finished.

"I know a guy who will give me money," Teresa declared.

Mags shook her head immediately and walked over to Teresa. She put her hands on her shoulders and captured her gaze. She was small, like Zara had been, and one of the younger women in their group. "No. Selling your body is not the way. Del Rio may have forced us to do that, but that's *not* who we are any longer."

"What are we supposed to do, then, Mags?" Teresa asked angrily. "Every time we manage to get anything to make our lives easier, Ruben and his friends come and take it all. We can't get jobs, and we can't continue to scavenge from the trash for the rest of our lives. Sometimes I think things were easier with del Rio, that we should've tried harder to stay."

Mags shook her head and tightened her hold on Teresa's shoulders. But she also looked around at the others while she spoke. "One more day," she said, quietly but firmly. "That's it. We take one day at a time; we just have to hold on one more day. Things will get better. Yes, we'll have some setbacks, but living here with nothing but the clothes on our backs is better than being used by del Rio. Better than him selling our bodies and giving us nothing in return."

"But we had food," Bonita said softly. "And a roof over our heads that didn't leak when it rained."

"And we didn't have to worry every day about Ruben and his friends stealing from us," Maria added.

"So you'd rather deal with del Rio's customers, who took what they liked no matter what *you* wanted? The ones who beat the crap out of us just because it made them feel strong and powerful? The men who didn't bother to ask our names before making us strip and get on our hands and knees? We didn't even *have* names. We were merely holes for them to stick their dicks into. Faceless and nameless. I'd rather live here, hungry, getting wet when it rains, than let *any* man touch me again," Mags said fiercely.

"We know you're going back there three days a week!" Teresa retorted. "Are you going to try to tell us you aren't getting food and special treatment while you're there?"

Mags's chest instantly tightened. She didn't want to talk about that. About the deal she'd made with the devil himself. But Teresa and the others had a right to question her. She'd do the same if she was in their shoes. "I am *not* going to del Rio's compound. He's not selling my body anymore. I eat *nothing*. I get *no* special treatment. When I do have to see him, he treats me like the dirt on the bottom of his shoes," she assured them.

"And yet you go wherever it is you're going, week after week. Why?" Bonita asked.

Mags wanted to tell them. Wanted to explain why she walked five miles and back to a house del Rio owned, three days a week. But she couldn't. It wouldn't be just *her* life on the line if del Rio ever found out. He'd told her in no uncertain terms that if she told anyone where she was going and what she was doing, she'd regret it. And she knew without a doubt he would keep his word, and that he had ways of hurting her that were a thousand times worse than merely allowing men to use her however they wished. She wouldn't risk it. Not for anyone.

"I would do anything for you guys," Mags told her only friends honestly. "And I'd tell you if I could. But I can't. You *know* del Rio has eyes and ears everywhere. I can't risk it. But I swear on my honor that I'm not getting special treatment. No food. If I was, I'd bring it back here and give it to *you* before eating it myself."

She didn't think the others were going to let it go, but finally, Carmen, who'd been a captive of del Rio's for as long as Mags had, nodded. "If you say you aren't holding back on us, then I believe you. Just . . . be careful. Del Rio is not to be trusted. You know this. He is a snake, and making any kind of deal with him is dangerous."

"I know," Mags whispered. And she did. She knew all too well . . . but it was too late.

"Okay, then let us get going," Carmen said. "Teresa, stay here with Maria. It'll be safer. The rest of us will find something for us to have for dinner. Promise."

"Be safe," Maria and Teresa said at the same time.

Everyone nodded, and one by one they slipped out of the hut and headed for their destinations. Mags left before Gabriella and waited in the alley with the bicycle for her to arrive. Within ten minutes, she snuck around the corner and, without a word of protest, climbed into the secret compartment of the trailer and got settled.

Mags shut the hinged lid and made sure the trash on top was strategically placed, so it looked like she was merely pulling a load of worthless plastic and wood. "Here we go," she told Gabriella.

It wasn't easy pulling the trailer with more than a hundred pounds inside, and Mags felt every year of her age, but there wasn't anyone else around to do what needed to be done.

"One day at a time," she muttered. Then, clenching her teeth and ignoring the pain in her thighs, she headed for the nearest dump.

Chapter Three

Dave was jumpy as hell. And impatient. He wanted to get the hell out of the airport and head to the barrio as soon as possible. But they'd had to go through customs, then rent a couple minivans, which took forever. Then they'd gotten stuck in a traffic jam, which irritated the hell out of all of them. *Then*, because someone hadn't filled one of the minivans with gas, they'd almost broken down on the highway.

Nothing was going right, and it was all Dave could do to keep his cool. When they were finally pulling up to the motel where they'd be staying, near the barrio, Dave mumbled, "If all goes well, we can be out of this fucking place and back to the States by morning."

Zara stared at Meat in bewilderment. "Is he serious?"

"I'm guessing."

She shook her head. "I'm sorry, but I really don't think that's how this is gonna go," Zara told them, reiterating the opinion she'd shared on the plane.

"Why do you think so?" Meat asked.

"I don't want to be the downer here, but Dave, your wife has been living a completely different life for ten years. She never told any of us about her life in the States, or about you. None of us talked much about what brought us to the barrio either, but I know Mags . . . suffered."

Dave frowned at Zara's words. He knew she'd suffered. Not a day had gone by over the last decade *without* him thinking about what she'd been through. And the thought of his beautiful wife hurting was enough to make him want to kill someone. But to be so close, yet feel so far away from her still, was killing him.

"And no, I can't tell you specifically *how* she suffered, because I don't know the details. But I think it's obvious. She once said that the only reason she was allowed to leave del Rio's employment was because she got too old. The bastard's actually somewhat picky about the women he forces to work for him, which is why the others—Teresa, Bonita, Maria, and Carmen—were all kicked out too. I don't know what happened with them, but they're all very thankful they were fired. Life in del Rio's compound was hell. And not something any woman can truly ever fully recover from. I just . . ." She shook her head. "I just don't think Mags is going to take one look at you and simply agree to leave right that second."

Dave hated pretty much everything Zara had just said. He knew this wasn't going to be easy, but Raven was his *wife*. They loved each other. The five years they'd been married had been the happiest he'd ever been in his life. Why *wouldn't* she want to get the fuck out of Peru after everything she'd been through and go home with him? He had no answers to that question, and it bugged him.

"She's right," Arrow said. "I know what my Morgan went through, trying to recover from everything that happened to her, and if your wife was in the sex trade for years, she's going to be a completely different person. She might not be anxious, or even *able*, to resume your life together."

Dave clenched his teeth. "You're all tiptoeing around what I already know. I know why my wife was kidnapped. She's fucking beautiful, and some asshole decided she'd be the perfect addition to his stable of women. I have no doubt she was raped and abused for years. I don't know for sure what happened between the time she was taken from me and when she showed up in the barrio, but what you aren't understanding is that *I don't give a shit*. I vowed to be with her for richer or poorer.

Through sickness and health. To love her until death do us part. And dammit, death hasn't parted us, and I love her just as much today as I did that day ten years ago when she was ripped away from me!

"Love isn't about just being with someone when things are good. And I love Raven. With everything I am. I've spent the last decade looking for her. I'm also not stupid. I know she's not going to take one look at me, throw her arms around me, and let me carry her off into the sunset. But I'm not going to wait one more minute to let her know that I'm here. That she's safe. That things are going to be all right from here on out."

"At least let me approach her first," Zara begged. "I can explain what's going on and that you're here to talk to her."

"No," Meat said emphatically. "You aren't going back into that barrio by yourself. No fucking way."

Zara turned to face her fiancé. "I didn't mean going by myself. I'm guessing Ruben and his gang of assholes are still around, and if I ran into them on my own, I'd be in big trouble. But I truly think letting me see her, talk to her alone while you guys all wait nearby, would be best."

"I can't stand the thought of you going back there," Meat said a little less harshly.

"I know, but think about it. If all seven of you show up at once, demanding to know where Mags is, people are gonna freak. But if I go in and *explain* what's going on, Dave will have a better chance of being able to talk to Mags without it turning into a huge battle of wills. And believe me, Mags is stubborn. She's had to be. Besides," she went on, "the women don't really trust men. They haven't lived easy lives. From the time they wake up until they go to sleep, people are trying to steal what little they have. Take what they don't want to give. All of you showing up, looking pissed off because of their situation, isn't going to work."

"As much as I don't like it, she has a point," Arrow said.

Zara turned to Dave. "I *know* you want to see your wife and that it's painful to have to wait, but trust me, it's for the best. Mags is one of the most amazing women I know. She helped me more than I could ever explain. But she's also hurting. I saw it every time I looked in her eyes. If you show up out of the blue and attempt to force her to leave . . . it's possible you'll lose her forever. She's not the Raven you used to know. She's Mags."

"She'll always be my Raven," Dave argued. "And it doesn't surprise me that she helped you—that's the kind of person she is. But it's been *ten years*, Zara. You can understand better than anyone how badly I need to see her for myself. To touch her."

"I'm not asking you to wait days," Zara said. "Just a couple hours or so. Let me go in, talk with my friends, tell them how wonderful you all are. Ease the way a bit."

"We could go shopping in the meantime," Meat suggested. "Not to bribe them, but I'm guessing there are things they could use."

Zara nodded eagerly. "That would be awesome. I can make a list. But . . . Ruben and his cronies raid the shacks all the time. Anything we get for them will have to be easily hidden, so don't go overboard."

Dave did his best to control his impatience. The thing he liked least about sending the Mountain Mercenaries on missions was the lack of control he had over so many aspects. Even though he wasn't a soldier, he hated simply sitting around waiting to hear whether the mission was a success or not. He could do all the research he wanted before they left, but once they were on the scene, unless they required information or help from one of his contacts, he could do little but wait to hear about the outcome.

That was kind of how he felt right now. He didn't want to wait. He wanted to see Raven again with his own two eyes. His skin was crawling, he was sweating madly, and he felt as though if he didn't see her right this second, he would literally implode.

But he also knew Zara was correct. They couldn't all just show up out of the blue. Seven huge men would stick out like a sore thumb in the barrio. They'd also scare the women, and the last thing he wanted was to force more hurt on his wife.

"Fine. But I need you to bring something to her for me. I'm guessing she'll be skeptical, possibly won't even believe that I'm really here." Dave reached for his wallet and pulled out a squished penny. He'd carried it with him every day for ten years. He and Raven had gotten it while they'd been in Las Vegas. Right after, she'd put a twenty into a slot machine and won a thousand bucks. She'd laughed and said it was all because of the penny. That it was their lucky penny now.

He handed it to Zara, and she looked down, inspecting it, then back up at him. "I'll make sure she gets it," she said softly.

They got out of the minivan, waiting for Black, Ro, Ball, and Gray to exit theirs before trooping into the lobby of the run-down motel. After Dave checked them into several rooms, Arrow said, "We should wait until dusk. We might be less conspicuous."

Dave wanted to protest. Wanted to tell his team that they were going to put their shit in their rooms and come right back down so they could get on with it, but he knew Arrow was right.

He wanted to believe that Raven would take one look at him and beg him to take her home. Hopefully that would be the case, no matter what Zara suggested. He wanted to be on his way back out of the country as soon as possible.

The very thought of seeing Raven, of putting his arms around her again, was overwhelming. The day she'd disappeared, Dave had lost a part of himself. He'd gone crazy for a while. Crazy with grief and anger. He wanted to be calm now. He was closer to his wife than he'd been for years, but all he could feel was renewed anger that she'd been taken from him, and throat-clenching nervousness about seeing her.

As they all filed out of the lobby to go to their rooms and prepare for the trip to the barrio late in the afternoon, Dave couldn't help but be apprehensive. It felt as if the longer he waited to see Raven, the greater the chance she'd simply disappear into a puff of smoke once again.

~

Zara headed out of the motel a few hours later. She was walking a block or so in front of Meat, but she knew he was behind her, watching and making sure she was safe. She'd known she wouldn't talk him into letting her go to the barrio by herself, but she'd been able to talk him into following her at a distance.

When she and Meat had gotten to their room, she'd convinced him that it would be a good idea to head to the barrio even earlier than they'd discussed with Dave. They both knew how anxious the other man was to see Mags, and it was going to be almost impossible to hold him back if he accompanied her to the barrio for the first time.

Meat wasn't happy about deceiving the leader of the Mountain Mercenaries, but all things considered, he agreed it was a good plan.

Zara couldn't help remembering, however, how badly Meat had been hurt the last time he'd been in the barrio. She didn't quite blend in as well as she used to herself, but she had no doubt that if someone harassed her, Meat would be at her side in a heartbeat. He would never allow her to head into potential danger alone. She wanted to be mad about that, insist she could do this; after all, she'd wandered the streets of the barrios for fifteen years all by herself. But she knew that wouldn't make one bit of difference to Meat. And she loved him all the more for it.

Praying he would stick to the shadows and remain unnoticed, she turned her thoughts to Mags. She felt bad for Dave. She really did. But she had to think about her friend too. No way would she do anything that would cause the other woman emotional pain. She'd been through way too much already. While Mags was smart and empathetic, there was also a deep well of pain she kept hidden from the world. Zara recognized it because she'd harbored similar pain. But what caused Mags's suffering, specifically, Zara didn't know. She'd never felt comfortable asking.

Hopefully being reunited with her husband would allow Mags to begin to heal.

The sounds and smells that assaulted Zara as she made her way toward the barrio were both scary and familiar at the same time. Once upon a time, this had been her world. Despite having no trouble navigating it, the area now felt alien. Foreign. It wasn't a good feeling.

Once she entered the barrio, she continually looked around nervously as she walked, relieved when she didn't see Ruben or any of his friends. Most people would be inside their huts sleeping through the hottest part of the day. She hoped to find at least one of her friends inside the hut they all used to share. But it was possible they'd moved on to another barrio, another hut.

Zara approached the shack that she'd last been in a few months ago, and memories threatened to overwhelm her. She knocked lightly on the piece of corrugated metal being used as a door and called out in Spanish, "Hello? Gabriella? Carmen? Is anyone there?"

In seconds, the metal was pushed to the side, and Zara was staring into Teresa's eyes.

"Madre de Dios," the other woman said breathlessly, then burst into tears.

Zara pushed her way inside and quickly saw that everyone but Mags was there.

They all started talking and crying at once. It was several minutes before Zara could control her own emotions enough to explain what was going on. She fell back into using Spanish as easily as she'd picked up English.

"What are you doing here?"

"Did you not go to America?"

"You look beautiful!"

Zara smiled at her friends. "Give me a second, and I'll explain everything!"

Everyone quieted down, and Zara spent a few minutes quickly telling them about Meat, and Colorado, and about her grandparents and uncle. When she was done, everyone was just staring at her incredulously.

"I'm rich," she said softly. "All those years, and my grandparents didn't try all that hard to find me. So I've decided to use the money for good. I don't need it all. I'm here to see Daniela and you guys, and to set up a clinic so people like us can get medical care when we need it. And in the future, I'd also like to set up a food bank too." She wasn't exactly lying. She did want to set up a clinic, but that wasn't the real reason she was there.

Everyone started talking at once again, and Zara could only smile. She'd missed these women. They'd been such an important part of her life for so long. Allye, Morgan, and the others back in Colorado had done a lot to make her feel welcome, but these women had been through a lot together.

"Wait until Mags sees you!" Gabriella said in excitement.

"Where is she?" Zara asked.

"It's Wednesday," Carmen explained.

Zara nodded. "That's right, I'd forgotten." And she had too. No one knew where Mags went three days a week. She wouldn't talk about it, and everyone had just gotten used to the fact she was gone on those days. No one asked too many questions in the barrio.

Zara hadn't planned on staying in the barrio for long, but she also wasn't going to leave without seeing and talking to Mags. She couldn't go back to the motel and tell Dave he'd have to wait until tomorrow. It was bad enough he'd have to wait the rest of the day for her to get back, but it couldn't be helped.

She also worried about Meat hanging around outside, watching over her, but she just had to accept that he could take care of himself.

A part of her had been scared the women wouldn't be here anymore, and she was relieved that wasn't the case. If it had been, Zara knew Dave would've lost his mind.

"How have things been here?" Zara asked. "Are Ruben and his friends just as bad as they were?"

Maria frowned. "Worse. The other day, they broke in and stole or destroyed just about everything we had."

Looking around, Zara could see that the hut was nearly empty. She shook her head in frustration. "I'm so sorry."

Bonita shrugged. "It is what it is."

"Well, I have good news for you, then. I've not only returned with my boyfriend, but all of *his* friends too. And today they're shopping. I gave them a list of things I thought you could use or would want. We'll have to figure out a way to hide everything from Ruben's bullies so they don't come in and rob you again, but I think you'll be happy with what they bring."

And just like that, the excited chatter started up again.

Zara was thrilled to see her friends so happy, even if it was momentary. Life wasn't easy in the barrio, and it felt amazing to be able to give back to them after all they'd done for her.

She hadn't told them that she also had plans to buy a house near Daniela's that she hoped to move them all into—she was saving that bit of news for later. She couldn't save everyone in the barrio, but she *could* do something for the women who'd shown her what true friendship was about.

She talked with her friends for at least an hour, and Zara knew it was getting late. She was still worried about Meat, and about Dave simply showing up out of the blue if he found out they'd ditched him. The last thing she wanted was for Mags to accidentally run into him. She needed to be warned that he was here. But a part of Zara didn't want to leave. She'd enjoyed reconnecting with Bonita and Carmen and the others. While she didn't miss her old life, she *did* miss these women.

Just when Zara thought she was going to have to leave and come back the next day to talk to Mags, the piece of metal covering the door slid back, and Mags was there.

Zara quickly stood and smiled uncertainly at the other woman. She'd always been a kind of mother figure to her. Zara valued her opinion and deeply cared what Mags thought of her.

"Zara? Is it really you?" Mags asked.

"It's me."

"Come here and give me a hug!" she ordered.

Zara sighed in relief and went over to hug the older woman. She smelled like sweat and the funk that permeated everything in the barrio, but Zara barely even noticed.

"I missed you," Zara said softly in English.

"And I, you," Mags returned.

"You don't seem that surprised to see me," Zara noted.

Mags chuckled, but the humor didn't seem to reach her eyes. In fact, the other woman seemed exhausted. More tired than usual.

"That's because I'm not. There are three men lurking around the barrio who obviously don't belong here. And if I'm not mistaken, one of them is the man who took you back to the United States."

Zara closed her eyes and huffed out a breath. If Mags had seen three men, that meant Dave was probably out there somewhere too. "I knew Meat was waiting for me, but I told him to stay hidden," she said.

"I take it things went well with him?" Mags asked.

Feeling shy, Zara nodded.

"Good. I got good vibes from him," Mags said. "Now, why are you here?"

The other women all started talking at once, telling Mags all about the clinic Zara planned to build and the food pantry. When they were done, Mags brought a hand up and cradled Zara's cheek. "You always cared about everyone who had less than you."

Zara grabbed Mags's hand and held on tightly. "That's not the only reason I'm here."

Mags tilted her head in question.

In English, Zara said, "Meat's friends are part of a group who travel around the world, rescuing women and children who are being abused or who've been kidnapped. Their leader's wife disappeared ten years ago . . . and he's spent the last decade frantically looking for her. He hired my boyfriend and the others for the team because he didn't have any military experience himself."

With every word Zara spoke, Mags's face got whiter and whiter, until she looked as though she was going to keel over.

"I recognized you from a picture that was behind the bar at The Pit. The second Dave heard where you were, he made arrangements to come down."

Mags abruptly crumpled to the floor. Her knees simply gave out.

Zara kneeled down in front of her and reached into her pocket, bringing out the pressed penny Dave had given her. She held it out. "He told me to give this to you, to prove that he's your husband."

Mags stared at the piece of copper as if it was a snake that would bite her hand off if she reached for it.

"He's here, Mags. And unlike my own relatives, he hasn't *ever* stopped trying to find you."

~

Mags stared at the penny, and memories flickered through her brain as if she were watching an old movie. Dave smiling at her reaction to seeing the penny-smashing machine. Mags reaching into his pocket looking for change . . . and teasing him at the same time. Telling him they had to get a lucky penny so they could win big. And they had.

She remembered how Dave had sworn he'd carry the penny with him always, before he'd tucked it into a pocket in his wallet.

She closed her eyes in despair. She'd pushed thoughts of her husband to the very recesses of her mind, for the most part, for her own sanity and self-preservation. Thinking about Dave and the love they shared was extremely painful; it had been especially difficult in the first year they'd been separated. The things she'd been made to do and endure had been so horrific that any thoughts of the way her life used to be were pure torture. She hadn't wanted to remember how good he'd made her feel. How special and loved she'd been. All she could think about was surviving one day. Then the next. And the next.

But after years of keeping those memories at bay, they'd begun to sneak back in . . . particularly in the last few years. And after seeing Zara find love with her man, Mags couldn't help but think about her long-lost husband even more frequently, about how things used to be.

And seeing that penny in Zara's palm brought back so many painful recollections, Mags thought she was going to be physically sick.

"I can't see him. I won't!" Mags whispered.

Then what Zara had said sank in.

If the men lurking around the barrio were any indication, Dave was already here.

Here.

At one time, she would've been ecstatic to see him. To know he was here to take her away from Peru and what her life had become. But not anymore. She couldn't leave. *Wouldn't.*

Frantically, Mags looked around the hut and tried to think. She had to get out of there before Dave arrived. Had to hide.

The others stared at her with wide, confused eyes. They didn't understand, but then again, they didn't know her entire story. She'd had to keep it quiet. Not even the women who'd become more like daughters and sisters to her knew everything that had happened to her.

"Zara?" a male voice called quietly from the other side of the flimsy piece of metal they used as a door.

Mags immediately stood up and backed away. Her heart was beating a million times a minute, and she couldn't get enough air in her lungs. She would've fled out the back of the hut through the small concealed door they'd made just for situations like this, when an exit out the front wasn't possible, but Maria and Bonita were standing in front of it.

Zara slid the piece of metal back, and Mags recognized the man who they'd smuggled out of the barrio a few months ago. He was tall, but not as tall as her Dave.

No. No, no, no, no!

Mags couldn't deal with memories of Dave popping up every other second. She'd barely survived losing him the first time. She wouldn't be able to do it a second.

But then the decision was taken out of her hands.

Crowding in behind Zara's man were three others. But Mags only had eyes for one.

Whereas before, she was breathing too fast, now she couldn't draw in even the slightest bit of oxygen.

How many nights had she lain on the floor, beaten and bleeding, praying to see Dave again? How many times had she vowed to do whatever it took to survive until her husband could find her? How many times had she wished she was dead rather than have to give to other men what she'd vowed would only belong to her husband?

Too many times to count.

She'd stopped wishing and hoping for anything when it came to her own safety about five years ago.

But now, here he was. The man she'd loved with all her heart. The man she *still* loved, but couldn't have. He shouldn't be here. He should've moved on by now. Found another woman to comfort him and love him.

"Raven," Dave said in a broken whisper. Then he took a step toward her.

Panicked, Mags frantically scrambled backward and ran into Gabriella and Teresa, who were standing directly behind her. They caught her before she could fall to the ground.

The look on Dave's face as she backed away almost destroyed her.

He was devastated.

He fell slowly to his knees and bowed his head as if it were too heavy for his neck to hold it up. When he looked up again, she saw so many emotions in his eyes. Frustration, fear, determination, love.

It was the last that almost did her in.

Zara's man gave his fiancée a sheepish look. "Clearly, we were followed. I tried to keep him back, to give you more time to talk to her," he said, "but the second he saw her walking by, I couldn't stop him. I stalled him as much as possible."

Mags couldn't look away from her husband. Her eyes drank him in. He looked good. *Really* good. But he was changed. Harder. She knew without a doubt that she'd done that. Not on purpose, but her disappearance had taken its toll on them both.

His biceps were just as big as she remembered. How she'd loved to snuggle up against him and rest her head on those arms. He could lift her up without seeming to struggle in the least. His hair had gray streaks that weren't there the last time she'd seen him, and fine lines surrounded his eyes and mouth. His beard also had gray streaks, and it just made him all the more sexy to her.

But it was the large scar that snaked down his neck and into the neckline of his shirt that had her staring at him with concern. What had happened? The scar was nasty, and it looked as if it had probably come very close to killing him. How had he gotten it? Had anyone sat in the hospital with him as he'd recovered?

Everyone in the room faded away as Mags stared at the man she never thought she'd see again. She was very aware of how horrible she probably looked. She hadn't washed her hair in who knew how long. She had dirt caked under her fingernails, and she knew she smelled, both from sweat after her long walk today and from never having clean water to bathe in. She was so far removed from the carefree woman she'd been the last time she'd seen Dave, it wasn't funny.

But he wasn't looking at her in disgust. More like awe.

Swallowing hard, Mags tore her gaze from Dave's. There were three other men standing in the hut, making the already small space extremely cramped. There were four bags sitting near the doorway that had obviously been brought by Zara's friends.

"I'd like you to meet some friends of mine," Zara said in Spanish. "This is Meat, my boyfriend. He's the one we dragged out of the alley, who I brought to Daniela for treatment. We . . . um . . . we're living together, and I love him. These are his friends, Arrow and Gray. And that's . . . Dave. They're here to help me with the legwork on the clinic."

Mags was glad Zara didn't say anything else about who Dave was. She wasn't ready.

Would *never* be ready.

Their friends weren't dumb, however. By her reaction to the man, it was obvious he wasn't just another friend of Zara's.

The women all said hello, and the man who Zara called Gray turned, picked up the bags, and held them out.

"I told you that I gave them a list of things I thought you could use," Zara said. "We'll have to bury everything, or take things to Daniela's for safekeeping so Ruben and the others don't steal them."

Teresa reached out and took a bag, and Gabriella and Bonita followed suit. They looked inside, and their eyes widened almost comically.

Mags looked back at Dave . . . and once again couldn't breathe. He hadn't taken his eyes off her. It was as if he was drinking her in. But instead of his gaze comforting her, she felt exposed. Naked. She felt as if he could see straight through her to her deepest, darkest secrets.

Things she'd never speak of. Not to him or to anyone. They were her shame to carry.

Zara was acting as a translator, but Mags couldn't even hear what she was saying with the rushing sound in her ears.

Dave didn't get off his knees. He stayed on the floor, looking at her intently. Mags knew if she had to endure it for one more second, she'd go stark raving mad.

"Raven," Dave said softly. "I wanted to believe Zara. Wanted to believe that the woman she knew as Mags was really you . . . but I also didn't want to get my hopes up too high. I've been disappointed so many times, I knew I couldn't handle it again. But it's you. It's really you."

Mags stared at him without blinking.

"Can I . . . Are you all right?"

She wanted to snort at that. Was she all right? No, of course she wasn't.

"It's a lot to process, Dave," Arrow said, putting a hand on his shoulder. "You need to give her some time."

"I can't leave," Dave said, his voice breaking. "I just found her. I can't go!"

Mags stiffened. He couldn't stay. She had to make him understand. "I don't want you here," she said in as hard a voice as she could muster. Unfortunately, it came out more like a plea than a demand from the in-charge woman she'd had to become over the years.

She was shocked when tears formed in Dave's eyes and spilled over his cheeks. He didn't reach up to wipe them away, simply continued to stare at her.

"Ten years," he said softly. "Ten years, twenty-two days, four hours, and thirty-six minutes. That's how long you've been missing. And I've been searching for you for every single second of that time. I've prayed to hear your voice again . . . and the reality is so much better than my dreams."

His words both soothed a hurt she didn't know she'd harbored and stung like a thousand bees. Dave had obviously suffered. The man she used to know never would've cried. Especially not in front of others. She couldn't talk through the lump in her own throat.

"You should go. Just for tonight," Zara said. "Mags needs time to process everything."

Dave opened his mouth to protest, but Gray spoke before he could.

"That sounds like a good idea. We can come back tomorrow."

"You're not staying here," Meat told Zara.

"I'll be fine," she told him gently.

"No."

Mags approved of Zara's man. He was protective and obviously concerned about her safety. As much as Zara was a product of the barrio, it wasn't safe. Not even for her.

"Maybe they can all come to the motel with us?" she asked.

"If we're gone too long, Ruben or someone else might take over our house," Maria said.

Zara's shoulders drooped. "Yeah."

"We'll come back first thing in the morning, and we'll bring food," Meat reassured both Zara and the other women. "If there's anything else you can think of that you need, we'll go shopping again tomorrow and get it for you. We need to visit Daniela as well."

The women all agreed, and Mags knew they were anxious to go through the bags of supplies the men had brought them and talk about exactly what was happening.

"I don't want to go," Dave argued.

Meat put his hand on Dave's shoulder and squeezed. "She needs time," he said quietly.

No one said anything for a long moment.

Then, from his position on his knees in the doorway, Dave said, "I love you, Raven."

Mags braced herself to look at him again.

"I love you. I know enough about what happens to young women who get taken without their consent to know your life has been hell. But I've found you—and I'm going to do whatever it takes to prove you're now safe. That my love for you hasn't stopped simply because you've been gone."

"People change," she said softly. "I'm not the woman you once knew."

"And I'm not the same person you married," Dave countered. "I'm harder. More stubborn. A hell of a lot less trusting. But one thing will *never* change, and that's how much you mean to me, and how much I love you."

"I don't love you anymore," Mags lied.

Dave didn't even flinch. "You will."

Frustration rose within her. She needed him gone. Why wasn't he getting mad? Leaving? She had too much to lose if he didn't go. "My life is here in Peru," she said as sternly as she could manage. "I'm not leaving."

Dave eyed her for a long moment, and Mags refused to squirm under his scrutiny. Then he slowly stood, and Mags forced herself to stand her ground and not cower from the intensity of his gaze. The tears had dried up, and a very determined man stood in front of her now.

"I didn't tell your parents that I was coming to Peru. They've had their hopes raised too many times and dashed just as many. And my parents have suffered right along with me. But they don't matter. No one matters but you. My life is wherever *you* are," Dave said without a trace of irritation or insecurity. "If I have to move to Lima in order to be with you, I will."

At any other time, Mags would've thrown herself at her man and begged him to take her away from the barrio. From Lima. From Peru. But she couldn't.

She was in hell. This was like being offered everything her heart desired, but she knew if she dared reach for it, she could lose something else she loved just as dearly.

She heard Gabriella begging Zara to translate what was being said, but Mags didn't look away from Dave.

"Te amo," he said softly, bringing quiet sighs from the other women.

Mags shook her head stubbornly.

She knew Dave would've stood there all night if his friend Gray hadn't taken hold of his forearm and tugged him toward the exit. "Come on, Dave. Give her some space. We'll come back tomorrow."

Mags held eye contact with Dave until he was outside the hut and Gray had literally dragged him away. She let out a huge breath of relief.

Then panic returned just as quickly.

He'd come back.

She knew he wouldn't stop until he got her to admit she still loved him too. That she would go back to the States with him. It was all fine and good for Zara to have left her life in Peru behind, but Mags didn't have that option.

"Please don't run," Zara said in Spanish before she left. "Promise me you'll stay and talk to him."

Mags didn't agree or disagree, but eventually Zara sighed and said goodbye to the rest of the women and slid the piece of metal over the entrance.

The others all started peppering her with questions, but Mags didn't have the energy or will to answer them. She wandered over to her pallet and lay down. Her stomach growled, but she ignored it. There was no way she could eat. Not now.

Just when she'd gotten used to the life she was leading, something came along to disrupt it once more.

She had no idea what she was going to do. She couldn't leave, but she didn't want to stay either. Dave appearing out of nowhere was a dream come true, but it also placed her smack-dab in the middle of her own personal nightmare.

Dave might've spent the last decade trying to rescue women in situations like hers, but she didn't think he could truly understand what she'd been through, and there was no way he'd be able to come to terms with the choices she'd made. The shame she felt every day shrouded her like a heavy blanket, slowly and surely weighing her down and suffocating her.

But she knew Dave wasn't going to simply turn around and go back to America quietly. Even if she continued to tell him that she didn't love him anymore, didn't want anything to do with him. No, he'd want explanations and answers. Two things he wasn't going to get. Not if she could help it. The last thing she wanted was for him to look at her with disgust, which was what he'd do if he knew why she didn't want to leave.

The other reason she knew he'd stay was because Dave could always read her. He'd always seemed to know when she wasn't being truthful. She could tell him over and over that she didn't love him, that she wanted him to leave, but he'd know she was lying. That she desperately needed him to make things right in her world, even if that was impossible.

As Mags listened to her friends oohing and aahing over the things Dave and his friends had bought, a rare tear formed and slipped down the side of her face. Nothing was easy in the barrio, and the arrival of the only man she'd ever loved had just complicated things. Tenfold.

Chapter Four

Dave went back to the motel docilely enough, but inside he was making plans. If Raven thought for one second he was leaving without her, she was mistaken. He hadn't looked for her for *ten years* just to walk away now. He didn't know what was going on in her head, but he knew enough about trafficking victims to know many had serious psychological issues because of what they'd been through.

But one thing that wasn't in question was whether Mags was his Raven. She was. She'd been through hell, suffered more than anyone should, and had the lines on her face to prove it, but to him, she was still the most beautiful woman he'd ever seen.

He didn't care about her tattered and dirty clothing, or the way her hair lay lank and greasy against her back. What he *did* care about was the look of absolute agony in her eyes.

He knew what had probably happened to her over the years. She'd been sold like a piece of meat and had most likely been used and abused by countless men who only cared about getting off.

The thought of his Raven being taken against her will was a tough pill to swallow, but the woman he'd seen today had somehow managed to survive everything she'd been through for an entire decade. And he could still see flickers of the Raven he used to know buried somewhere inside.

But it was the soul-deep conviction in her eyes that there was no way he could ever want her now that killed him. The secrets she hid from him, and everyone around her, were deeply ingrained in her psyche. They'd once been best friends. Closer than he'd been to anyone in his entire life. She knew all his hopes, fears, and dreams, just as he knew hers. But now there was a chasm between them that seemed as wide as the Pacific Ocean, and that hurt. Bad.

There had to be a reason why she didn't want to leave Peru—and he was going to find out what it was. He hadn't lied. If he had to move to Lima and live here for the rest of his life to be with his wife, that was what he'd do.

He knew she was lying to him for some reason. He'd always been able to read her like a book. It used to annoy her and amuse him. He wasn't amused anymore. Because he knew down to the marrow of his bones that she didn't want to stay in Peru. She longed to go back home to Colorado, but for some reason she was holding back.

And he'd be damned if he left her for even one more night.

He'd spent ten years not knowing where she was, not knowing if she was hurting or hungry, and now that he'd found her, he wouldn't spend another night away from her if he could help it.

Dave said his good nights to the others and followed Ball up to the room they were sharing. The team had met outside in the parking lot to discuss what had happened in the barrio. No one was happy that Raven hadn't agreed to come back to the motel, but they were somewhat mollified by the fact they'd return in the morning.

Black, Gray, and Meat, with Zara along to translate, were going to see Daniela first thing. They wanted to check out the neighborhood where her house was located and talk to her about what she needed in a clinic.

Ball tried to make small talk, to ask about Raven, but Dave responded only with a few grunts and shrugs until Ball got the message and gave up. Dave wasn't ready to talk about Raven yet. Not until he figured out what the hell was going on. It was especially frustrating because he couldn't use his computer skills to figure it out either. Oh, he had his computer with him, and all the connections he'd made over the years who would help investigate, but neither had helped him find Raven during the last ten years, and even though he knew where she was now, no amount of hacking or research skills in the world would help him win his wife back.

He had to talk to Raven, get her to open up about what was really going on.

He already knew more than he wanted to know about Roberto del Rio, the man he was now convinced had been behind his wife's kidnapping. The asshole had an extraordinary amount of clout in Lima, and it wasn't a secret that he ran a flourishing whorehouse. The police had raided his sprawling estate more than once, but every single woman they'd found in the past had sworn she was there of her own free will. Which didn't prove anything other than they were either scared to tell the cops the truth, or the police were being paid off by del Rio. Both likely prospects.

Dave tried to take solace in the fact that Raven wasn't at del Rio's compound at the moment. But that didn't make him feel much better about her safety. Not after seeing where she was living. He was well aware of how dangerous the roving gangs of men like Ruben were. Meat and Black were proof of that.

After they'd followed Zara and Meat into the barrio, Dave, Arrow, and Gray had scoped out the area during their long wait. There were several unsavory-looking men lurking around, and if he had to guess, Dave figured they were probably the same men who'd attacked Black and Meat when they'd been there on their last mission. He had no proof, but it didn't take much guessing to know which guys were up to no good. None of the residents of the barrio would meet their eyes, and when they saw the young men, they either scurried off in another direction, or they disappeared into one of the poorly constructed huts that lined the alleyways.

Dave wasn't leaving Raven, or the other women, unprotected for one more day. Raven might not want him there, but tough shit. Their mere presence in the barrio had brought unwanted attention to Mags and her friends. He wasn't going to let anything happen to them, not on his watch.

Not only that, but he wasn't completely sure Raven wouldn't bolt. The look in her eyes that evening had said she wanted to be anywhere but in that hut. Dave hated it. He'd always sworn he'd never force a woman to do anything she didn't want to do . . . but this was his wife, and he'd waited what seemed like forever to see her again. He wasn't going to let her slip away and put herself in danger just to try to avoid him.

He waited until Ball was on the phone with Everly, and then said as he walked toward the door, "I'm going to grab a Coke from the vending machine. Want one?"

He hated tricking his friend, but he knew Ball wouldn't allow him to go to the barrio by himself. And this was something he had to do. He might not be a former Special Forces soldier, but he also wasn't completely helpless.

As Dave hoped, Ball merely shook his head, distracted by the conversation he was having with his girlfriend. Dave slipped out the door and into the stairwell. Within minutes, he was walking along the dark streets near the motel and headed for the barrio. He wasn't scared in the least; he had too much pent-up energy to worry about someone robbing or attacking him.

In fact, he'd welcome the prospect.

But of course, since Dave's arms were the size of most people's thighs, anyone who was out and about quickly walked in the other direction after they caught a glimpse of him.

The barrio was quiet, the occasional smell of smoke from random fires wafting through the air. The sky rumbled with far-off thunder, but Dave didn't think it was supposed to rain. He easily found the alley he was looking for. In the dark, everything looked the same, but he'd memorized where his Raven was.

He knew what he was about to do wasn't exactly the smartest thing. He was alone, and Ruben or anyone else could come upon him and try to fuck with him, but with the way he was feeling right now, he almost *wished* someone would try something. He thought it was more important to let anyone watching know that the women in this shack were off-limits. That they were protected. He could hide in the shadows, but no . . . he wanted to be visible, so any local punks would think twice about harassing the women in the future.

He didn't knock on the makeshift door. Didn't bring any attention to the fact that he was there. He simply lowered himself to the dirt outside the hut he'd been in earlier that afternoon and lay down parallel to the doorway. He listened to the female voices talking quietly from inside the hut at his back, but didn't hear Raven. For a second, he worried that maybe she'd left, but then she spoke. He couldn't understand what she was saying since she was speaking in Spanish, but he'd know her voice anywhere. He'd dreamed about hearing it again. Raven teasing him about some inside joke between the two of them . . . or hearing her say she loved him.

Relaxing as best he could on the hard-packed dirt, Rex lay his head on his biceps and closed his eyes. He hadn't slept well for the last ten years, only getting snatches of sleep here and there, and he wasn't about to start now. If anyone walked by, or in any way threatened what was his, he'd wake up and deal with it.

He hadn't found his beloved after all this time to lose her in some stupid random robbery. She was his to protect, his to love. And even if she didn't return his feelings, even if he had to make her fall in love with him all over again, he wasn't leaving her side.

It wasn't too much later when Dave sensed he had company. He sat up quickly—

And saw Ball and Gray standing nearby.

He stood up and walked over to the men. "Go back to the motel," he ordered.

"Fuck you," Ball said with a shake of his head. "We all knew you were going to come back out here. There's no way, after ten years, that you were going to let her out of your sight."

Dave shrugged. "This isn't your problem."

"Not our problem?" Gray repeated, sounding way the hell pissed off. "Is that what *you* thought when Allye was taken by that asshole who wanted to keep her as some sort of sideshow freak? Or when Everly's sister was kidnapped?"

Dave ground his teeth but shook his head.

"Right, so why would you think any different about this? We came down here to help. It's obvious how much Raven means to you, so you sneaking out to put your ass on the line like this wasn't only stupid, it was offensive as hell."

Dave thought about his friend's words, and knew he was right. After a long pause, he haltingly tried to explain his thought process. "Every night for the last ten years, I've slept beside an empty spot in my bed. I've worried about what my wife might be going through and if she's in pain. I haven't been able to stop thinking about her crying for help, wondering if I was looking for her or not. It's been torture. Not physical torture, like you've both endured in the past, but mental. I simply can't *not* be here. The thought of losing her again is unbearable.

"I know this isn't that smart. But because she can't stand to look me in the eyes for more than a few seconds at a time, and because she's obviously scared to death of something . . . maybe me . . . I can't hold her in my arms and reassure her that everything will be all right. Maybe it'll *never* be all right for her—but there's no way in hell I'm leaving her alone again."

Gray sighed and Ball nodded.

"Fine, but at least let one of us stay out here with you," Gray said in a much less pissed-off tone.

"I appreciate that, but no. I'm fine. No one is going to mess with me," Dave said.

Ball shook his head again. "Sorry, but also no. You saw what happened to Black and Meat. In fact, it happened in this exact same alley. You lying here without any weapons is like waving a red flag at a bull. You're bringing more attention and danger to Raven and the other women than if you weren't here."

Dave's hands clenched into fists. He didn't like what his friends were saying, but deep down, he knew they were right. "I'm trying to send a message to the assholes in this barrio that these women are off-limits. Besides . . . I can't leave. I just can't," he said.

"Then neither are we," Gray said.

"We won't sit here with you, but we'll watch from the shadows," Ball assured him. "Gray and I will stay tonight, and we'll work out a rotation with the rest of the team for as long as it's needed."

Dave swallowed hard. He hadn't expected this. He'd felt alone in his quest to find his wife for so long. The cops and detectives had done their best, but it hadn't been good enough, and when enough time had passed, and her case had gone cold, they'd simply had to move on to other cases.

"What are you doing?"

All three men turned at the question—and Dave saw Raven looking out of the hut he'd been sleeping in front of a few minutes ago.

He crossed his arms over his chest and said truthfully, "We're hashing out a plan to make sure you and the others are safe at night."

His wife rolled her eyes, and Dave's knees almost buckled. He'd forgotten about her sassy side. How could he have forgotten? She used to do that all the time. Roll her eyes at him when he'd been too overprotective, or just to be silly. Seeing her do it now gave him a glimpse of the woman he used to know, and filled him with hope that she was still inside the battered outer shell she'd donned to deal with the nightmares she'd been through.

"We don't need you bringing that kind of attention to us," Raven said shortly. "Just leave."

"Not happening," Dave said, slowly walking toward her. He didn't want to spook her, but he absolutely wanted her to know that he wasn't going anywhere.

"Seriously, Dave, just go. You're going to make Ruben and his friends wonder what the hell you're guarding. They'll become curious enough to break in again to steal what you and your friends brought today."

"Again?" Dave asked in a low, furious tone.

Raven seemed to realize what she'd said and quickly dropped her gaze from his.

He did his best to control his anger. "I can't leave," he told her honestly. "I lost you once because I took my eyes off you. I learned my lesson, and I'm not going to do it again."

"I'm not a four-year-old kid, Dave," Raven said. "I'm a grown woman who's learned a whole lot about the world in the last decade. I can take care of myself."

At those words, Dave's head dropped, and he brought a hand up to rub the back of his neck. He hated everything about this. All of it. He'd imagined their reunion so many times, and not once had Raven *not* been happy to see him. In every scenario he'd imagined, she'd smiled at him and leapt into his arms. He was struggling and completely out of his element, and he didn't like it one bit.

"I can't leave," Dave whispered.

Without another word, Raven slid the metal door shut, and the sound of it closing made bile rise in Dave's throat. He forced it back and straightened his shoulders. She might not be happy with him, but it didn't matter. He was staying.

He'd known that if he ever found his wife, they'd have an uphill battle to get back to the couple they'd been before. That she'd have demons. But Dave realized now that he'd naively thought his love would magically make her get over them. That she'd be just as happy to see him as he was her.

The fact that she seemed annoyed he was there hurt like crazy.

But it didn't make him want to leave. All it did was make his determination to get to the bottom of what was going on even stronger. He loved Raven, and she still loved him. He could sense it. See it in her eyes. But she was holding back.

Maybe she was ashamed. Maybe she truly *had* fallen out of love with him, despite what he thought he saw in her eyes. But it didn't matter. He'd do whatever it took to make her fall in love with him again. He needed her. Was nothing without her.

Dave settled back on the ground in front of the door of the shack and watched as Ball and Gray disappeared into the shadows of the barrio. It would be a long night, but Dave knew it was nothing compared to what his wife had endured. He'd sleep on the hard ground every night for the rest of his life if it meant keeping Raven safe.

~

"Are they really staying out there all night?" Teresa asked incredulously after Mags had closed the door and gone back to her pallet.

"Apparently," she muttered.

"You're mad," Carmen noted. "Why?"

"Because all he's going to do is bring attention to us. Ruben and his friends are going to think we've got something valuable in here," Mags said in a huff.

Carmen continued to stare at her until Mags got a little defensive. "What?"

"This man is your husband, yes?" Carmen asked.

Knowing the other women were all listening intently, Mags simply nodded.

"And he hasn't seen you in over ten years?"

Mags nodded again.

"I don't understand what you're so upset about," Carmen continued. "From everything I've seen, he and his friends seem to be good. Is that not true?"

Not wanting Carmen or the others to think ill of Dave, Mags immediately shook her head. "No, he is. It's just . . . sleeping outside our hut is like waving a neon sign that says, 'Come rob us!'"

"I know I'm the youngest," Gabriella said, "and I don't have as much experience as you all do. But I was born and raised in the barrio, and *never* have I seen a man do as your husband is doing. Most are more concerned about finding alcohol or trying to find a way to make money. And I saw the way he was looking at you today."

Mags didn't want to ask, but she couldn't stop herself. "And how was that?"

"As if you were a walking, talking miracle. Zara said he's been looking for you for ten years. That he has never stopped. He even sent his friends to different countries to do what they could to help women and children. I don't understand why you are not happy to have him here."

Mags couldn't explain it. How would Gabriella understand the shame she felt down to the marrow of her bones?

All these years later, Mags still couldn't help but think she should've done something different when she was first taken. She'd fought hard those first few days. Been an absolute maniac—when she wasn't drugged and knocked out. Anytime anyone came near her, she'd lashed out, done whatever she could to try to get away. But maybe she should've been more docile. If she had, perhaps her kidnappers would've let her go. Maybe she wouldn't have been taken out of the country. Maybe it would've changed the trajectory her life had taken.

By the time she'd realized her fate, it was too late. She was in Peru and hidden away in del Rio's compound. It had taken several months to "train" her for her new role, and Mags couldn't shake the disgrace she felt over finally giving in, not fighting anymore.

How could she admit to the love of her life that she'd been beaten down until she'd let other men do whatever they wanted to her—and she hadn't fought them? That she'd pretended to enjoy their hands on her body, the same body he'd spent many a night revering with his hands and mouth?

The bottom line was that she couldn't.

And she knew he'd *never* be able to forgive what had happened over five years ago. He wouldn't understand. No way.

"It's complicated," she finally told Gabriella.

"Well, I'm glad he's out there," Maria said firmly. "I can sleep tonight and not have to worry about Ruben, Marcus, Fortuno, or any of the others breaking in here, thinking they can have what del Rio so easily sold for so long."

"Me too," Teresa admitted.

"Me as well," Bonita chimed in.

Everyone but Gabriella had belonged to del Rio at some point. Mags had gotten too old to be desirable to his customers. Teresa and Maria hadn't been exotic enough, Carmen had managed to slip away from the compound, and they guessed del Rio didn't care, because he hadn't bothered to send his henchmen to drag her back.

And Bonita had gotten so sick, del Rio had assumed she would die, and he'd literally discarded her as if she were a piece of trash. Daniela had found her near one of the dumps, nursed her back to health, and introduced her to Mags.

These women had been a lifeline for Mags. But she hadn't been completely honest with them, not for a long time. There was a huge secret she was keeping. A secret she didn't think they'd understand or approve of.

But if they felt more comfortable with Dave sleeping outside their door, guarding it, then she wouldn't complain about it anymore. Deep down—deep, *deep* down—Mags was also glad he was there. She still couldn't believe it, but the fact that he hadn't stopped trying to find her made her heart skip a beat and hope flare deep within her soul.

Mags nodded at her friends and made a mental note to leave the hut through the secret back exit very early the next morning. It wasn't one of the days she traveled miles and miles to take care of the very important business she'd tended to every week for the last four and a half years. She just couldn't be around Dave. He made her wish for things she couldn't have. She had to remember who she was. She wasn't his Raven anymore. Her wings had been clipped, and she was now Mags. Ex-whore. Dirt-poor member of the barrio. Leader of her small group of friends.

Lying back down, Mags rested her head on her arm and closed her eyes. Not surprisingly, instead of thoughts of her life in Peru and the abuse she'd suffered, all she could think of was Dave. One particular memory stuck out in her mind, and she let herself get lost in it briefly. It had been their three-year anniversary, and Dave had gone all out, not only cooking a fancy meal for the two of them, but also setting up a surprise.

"Come on, tell me where we're going," Raven begged.

"Nope, you're just going to have to wait," Dave said with a laugh. They were in his car, and he was holding her hand as he drove.

"I hate waiting," she said with a pout.

Ten minutes later, they'd pulled into the parking lot of his bar, The Pit.

"Seriously? We're at the bar?"

He chuckled. "Yup."

"And here I was thinking I was gonna get to go somewhere cool," she mock-complained.

Dave came around to her side of the car and took her hand as she climbed out. "You're such a doubter," he said with a smile. "When have I ever let you down?"

"Never," she said without hesitation.

"Exactly. Now come on."

Raven followed behind her husband and took the time to check out not only his ass, but his broad shoulders and the arms she'd never get sick of looking at. He was so strong, he made her feel feminine and petite every time she was near him. She loved how he could throw her over his shoulder or move her exactly where he wanted her in bed without breaking a sweat.

She also loved some of the more adventurous positions they'd tried because she could trust him to not drop her.

Dave opened the door to the bar and gestured for her to enter ahead of him. Throwing him a flirty smile, she walked inside—and stopped in her tracks at what she saw.

Someone had strung white Christmas lights all over the front part of the bar. As she stood there, dumbstruck at how beautiful and transformed the space was with the fairy lights twinkling, Dave went over to the jukebox and pushed a button. Their wedding song filled the air . . . and all Raven could do was close her eyes and try not to cry.

"Dance with me?" Dave asked.

Raven opened her eyes and saw her husband standing in front of her, holding out his hand. She took it, and he wrapped his other arm around her waist, pulling her into him until they were plastered together from hip to chest. She laid her head on his shoulder as they swayed back and forth.

"It's not fancy, but I couldn't think of anything I wanted to do more than hold you in my arms. I didn't want to take you to a show where we'd be surrounded by strangers and I couldn't kiss you whenever I wanted," he said softly.

"There hasn't been much kissing yet," Raven said with a small smile.

His eyes glinting, Dave leaned down slowly and brushed his lips against hers. Once, then twice.

His beard tickled, but she loved it. "Stop teasing," Raven complained.

She saw his pupils dilate for just a moment before his head dropped, and he kissed her so passionately, her knees went weak. But of course, Dave didn't let her fall. He immediately picked her up, without breaking their kiss, and carried her to the back room of the bar, where there were rows upon rows of pool tables. He set her down on the nearest one and proceeded to show her exactly how much he loved her.

Then he took her to his office in the back room and sat in his office chair while she gave him an out-of-this-world blow job. Then he led her back into the bar with the twinkling lights and danced with her for another hour. At one point, he got out the Polaroid camera he kept behind the bar that he used to take pictures of his patrons, and as she laughed hysterically, he took her picture.

He'd proudly pinned it behind the bar and told her that now when he was working, all he needed to do was turn around to see her beautiful face whenever he wanted.

The night had been magical. They'd talked about expanding their family. They both wanted at least two kids, but she wouldn't mind three. They'd made love back at their house that night without using a condom for the first time. Secure in the knowledge that their love would last forever, and hopefully, within a year, they'd be expanding that love to include a baby.

A tear fell from Mags's eye before she could wipe it away. Of course, that wasn't how things happened. There had been no babies, even though they'd tried damn hard to make them, and she'd been stolen away during what had been one of the most fun trips of her life. She'd been so excited to visit Vegas. She never would've guessed an innocent trip to celebrate their anniversary would end so horribly.

Mags listened carefully and didn't hear anything from outside their hut. She knew Dave wouldn't have left. She felt guilty that he was sleeping out in the open on the hard dirt. But it also felt . . . good. She'd never expected to see her husband again. Had resigned herself to living the rest of her life here in Peru. She wanted to cling to him, to tell him to take her away, that she'd prayed to see him again every day since they'd been separated. But she couldn't. Not only was she not the same person he'd fallen in love with, she had . . . responsibilities here.

Raising her head, Mags looked around the hut. She could barely make out the other women, but knew they were there. Sighing, she laid her head back down. Seeing Dave every day would make her weak. Weaker than she was already. She couldn't let him talk her into going with him . . . and she knew he would try. She loved the man with everything she was, but he didn't belong here in her world.

Making one of the hardest decisions she'd ever had to make, Mags closed her eyes. Tomorrow, she'd slip out the back side of the hut early, before Dave was awake. She'd stay away all day. If he couldn't talk to her, he couldn't convince her to go back to Colorado.

Eventually, he'd get the message and leave. It was for the best. For him *and* for her.

She refused to admit how depressing that thought was.

Chapter Five

Dave sighed in frustration. He'd been in Lima for a full week, and he'd only seen Raven a small handful of times. She was avoiding him—and it was starting to piss him off. He was trying to be patient, giving her space to work through the fact that he was there, that he'd found her, but the bottom line was that her refusal to be anywhere near him gutted him.

When he'd imagined what his reunion with his wife would be like, at no time did he ever even consider that she wouldn't be thrilled. He figured things might be awkward, that she'd be uneasy, but eventually she'd come to realize how lucky she'd been, and they'd go back to Colorado. But of course, that was far from how things were turning out, and Dave wasn't sure what to do about it.

He'd spent every night since he'd arrived sleeping outside the hut Raven called home. And every morning, when one of the other women slid open the metal door, he found that his wife had snuck out so she didn't have to talk to him.

The *other* women seemed to like him. Even if they couldn't exactly have any in-depth conversations, they found ways to communicate. The Mountain Mercenaries brought food and water every morning, and Teresa and the other women cooked. They laughed and smiled and seemed genuinely happy to have them there. On the contrary, Dave had seen his wife for only a few minutes each night. She always looked stressed and haggard, and he wanted to whisk her away to the motel and force her to talk to him.

He'd realized after waking up the first morning that there was a back way out of the hut, but instead of having one of the other guys tail her, he'd decided to give her some space to work through whatever was fucking with her head . . . but now, several days in, he was done with that.

Zara had come over to eat breakfast with the women this morning—escorted by three of Dave's team; no one was ever left alone in the barrio—and she happily acted as translator. She seemed surprised and dismayed to hear that Raven had been gone every day that week. According to the other women, she never talked about where she'd been, but it was obvious she wasn't eating well, and that she seemed at the end of her rope.

"How are the clinic details progressing?" Dave asked Zara when they were seated on the dirt floor of the hut eating.

"Good. Daniela is thrilled. Says there's a bigger house not too far from the one she's using now that would be perfect."

An idea hit Dave then. "What's going to happen to the house she's using now?"

Zara shrugged. "I guess someone else will move in."

Dave leaned toward her. "I want to buy it."

Zara blinked in surprise. "What?"

"I want to buy it. Teresa, Bonita, Gabriella, Carmen, and Maria can move into it. It'll be safer than this. At least it has a locking door, doesn't it?"

"I was already planning on buying them a house," Zara replied.

"Well, now you don't have to. You can save your money. Or give it to Daniela for the new clinic," Dave told her, not backing down.

Zara stared at him for a moment, then finally nodded.

The other women looked between him and Zara, trying to follow the conversation and failing. But when Dave said their names, Bonita asked Zara a question.

She turned to them and answered in Spanish.

All five women looked at Dave in shock. Their eyes were wide, and Carmen's mouth was hanging open.

"*¿Por qué?*" Maria asked quietly.

"Why? Because it would be safer," Dave explained as Zara translated. "Because no woman should be afraid to close her eyes to sleep at night. Because you're Raven's friends. Because you need a break, and I can afford to give it to you. I wasn't there to help when you needed it the most, but I can help now, and I will."

Gabriella was quietly crying, and the other women looked on the verge of bursting into tears themselves.

Dave was happy to help. He wasn't doing it to try to bribe his way back into his wife's affections. Hell, she wasn't even giving him the time of day to do more than say hello in the evenings. But these women were her friends. They'd helped both his Raven and Zara, and that meant more to him than anything. He'd do whatever it took to try to make sure they were safe and in a healthy environment.

Before anyone could say anything else, there were shouts from outside. Suddenly, all the women looked terrified.

"What's going on?" Dave asked Zara.

"Ruben," she whispered. "Maybe they don't know we're here."

But right after Zara spoke, a male's voice rang out, and Dave recognized Raven's name.

His hands fisted, and he stood, happy that the confrontation he'd been expecting way before now was finally happening.

Zara pulled out her phone, probably to call Meat.

"Stay in here," he ordered the women, and pointed to the ground to emphasize his point, since they couldn't understand him.

No one moved a muscle as he slid back the metal door and stepped outside. He took the time to close the door behind him. He knew if things got out of control, Zara and the others could go out the back of the hut, so he wasn't too worried about them getting trapped inside the ramshackle shelter.

Looking up, Dave saw a cluster of slender men wearing dirty clothes and smirks on their faces. This had to be Ruben and some of his cronies. They were the barrio bullies, and the police and military didn't seem to care what they did. Zara was sure they were being paid by del Rio to help deliver helpless children and women as well. That was one of the reasons why the Mountain Mercenaries' last mission to Lima had almost failed spectacularly. Both these men and the military group they'd been working with had had no intention of letting the team succeed in rescuing the women and children who'd been slated to be delivered to del Rio.

That thought pissed Dave off all the more. How dare these men sell their own up the river? How would they feel if it were *their* wives or children who were sold? Then again, it was obvious these bullies weren't married, and they definitely didn't have any children they loved and cherished. They were too full of themselves to care about anyone, and they obviously craved the power that came with being petty tyrants.

Dave narrowed his eyes at the men. These were the ones who'd hurt Meat and Black. He felt it in his bones. They had also tormented his wife and her friends, not to mention the other residents of the barrio. He wasn't scared of them, no way in hell. In fact, he needed a handy outlet for his frustration.

The man in front of the others—Dave assumed it was Ruben himself—said something in Spanish, and Dave merely crossed his arms over his chest. He didn't need to know what they were saying; he understood them from their tone. They weren't happy he was here and wanted to scare him into leaving. Well, tough shit. He wasn't leaving without his wife, and since she didn't seem to want anything to do with him, he was apparently going to be here for the long haul.

He frowned at them and didn't back down, which seemed to piss them off even more. Instead of listening to their words, which he couldn't understand anyway, Dave concentrated on their body language.

Ruben gestured to two of the men, and they fanned out, attempting to box him in. Dave dropped his arms and rotated his head, working out the kinks in his neck from sleeping on the hard ground. He looked forward to the upcoming fight. He hadn't worked out in a while, and beating on these men would help assuage his frustration and anger about the situation he'd found himself in. Black and Meat might've been taken by surprise by Ruben and his gang a few months ago, but Dave was more than ready.

The man on his right made the first move, leaping toward Dave with a yell. He held a thick tree branch and swung it at his head. Dave turned into the hit, making the weapon literally bounce off his back, before turning and grabbing the smaller man around the neck and smashing his other fist into his face. The man went down like a stone—and after that, the fight was on.

Dave fought like a man possessed. These were the people who'd been terrorizing Raven and her friends for years. They thought they were the prime rulers of the barrio and didn't think twice about taking what they wanted, whether that was food, money, possessions, or even women.

Dave wasn't a soldier, had never studied hand-to-hand combat, but he was a strong man who owned a bar and had dealt with his share of violent and drunk men. He was also determined to teach these assholes a lesson. He felt as if he had the strength of ten men. Every time he hit someone, he imagined it was del Rio—or one of the men who'd violated his wife.

He punched and kicked at Ruben and his friends, feeling satisfaction with every landed blow. His shirt was covered in blood from making contact with vulnerable flesh, and he knew his knuckles were ripped to shreds, but still he didn't stop.

He wasn't losing the fight, but he also wasn't gaining much ground . . . mainly because as soon as he knocked one of the punks out, another would join in the fray.

How long Dave fought, he didn't know, but finally, out of the corner of his eye, he saw Meat, Ball, and Gray running up the alley toward him. They'd been patrolling the barrio and had likely been alerted by Zara's phone call.

Reinforcements had arrived, and it gave Dave a renewed burst of energy.

With their arrival, the advantage quickly turned to the Mountain Mercenaries. Five minutes later, the bullies who remained standing had run off. There were several men lying unconscious in the dirt at their feet, and Gray held a semiconscious Ruben with an unbreakable grip of his biceps.

Dave heard the metal door behind him slide open, and he didn't even bother to look back to see which of the women had been brave enough to risk it. He stalked up to Ruben, grabbed his neck in a brutal grip, and forced him to meet his gaze.

"Stay away from my woman," Dave growled.

Zara translated his words from behind him. Dave wasn't surprised to know it had been her who'd exited the shack. She'd probably been watching the entire time. Thank God she'd been smart enough not to come out and join in, though. Dave would've protected her rather than concentrate on beating the shit out of anyone who got close enough to touch him.

Ruben glared up at Dave.

"I mean it. These women are off-limits to you. Now and forever. If you even look at them cross-eyed again, you'll regret it."

Ruben sneered and said something in Spanish.

Zara translated. "You made a mistake today, gringo. I have power here. The second you're gone, the women will be too. Del Rio will make sure of it."

Dave tightened his hold on Ruben's neck until the other man's face turned purple. "Listen to me, and listen good," Dave said in a low, deadly tone. "I know you think you're a big shot here in the barrio, but I have more power than you'll *ever* have. I've got friends all over the planet. You think you're safe because you've got friends in the Peruvian military? They're nothing compared to *my* friends. You've got a pretty comfortable life in the barrio, but I can have you and all your buddies thrown in prison with one phone call. As long as you leave my friends alone, you can continue to be the big man in your small world. But if you even *look* at them the wrong way, and I hear about it, you're done."

It took a moment for Zara to translate, but Dave saw the second his words registered with Ruben. Some of the bravado left the man. He continued to glare, but Dave could see the unease in his eyes.

"And del Rio is a coward. He hides behind people like *you*, relies on you to do his dirty work while he sits in his huge mansion with more money than he knows what to do with. You're an idiot for doing his bidding. Listen hard—my men and I didn't kill any of your friends today, but make no mistake, if we're attacked again, we won't hesitate to do what needs to be done. And those contacts I mentioned? They'll make sure we stay out of prison—so make your choice carefully."

The second Zara finished translating, Dave shoved Ruben away from him, and Gray let him go at the same time. Ruben went sprawling to the ground and stayed down for a long moment before pushing to his feet and walking away without a glance at his fallen comrades, still unconscious in the dirt.

Zara ran up to Meat and put her arms around him.

"Where are the other women?" Dave asked.

"They went out the back," Zara said.

"Why didn't you go too?" Meat scolded.

She glared up at him. "As if I was going to leave."

Meat shook his head and rolled his eyes at her stubborn response.

Dave shook out his hands, ignoring the pain that coursed through them, and started walking down the alley.

"Where are you going?" Ball called out.

"To get in touch with some of my contacts," Dave said without looking back. "The women need to get out of here. Now. The new clinic needs to happen now so Daniela can move into it, and the others can have her house. I'm sick of tiptoeing around everyone. This shit ends today—and that clinic will be up and running sooner rather than later. This isn't why we came, but I'll be damned if I leave Raven's friends to fend for themselves when we're gone."

He tuned out the men talking behind him as they headed toward the exit to the barrio.

Raven would be gone all day, as had been her norm for the last week, but Dave was done giving her space. He needed her home. Safe. In Colorado. He'd told her that he'd stay in Peru if that was what she wanted, but that option was no longer on the table.

He wasn't staying here, and neither was she.

She'd been on her own for way too long, but that was done. She was his wife. He loved her. They could work everything else out . . . but she had to stop hiding from him. Tonight, when she reappeared from whatever hidey-hole she disappeared to every day, he'd make sure she knew without a doubt how he felt about her, and that he wasn't going to let her push him away anymore. They could work through whatever she was hiding.

Nothing was going to keep him from his wife. *Nothing.*

Chapter Six

Mags ignored the growling of her belly as she crept through the barrio. She'd been staying away from the hut longer and longer each day because she felt the pull toward her husband stronger with every second he stayed. Even though she hadn't spent much time with him, everything he'd done since he'd burst back into her life reminded her why she loved him so much.

He was protective and kind. Loyal and strong. He'd changed, yes, but then again, so had she. For him, however, all his good traits just seemed to have gotten more intense. Sleeping in the dirt outside the hut she'd been staying in? That was crazy, but he didn't even seem to give it a second thought.

She knew it was only a matter of time before she gave in and told him how much she still loved him and how scared she was. She'd thought if she avoided him long enough, he'd eventually get the message and leave her alone.

But she was kidding herself. She knew she was. There was no way Dave would leave. Not now. Not when he'd found her after ten long years. That wasn't the kind of man he was. Even if he'd gotten remarried and had a family, he would still do everything in his power to bring her back to the States, to make sure she was safe. But knowing he didn't have a family, that he hadn't moved on, made it all the more obvious he was never going to leave her here. That he'd do whatever it took to get her to talk to him.

She was so conflicted. Truth was, she *didn't* want Dave to leave . . . but she wasn't sure she was brave enough to tell him why she had to stay.

The sun had set, and the barrio was dark, but she made her way up the alley to the shack easily. Strangely enough, she could hear laughter coming from a few of the huts near hers. She couldn't remember the last time she'd heard happiness in their dismal, depressing world.

And come to think of it, she hadn't seen Ruben or his friends lurking around either. Usually she'd see at least one of them as she slipped into the barrio. They kept watch over everyone who came and went, but she hadn't seen any prying eyes tonight.

A little concerned, Mags eased through the back entrance to the home she shared with her friends—and stopped in her tracks.

Dave was there. He wasn't sleeping outside like he had for the last week. He was sitting in the middle of the floor playing cards with Gabriella, Maria, and Teresa, while Bonita and Carmen sat nearby sewing. Everyone was smiling and seemed to be having a good time, even though they couldn't understand a word Dave was saying.

The second the group saw her, though, the smiles fled from their faces, and they looked at her in concern.

"Are you all right?" Carmen asked.

"Of course. Why wouldn't I be?" Mags asked. She couldn't stop herself from staring at Dave. Her eyes were naturally drawn to him. And as she examined him closely in the dim light, her heart stopped for just a second before it started up double time.

He had a black eye and what looked like the beginning of bruises on his face. His knuckles were split, and it was more than obvious he'd been in a fight.

"What happened?" she asked in Spanish, then English.

Dave didn't answer, merely kept his intense gaze on her, and Mags felt as if she were pinned to the spot.

"Ruben decided he was done watching and attacked Dave," Teresa informed Mags. "We didn't stay around to see, but Zara said he was amazing. He took on Ruben, Eberto, and Alfonso all by himself. Then Marcus and Fortuno and some others joined in. But Zara called her man, and they came running. They beat them up, Mags! It was great!" Teresa's words were all strung together as she got the story out as fast as she could.

Mags's eyes ran over Dave from his head to his toes, wanting to make sure he really was all right. Ruben was an asshole and a typical bully, and when he wanted, he could definitely make life hell in the barrio. She couldn't decide if what Dave had done would make things better or worse.

But then she remembered the laughter she'd heard. It seemed as if, for the time being, things were better.

"We need to talk," Dave said as he slowly stood.

Mags had always loved the way her husband seemed to tower over her. At six-three, he was a tall man, but with his muscles and brawn, he seemed even bigger. It had always made her feel safe . . . but after all she'd been through, his size intimidated her now.

As if knowing how she was feeling, Dave took a step back. "I will *not* hurt you," he said, slowly and carefully.

"I know," Mags responded immediately.

Dave shook his head. "You obviously *don't* know, if your body language is any indication."

Forcing herself to relax, Mags shook her head sadly. "I'm not the same person I was ten years ago," she told him.

"Neither am I," he countered. "But my love for you hasn't changed. In fact, I think it's grown in intensity. I've spent every moment of the last ten years searching for you. So long that it's hard to believe you're actually standing in front of me. Though I'm just now figuring out that you might be here physically, but mentally, you're still lost to me."

Mags stared at the man she loved more than almost anything and knew she was hurting him. Had known this would happen. It was one of the reasons she hadn't tried to get in touch with him after she'd been let go from del Rio's employ. She was so messed up in the head, she couldn't even remember who she'd been before coming to Peru. Her life as an insurance underwriter and Dave's wife was as foreign to her as her current life would've been to her old self.

"Talk to me," Dave begged. "Tell me why you've been avoiding me. Why don't you want to leave here? What is it? What's keeping you in Peru?"

This wasn't the time or place to have this conversation, but Mags didn't know what to do to stop it. The other women were watching her and Dave carefully, their heads going back and forth as each of them spoke. Even though they couldn't understand what was being said, the emotion behind their words was clear.

Mags shook her head. She couldn't tell him. Couldn't bear to see the love in his eyes turn to disgust.

"Damn it, Raven, I've spent the last decade turning over every rock I could to find you! I've learned more about the sex trade than I ever wanted to know. I've rescued hundreds of women and children and reunited them with their families. I've seen some flourish after coming back home, and others who couldn't seem to acclimate. Some women went back into prostitution when they returned simply because they couldn't cope."

Mags flinched.

Dave's voice gentled. "I know what happened to you, sweetheart. And I wish to God it hadn't. I want to kill every single motherfucker who put his hands on you. But none of that changes how I feel. You're my wife. The woman I promised to love through good times and bad. And if you think I'm just going to turn around and leave, you're deluding yourself."

"You have no idea what I've been through," she said bitterly.

"Unfortunately, I do," Dave said sadly. "Right after you were taken . . . they probably threatened both me and your parents. You thought if you did what they said, you'd be okay. I'd pay whatever ransom they demanded, and you'd be home within a few days. But then they probably drugged you. When you finally came back to yourself, you were here. Although you had no idea where 'here' was.

"You were raped repeatedly the first month or two, and you probably fought like hell every time. Eventually, you realized that I wasn't coming for you. That the situation you were in was permanent. After a while, it became easier to just do as you were told. That you would get beaten less and maybe even get more food if you complied. Except, complying ate away at your soul . . . but you still did it anyway.

"As the years went by, you probably thought less and less about your old life, only about getting through each day. You might have earned better treatment through your compliance, and you settled into your life as a slave and prisoner. Then one day, you were either too old or too boring to be a draw to the customers anymore. They'd had their fill and wanted younger and more exciting partners. You were kicked to the curb with nowhere to go and no way to contact me or anyone else from your old life. So you made do with what you had. Made friends, settled in.

"But, Raven, this is *not* your life anymore. I'm here. I'm going to take you home, and we'll figure out how to help you live your life again."

Mags got more and more pissed as Dave spoke. Yes, he was mostly correct. Scarily spot-on, in fact, about how most of her life had gone after she'd been taken.

But he was way off base about why and how she'd gotten out of the business. Del Rio had in no way kicked her to the curb, as she wished he had. She was as tied to him now as she'd been the first night she'd been locked in a room in his compound.

But it was her husband's casual recital of the nightmare she'd lived through that infuriated her the most. To have her own personal hell reduced to two minutes of narrative was depressing.

She supposed she should be glad he wasn't going on and on about her personal hell.

"You might've learned a lot about trafficking over the years, but I'm not one of your charity cases. I'm no victim," she hissed.

"Then talk to me," Dave retorted.

"You wouldn't understand."

"Don't do that," Dave said, sounding pissed.

It was the first time he'd spoken to her in any way that illustrated his frustration, and for some reason, Mags preferred it. Almost liked the idea that he was losing his control.

"Don't do what?" she asked.

"Don't shut me out. I prayed every night that tomorrow would be the day that I'd find you, and when Zara recognized you in that photo, I finally had a shred of hope that *this* time, I actually would."

"Dave, what if I didn't want to be found? Did you ever think about that?"

"No." His answer was immediate. "You wanted to be found as much as I wanted to find you. But I don't know what you're keeping from me. I even asked Zara, and she said she didn't know."

"You interrogated my friends?" Mags asked, wanting to scream at him to drop it, to leave it alone.

"That's a pretty harsh word. Yes, I talked to them. Asked them what they knew about you and where you disappear to during the day," her husband said without any trace of guilt in his tone. "But you have to know, I'll do whatever it takes to figure out what's going on and to keep you safe."

Dave had gotten a lot more stubborn over the years. Mags didn't remember him ever being this insistent when they'd been married. He'd been loving and hadn't pushed her when she was grumpy or simply tired and didn't want to talk. She found his persistence frustrating, and she didn't know how to get him off her back. How to get him to leave.

Except for maybe one way . . .

She could tell him the truth.

Feeling cold and dead inside, she asked, "You want to know what's going on, Dave?"

"Yes," he said immediately.

"You won't be able to handle it," she warned him.

"Try me."

He was so sure that nothing she could say would affect him, and that pissed Mags off so badly. He had no idea what she'd been through. It didn't matter how many other victims he'd talked to. He didn't know about *her* choices. The sacrifices *she'd* had to make over the years. Dave thought he knew everything about sex trafficking and how the world worked—but he didn't know what had happened to *her*.

She knew part of her anger was because her husband had managed to rescue hundreds of other women and children, but he hadn't found *her*. He was here basically by accident.

She also knew her feelings were irrational. It was obvious Dave had done whatever he could to find her; that deep down, she was still struggling to come to terms with the way her life had turned out.

So she lashed out at the one person who, despite everything, was still one hundred percent on her side.

"Fine. I didn't get fired from del Rio's operation because I was too old, even though that's certainly the case. I made a deal with him. A deal with the devil."

Dave stilled—and for the first time, she saw uncertainty creep into his gaze. "What kind of deal?" he asked.

"I promised that I would allow him to increase the number of clients I saw every day for seven months, in return for him letting me retire."

Dave frowned and swallowed hard. "And? There has to be more to it than that. Men like del Rio don't let their employees make those decisions."

He was right. And that irritated her again. "Yeah, well, del Rio's 'employees' don't usually beg to be able to keep the baby one of their customers knocked them up with," Mags shot back.

There. She'd said it.

And she got exactly the reaction she was expecting.

Dave's eyes widened in shock and his mouth fell open. "Baby?" he asked.

At the word, the other women straightened and gaped at Mags.

She ignored them and kept her gaze on her husband. "Yeah, Dave. I got pregnant. It was a miracle."

And it was. She and Dave had tried for two years to have a child, with no luck. Doctors had said there was a problem with both Dave's sperm count and her fertility. The odds of them having a child together had been extremely low. It had devastated them both, but after a couple years, they'd decided to try the adoption route.

But then she'd been taken, and that had been that.

"How?" Dave whispered.

Mags shrugged. "Del Rio doesn't require customers to use a condom, although most did when I insisted. Apparently, one of the men who'd paid for the privilege of being with me managed the impossible—and I wanted that baby. Badly enough to tell del Rio I'd be willing to take on more men, make more money for him, until my ninth month. You wouldn't believe the number of guys who have fantasies of getting it on with a pregnant chick."

She was being deliberately crude now. She just couldn't make herself stop. She wanted to hurt Dave. And she wasn't even sure why. Maybe because she knew after this conversation, he'd probably go back to the States as soon as possible. She'd be left alone again. There was no way he'd want to be with her after hearing all this. And she needed him gone. Needed to stop thinking about the past and dreaming about an impossible future. She was a former whore, no matter that she hadn't wanted to participate in del Rio's sick operation in the first place.

"So I let as many men as del Rio wanted into my bed for seven long months—and I pretended to love it. When it was time for me to have the baby, he locked me in my room and told me if I survived the birth, he'd consider letting me go. I was so scared . . . I had no idea what in the world I was doing. But I did it. My son was born, and he was perfect, from the top of his head to the tips of his toes."

"Where is he now?" Dave asked in an eerily subdued tone.

This was the hardest part of all. The part that made Mags so mad, she could literally kill del Rio with her bare hands.

"Del Rio has him. He said that I could leave, but I couldn't take my baby with me. He has him in a house not too far from his compound. He's being raised by some of the other women who work for del Rio. He's also watched twenty-four hours a day. He's as much a prisoner as I was, except he's getting three healthy meals a day, and he's safe. Del Rio doesn't give a shit about David, but he doesn't want *me* to have him either. He loves knowing I still can't leave, despite getting away from him. He lets me see my son three times a week, on Mondays, Wednesdays, and Fridays. I'm not allowed to eat any of the food there, and I can't take anything with me.

"My son is the most important thing in my life—and I am *not* leaving him. I can't."

As she talked, Dave's face had gone as white as the snow that used to fall outside their house in Colorado Springs. It had been ten years since Mags had seen snow, but she remembered how blindingly white it was after a fresh snowfall. And that was exactly how her husband looked now.

"You named him David?" he finally asked.

Shit!

Mags hadn't meant to let that slip.

Reluctantly, she nodded. "I have no idea who the father is. I was knocked up by one of the hundreds of men who paid del Rio to fuck me," Mags said plainly. "But he's *mine*. I gave him my maiden name, Crawford. And I don't know how, but one of these days I'm going to get him out of there, and we're going to live a life free of del Rio."

"How old is he?"

"Four and a half."

Mags held Dave's gaze firmly. She wasn't ashamed of her son. It didn't matter how he'd been conceived and what she'd had to do to keep him. All that mattered was that he was hers, and he was a beautiful, mostly happy little boy.

Without another word, Dave dropped his gaze, nodded at the other women still sitting on the floor staring at him and Mags, and turned toward the door.

Then he slid the piece of metal away from the opening and left, quietly shutting the door behind him.

Mags's stomach dropped. She instantly felt as if she was going to throw up.

Dave had done exactly what she'd told herself she wanted. He'd left. He couldn't deal with the fact that she'd had another man's baby . . . and she'd never been more devastated.

"What just happened?" Bonita asked urgently.

"He's gone," Mags said softly in Spanish.

"Go after him!" Teresa urged.

Mags shook her head. "I can't."

"You have a baby?" Gabriella asked gently.

Looking up at the youngest member of their little group, Mags nodded. "You understood?"

Gabriella shrugged. "Some. I used to listen to you and Zara talking, and have picked up words here and there. Where is your son? Why don't you have him here?"

Zara wanted to cry. Wanted to lie down and sob about how unfair life was, but the women gathered around her had experienced just as much heartache as she had. Instead, without answering Gabriella, she wandered over to the fire, where a lone meal sat nearby, wrapped in aluminum foil, ready to be eaten.

During the last week, Dave had always made sure to bring her something to eat every night. Even though she'd been avoiding him and treating him like shit, he'd still taken care of her.

She sat down and slowly peeled back the foil.

Closing her eyes, Mags felt her chest grow tighter. Dave had somehow found her chicken nuggets and fries. It had been her favorite meal, and he used to tease her that she would turn into a chicken nugget if she didn't cut back.

The food was lukewarm and a little chewy, but Mags didn't think she'd ever tasted a better nugget in her life.

Realizing she'd finally lost the man she still loved with all her heart, she began telling her friends the story about how she came to have a son.

~

Dave entered the motel room he hadn't spent much time in, slamming the door shut behind him hard enough to shake the wall.

Ball sat up on his bed and asked, "What the fuck? What's wrong? Where's Raven?"

"In the barrio," Dave said shortly.

"And the others?"

"Also there."

"You come here to change clothes or something?" Ball asked.

"No. I'm sleeping here tonight. Arrow's still over there keeping watch."

"Shit," Ball said, and swung his feet off the edge of the bed to put on his boots. He picked up his phone and clicked on a name. Within seconds, he was talking. "Gray, it's Ball. Dave's back. No . . . I don't know. Arrow's got eyes on the women; I'm gonna go check in with him. Yeah, I'd appreciate that. No, he didn't say, and I'm not sure now's the time to ask. Okay, I'll meet Ro in the hall. Thanks. Bye."

Dave didn't even flinch at his friend's conversation. He was numb. He lay down on the bed and put his arm over his eyes.

He couldn't get the devastated look on Raven's face out of his head. She'd sounded defiant enough, and was almost casual about telling him how many men she'd slept with, but he knew simply by looking at her that each one had eaten away a bit of her soul.

A baby. A son.

His wife had a *son.*

He knew he was a coward for leaving without a word. She'd probably never forgive him for that mistake. But in that moment, he couldn't wrap his head around the fact that his Raven had a child.

It was something he'd so desperately wanted to give her, and he'd failed.

He'd held her the night after they'd visited the doctor and been told that a biological child just wasn't going to happen for them. He'd been so worried about her because she wouldn't stop sobbing.

He'd spent the last two years before her kidnapping praying he'd somehow be able to give his wife what she wanted most in her life—and he couldn't.

Not only that, but some *stranger*, someone who didn't love Raven, who didn't give one little shit about her, had succeeded where he'd failed.

The pain was so overwhelming, it had been hard for Dave to remain standing.

He would've done anything, paid any amount of money, to give Raven the child she'd wanted so badly. And instead she'd found her heart's desire in hell.

He was having a hard time processing all of it. He shouldn't have left her—he knew that the moment he'd slid her door closed . . . but he'd needed space to come to terms with how badly he'd failed his wife.

He hadn't been able to find her.

He hadn't been able to give her a child.

It seemed she'd been mostly getting along just fine without him.

It was all too much.

"Dave?" Ball said softly. "I'm headed to the barrio. If you need anything, call Gray, okay?"

Dave nodded, but he wasn't really paying attention to his friend. He was still trying to process what he'd just learned.

He'd been so arrogant when he'd told his wife that he understood what she'd been through. He didn't know a goddamn thing.

Intellectually, he knew what had happened to her. That she'd been used and abused. But emotionally, he had no clue. She'd willingly allowed herself to be used in order to save the life of her baby. She'd probably been terrified when she'd been locked in a room to have her child alone. But she'd done it. She'd done what had been necessary, just as she'd been doing every day since she'd been taken.

She didn't need him to look after her. To protect her. She'd done a hell of an amazing job all by herself.

A kid. *Fuck.*

Four and a half. Her son was four and a half. He'd be talking, and was at a very impressionable age. Were the other women taking care of him properly when Raven couldn't be with him? And why was del Rio holding on to him? What was his ultimate plan? Was he doing it just to torture Raven? That was possible, but for some reason, Dave didn't think so.

He'd done a lot of research into del Rio, and knew others like him. The man didn't do anything out of the goodness of his heart. He was keeping Raven's son for a reason. And knowing that del Rio had no problem trafficking children as well as women didn't bode well for the child.

Raven's son.

David.

Dave sat straight up in bed, his wide eyes staring forward, not seeing a thing.

She'd named her son after him.

He hadn't been there to save her. Hadn't been able to find her. And yet, she'd still named the most important thing in her life after *him*.

The fog Dave had been lost in since hearing his wife had borne a child fathered by another man slowly started to lift. He'd been in shock, hadn't been thinking clearly.

He winced. He'd simply turned and left the hut when she'd told him about her son. He should've taken his wife in his arms and told her everything would be all right. Yes, he'd needed to process what she'd told him, but he should've done that *there*, with her. He'd made a lot of mistakes in his life, but leaving her when she'd finally opened up to him was the absolute biggest.

Standing up, Dave went over to the table and grabbed his laptop. He needed to go back to Raven and make things right with her, if that was even possible, but first he had a lot of work to do. He needed even more information on del Rio.

And he needed to get in touch with his contacts to see about getting another passport prepared.

This one would be harder, since the baby hadn't been born in the United States and there probably wasn't even a birth certificate.

The reason why Raven didn't want to leave Peru was crystal clear now. He had no doubt she would've found her way out of the country and back to him if it wasn't for her son. There was no way Raven would leave an innocent child in del Rio's clutches, especially her *own* child.

Dave was an ass. He didn't deserve Raven, but he'd work hard for the rest of his life to make sure she, and David, never wanted for anything.

He couldn't help but think that he and Raven had wasted a lot of time, but that was done. She had her reasons for keeping David's existence from him, but now that he knew about him, knew why she didn't want to leave Peru, he'd move heaven and earth to get mother and son home.

The team had already been in the country for longer than he'd planned. Dave had thought they'd arrive, he'd be reunited with Raven, and they'd leave. Things were more complicated now, but Dave wasn't the handler of the Mountain Mercenaries for nothing. He'd be able to figure this out too.

His first job was getting David Crawford Justice a passport.

The second was getting the child away from del Rio.

The third was doing everything in his power to make his wife love him again.

Dave paused and took a deep breath.

David Justice.

He'd been an insensitive ass when he'd learned about Raven's child. He'd been stunned, he couldn't deny it. *He'd* wanted to be the one to give his wife a baby. He'd acted like a petulant brat who didn't get a piece of candy after dinner. But now that he'd had a little time to get used to the news, he understood that David was a fucking miracle.

Dave didn't care who the biological father was—*he* would be the boy's father from here on out.

Thinking about a child with Raven's DNA out there in the world made him protective and more than a little obsessive. No one and nothing would hurt him. Because hurting the boy would hurt Raven, and that was unacceptable. She'd been through enough hell in her life, and he'd be damned if she spent one more minute worrying about her child's future.

Dave longed to go straight back to the barrio and reassure Raven that he'd get not only her out of Peru, but David as well. He couldn't. Not yet. Ball, Ro, and Arrow would keep the women safe as he took care of what needed to be done for their son.

That thought hit him hard.

Their son.

When his brain had made the switch from *her* son to *theirs*, he wasn't sure. It was almost instantaneous. But now that the thought was there, it was as good as done.

After they'd found out they couldn't have children together, they'd talked about adoption. They'd decided it didn't matter how a child came into their lives, just that they would be a mother and father. This was no different. David might not be his biologically, but Raven loved him, and he loved his wife. Therefore, the child was now a part of Dave's life. Period.

Determination rose up within him. Del Rio had taken enough from his family. He wouldn't take this too.

He opened his email program and shot off a quick message to his contact who had gotten him a passport for Raven. He needed a picture, and proof that David was Raven's biological child, but he had no doubt that he could obtain both. Getting the child out of the prison he was being held in would be trickier, especially considering how heavily guarded del Rio's properties were. But knowing his Mountain Mercenaries, they'd figure out something.

For the first time since reuniting with Raven, Dave felt confident that they'd make their way back to some semblance of the relationship they'd had before she'd disappeared. There would be bumps in the road, but they'd get there. Together.

Chapter Seven

Mags wasn't sure what woke her up.

She'd lain on her pallet tossing and turning for way too long before finally drifting off to sleep the night before. Today was Friday, and she'd get to see David. Would be able to hear his boyish giggle, see his beautiful smile. He was the only thing that helped her get from one day to the next.

However, her heart was aching because of Dave.

She'd secretly hoped he would somehow understand, and would want both her *and* her son. She knew it was too much to ask. That even as great as her husband was, he'd never be able to accept another man's child as his own. And after he'd left without a word, Mags knew she'd been right. How could any man want to be with her after hearing the stark truths about what she'd done?

Dave was amazing, but if Mags could barely deal with what her life had become, how could he?

Sighing heavily, she started to turn over—freezing when an arm curled around her waist and a body pressed against her back.

"It's me," Dave whispered.

Instead of freaking out and pulling away in terror when he touched her, something deep inside Mags instantly settled. As if her body recognized that Dave wasn't an enemy. She wasn't completely comfortable with him touching her, but she didn't feel threatened either.

She used to be a cuddler, but since her kidnapping, the feel of a man crowding her made her physically sick. She felt a little queasy at the moment, but not enough to hurl last night's dinner.

"How did you get in here without anyone hearing you?" she asked, trying to ignore the feelings stirred up by the large man behind her.

"I'm just that good," Dave said with slight humor in his tone. "Now hush and listen to me."

Mags opened her mouth to respond, but he didn't give her a chance to say anything.

"I'm sorry I left like I did earlier. I was shocked. Hell, I was flabbergasted. Never in my wildest dreams did I think a *child* was the reason you didn't want to leave Peru. But once I got back to the motel and had a chance to think, I realized David is a miracle . . . just like his mother. And you were right, I was an ass to say that I knew what you went through. I don't know a damn thing. But one thing I *do* know is that I love you, Raven. And no matter how long it takes, I'm going to get you *and* our son out of here and back home where you both belong. We all deserve a happily ever after, and I'm determined to make that happen."

Mags couldn't believe what she was hearing. She'd only partly been listening, trying to fight her body's reaction to having him near, but when he'd started talking about her son, she couldn't *not* listen.

"*Our* son?" she whispered.

"Our son," Dave confirmed.

"Dave," she choked out, but he wasn't finished.

"I want to go with you today. To see him."

She shook her head violently. "No, you can't! Del Rio will find out, and he won't let me see him anymore!"

Dave gently turned her so she was on her back looking up at him.

Mags couldn't help it. She panicked. It had been a long time since she'd been at the mercy of a man, but some things just couldn't be forgotten.

The second she started to lose it, Dave realized what was happening. He rolled them gently until she was straddling his stomach.

The change in position made her panic recede a bit. She still wasn't comfortable, still felt way too vulnerable, but he'd put his arms up and out to his sides, so he wasn't touching her. He wasn't holding her on top of him in any way.

"Easy, Raven. I won't hurt you," he said quietly.

Reaching deep down for her bravery, Mags made herself stay right where she was.

Even after a decade, after all the men who hadn't cared one bit about her feelings or what she wanted, she *knew* Dave wouldn't hurt her. "You can't come with me," she reiterated.

"I'll stay hidden when we get close to the house," Dave said. "But I need to know where David is. What kind of guards there are, what the obstacles will be to getting him out. Sweetheart, rescuing children from kidnappers is what the Mountain Mercenaries and I do. Besides, I can't stand to be apart from you even one more day. I've tried to give you space, haven't followed you, even if everything inside me was telling me to do so. Please. Even if you're inside the house, and I'm outside, at least I'm near you."

Mags closed her eyes and tentatively rested her palms on Dave's chest. He was so warm, and she could feel his heart beating under her hand. Memories of making love with him just like this flashed through her brain before she ruthlessly cut them off.

That was a different world. A lifetime ago.

"We need to talk," Dave said gently. "We can talk some while we walk, and tonight I want to take you back to my motel room. You can shower and sleep on a real bed. We can talk about whatever you want. I'll tell you all about The Pit and what I've been doing since you were taken. You don't need to say another damn word about what happened to you in the last ten years if you don't want to, but I'd love to hear all about David. About his first word, his first steps, what kind of food he enjoys. I've missed out on so much . . . and I just want to know everything about him."

"You still have The Pit?" Mags asked.

"Yeah. It's kept me sane," Dave admitted.

"Will you tell me about how you got this?" Mags asked, running a finger over the large scar on his neck.

"I'll tell you everything and anything you want to know," he said, his eyes confirming his sincerity.

"You *have* to stay hidden," Mags told him, not able to believe she was giving in.

"I will," Dave said confidently.

"And when we get close, you can't walk with me."

"Okay. But I need you to do something for me too."

Mags's belly tightened. "What?"

"I need you to get me David's DNA."

She frowned. "Why?"

"Because I need it to prove that he's your biological son. I believe you—it's not that. It's just that it'll be easier to get him a passport that way."

"A passport? Easier?"

"Yeah, Raven. We've left countries on the down-low before without having the proper documentation, and we could do so with David, but since we entered the country officially, with our passports being stamped and everything, it'll be easier to go through official channels so we don't have to be separated from David while we travel back home. I've already talked to my contact, and he's working on everything from his end, but it would speed things up if we had his DNA."

Mags swallowed hard. "You've already talked to someone?"

Dave's face gentled. "Yeah. I'm ashamed of my reaction to you telling me you had a son, but I got my head out of my ass as soon as I could."

Once again, Mags wanted to cry, but instead she asked, "What kind of DNA? I'm not allowed to bring anything in or out of the house."

A muscle in his jaw ticked at hearing that, but he simply asked, "What about a tissue? You could help David blow his nose and then stuff the tissue in your pocket. I doubt anyone would care about a used wad of tissue, would they?"

Mags slowly shook her head. No, they wouldn't. It was actually genius. "I can do that."

"Good. Are you allowed to take him outside at all?"

She nodded. "Just in the backyard. And there's an armed guard watching us the entire time. There's also a concrete wall around the yard, but he can go out there and play."

"Perfect. I'll get his picture when you take him outside, then. If possible, after he runs around a bit, sit with him in your lap, facing the wall. That way I can zoom in on his face while he's not in motion."

Nerves rose up within Mags once more. "If you're caught—"

"I won't be," Dave said with conviction. "I'm not going to do anything to jeopardize us being able to leave the country," he told her. "Trust me."

"I do."

"Do you?"

Mags swallowed and nodded.

Slowly, one of Dave's hands rose toward her face, and he palmed her cheek. Mags leaned into his hand.

"This right here is a miracle," Dave said softly. "I wanted to believe you were alive, but I wasn't sure. You could've been killed an hour after they took you and buried somewhere in the Nevada desert. But I had a feeling, deep down, that you were alive. I dreamed about you. That you were bleeding and hurting, and you'd look me in the eyes and tell me to hurry up and find you. I'm so damn sorry I took so long. And *I* really didn't even have anything to do with it. It was all Zara. I owe her more than I can ever repay. It took me ten years, but I'm here, Raven. And I'm not going anywhere."

Mags closed her eyes, reached up, and grabbed hold of Dave's wrist. She wanted to tell him that it might've been Zara who recognized her picture, but it had been Dave's tireless work in hunting down missing women and children that led them to where they were right now. If he hadn't formed the Mountain Mercenaries, hadn't made the connections he had, Zara might still be living in the barrio and wouldn't have met Meat. Wouldn't have gone back to the States.

Everything was connected, and it truly was a miracle that out of the billions of people in the world, he'd somehow managed to find her.

How long they sat like that, her holding on to his wrist while he palmed her cheek, Mags didn't know, but eventually the unease she felt about being astride him, at his touching her, disappeared. She felt . . . content. Safe.

It had been ten years since she'd felt this way, and she didn't want to move. Ever.

"What time do you usually leave?" Dave asked after a while.

"Before the sun comes up," she whispered.

"Then we should get going."

Her eyes flew open, and she looked around. The interior of the hut was lighter than it had been when she'd woken up to find Dave behind her.

"Don't panic," he told her, steadying her with a hand at her waist. "We'll get there in time. Relax."

Nodding, Mags still climbed off him. He stood, reached for something in his pocket, and held it out. She couldn't make out what it was and didn't reach for it.

"It's a protein bar. I've got a couple of them. I heard you say that bastard doesn't allow you to eat while you're there. That's fucking wrong, so I grabbed some of these to help tide you over. You can eat a couple while we're on our way."

It was such a little thing, but the longer Mags spent around Dave, the more she remembered that was just how he was. He was always doing things like that. Little things that a lot of people wouldn't think twice about. But it seemed over the last ten years, his respectfulness and politeness had morphed into uber-protectiveness and caveman tendencies. She smiled slightly. She couldn't deny it felt good.

She'd spent years in hell, relying on no one, trusting almost no one, bearing the burden of doing what she thought was best for her son all by herself. Knowing that Dave had not only heard what she'd said about her visits with David but had done something to try to make her life easier felt amazing.

She took the food and nodded in thanks, not able to put into words what was going through her head.

Dave nodded toward the protein bar and waited. She realized that he wasn't going to go anywhere until she'd eaten. She ripped open the snack. The smell of chocolate and peanut butter wafted up to her nose, and her mouth automatically started watering. She'd eaten some very good meals over the last week . . . Dave and his team had taken very good care of her as far as meals went. But after taking a bite, she closed her eyes and was surprised at how much she enjoyed the protein bar.

She hadn't eaten a lot of health food ten years ago, and for some reason, she'd expected the protein bar to be awful. Dry and tasteless. But whatever was in this one was anything but. It was like eating a candy bar.

She opened her eyes to see a look she'd never seen on her husband's face before.

Sorrow and . . . pride?

Mags didn't know what that was about. The sadness she understood; she was pretty pathetic. But there was no way he could be proud of her for anything she'd done in the time they'd been apart. All she'd managed was to tread water and keep from sinking below the stormy sea that had become her existence.

After she'd finished the protein bar, Dave stuffed the wrapper in one of the pockets on his black cargo pants, and they headed out the door.

Mags hadn't realized that Ro was outside, and it was obvious he'd spent the night on the hard dirt, just as Dave had been doing. Her husband briefly stopped to thank Ro for staying the night and to tell him what their plans were.

"It's Raven's day to visit David, and I'm going with her to do recon. We'll be back this afternoon."

Ro nodded. "Okay. We're going to meet with Daniela about the logistics of moving the clinic to a bigger building. We'll take care of that and keep watch over the women here. Once you figure out what the situation is with David, we can have a chat about our next steps to get us all out of here."

"Everything good with Chloe?" Dave asked.

"Yeah. Just missin' her."

Dave clapped a hand on Ro's shoulder. "I know. With any luck, we'll be out of here sooner rather than later."

"Wasn't complaining," Ro noted. "Be careful today. Don't let anyone see you lurking around the house. If they know somethin's up, they could tighten security, and that's one problem we don't need."

"I won't. Later."

"Later."

It was obvious between last night and now, Dave's friends had been informed about David. Mags should've been upset about that, especially after having to keep the secret for so long, but at the moment, she couldn't care about anything other than getting to her son.

The interaction between Ro and Dave was interesting. She knew her husband was in charge of the other men as far as the group went. But she didn't know how those dynamics worked. Dave had never been in the military, and she wasn't sure why they willingly followed his lead. But all she saw between Ro and Dave was respect. The kind that didn't come from brute force or intimidation, like she witnessed every day from del Rio's men.

Not for the first time, Mags really understood that what Dave had said was right. He *wasn't* the same man he'd been.

He'd always been protective of her, but now he was even more so. He didn't touch her as they walked, but his gaze was constantly moving from side to side, as if looking for danger. When they got to the sidewalk outside the barrio, he insisted she walk next to the wall, instead of the street. He put out an arm to keep anyone passing from touching her. And when a bicycle came toward them a little too fast, he stepped forward and put himself between her and the rider.

Over the last ten years, no one had treated her with any delicacy. She'd been more like an object than a living, breathing person. She was a way to make money, a slave to del Rio, and she'd had to do whatever he told her to do if she wanted to live. Even after being kicked out of his compound, she wasn't free. She had to toe the line in order to protect her son. She'd scrounged in trash cans for food and faded into the background to escape too much interest from men like Ruben.

Longing hit Mags hard then. She wished life had been different. Wished she'd been able to see her husband change and grow over the last ten years, like normal couples. But if she was honest with herself, she liked the man it seemed Dave had turned out to be. A little rough around the edges, a bit too inwardly focused, but still gentle, protective, and loyal to his friends. She hadn't missed how he'd asked about Chloe, who she assumed was Ro's girlfriend or wife.

The walk to the house where David was being raised didn't seem quite as long today as it had in the past. She and Dave didn't talk much, but just having him there, watching for trouble, allowed her to relax and not be quite so on edge. The walk was roughly five miles, but she'd never minded it. She'd walk twice that if it meant being able to see her son.

When they got within half a mile of the house where David was living, Mags reluctantly turned to Dave. "I need to go by myself from here."

He frowned but nodded. Pulling out another protein bar, he said, "Eat this before you get there. I don't like the thought of you going hungry."

Mags wanted to cry as she stared at the food, but controlled herself. She took it and stuffed it into one of her pockets. She'd eat it once she started walking again. She couldn't take it in with her. She was always searched, both entering and leaving the house.

"And take this." Dave held out a wad of tissues. "They shouldn't care that you've got them in your pocket."

Reaching for them, Mags held her breath when Dave gently took hold of her hand. "Be careful," he whispered. "I know you've been doing this for a while now, and you're a grown adult, but I can't help but worry about you and David. I can't lose you again. It would destroy me. Don't do anything unusual that will bring attention to yourself. We're in the home stretch, and if all goes well, we could all be on our way back to the United States in a few days. If you act differently, someone might think something is up. Is del Rio around when you're there?"

Mags wanted to argue. Wanted to tell Dave that she hadn't agreed to go back to the US with him. He was acting as if it was a foregone conclusion.

But the fact of the matter was, Mags wanted to go home more than anything. She wanted to see snow again. Wanted to breathe in the scent of Dave's bar. Wanted to show David that life wasn't just about having to follow orders and be meek and quiet all the time. She wanted to be free. Wanted her son to be free to laugh and cry without worrying about being reprimanded for being too loud. Wanted to see him run around without a care in the world. He was way too quiet for an almost five-year-old. Too grown up.

Dave's words also made her melt a little inside. It had been a long time since anyone had worried about her, and the fact that he'd included David in his worry was a miracle in her eyes. She'd never thought he would be mean to the boy, but for him to willingly embrace another man's child, to be one hundred percent committed by calling him "our son," wasn't something she could've dreamed up in her wildest fantasies.

Remembering his question about del Rio, Mags said, "He's not usually here on the days I am. Sometimes he'll show up just to remind me that he's the one allowing me to see my son, but David has said a few things that make me think del Rio pops by to visit him when I'm not there."

"All right. If he does happen to come today, just do whatever you usually do. I'm working on some things that will hopefully pan out, but in the meantime, we don't want to give him a heads-up that anything's different."

Mags eyed him. "What are you working on?"

"I'll tell you later. There's no time now, and I don't want you to worry about anything but making sure our boy has a good day with his mom. Okay?"

It was a good answer, though it didn't assuage her worries.

Moving slowly, Dave leaned over and gently kissed Mags on the forehead. "I love you, Raven. I know it might be awkward hearing me say it, but I can't help it. I've loved you since the day I met you, and I will until the day I die. I'd never do anything to put you or our son in danger. Just know I'm here and I'm watching. I'll wait for you this afternoon right here. Okay?"

"Okay," she said softly. She'd spent the last ten years with absolutely no affection. Just enduring men doing what they wanted, when they wanted. Dave's gentle caress felt like heaven.

She turned and walked toward the house where her son was waiting. He knew their routine just as well as she did, and she knew he looked forward to her visits. He was too young to understand why he only got to see her a few days a week, and Mags was all too aware that it wouldn't be long before del Rio would change their arrangement. He'd hinted at it the last time she'd seen him, and it scared the shit out of her.

She was terrified del Rio had set his sights on making her son work for him.

She'd find a way to kill del Rio before she allowed him to sell David like he'd sold her.

Pushing the thought to the back of her mind, she concentrated on eating the protein bar Dave had given her and making her way safely to the house. The house wasn't in a great area, and in the past, she'd always walked as fast as she could to try to avoid the men looking for trouble, but today she knew with complete certainty that she was safe. Simply because Dave was there somewhere, watching over her.

It was a little scary how quickly she'd found comfort in Dave's presence. But she'd felt alone for so long that knowing she wasn't any longer was the best feeling in the world.

Chapter Eight

Mags watched as David ran around the small fenced-in yard kicking an old soccer ball. He'd been overjoyed to see her, as usual, and seeing his chubby little face made her feel one hundred percent better.

Since there weren't any other children in the house, he was used to playing by himself. He usually wasn't quite so energetic, but she loved to see it. She hated that he had to stay inside most of the time.

She hadn't recognized the woman who'd escorted her to David's room after she'd been searched by two of del Rio's men upon arrival, but that wasn't exactly a surprise. The women were rotated in and out of the small house frequently. Probably so David didn't get too attached to any of them, and vice versa. Del Rio might be an asshole, but he wasn't stupid. The women probably enjoyed the break from the main compound, and if they got too friendly with either her or her son, it was possible they might try to assist her in getting her son out of there. Del Rio wouldn't risk her disappearing for good.

She'd never taken much notice of the men who'd watched her and David in the past. They were just always there, just as they were in the main compound. They were frequently too liberal with their hands when they searched her. She'd always tolerated it because she had no other choice. But today, their fingers squeezing her boobs under the guise of making sure she hadn't stashed anything in the cheap cotton bra she was wearing made her skin crawl. And when one of them kept his fingers between her legs a little too long, she shoved him away and told him that she no longer worked for del Rio.

The man had sneered and informed her that she would *always* be working for del Rio. When she'd looked away, he'd chuckled, as if he knew he'd gotten to her.

Lost in her thoughts, Mags hadn't realized that David had gotten tired of playing with the ball and had wandered back over to where she was sitting. He climbed onto her lap and rested his little head against her breast. Mags wrapped her arms around him and held him close. He hadn't bathed in a few days, she could tell, but she could still smell his little-boy scent under the dirt and sweat.

She hadn't seen any sign of Dave, but she hadn't wanted to seem too interested in the wall either. Standing in the yard, there were two men holding rifles, and the last thing she wanted was for them to get suspicious. She just hoped Dave would be able to get the picture he needed for David's passport without being seen. She was nervous and anxious, and she hated it.

"Had enough playing with the ball?" she asked David softly. Mags had been speaking English to her son since he'd come out of her womb, and as a result, he was bilingual.

"*Sí.* Tell me a story, *Mamá*," her son begged.

"What do you want to hear this time, *mijo*?"

"The story about *Papá*."

Mags smiled. "Are you sure you don't want me to tell you a *new* story? Maybe about a pirate and a princess?"

David shook his head. "No. *Papá*."

For the first time, Mags didn't feel sad when thinking about Dave. She'd been telling David stories about his "father" since he was old enough to understand her. She hadn't thought he'd ever get to meet Dave, but she felt better giving her son a role model to look up to. Lord knew the men who hung around the house weren't the kind of men she wanted him to emulate. But now, with the possibility that he just might get to meet Dave, Mags almost felt giddy.

"But first tell me what he looks like," David demanded, as he did every time they talked about him.

"He's big. Tall and muscular. His arms are as big around as tree trunks, and he's taller than even the wall surrounding this yard," Mags said fondly. "He's got a scar that runs down his neck into the collar of his shirt. It makes him look scary, but to those he loves, he's the most protective and gentle man you'll ever meet."

"Scar?" David asked with a furrow in his brow. "You never told me that before. How did he get it?"

Mags blinked. Of course she hadn't described it in the past, because she hadn't known about it. "Yeah, baby. It's pretty big."

"Did it hurt?"

"I'm sure it did."

"Did you kiss it and make it better?"

Mags felt tears well up in her eyes, but she closed them and refused to let them fall. "If I had been there when he got it, I would've," she told her son.

"I bet he put a Band-Aid on it. If I scraped my knee, would he bring me a Band-Aid?" David asked.

Mags smiled and hugged her son tighter. "Yes. Not only that, but he'd pick you up and carry you to a chair. He'd blow on it to make it feel better, and if you cried, he wouldn't scold you. He'd simply hug you until the pain was gone." Mags knew exactly what her son wanted to hear. He didn't get any love from the women and men he encountered on a daily basis, and she knew when he was scared or hurt, and cried, he was yelled at instead of reassured. He barely ever cried anymore, and she knew it was because he was abused when he did.

"Where is *Papá* now?"

They'd been over this many times too. She could've told David the truth today, that his *papá* was in Peru and would soon be taking them both home to the United States, but she didn't want him to accidentally let that information slip in his excitement. The last thing she wanted was del Rio getting wind of an escape attempt. And she didn't think Dave would change his mind about taking her and her son back to Colorado, but just in case he did, she didn't want to disappoint David.

"He's in the United States. See, *Mamá* got lost. And *Papá* is looking as hard as he can to find us. And when he does, we're going to go and live happily ever after with him."

David looked up at her. "Were you scared when you got lost?"

"Yeah, baby, I was. Sometimes I still am. But you know what keeps me going?"

"What?"

"Knowing that tomorrow is a new day. I just have to get through one day at a time. And one of these days, I'll wake up, and *Papá* will be here, and he'll take us home."

"And we can all live together? You won't have to leave at the end of the day?" David asked.

His question nearly broke her heart, but Mags did her best to keep her voice neutral. "Yeah, baby. We'll all live in the same house together. We'll have all the food we want, and you'll have a ton of friends to play with. We'll eat dinner together, and I'll tuck you into bed every night." Mags wanted to cry. She'd been telling her son the same fairy tale his entire life, but today was the first time she believed it might come true.

"Will I have to take pictures with him?"

Mags frowned. That was a new question. "What do you mean? What kind of pictures? Who takes pictures with you now?"

David shrugged, but she could feel the sudden tension in his little shoulders and in the way he pressed his head harder to her chest. "Del Rio comes here, *Mamá*. With another man. We play naked, and del Rio takes pictures. I don't like it, but I have to." His voice lowered as he admitted, "I said no once, and I didn't get to eat for a really long time.

Del Rio told me good boys do what adults say." Then he looked up at her and whispered, "He said you won't come see me if I'm a bad boy."

Mags felt as if she were going to explode. She was outraged, and scared, and freaked out.

Del Rio was training her son to do whatever his sick pedophile clients wanted him to do.

She took David's head in her hands and looked him in the eye. "Your body is your own," she said in a shaking voice, doing her best to stay calm. "*No one* is allowed to touch you without your permission. I don't care if they're an adult or not. And no one will keep me away from you, *mijo*. I will always be your *mamá*, and I will not let anyone keep us apart. Okay?"

David nodded. "'Kay."

"You can tell me the truth. Did that man touch you when you had your clothes off?" Mags wasn't sure she wanted to know the answer.

"He stood next to me in the photos, then I sat on his lap."

Mags inhaled deeply. She'd occasionally seen little kids around the compound, but since David wasn't being kept there, she'd hoped and prayed he might have escaped their fate. But deep down she'd always known there was a reason del Rio wasn't letting her leave Peru with her son.

She wanted to kill him with her bare hands.

She looked David in the eyes once more and said gently, "I love you. More than anything in this world. No matter how old we get, or what happens in the future, I will always love you. Hear me?"

"Yes, *Mamá.* Will you tell me the story of how you and *Papá* met now?" David asked.

It seemed like he wasn't visibly traumatized by what del Rio had done, but it was only a matter of time before things went further than naked pictures.

He turned on her lap and stared out into the yard, and Mags lowered her chin until it rested on her son's little head. Then she began to tell him the same story he'd heard countless times already.

"Your *papá* bought a building and had called where I worked to get it insured. It was my job to go inspect it to make sure it would be safe to let people inside. When I got there, I was nervous because it wasn't in the safest part of the city, and I was all alone. I got out of my car, and your *papá* came out of the building."

"And you were scared!" David interjected.

Mags chuckled. "Yes, I was."

"Because *Papá* is big. Big enough to lift cars and beat up bad guys!" David said enthusiastically.

Mags thought Dave would get a kick out of David's imagination. "Exactly. He came outside, and I was scared to be around him. But he noticed and made sure not to get too close. That made me feel better. In fact, when I inspected the outside of the building, he stayed by the front door, watching to make sure no one else came and bothered me, but also keeping his distance. He held open the door for me when I had to go inside and asked if I wanted something cold to drink. After I was done making sure the building was safe, we talked some more. He was funny, and he made me feel comfortable. He asked if I wanted to go on a date, and I said yes."

"And you went to a restaurant where you got a steak and he got fish!" David recited happily.

"That's right. And we talked all night. And by the end of the date, I wasn't worried about how big he was anymore. I knew he wouldn't hurt me," Mags said.

David turned again and looked up at her. "Just because someone is big and mean-looking doesn't mean they're going to hurt you."

"Exactly. And on the flip side, someone who is small and skinny might be able to hurt you much more than someone bigger."

"Mamá?"

"Yeah, baby?"

"Why are some people mean and others aren't?"

Mags shouldn't have been surprised at her son's question. He might only be four and a half, but he hadn't had the most stable or loving home. She'd done her best to shower him with love and affection, but she couldn't control what the other people who were raising him did. And unfortunately, they were around him more than she was. "I don't know. Some are probably born that way. Others learn how to be mean by watching those around them. Others are greedy and will do whatever they can to get money."

"I don't want to be mean," David said softly.

"You aren't," Mags soothed him.

"Sometimes I get really mad inside," her son admitted. "I miss you when you aren't here, and the other ladies who watch over me don't care if I'm hungry or if I get hurt, not like you. And it makes me mad. I want to hit them!"

Mags sighed in frustration. "Thank you for being honest, David. It's important not to lie. And I'm sorry they treat you that way. This will be hard for you to understand, but sometimes people do things because they don't have a choice. Someone else is making them be that way. Or they're hurting inside so much, they don't have the energy to care about anyone else. They're simply trying to get to tomorrow. One day at a time."

Her son thought about her answer for a moment, then nodded. "Like when del Rio comes and yells at everyone, and they have to do what he says."

Mags stiffened. "Does he come by a lot?" she asked, wanting to know how much time she and Dave had to get her son out.

David shrugged. They were both quiet for a minute or two. Then he asked quietly, "Do you think *Papá* will find us soon?"

"I'm sure of it," Mags couldn't help but say. In the past, she'd always tried to be optimistic, but cautiously so, not wanting to raise the boy's hopes. But now that Dave *was* here, and seemed ready to take both her and her son back to the States, she couldn't help but give David something to look forward to.

"Do you think he'll like me?"

"Oh, sweet boy, of course he will. Why wouldn't he?"

David shrugged again.

"Look at me," Mags ordered her son. She waited until he looked up at her with his big blue eyes. She liked to think he looked more like her than whoever his biological father was. He had black hair and blue eyes like she did. He even had a dimple in one cheek, just like she did. Before he was born, Mags had been afraid that looking at him would remind her of the hell she'd lived through, but the opposite had been true. The first time she held him in her arms, she'd fallen in love. Immediate and all-consuming. She didn't care how he was conceived, just that he was alive and healthy . . . and hers.

"You are an amazing little boy. You're smart, handsome, and compassionate. Why wouldn't *Papá* like you?"

"Del Rio called me a bastard. He says the only way anyone will ever love me is if I do what they tell me to. What *he* tells me to."

Mags wanted to scream. Del Rio had no right to say such a thing to her son!

At one time, she'd been happy she'd had a son instead of a daughter, thinking he would be safe from del Rio and his sex-trafficking business. But it was very clear that wasn't the case. She'd been deluding herself, thinking the vile kingpin had no interest in her son.

Over her dead body would she let anyone touch David. No more than they already had. No way in hell. She'd die trying to save him from that fate.

"Don't you listen to him," she said a bit more furiously than she'd intended. She did her best to get her anger under control. "He's wrong. And you have a mind of your own." She tapped his little head with her finger. "You're smart and can think for yourself. If someone tells you to do something you know is dangerous or wrong, you don't have to do it. But here's the thing . . . sometimes in life, you could find you must do something you don't want to do. It doesn't make you a bad person. If someone else is making you do it, *they* are the bad ones. Not you. Understand?"

David nodded, but Mags could still see the hurt and confusion in his eyes.

"I love you, David. You are the best thing to happen to me. I wouldn't change one day of my life if it meant you wouldn't be here with me. Hear me?"

"Yes, *Mamá*."

"I mean it. I've had to do some things I'm ashamed of, but I'll *never* be ashamed to call you my son. No matter what the future holds. You always hold your head up and know that you are David Justice. You're smart and important."

He threw his arms around her neck and buried his head in her shoulder. He wasn't crying, but they were both fairly emotional. Mags just wanted to pick him up and carry him straight out the door, but knew she couldn't.

She'd already hated del Rio with everything in her, but at that moment, knowing what he was attempting to do to her son, she vowed to see him dead.

She pulled back and took David's little head in her hands once more. She gazed into his blue eyes and said, "The world is sometimes scary and confusing. But no matter what happens from this day forward, know that your *mamá* loves you. If you get lost, I'll find you. If someone hurts you, I'll be there to make you feel better. If you have to do something you don't want to, I'll still love you. All you have to do is hang on until tomorrow. One day at a time, okay, baby?"

"Okay, *Mamá*. What about *Papá*? Will he love me too?"

Two days ago, Mags wouldn't have known how to answer his question. Today, she could answer it with confidence. "Yes, *mijo*, *Papá* loves you very much and will do whatever he can to keep you safe. You can trust him with your life, he will never hurt you. Ever."

David nodded.

A door opened behind them, and a woman said indifferently, "It's time for the boy to eat."

Mealtimes were usually torture for Mags. In the past, she'd been so hungry that her stomach had physically hurt when she looked at the food on the table that she wasn't allowed to touch. But since Dave had found her, he'd made sure she had plenty to eat. And the protein bars he'd given her that morning meant she wasn't even hungry now.

Not that she could've forced anything past her lips anyway . . . not after hearing what del Rio was grooming her son to do.

Grateful for the fact that she'd be able to sit through lunch without David having to listen to her stomach growl, she stood up and held her son's hand as they walked back into the house. It was a prison for them both, but for now, she was glad he didn't realize it.

Leaving her son was harder than normal that afternoon. Usually Mags could rationalize within herself that she'd see him again in a few days, but after learning del Rio had been visiting the house and taking pictures of her son, and trying to fill his head with garbage, she was all the more reluctant to leave.

But of course she had no choice. Right at five, one of del Rio's men told her it was time to leave. She held her son a little longer than usual and reminded him that he was smart and how much she loved him. She was escorted to the door, and the sound of the locks clicking into place behind her made her cringe. She wanted to turn around, bang on the door, and demand they let her son go. Pick him up and run away as fast as she could. But of course she couldn't do that.

Wrapping her arms around herself, Mags turned and walked down the sidewalk toward where she'd left Dave that morning. He'd said he'd be waiting for her, and for the first time in forever, she needed someone to hold her. To tell her everything would be okay. To share the burden of the suckage that was her life. Usually she remained stoic about the way things were and the difficulties she endured, but with the arrival of Dave, and the hope he'd sparked within her, she was no longer content going along with the status quo. Nor could she afford to be, considering del Rio's plans for her son.

She felt as if there was a black cloud surrounding her, and the longer she tried to ignore it, the more it would consume her. Something bad was coming. *Was already here.* She could feel it in her bones. Which made it harder than ever to leave David.

Turning a corner, Mags gasped in surprise and fright when she bounced off someone. She would've fallen to the ground, but whoever she'd run into grabbed ahold of her arms. She struggled for a split second before it registered that it was Dave who held her.

The moment she realized who it was, she relaxed, and he put his arm around her waist, plastering her against his side as they walked. He didn't say anything, simply steered her toward a minivan idling nearby. She climbed in and recognized Ball, who was behind the wheel.

As soon as the door was shut, the car started moving.

"You okay?" Ball asked.

"Not really," she said, doing her best to get control over her emotions and the need to be held by her husband. She jerked as she realized Dave was pulling a seat belt across her lap and fastening it. It had been so long since she'd ridden in a vehicle, she hadn't even thought about buckling up.

He then pulled out another protein bar and handed it to her before he snapped his own seat belt into place.

"Right, how *could* you be all right?" Dave said angrily. "That asshole has locked up your son and only allows you to see him three days a week. And the fact that he kidnaps children from the barrios to sell them doesn't bode well for David."

She looked from Dave to Ball nervously, not sure she wanted to talk about what she perceived to be her greatest weaknesses—namely, that she had no idea how to save her son from a fate worse than death—in front of the other man.

"That asshole isn't going to put one finger on your son," Ball said tersely from the front seat. His words put her at ease. He was obviously angry, but not at her. At the situation. Mad that she and her son were being separated, and he was being held hostage by del Rio.

Anger on David's behalf, she could deal with.

She looked up at Dave worriedly. "David said some stuff today that terrified me."

Dave put a hand over hers in her lap. "All right. We'll talk about it when we get to the motel."

"Oh! And I got the tissue like you wanted," Mags told him, starting to reach into her pocket with her free hand.

"Good. Leave it for now. We'll give it to Gray when we get to the motel. He'll overnight it to my contact in the States."

Mags nodded and took a bite of the protein bar. It tasted delicious and helped curb her hunger, which had just begun to return after not eating since that morning. "Were you able to get a picture?" she asked after she'd swallowed a bite.

Dave nodded. He wasn't talking much, which made her nervous.

"Was it all right? I tried to keep him outside for as long as possible. I also tried to look for you, but didn't want to be obvious."

"You did perfect," Dave said, lifting her hand and kissing the back of it.

"What's wrong?" she whispered.

"Nothing."

She bit her lip. Something was definitely wrong. She hadn't seen Dave in years, but in the time she'd been around him in the last week or so, she'd begun to read his moods pretty easily. And something was definitely not right at the moment.

She kept quiet for the rest of the ride back to the motel. It felt amazing not to have to walk the five miles to the barrio, she couldn't deny it. Ball pulled into a parking lot in the back of the motel, and she wasn't really surprised to see Gray already there, waiting for them.

Dave helped her out of the minivan and kept hold of her hand when she was standing next to it.

"Give him the tissue," Dave said, sounding a little calmer than he'd been in the van.

Mags reached into her pocket and pulled out the used tissue David had blown his nose in earlier. Not too much grossed her out after everything she'd seen and done, but for some reason, boogers and snot still made her want to gag.

She held it by a corner as she placed it in a plastic bag Gray held out.

Chuckling, Gray said, "For me, it's vomit. I can handle shit, spit, blood, and anything else the human body can expel . . . except for puke. It makes *me* want to hurl every time."

"How're you handling baby spit-up?" Dave asked with a slight grin.

Gray made a face. "I'm handling that okay. I mean, when he's burped after eating, it's basically just milk, so it's not quite as gross."

"You're gonna be in big trouble when Darby gets the flu," Ball said with a chuckle. He hadn't moved from the driver's seat, and it was obvious he was going to drive Gray somewhere so he could mail the tissue.

"Nope. Allye and I already made a deal. I'll change diapers whenever I'm home for as long as I need to, and she'll take care of any puke that might happen," Gray said with a smile and a wink. Then he sobered. "How's David?"

Mags flinched. She wasn't used to talking about her son so openly. Hell, before today, none of the women she lived with even knew about him. "He's okay."

"Saw the pictures Dave sent. He's adorable . . . and the spitting image of his mom," Gray said. Then he gave Dave a chin lift and climbed into the passenger side of the minivan.

Dave didn't give her a chance to respond, merely pulled her toward the door to the motel.

Still feeling uneasy, Mags let Dave lead her up the stairs to the second floor and to a room right next to the stairwell. He opened the door and held it open, gesturing for her to enter first. She did, and at first glance, the room was nothing special. It had two queen beds, a tiny television on a dresser, and an even smaller table and chair in the corner.

Dave walked over to a bag on the floor and plopped it on the mattress. It had some sort of biometric lock, and Dave used his finger to unlock it. He pulled out a laptop and placed the bag back on the floor.

Mags stood in the middle of the room feeling ill at ease. For the first time, she was acutely aware of how she must look . . . and smell. Personal hygiene wasn't something she gave a lot of thought to, simply because she didn't have the means or ability to do much about it.

But standing in the clean motel room, seeing Dave settle on the clean bedspread, made it painfully obvious she was filthy. She didn't know what to do, where to sit, what to say. She felt extremely awkward, which she hated.

Dave had opened the computer and was busy clicking keys. He didn't even look up when he said, "If you want, you can go ahead and shower. There's soap and stuff in there."

God, how she wanted to take that shower. It had been so long since Mags had been able to take a hot shower . . . and not worry about who might want to join her in it and what they might want to do to her.

Still, she hesitated. "I thought we were going to talk," she said.

Dave looked up then—and Mags almost staggered back at the look in his eyes. The longing was easy to see. But it was the frustration and agony that really struck her.

"There're so many things I want to do for you, Raven. I want to feed you. Clothe you. Give you a safe place to heal. I want *my* friends to be *your* friends, and I want to give our son the comfort and safety he's been missing. And more than anything, I want to hold you."

He sighed heavily. "But I know out of all those things, the only ones I can do at the moment are feed and clothe you. I had Ball pick up some things I thought you might like to wear today, and they're in the bathroom on the counter. I guessed on the sizes. Take your time. I'll take you back to the barrio anytime if you want to go—you aren't a prisoner here. But I'm hoping after you shower you might stay and . . . talk. Just talk. Ball said he'd bunk with one of the others tonight. You don't have to be scared of being alone with me. We'll just talk."

"I'm not scared of you," Mags said. There was so much more in what he'd just said, but she couldn't think about it all without wanting to cry. So she focused on the simpler stuff. "I'm sure whatever Ball got is fine, but I'd prefer putting my own things back on."

"If you want, you can clean them in the shower and wear the new stuff just while your own clothes are drying. Then you can change back into them . . . before you go."

It was obvious how hard those last few words were for Dave. "It's not that I don't want to wear what Ball got for me," she tried to explain. "It's just that I'm more comfortable in my own things."

He nodded. "I know. Go on, sweetheart. Take your time. I need to send these pictures and talk to a few of my contacts."

Mags knew she'd disappointed him. And she hated that.

Then something struck her for the first time. "Do my parents know?"

Dave tilted his head as he studied her. Mags had forgotten how he'd do that when he was contemplating what to say. It was one of the million and one things she loved about him . . . and she'd forgotten it. Sadness threatened to overwhelm her.

"Know that you've been found? Yes. I emailed them the second night I was here. They're anxious to see and talk to you, and I told them that they'd have to wait for you to be ready. Acclimating back to your old life will take some time. But they've been in touch since."

"You didn't tell them about David?" she asked.

"No. It's not my place."

"But you told your friends."

Dave nodded. "I did. Because I need their help to get him out of the country. After seeing where del Rio is keeping him, it's not going to be as easy as I'd hoped. I doubt we'll just be able to walk into that house and take him out."

Mags nodded her head, agreeing.

"Right. So I had to tell them. They had to know it's no longer a matter of waiting for you to be comfortable coming with me. We have to rescue a child. Our son."

The way he kept claiming David as his own threatened to undo Mags. "I'm afraid to ask what they think of me. Of you still wanting to be with me, knowing I had a child with someone else."

Dave put his laptop to the side and slowly walked toward her. He stood close, but didn't touch her. "Raven, they understand. They've been working trafficking cases for years. They know exactly how things work and the consequences of them. You want to know what they think of you? They're fucking impressed, that's what. You're amazing. Strong as hell. Somehow you've managed to keep your humanity and compassion even after what was done to you. They know David is your son, and is mine now too. We take care of our own. Period. There will be no uncomfortable questions you'll have to answer, and each and every one of them will protect David as if he's their own. You have my word."

And with that, tears formed no matter how hard she tried to hold them back. She'd been scared for herself plenty of times, but knowing David had the protection of each and every one of the big, strong men who'd come to Peru specifically to look for her had Mags feeling more emotional than she could remember feeling in a very long time.

Dave raised one hand and used his thumb to slowly wipe the tears off her cheek. "You aren't alone anymore, Raven. You've got a big family now. They're a pain in the ass sometimes, and way too nosey, but they're loyal as the day is long and fiercely protective of each other." He gestured to the bathroom. "I have it on good authority that the water in this motel is nice and hot, and you can take as long a shower as you want, and it won't run out."

Mags did her best to smile. "Zara?" she asked.

Dave returned the grin. "Yup. Meat said she stayed in there so long the first time, her fingers pruned up badly enough that he thought they'd never recover."

She knew he was teasing, and she appreciated him attempting to lighten the mood.

"You've always been so fucking beautiful," Dave said out of the blue. "But I had no idea what beauty was until I saw you with our son today. He's perfect, Raven. So fucking perfect, I almost couldn't breathe when I saw the two of you sitting together."

And just like that, Mags was crying again.

"I swear on my life that I'm getting both of you out of here. Del Rio will be nothing but a bad memory, and I'll spend the rest of my days making sure you and our son have everything your hearts desire."

All Mags could do was nod. She couldn't see him anymore through her tears, so she blindly turned toward the bathroom.

She needed to get away from him and his beautiful words. She needed time to compose herself. As if realizing she was on the brink of a breakdown, Dave let her go without another word.

Mags closed the bathroom door and didn't bother to lock it. Seeing the stack of clothes on the counter made her cry harder. She turned on the water in the shower, and when it was the perfect temperature, she stepped into the tub fully clothed. Raising her face up to the spray, she let her tears fall hot and fast.

Chapter Nine

Dave wanted to kick himself. He hadn't meant to make her cry. He just couldn't hold back from telling her how touched he'd been, seeing her and David together. The second he'd laid eyes on the boy, Dave had fallen in love. He could so easily see his wife's features in David, and witnessing the obvious love they had for each other had made him vow right then and there to do whatever it took to keep them both safe.

The fact that she'd even *had* a biological child was a miracle. They'd been ready to adopt, and would've loved whatever child they'd been fortunate enough to welcome into their home, but seeing a boy who looked so much like Raven was a blessing. The circumstances of his birth had nothing to do with the child he was today. Dave still wanted to kill everyone who'd dared touch his wife, but seeing David made him realize that out of the darkness, there was always some light.

He'd known neither he nor Raven were the same people they'd been ten years ago, but seeing her with her son really hammered that fact home. It wasn't just the two of them; they now had a small human to protect. What Dave wanted no longer mattered. His life would be all about making sure both his son's and wife's needs were met—that they were secure in the knowledge that they were loved and safe.

And right now, David was anything but safe. That much was obvious after seeing the lengths to which del Rio had gone to house him. There were armed guards patrolling the house, and every second David and Raven had been in the yard, there had been eyes on them. It was odd that del Rio would keep a single child locked behind what basically amounted to prison bars.

The reasons why del Rio might do such a thing were unthinkable and repulsive, but little surprised Dave. The Mountain Mercenaries had been sent to Peru in the first place because of the trafficking of children.

As a result of his reconnaissance today, Dave realized it wasn't going to be as easy as he'd hoped to take back what was rightfully his. And he knew without a second thought that David was *his*.

He'd managed to get the pictures he needed for the boy's passport, and a lot more besides, but getting him out of the house was another thing altogether. He'd called Gray and the others while Raven was visiting with her son, and they'd had a mini brainstorming session about what to do, but nothing certain had been decided.

While Dave wanted to flat-out kill anyone who kept him from his son, and kept the boy from his mother, it wasn't that easy. The Mountain Mercenaries didn't usually kill unless absolutely necessary. They weren't hired killers. Not at all. Their main objective was rescuing women and children from those who were oppressing them.

It looked like they were most likely going to have to kidnap his son, which sucked. Dave hated to have to traumatize the child, and having the Mountain Mercenaries storm the house where he was being kept would most likely do just that, but it wasn't as if del Rio was going to give the boy up voluntarily.

The more Dave thought about it, the more he knew del Rio had a plan for David. He didn't know what it was, only that it was horrifying. The man had decided to raise David separately from the other children he either kidnapped from the barrios or took from his women, and there was a reason.

He must've been lost in his head for longer than he thought because the next thing Dave knew, the door to the bathroom squeaked as it opened, and then Raven was there.

Her hair fell against her back. It was still wet, but the ends were beginning to dry, curling slightly. Her face was pink from the heat of the shower. She'd put on the clothes Ball had bought—a pair of leggings and a tan T-shirt with a big llama on it . . . the other man's idea of a joke.

If Dave closed his eyes, he could picture her looking exactly the same way when they'd been on vacation in Vegas. She'd come out of the bathroom wearing nothing but a white T-shirt. She'd coyly smirked at him and teasingly crooked her finger, beckoning him closer.

The smell of the motel's soap wafted through the air, making him wish he'd told Ball to get something flowery for her to bathe with.

She looked hesitant and unsure, which Dave hated. She used to be so sure of herself and her sexuality. She had him wrapped around her little finger, and they'd both been more than happy with that.

Dave patted the mattress next to him on the queen-size bed. "Come sit, Raven."

She slowly padded toward him, gingerly sitting on the bed, but as far away from him as she could get. That bothered Dave more than he wanted to admit, but he didn't let his feelings show on his face. The last thing he wanted was to make Raven uncomfortable. Just her being there was a huge step. She could've gone straight back to the barrio to sleep with her friends instead of agreeing to come to the motel.

"It feels weird to hear you call me Raven," she admitted softly.

Dave smiled. "I know, but that's who you are to me. My Raven."

"She's gone," Raven said. "Mags has taken her place."

Dave shook his head. "She's not gone. She's there. Deep down, maybe, but she's there."

His wife just looked at him. Then, changing the subject, she asked, "Will you tell me how you got the scar?"

Sighing, Dave looked away from her for the first time. He didn't mind telling her, but he'd hoped they'd start with small talk first. Fingering the gnarly scar on his neck, Dave tried to think of a good place to start.

"You don't have to talk about it if it makes you uncomfortable."

"I'm an open book to you, Raven," Dave told her, turning back to meet her gaze. "I've done things in the last decade that I'm not proud of, but I wouldn't change one thing if it meant I wouldn't be sitting here with you right this second."

Raven blinked in surprise, but then she nodded and moved to put her legs under the covers. Seeing her get comfortable made something in Dave relax a bit. She didn't look like she was getting ready to jump up and leave. He'd talk all night if it meant keeping her by his side.

"The first few months after you disappeared . . . weren't good," he said hesitantly. "And I know it's ridiculous for me to say that, considering what you were going through. Me being sad and confused and angry seems petty in comparison."

She leaned over and put her hand on his arm. "I can't imagine what you went through," she said softly. "I mean, I wasn't exactly at Club Med myself. But to have me there one second and gone the next had to have been terrible for you."

"It was hell," Dave said. "Absolute hell. I couldn't stop thinking about what you might be going through. Wondering if you were dead or alive . . . and if alive, were you wondering why no one was showing up to save you? I went a little crazy. I took several trips back to Las Vegas and basically harassed the police. When it was obvious they couldn't do anything more than they'd already done to find you, I kinda lost it. I decided if they weren't going to get off their asses and find you, I'd have to do it myself. Which wasn't fair to them. They'd gone above and beyond to track you down, but you seemed to have disappeared into thin air. Then I got it in my head that a local motorcycle gang had taken you and was keeping you hostage in one of their compounds."

He stopped talking, remembering how low he'd sunk to try to infiltrate the Vegas Panthers Motorcycle Club.

Raven's hand moved from his arm down to his hand. She intertwined her fingers with his and squeezed.

Dave stared down at their clasped hands, and the ball of hate he'd held inside him for ten long years seemed to shatter into a thousand pieces and simply dissolve.

Having his wife back with him, touching him voluntarily, trying to comfort *him* when he should be the one doing everything in his power to take care of her . . . he'd forgotten the power she'd always had over him. How with only one touch, she could make him melt.

"I did some things I'm not proud of, but I never killed anyone. I'd spent over a month hanging out and drinking with the men in the MC. We were at a bar one night, and while I was drinking, I started thinking about you. I was pissed off and frustrated. I'd wasted a month of my life trying to infiltrate the gang and find out if they were involved in sex trafficking, and all I'd gotten for my efforts was a raging headache every morning. I knew no one trusted me, and I couldn't handle it anymore."

"What'd you do?" Raven asked softly.

"I confronted the president of the club. Got in his face and demanded to know where you were. Let's just say he wasn't too happy that I wasn't who I'd portrayed myself to be, or that I'd gotten in his face. His sergeant at arms and VP took me out back and beat the shit out of me. They thought I was from a rival gang that was trying to get intel about the Vegas Panthers. They left me with this as a souvenir."

Once more, Dave fingered the scar on his neck. It went down past the collar of his shirt to the top of his chest. He'd been very lucky they hadn't really wanted to kill him. If they had, he would've bled out within minutes.

"I knew then I had to change my tactics. After getting stitched up, I went home to Colorado Springs and put all my energy into learning how to use the web to my advantage. I needed to see if I could track you electronically. I learned how to glean information on almost any group or individual by hacking into their bank accounts, social media, email, phone records, or following them by hacking traffic cameras, even home-security cameras."

"How'd you come to team up with your friends?" Raven asked.

Her eyes were focused on his face, and she truly seemed riveted.

"After a while, I started finding out about other women who'd been kidnapped. I ran across stories about children who'd been taken out of the country by their noncustodial parents. I hadn't found you, but I'd stumbled across other networks of traffickers. Other women who were someone's wife, sister, daughter, friend. I couldn't just leave them to suffer, not when I knew where they were and what they were going through. But after my ill-fated attempt to do things on my own, I knew I'd never be able to pull off a full-blown rescue. So . . . I hacked into a few military databases."

"Holy crap, wasn't that dangerous?" Raven asked, squeezing his hand.

Nothing felt better than her hand in his. Dave nodded. "Yeah, if I'd gotten caught, I would've been in deep shit, but I was lucky. I looked up records of some of the most decorated Special Forces soldiers and sailors. If I was going to send them into dangerous situations, I needed to know they could hold their own. I didn't want them to know who I was, though. I mean, who would agree to work for a blue-collar bar owner who'd never been in the military?

"So, I convinced them all to come to The Pit for an 'interview.' They were pissed off when 'Rex' never showed, but what they didn't realize was that I already knew they could do the job. It was their chemistry with each other that was in question. I wanted a group of men who would have each other's backs with no question. Who could work together in the most stressful of situations."

"And they could," Raven concluded.

"Yup. They bonded over their irritation that I never showed and played pool and talked all evening. Before they left, I knew they were the team I needed."

"How are you able to pay them?"

Dave shrugged. "Investments and luck. I met a few people on the web who taught me the stock-market version of card counting. It took a while, but once I started earning money, things snowballed. There've also been donations over the years." He squeezed Raven's hand. "Money's not an issue. I can take care of you and David and give you everything you've ever wanted. I currently live in a small apartment not too far from The Pit, but I can buy a piece of land and have your dream house built."

"I don't need much," Raven said softly. "The only thing I want is to be safe and for David to be able to run and play and to be free."

"Deal," Dave said immediately. After a moment of hesitation, he asked, "Can you tell me what happened? Not necessarily the details, just in general? If nothing else, even though it was a decade ago, it might help me understand more fully how the network operates and how they're targeting women, so I can do my best to stop them."

~

Mags knew the question was coming. But strangely enough, she felt as if she could share with Dave. She hadn't talked about how she'd been taken or what had happened to her with anyone in ten years. She'd kept it all bottled inside. But after hearing the lengths to which Dave had gone to try to find her, somehow it made her feel . . . settled. He hadn't simply shrugged and gotten on with his life while she'd been suffering.

He'd been hurting just as much as she was . . . in a different way, yes, but the agony was there all the same. She eyed the scar on his neck and shivered. He'd been lucky. The scar was deep and gnarly, and he could've bled out.

They were both lucky.

Mags knew some people would think she was crazy. How could she be *lucky* after being kidnapped and forced into the sex trade? She was alive, that was how. And she had a beautiful, innocent child as a result. That in itself was a miracle. And somehow, through a series of events she'd never understand, her husband was here right this second. She was holding his hand. And he was looking at her with as much love and respect as he'd had for her ten years ago.

In all her fantasies, she'd never thought Dave could still love her after everything that had happened to her. But here he was. Sitting next to her, still proving with every word out of his mouth that he was as devoted to her today as he'd been a decade ago.

Yes, she was lucky. She knew better than most how many women died while in captivity. They didn't get a chance to see their families and loved ones again. They were used and abused until they just gave up.

"If you can't, I'll understand," Dave said gently when the silence stretched on.

"I'd finished going to the bathroom and had just exited the restroom," Mags said, starting her story. "A man came up to me and put his arm around my shoulders. He was strong, and even though I tried to pull away from him, I couldn't. He said if I didn't come with him, his partner would kill you. I was confused and scared and didn't know what to do. Before I knew it, I'd been led out of the club and was being hustled through the casino. He walked me right through the front door of the hotel to a car and shoved me inside.

"There were three other men in there, and no matter how many times I asked what they wanted and where you were, no one would answer me. I don't know how far we drove, but it wasn't too far, I don't think. I was taken to a house and a basement. They shoved me into a dog crate and locked it."

Mags heard Dave inhale sharply, but she didn't look at him, knowing she needed to get the whole story out. She focused on their hands clasped together instead. Seeing her husband's large, calloused fingers curled around hers kept her grounded.

"I didn't make it easy for them," she recalled. "I screamed and shouted and demanded they let me go. I think they got tired of listening to me, and someone came down and shot me with some sort of dart. I don't remember a lot of the trip out of the country, but I do recall coming to once and seeing a huge tractor trailer. They were loading me and a few other cages with other women in them into the back, behind a hidden partition. I'm assuming that's how they got us out of the country and into Mexico.

"When I finally woke fully, I was in a bedroom, and my arms were chained to a bed. I hadn't eaten in a very long time, and I was dehydrated, but that first night taught me what was to come.

"I don't remember how many men came into my room that night. I thought if I stayed nonresponsive, they'd stop, not wanting to be with a woman who just lay there limply. But they didn't.

"It seemed like hours later, but it was probably much less than that, when del Rio came into my room. It was the first time I met him. I was lying on the bed naked, scared to death and hurting. He told me that I now belonged to him, and my job was to make the men who came to see me happy. If I did, I'd eventually be allowed a bit more freedom to move around, to talk with others, to eat. If I continued to be a pain in the ass, then I'd stay chained to the bed and would only get a few scraps of food a day. Either way, I'd be forced to open my legs to whoever came to see me."

Mags spoke faster. She could feel the tension and fury coming from her husband. She couldn't blame him. But she had to tell him. Needed him to know what had happened to her and what he was getting into. If he decided he couldn't handle it, she needed to know now, before she went back to the States.

"I fought after that. Refused to simply lie back and take what was happening to me. But eventually, I broke. I was starving. A customer came into my room with an apple. Just one. But he held it up and said if I let him take me without a fight, he'd give it to me."

Tears formed in her eyes at remembering the humiliation. "I was so hungry . . . I agreed," she admitted softly. "I figured if I hadn't been found by that point, maybe I wouldn't ever be. I had no choice. If I wanted to live, I had to adjust to my new situation. So the next time del Rio came to see me, I told him I'd do what he wanted.

"I'll never forget the grin on his face. He knew he'd broken me. He'd done it time and time again with hundreds, maybe thousands, of women, and he held all the power."

"Look at me," Dave said in a tone Raven couldn't read.

She didn't want to, but she finally looked up at him, expecting to see anger or disgust on his beautiful face. But what she saw when she looked into his eyes surprised her.

"I'm outraged beyond belief at what happened to you. But I'm so incredibly proud too."

"How can you be? Did you not hear what I did? What I *voluntarily* did?"

"You didn't do *anything* voluntarily," Dave said without hesitation. "Just because you physically stopped resisting doesn't mean you enjoyed it or wanted it. You did what you had to do to stay alive. We both know if you'd continued to fight, you'd be dead right now. Del Rio wouldn't have any problem letting you starve to death. He doesn't have a conscience. You were just a thing to him. But you know what? *You won.* He thought he broke you, but he didn't. He made you stronger. You're here. You have a group of friends who would do anything for you, and you have an amazing son. Fuck him."

Mags couldn't believe what she was hearing. Dave should be mad. Should be upset with her for not fighting harder. But instead, he was praising her. She couldn't wrap her mind around it. "I know you have to be wondering why I didn't try to get in touch with you after I got out," she said hesitantly.

Dave shook his head immediately. "No, I understand."

Mags was skeptical. "You do?"

"Yes. When Zara came back to Colorado, it took her a while to acclimate. When she was ready, she had a press conference to answer some of the questions about where she'd been for fifteen years. One of the reporters had the balls to ask her why she didn't try harder to tell someone who she was. To get help. She didn't fly off the handle, but she cut that reporter to shreds with her answer."

"What'd she say?" Mags asked.

"I don't remember her exact words, but the point she got across loud and clear was that she did the best she could with the knowledge and resources she had at the time. She'd been a child. Scared to death and trying to survive in a foreign world she'd been dropped into without warning or preparation. And she made sure everyone understood that the question was offensive. We can second-guess her decisions all we want, but the bottom line is that we weren't there. We don't know what she was going through, and therefore we can't armchair-quarterback it. And now that I know about David, I understand your decisions even more."

"I couldn't leave him," Mags whispered. "He's innocent in everything. If I left him, I'd be throwing him to the wolves. No one would take care of him the way I would. No one would tell him he was smart and strong."

"I get it," Dave said.

Mags looked down at their clasped hands once again. "And . . . I was ashamed. I had no idea if you'd moved on and found someone else. I didn't want to come back into your life if you were happy and remarried. And I really didn't like what I'd had to do to survive."

"I haven't been with anyone since that last night we spent together in Vegas," Dave said.

His words were akin to a bomb being dropped in the room.

Mags's eyes whipped up to his. *"What?"*

"I haven't touched another woman since you disappeared," Dave clarified.

"But . . . it's been ten years!"

"I know. How could I make love to someone else when all I wanted was you? I didn't know if you were dead or alive, but it didn't matter. If I had touched someone else, I would've felt as if I was cheating on you. And I'd rather rip my dick off than ever dishonor you that way."

"Dave," Mags whispered, overwhelmed.

"Hear me now, Raven," Dave said. "I would do anything for you. *Anything.* Face down a pissed-off motorcycle club, learn everything I can about the dark web and hacking, hire former Special Forces men to hunt down and find missing women and children in the hopes that someday, one of them might be you. I'd even die if it meant you and our son could survive. Giving up sex was *nothing* in the scope of what I'd lost, sweetheart."

Moving slowly, Mags scooted closer to her husband and rested her head against him. He shifted until his arm was over her shoulder. She tensed, not comfortable with being trapped under his arm, but when he didn't grab at her or otherwise do anything that would make her nervous, she slowly relaxed.

Her mind was whirling with everything she'd learned tonight. Not only had her husband not forgotten about her, he'd completely changed his life, changed who he was, to try to find her. She regretted not trying to get in touch with him right when del Rio kicked her out of his compound without a Peruvian sol to her name. But she couldn't change the past. She was still ashamed of what she'd been forced to do, but somehow, sitting with Dave in this motel, clean from a shower, and lying on the softest bed she'd been on in a decade, the shame seemed less.

She couldn't believe Dave hadn't been with another woman in all the time she'd been gone. She wouldn't have been upset if he had—life went on, she knew that as well as anyone. But the fact that he'd abstained only proved how deep his devotion ran.

For just a moment, a spark of hope flared within her breast. Was there a chance they could pick back up where they'd left off ten years ago?

But then reality set in.

"I'm not sure I want to have sex ever again," she whispered.

Dave's arm tightened around her briefly in a kind of sideways hug. "I couldn't give a shit about that. I've done without for ten years, and I've managed just fine with using my hand when I really need to get off. I don't love you because of the sex, sweetheart. I love you for *you*. All I want is you back in my life. You're enough just the way you are. And honestly, I don't blame you one bit. If I'd been through what you have, I wouldn't want to be touched either. The fact that you're here with me, letting me sit next to you, is a miracle. One that I've prayed for every day for the last ten years. We'll forge our way to a new relationship, together."

Gah! She'd always known her husband was amazing, but she'd forgotten just how much. "Do you think you'll continue on with the Mountain Mercenaries?" she asked after a minute.

"Yes," Dave said without hesitation. "I've found you, but that doesn't mean there aren't other women out there who need to be rescued. They have loved ones who desperately want to know what happened to them. Where they are. I can't abandon them now that I've found you. I just can't."

Mags didn't bother to brush away the tears that fell from her eyes, soaking into the cotton material of Dave's shirt.

"And more than that, I've been thinking . . . it makes little sense to give Daniela's old house to Maria, Carmen, Bonita, and Teresa."

Mags stilled. "Why?"

"Because they should be able to go *home* if they want. Back to Brazil, Venezuela, and Mexico. They have families, just as you do. I can get in touch with their relatives and let them know they're alive."

Shit, Mags was going to lose it again. She managed to say, "And Gabriella?"

"She was born in the barrio, right? I thought if she wanted to, and if you were agreeable, maybe she could come back to Colorado with us. It might be good for you to have someone with you, in addition to Zara, from this part of your life. Someone positive."

And just that easily, Mags fell head over heels in love for the second time with her husband.

"I'd like that. And I think she will too," she managed to say.

"Good."

"What's next?" she asked.

"I need to get with my contact and tell him we're adding another person to our traveling party. She'll need a visa, and I'll have to grease some wheels with my contacts at the State Department. And getting the others back to their home countries won't be a walk in the park, but I think I can bribe some officials here in Peru to make that happen pretty easily."

"And David?" Mags asked nervously.

"That's a little trickier, but I swear, we aren't leaving without him."

Mags had a million more questions, but she was exhausted. Emotionally and physically. And she was more comfortable than she could remember being in a very long time. Dave's arm around her didn't feel threatening. It felt safe. She could hear his heart beating under his chest, and when he shifted to lie down, she didn't panic.

Moving with him, she lay under the covers while he stayed on top. Her head was on his wide chest, and a flashback of sleeping this exact way with him, except they'd both been naked, whirled through her head.

Safe. In Dave's arms, she was safe.

Her eyes closed, and she was asleep in seconds.

~

Dave held as still as possible and simply memorized the feel of having his wife in his arms. He couldn't believe she was letting him hold her like this. He felt as if it was Christmas and every other holiday wrapped into one.

He'd spent the last decade dreaming of this exact moment, of having Raven in his arms, safe, and the reality was so much better than his fantasies.

She'd gone through hell. Absolute hell. He couldn't even begin to process it. But he hadn't lied. He was as proud as he could be of her. She'd survived. Somehow, miraculously, survived. Dave hated that she was ashamed, but he'd spend the rest of his life making sure she knew how much he loved her and how proud he was.

It was unbelievable that she was actually here. That he was holding her. He'd always known his wife was tough, but after hearing her story, and after learning she'd birthed their son alone, he was even more impressed. On top of it all, she'd done whatever she could to protect David as well—not an easy task when someone like del Rio was controlling every second of the little boy's day-to-day activities.

Dave was more than ready to get his wife and son out of this country and back home to Colorado. Unfortunately, they needed to wait until they had David's passport. They'd come into the country pretending to be tourists, and while it might look odd to have two additional people go home with them—three, if Gabriella came too—it could still work, especially if they bribed the customs officials at the airport.

First, they'd have to come up with a plan to get David out of the house where he was being held captive. Dave didn't want to kill the people who were guarding him if it was at all avoidable. The women were certainly under del Rio's thumb and only doing what they had to in order to stay alive.

Del Rio had more people in his pocket than not, and there was a chance, if he got wind of the plan to get David a passport and take him out of the country, he'd do something to hold up the process.

It was looking more and more like the only choice they had was to raid the house where del Rio was keeping David. But there was no telling what the men and women who were standing guard over the boy had been instructed to do if something like that happened. If anything happened to David, Raven wouldn't survive. He knew that for a fact.

Dave would do whatever it took to get David back to the States safely. It didn't matter if he had to lose all his dignity and *beg* the head of the biggest sex-trafficking faction in South America to let him take the boy. He'd do it. The most important thing was getting Raven and David home. No matter what it took.

As much as he wanted to call his team and raid the house tonight, he knew they needed to wait until they had the official paperwork to get his son out of the country. While del Rio was an asshole who abused children, David had been living in the house for four and a half years. They had no evidence del Rio was going to make a move in the next week or so. They'd be better off doing recon, planning the attack on the house, and making preparations to get the hell out of the country the second they had David in their hands. And they couldn't do anything that would make del Rio suspicious in the meantime.

The kingpin might already know someone was in town, hanging around Mags, but with a little luck, it would take him a while to figure out who they were.

If he knew the Mountain Mercenaries were back, and that they had a connection to David's mother, things could get ugly fast.

Wishing he could wave a magic wand and have his wife and child safely ensconced in his house in Colorado Springs, Dave knew he should get up and continue emailing his contacts to set things in motion to return Raven's friends to their families. But as long as his wife was sleeping in his arms, he wasn't going to move a muscle. He treasured this. Hadn't dared dream it would ever be possible.

Closing his eyes, Dave inhaled Raven's clean, soapy scent into his very soul. No one would hurt her again. He'd die before that happened.

Chapter Ten

Mags spent the next several days getting to know her husband again. He was much like she remembered, but so much more. He was insightful and compassionate, more so than when they'd been together.

She'd been to see David four more times, except now Dave dropped her off and picked her up so she didn't have to walk the ten miles. She knew her husband and his team were busy gathering intel for whatever it was they were planning in regard to her son, but she never spotted them while she was with David, and he didn't share any of those details with her.

They *did* share with Teresa, Bonita, Carmen, and Maria the plans to help them get home, and all four women had been overwhelmed with gratitude. Dave had written down their names, addresses, birth dates, and everything else he'd needed to not only find their families—or friends, in the case of Bonita, whose own family sold her to del Rio—but to procure the necessary paperwork to get the women out of Peru. Mags had watched as he did what he did best . . . use the computer to get information and make shit happen.

Gabriella had also been overwhelmed when Mags had asked if she wanted to go to the United States with her and the rest of the Mountain Mercenaries. She'd agreed immediately. Later, she'd told Mags that she was scared to death, but that there was nothing left for her in Peru, and she wanted a chance to make a better life for herself.

Mags had thought nights would be hard, sleeping in the motel room with Dave, but surprisingly, she'd slept better than she had in a decade. Tucked up against him, on the softest mattress she'd felt in ages, the scent of her husband in her nose . . . Mags didn't have any trouble sleeping whatsoever.

Today, while Zara and Dave's friends finalized the details for the new clinic she was funding, Dave had decided to take Mags down to Miraflores. It was the more touristy part of Lima. She would've been content to hang out in the motel room all day, but he said that he wanted to leave her with some good memories of Peru.

It was sweet of him. She knew he was just trying to keep her mind off the fact they were still waiting on the paperwork for her and the others to come through. And more important . . . she suspected they hadn't yet figured out the best way to get David out of del Rio's clutches.

At the moment, Dave was in the room next door talking with his friends about that very thing. Their voices had started out muffled, but the more time that went by, the louder they got. The frustration and anger she could hear from the other room made her nervous, and she was glad there was a wall between them.

She shamelessly eavesdropped on their conversation. They were talking about her son, and anything that had to do with him, had to do with her.

She'd finally told Dave just last night what David had said about the pictures del Rio had been taking, and he'd barely contained his rage.

Her husband had been very careful to not let his emotions get out of control around her. He did his best to be sweet and easygoing, but after hearing about what had been done to David, she could see the anger shimmering in his eyes, radiating from his entire body. Instead of getting scared, it reassured her. She *wanted* Dave to be mad. Wanted him to do whatever it took to get David away from the situation. Lord knew she hadn't been able to do it on her own, so she'd take all the help she could get.

"I know you think that's an option, but it's not a good idea," Ball said loudly in the other room.

"The only other option is scaring the shit out of my son," Dave argued. "And I have to consider any other alternative that would prevent that."

"You've been our handler for years," someone else said. Mags couldn't tell who it was. "And you've preached time and time again that we're a team. We go in together and get out together, so why are you pushing for this so hard right now?"

"There are situations where sometimes it's necessary for just one person to go in," Dave said.

"Like when?" Ro asked. Mags knew it was him because of his accent.

"Like when Gray climbed aboard that boat and found Allye," Dave fired back. "Like when Arrow had to split off from the rest of the team in the Dominican Republic to keep Morgan safe. When Black went into that burning building to get Harlow."

There was silence for a beat, then someone said, "Those are completely different."

"No, they're not," Dave said heatedly.

"Bullshit. Gray didn't go onto that boat expecting to find a female captive. If we'd known Allye was there, the plan would've been very different. Arrow didn't want to split off from the team; we were forced to split up because of the circumstances. And Black didn't go into a burning building . . . he caught those kids from outside. Your examples are a crock of shit, and you know it."

Mags held her breath as she listened intently.

"And how about the fact that you're not trained?" someone else asked. "The last thing you want to do is fuck up the most important mission of your life because you don't trust the team you've relied on for years to come through, just when we're needed the most."

Mags winced. Over the last few days, she'd gotten the impression that Dave felt somewhat at a disadvantage because of his lack of military skills, but from what she'd seen, he was perfectly competent regardless.

"That right there is one of the main reasons Rex was born," Dave told his friends. "I knew you would have a problem taking orders from Dave the bartender. But here's the deal—I know what I'm doing. I've paid attention over the years. I've studied. And I've got a motivation in this mission that none of you have. David is *my* son, and Raven is my *wife*. I'd never do *anything* to put either of them in danger. I know where my strengths and weaknesses lie. And if any of you tried to go in there and talk to that asshole, he'd see through you in a heartbeat. He'll know you're military. You all have an air about you."

"And you don't think he'll see that you care a little too much for the boy?" someone asked.

"I can make him see what I want him to," Dave insisted. His voice lost a bit of its edge, but he was still talking loud when he said, "I'm not an idiot, I know what's at stake here. I also know if I fuck things up, you'll all be there to get my family out of the country."

"Damn straight we will," Ro said.

"You aren't going in alone," Ball growled. "I hear what you're saying about this being your family at stake, but going in by yourself isn't smart—and you know it."

There was a long pause before Mags heard Dave speak again. "Losing David would destroy Raven. I lost her once, and I'm not willing to lose her a second time. I'd happily sacrifice myself to get David away from del Rio."

"We know you would," Ro told him. "But you don't have to. That's why you formed the Mountain Mercenaries. For situations exactly like this one. As soon as we get word that David's passport is processed and ready to go, we'll get him out of there."

Mags didn't hear Dave's response, but she did hear the door next door being opened, and she tensed, waiting for Dave to come back into his own room, where she was waiting for him.

Within seconds, he was there.

"Are you all right?" The question popped out of her without thought. "That sounded intense."

"Damn paper-thin walls," Dave muttered, then he came toward her. He kneeled down in front of where she was sitting on the bed, careful not to crowd her or touch her. "We're going to get David out of here. Okay?"

She studied his eyes and saw no doubt. No hesitation. She needed his strength and confidence more than she'd been willing to admit. "Okay."

"Good. Now, how about we head out. You ready to play tourist for a while?"

She'd been in Peru for a decade and hadn't once thought about having a carefree day. What she really wanted to do was see her son, but since that was out of the question, she nodded.

Dave stood and held out his hand, waiting for *her* to touch *him*. It was one of the thousand-and-one things she appreciated and loved about him. He never rushed her. Never forced her to do anything she didn't want to. She knew if she said she wanted to stay at the motel, they would. If she said she wanted to go hang out in the barrio, he'd agree, and stay with her to make sure she was safe. The only thing he wouldn't do was let her put herself in danger. Not for David, not for him.

She'd been determined to keep Dave at arm's length. She wasn't sure she could pick up where they'd left off that day in Las Vegas. But with every day, every hour, she spent with him, her defenses were crumbling. She liked the man he'd become. A lot. She needed his hardness and outward strength to keep herself going.

She reached out and put her palm in his, and goose bumps sprang up on her arms as he closed his hand around hers and squeezed lightly.

~

Hours later, Mags was walking hand in hand with Dave through a park in Miraflores. The area was teeming with tourists and locals trying to hawk their wares. People begged, much as she'd done more times than she could count. But even though they were surrounded by people, she wasn't nervous, as she usually was.

Her husband led her over to a bench in the shade, and they people-watched for a few minutes before he pulled a piece of paper out of his pocket and handed it to her.

Confused, Mags asked, "What's this?"

"Open it and see."

Slowly, Mags unfolded the piece of paper and stared down at the words typed there in confusion. Then what she was looking at registered. "Oh my God," she whispered.

"You know the other day I asked for more details about David's birth," Dave said. "I wasn't just curious, although I'm hungry for any detail you can tell me about him. I needed to know so I could get that." He nodded at the paper.

Mags was looking at her son's birth certificate. One that Dave had obviously figured out a way to have made, because del Rio certainly hadn't bothered to record the birth of her child. His name was there, along with his weight—which Mags had to guess at—and Daniela's address in Peru was listed as hers. But that wasn't what had her almost hyperventilating.

Dave had put himself down as the father.

"I know it was presumptuous of me," he said as if he could read her mind. "But I didn't want to leave it blank. We talked about having kids, and it's something I always regretted that we never got around to making happen. I haven't even met him yet, but I love him, simply because he's a part of you. I worry about him just like you do on the days you don't get to go see him, and I can't stand the thought of anything happening to him. Knowing what del Rio has planned makes me want to kill anyone who's dared to even look at him. Yes, having my name on the birth certificate makes it easier for my contact to get him a passport, but I don't give a shit about that. If you'd prefer to leave my name off and have me officially adopt him when we get back to the States, I can do that too."

"No!" Mags practically shouted. "I mean, this is fine. This is the most amazing thing anyone's ever done for me."

Dave brought his hand up and palmed the side of her face gently. "I love you, sweetheart. I'm so sorry it took me so long to find you."

She shook her head. "The fact that you never gave up means more to me than you'll ever know."

"As if I'd ever stop looking," Dave said with a little head shake. "No matter how much it cost or how long it took, I never would've stopped until I found you, or your body."

Mags believed him. She stared at the man she never thought she'd see again, and all the reasons why she'd fallen in love with him in the first place filled her head. Time had been good to him. He had some gray woven through his dark-brown locks and his beard now, and more lines creased across his face, but he was still just as handsome as he'd been on their wedding day. She'd always loved how brawny he was, and his body size made her feel all the more safe sitting in a park in the middle of Miraflores.

As she studied him, he moved. He knelt on one knee at her feet and reached into his pocket. He pulled out a ring and held it up between them. "Margaret Crawford Justice, will you do me the honor of remarrying me? We're both different people than we were fifteen years ago, when I first did this. Older and hopefully wiser. Definitely more cynical and cautious. I love you. *Have* always loved you and *will* always love you. I promise to take better care of you this time around, and I'll always strive to be the kind of man you and our son can be proud of."

Mags closed her eyes and put a hand over her heart, as if that could slow the frantic beating within her chest. She wanted to say yes. God, how she wanted to. But she had to make sure he knew what he was getting into.

When she opened her eyes and looked into his, she hated to see the insecurity there. "I have nightmares," she admitted. "And I'll probably be the most overprotective mother ever. I don't like large crowds, and I have a hard time trusting people. I don't need much; I've survived over the years with nothing but a few scraps of food to eat a day and a crappy metal roof over my head. I don't care about money or prestige, but I'm not sure I'll be able to be a real wife to you. I've got some real intimacy issues. Not only that, but I'll probably say the wrong thing to the wrong person and embarrass you . . ."

Her voice trailed off. There were a million other things she couldn't think of right now that might make him want to rethink his proposal, but if she was being honest with herself, she wanted that ring on her finger so badly. Her original wedding set had been missing from her finger when she'd woken up chained to a bed here in Peru, and she'd give just about anything to have it back. But having Dave put the twinkling diamond on her finger was a miracle she'd never dared dream would happen.

"If you have a nightmare, I'll hold you until it dissipates. And you won't be any more protective than I'll be of our son. I don't like crowds myself, and there won't be one more day in your life where you'll have to go without, whether that be food, shelter, or love. And believe me, I've said more than my share of embarrassing things to the wrong people. I once told the president of the United States that I didn't give a shit about his agenda, that I was more concerned about finding some of the thousands of missing women and children that the government didn't seem to care about."

Mags's eyes widened. "You did?"

Dave nodded. "Yup. But he just laughed and pledged to put half a million dollars toward renewing the effort to find missing children. Remarry me, Raven. Please."

"Yes." There was nothing else she could've said.

Dave reached for her hand and gently slipped the ring on her finger.

"When did you get this?" she asked.

"Yesterday, when you were with David."

Mags couldn't take her eyes off the diamond. It was simple. Not flashy in any way. It was probably only half a carat or so, set low in a traditional setting. She looked into Dave's brown eyes. "I love you," she whispered. "I never thought I'd get a chance to say that to you again."

Dave got up off his knee and sat next to her on the bench once more. He lifted one arm, then hesitated.

Doing something she hadn't done in years, Mags leaned forward and put both her arms around him. She put her head on his chest and held on as tightly as she could. She felt Dave return the embrace, and instead of making her feel trapped and panicky, his arms felt nothing but comforting.

She had the hopeful thought that maybe, just maybe, with her husband, she'd be able to enjoy being intimate with a man again. Not today. And not tomorrow. But maybe someday.

"I love you so much, Raven. I know this is a miracle, and I swear I'll never take you or our love for granted."

She hugged him harder, then looked up. "When can we go home to Colorado?" she asked.

A look of frustration flashed across his face before he wiped it clean. "I'm not sure. David's passport is taking longer than it should to process, and the last thing we want is to tip del Rio off and have him or the police and military he's paid off on our tail until we can leave. I'd like to send you home with Zara and—"

"No," Mags said emphatically, straightening and glaring at him.

"But—"

"I am *not* leaving without David," she told him.

Dave sighed. "I figured that would be your response," he said without seeming too upset.

"If you knew, why'd you even suggest it?" she asked.

"Because I hoped. I want you as far away from del Rio as possible, where you'll be safe."

"I wasn't safe in Vegas," Mags pointed out.

"Touché," Dave said.

"So what's the plan? I know you've been talking with your friends about it. Arguing about it."

Dave looked away from her then, and Mags felt uneasy for the first time.

"We're probably going to have to storm the house he's in. I know, I know," he said quickly when Mags opened her mouth to protest. "It's not ideal. The last thing I want to do is scare David, but del Rio isn't going to let us just stroll in and take him out of there. He's got a lot of people guarding him and the house, and he's spent a lot of money over the years raising him. He's not going to want to lose his investment."

Mags hated thinking about her son that way, but she knew Dave was right. Del Rio had already started trying to indoctrinate her son, telling him that children obeyed adults no matter what they said, taking pictures. It was only a matter of time until he did the unthinkable.

"You just need to know that I'm doing everything I can to get us all out of here as soon as possible. And now that we've got his birth certificate, I'm hoping things will happen much faster. If all goes well, we'll be headed back to Colorado as a family soon."

"And if all *doesn't* go well?" Mags asked.

"Then you and David will *still* be headed back to Colorado."

"Don't you do anything that will get you hurt or in trouble," she said, glaring at him. "I can't go back without you."

Dave put his hands on her shoulders and turned her more toward him. "You can and you will. I need you safe, Raven. You *and* our son."

"And I need *you*," Mags shot back. "Getting yourself killed isn't the answer here."

"I'm not going to die," Dave said calmly. "I'm a hard son of a bitch to kill."

Mags's eyes flickered to the scar on his neck before she met his gaze again. "Promise me you won't do anything stupid."

"I promise," he said immediately. "Stupid would be starting an international incident and getting myself and the rest of the Mountain Mercenaries thrown into a Peruvian prison. Not gonna happen."

Mags couldn't even imagine that. She leaned forward slowly and rested her forehead on Dave's chest. Her hands gripped his huge biceps as she said, "I can't have found you again, only to lose you so soon."

"You won't," he promised. "Now, come on, we need to get back to the motel to meet the guys. We're having a celebratory dinner tonight."

"We are?" Mags asked, letting Dave help her up. They started walking toward where he'd parked the minivan earlier, and he nodded.

"Yup."

"For what?"

"Our reengagement, my becoming a father, you being rescued, Gabriella coming back to the States with us, the imminent rescue of our son, the reuniting of the other women with their families, the purchase of the new clinic, and just life in general."

That all sounded amazing to Mags. "Are we going out?"

"Nope. We're all stuffing ourselves into Gray's room. The food's supposed to be delivered around six, and we need to go to the barrio and get the girls. Zara will bring Daniela with her."

"Everyone will be there?"

"Yup. Which is why I said we're stuffing ourselves into Gray's room," Dave said with a laugh. "We thought about going out, but the logistics of keeping you all safe would be difficult. So we're getting a shitload of food, and we'll sit and chat and laugh like one big happy family. Think anyone will mind?"

"Mind? Absolutely not. Honestly, we're all used to hunkering down and crowding together in a small space," Mags said.

"Good."

As they walked together toward the vehicle, Dave's head was on a constant swivel, making sure she was safe. Every now and then his thumb would brush over the ring he'd placed on her finger, and Mags could see the edge of David's birth certificate sticking out of the pocket of his shirt where he'd stashed it. Her life had done such a drastic one-eighty in only two short weeks, and Mags could hardly believe it.

But she hesitated to fully embrace it, because of the life she'd been leading for so long. If there was one thing she knew above anything else, it was that just when you thought life was going along perfectly, a curveball might be thrown at you, messing everything up.

Mags hoped and prayed that she was wrong this time. Both she and Dave, and also little David, had been through enough.

~

Later that night, Dave sat on the floor next to Mags in Gray's motel room and tried to memorize the moment.

Before this trip to Peru, he'd been worried what his friends would think when they found out the bartender who served them at The Pit was actually their handler, Rex. He hadn't really meant to keep it a secret for as long as he did, but once things got started, it just seemed easier to keep the status quo.

Luckily, everything between them so far had been pretty good. There was a bit of tension as his men disagreed with the best way to go about getting David out from under del Rio's thumb and back to the States, but other than that, Dave couldn't sense any kind of hesitation or distrust. They didn't seem to care that he hadn't been in the military. Apparently, he'd proved himself enough in the past, which was a relief.

Zara was sitting on Meat's lap on one of the beds, translating as they chatted with Teresa, Bonita, and Carmen. Ro and Gray were sitting near Gabriella and teaching her some English, while she taught them basic Spanish words. Arrow had left about five minutes ago to call his wife and make sure she and baby Calinda were all right. Black and Ball were sitting near Dave and Mags, who was translating for Maria and Daniela.

Empty containers of food were stacked up near the trash can, and the leftovers had already been packaged up for the women to take with them when they left.

Dave hadn't let go of Raven's hand and was simply enjoying soaking in the relaxed vibe of the room, which he knew was a gift. He also couldn't take his eyes from the ring he'd put on her finger earlier. He'd missed seeing his ring there.

When he felt Raven stiffen next to him, Dave realized that he hadn't been paying attention. Mentally berating himself, he sat up straight and looked around to see what had distressed his wife.

He realized that the room had gone mostly silent, and everyone was looking at Raven. "What?" he said a little too harshly.

"It's okay," Raven said, squeezing his hand. "Maria just asked why I never told them I'd had a child."

"It's not their business," he said.

Raven shook her head. "Actually, it is. They're my friends. I should've confided in them."

She turned to Maria and the others and began to explain in Spanish, while Zara translated quietly for the men.

"When del Rio kicked me out of his compound, I was both relieved and terrified. He hadn't let me take David with me, and even though I was happy to be retired from the life he'd forced on me, I didn't want to leave without my baby. But he didn't give me a choice. He told me that he'd be watching me, and if I did anything to try to take the boy from him, I'd regret it."

"We all know del Rio's an asshole of the highest order, someone who had no problem kidnapping children, but why would he want to hold on to David so badly, especially in a house basically just for him?" Arrow asked. He'd returned from making his phone call and was leaning against one of the walls.

Raven sighed. "I never saw another pregnant woman in the compound, or any babies, but there were occasionally children around. When a woman disappeared for months, then suddenly came back, rumors were that del Rio stashed them away until they had their babies. Some returned, but never said a word about where they'd been or what they'd been through. None of us wanted to ask them because it was obvious they were traumatized.

"When I got pregnant, at first he was pissed. I know he was making good money off me. He told me a doctor would come to the compound to 'take care of the problem.' I cried and begged him to let me keep my baby. I made a deal with him that I'd do whatever the customers wanted, as many times a day as *he* wanted, if del Rio would only let me keep him."

Raven swallowed hard, and when the four other women who'd been used by del Rio gathered around her, Dave stood and gave them some room. Everyone laid a hand on his wife in support, and it seemed to give all of them strength as she continued telling her story.

"There were many men who thought it was . . . interesting to have sex with a pregnant woman. Del Rio didn't shuffle me off to another part of the compound until I really started showing and it was obvious I was pregnant. I was kept very busy, and when the time came for me to give birth, del Rio locked me in a room and said that if I was going to have my baby, I'd have to do it by myself."

Carmen made a harsh noise. "What if there were complications?"

Raven shrugged. "Then we both would've died." She said it without any inflection in her voice. For her, it was what it was, but for Dave, it made his anger toward the monster that was del Rio flame even higher.

"So anyway, I had David, and del Rio kicked me out of the house. I'm still not sure why, considering other women had children and kept working. He brought David to one of his smaller houses and only allowed me to see him three times a week. I was even more confused about why he was allowing me to see my son at all, since he wouldn't let me leave with him, but I didn't dare ask. I breastfed him for as long as I could, but eventually he had to be put on formula since I wasn't there enough to feed him what he needed. I couldn't tell you about him," Raven said to her friends sadly. "If del Rio found out, I don't know what he would've done with my son."

"We understand," Maria said gently. "Any of us would've done the same thing."

Carmen looked distinctly uncomfortable. Then she blurted, "I heard a baby once."

Everyone turned to look at her when Zara translated.

"Where?" Dave asked when no one said anything.

"At the compound. I was locked in my room and couldn't investigate, not that I would've anyway, but I was lying on my bed, and I heard what I knew was a baby crying. I was confused because, as Raven said, we hadn't seen any women who were pregnant."

Raven looked at Dave, and he could see the agony in her eyes. "How many other babies do you think are out there?" she whispered. "Being raised by del Rio for some horrible purpose?"

Dave didn't want to even think about it, but he couldn't lie to his wife. He nodded. "I don't know. But I'd assume probably several. He's been trafficking children at least a few years."

"Where are they?" she asked, more to herself than anyone else. "Are they being kept in the compound? Why didn't he keep David there too?"

"Maybe he let others take their babies with them." He didn't believe that for a second, but said it to hopefully take some of the angst from his woman's eyes.

"Or maybe they're being raised in the same way as your son," Gray said quietly.

"The pictures . . ." Raven whispered.

"What pictures?" Arrow asked.

Raven closed her eyes and shook her head.

Dave answered for her. "Raven said that David told her del Rio had visited him with another man, and he took pictures of them both without any clothes on."

The words sounded even more obscene when explained to the group.

"Fuck," Arrow muttered.

The other men in the room also swore under their breaths.

"We can't wait anymore," Dave said. "We need to get my son out of that house and back to the States where he'll be safe."

"Agreed," Gray said.

"Absolutely," Black muttered.

Dave didn't want to think about del Rio and his plans for David, and possibly other children he had stashed around the city. They'd talked about what they were going to do, and although nothing had been set in stone, he knew time had run out. They couldn't risk del Rio deciding to do more than take pictures. He'd found his wife, and his son, just in time.

"Can you forgive me?" Raven asked the other women in the room. "I would've told you if I could."

A chorus of *sí*'s rang out in the room as everyone said yes, of course they forgave her.

"No one should have that much control over a woman's reproductive system," Daniela said, and Zara translated. "I see it all the time . . . women whose men refuse to wear condoms, and they have baby after baby. They can't feed the families they've got, and yet they can't do anything to prevent their families from growing bigger. And then there are the men who beat their women in the hopes they'll abort. That's just one of the reasons I'm excited about the clinic . . . I can give women more choices when it comes to family matters. Birth control and prenatal health is lacking here." She looked at Zara. "Thank you so much, child, for making this possible. My country wasn't good to you, and you have no reason to want to give back in any way, and yet you are." Daniela's eyes filled with tears. "Bless you."

By now, most of the women in the room had tears in their eyes, but Dave was only concerned about his wife. Raven looked emotional, but not completely devastated, which he could live with. She was either in denial about what del Rio had planned for David, or she was trying not to think about it. He suspected the latter. His wife wasn't stupid, but she'd been through a hell of a lot, and considering that she couldn't do anything to help her son, stressing about the situation wouldn't help.

He wasn't willing to stand around and let a conversation continue that was freaking Raven out, but because she seemed to be okay, he tried to make himself relax.

"How're you doing?" Gray asked from next to him.

Dave didn't take his eyes from his wife. "I'm good."

"No. *How are you doing?*" Gray asked again, deliberately enunciating each word.

Dave turned to look at him and raised an eyebrow.

"You haven't been away from your bar in . . . I don't know how long. You found your wife, who's been missing for a decade, and almost in the same breath found out she'd had a baby. A son you've now claimed for yourself. Not only that, but you've had to digest a hell of a lot about what Raven has been through while she was missing. And now, instead of being on the way home with your family, you're stuck here while we try to figure out what the hell del Rio is up to and how to get your son away from him without causing an international incident. So, I'm asking if you're all right."

Dave nodded. "I'm fine."

It was Gray's turn to raise a skeptical eyebrow.

"I'm not exactly happy. I'm sick of sitting around waiting for David's passport, and I want my son rescued. *Now.* But my wife is sitting right here in front of my eyes, and that's a fucking miracle. So I'm dealing."

"We'll have his passport tomorrow," Gray reminded him.

"I know," Dave said impatiently. "But I feel as if there's a huge clock over my head, and every second that ticks by echoes in my mind."

"We're going to get your son," Gray said. "No matter what it takes, we're going to get him out of del Rio's clutches."

Dave turned back to look at Raven. He couldn't go more than a minute or two without checking on her. The other women had moved back to where they'd been sitting on the bed and floor, satisfied that their friend was going to be all right. But he had a feeling it would be a long time before *he'd* be comfortable being away from her, letting her out of his sight, especially in public. "I'm scared," Dave admitted to his friend.

"I'd be worried if you weren't," Gray replied.

"I don't like risking any of you guys. You're not only my team, but you're my friends too. The last thing I want is to scare the hell out of my son by involving him in a firefight, but I know you and the others will do whatever you can to prevent that. And you've all got women waiting for you, and I don't want to have to tell any of them that the love of their life isn't coming home."

"This team's all about getting kidnapped women and children home. And your son is being held hostage. Yeah, he might be in a nice house and not chained up, but he's being held prisoner all the same," Gray insisted. "We aren't going to take any more chances than we would on any other op, but we're all more invested now. David's one of our own."

Dave inhaled deeply. He hated what they'd planned so far. To storm the small house and kill anyone who got between them and David. But he wasn't willing to wait any longer once the passports were in his hands. Especially after hearing the rumors about other babies. Del Rio was the devil, and whatever he had planned for David was pure evil.

"Thank you," Dave eventually said to Gray, meaning those two words down to his very soul.

"I don't think I've thanked you yet," Black said to Raven.

"For what?" Raven asked.

"For saving Meat. And for being willing to risk yourself to save my hide if my team hadn't come for me when they did."

Black was referring to their previous mission, when he and Meat had gotten separated from the rest of the team, and Ruben and his friends had jumped them. They probably would've killed the two Mountain Mercenaries if Zara and her friends hadn't dragged Meat away, and if the team hadn't found Black when they had.

Raven shrugged. "You were there to try to help, not hurt. It was the least we could do."

Black encompassed all the women in his gaze as he said, "In our line of work, it's easy to get cynical and think the worst of humankind. We see the worst of the worst, so it's nice to see people who, even when the odds are against them and they have nothing to gain, are still willing to help. Thank you."

Raven nodded, and the other women blushed when Zara translated for them.

"So, you guys are all married or have girlfriends, right?" Raven asked.

Dave wandered back over to where she was sitting on the floor and lowered himself to the carpet to sit next to her. It felt as if his heart was going to burst when she reached out and took hold of his hand. Every time she'd touched him voluntarily since they'd been reunited, Dave had felt as if he'd just won the lottery. He did his best to pay attention to the conversation going on around him, and not the feel and smell of his wife next to him. He'd dreamed about this moment more times than he could count, and it was hard to believe it was actually here.

"Yup," Gray answered. "My wife's name is Allye. She was a professional dancer out in San Francisco. We met when the boat she was on sank and we were stranded in the middle of the ocean together."

Raven's brows shot up. "Seriously?"

"Seriously. She'd been snatched off the street and was being delivered to the man who bought her, but I interfered with that. Unfortunately, he got his hands on her later anyway."

"But you found her?" Raven asked breathlessly.

"*We* found her," Gray confirmed. "She now teaches dance to special-needs children in Colorado Springs, and we just had our first child, Darby James."

Raven turned to the other men. They took the hint. One by one, they told her the very abbreviated stories of how they'd met their own women.

"Chloe was kept prisoner by her brother. I found her . . . and decided I was keeping her," Ro said succinctly.

"Morgan Byrd was one of the most famous missing persons in the United States. We stumbled across her while on a mission in the Dominican Republic," Arrow said. "And you know that she recently had our baby girl, Calinda."

"I knew Harlow when we were in high school," Black said. "She's a chef, and was working at a women's shelter when some developer was putting heavy—and illegal—pressure on the owner to sell. He ended up setting the shelter on fire, and Harlow had to jump out a third-floor window to escape."

"I helped Everly find her sister, who'd been kidnapped. We thought it was a sex-trafficking ring, but it turned out to be just a crazy man who was looking for his next wife . . . who he wanted to keep chained up in his house for the next twenty years," Ball explained.

Raven's eyes were huge in her face, as were the other women's when Zara finished sharing the men's stories.

"And you know Meat's story, and about how we met," Zara said with a chuckle. "I saved *him*, but when someone from my past decided she wanted my money, he had to rescue himself that time."

"You guys certainly don't lead boring lives," Raven quipped.

"With the exception of maybe Black, we all met the loves of our lives because of your husband," Gray said.

"Nope, even though I didn't meet Harlow while on a mission, I wouldn't have gone to the women's shelter to help with self-defense if I hadn't been a Mountain Mercenary," Black said. "I wouldn't have even been in Colorado Springs."

"True. Okay, then, as a result of Rex and his dogged determination to do whatever it took to find you, we've all found the women who make us complete," Gray amended.

Dave felt Raven looking at him, and he turned to gaze at her. She was staring at him with a look he couldn't interpret.

The other women in the room all began to talk at once. It was obvious they were impressed and touched by the stories of how the men had met their women. The mood was happy, and Dave loved simply hanging out with his men like this. He hadn't had a lot of chances to do this in the past, since he was simply the bartender. Being in the middle of the group and being included felt good.

But sitting next to his wife, who he honestly *had* begun to think he'd never see again, was the icing on the cake. He was happy for his friends that they'd found women to love, but he was even more thrilled for himself.

The only thing standing between him and a long, beautiful life—what was left of it—with his wife and child was del Rio. And getting out of Peru.

Not long after all the men had told their stories, the party started to break up. Daniela said she needed to get back before it got too late, and the other women agreed. They hadn't had any issues with Ruben and his friends since the gang's encounter with Dave, but no one wanted to push their luck. Black and Ro were going to escort them back to their hut and stand watch for the night. Ball and Gray would make sure Daniela got back to her house safely as well.

Everyone said their good nights, and Dave escorted Raven to the room they'd been sharing. She got ready for bed in the bathroom, and Dave stripped off his shirt and pants. He got under the comforter, but stayed on top of the sheet. Raven came out of the bathroom and climbed into bed. She didn't say anything about him not wearing a shirt, but he saw the hesitation in her movements.

"I can put it back on if you want me to," Dave said gently.

She took a deep breath, then shook her head a little desperately. "No. It's fine."

"Come here," Dave said, and held out his arm.

She hesitantly scooted closer to him, and he could tell the second she realized there was still a sheet between their bodies. He hated the relief he could see in her eyes, but reminded himself that they'd only been reunited for a couple weeks. That wasn't long enough to wipe out the memories of other men and the things they'd done to her.

She gingerly lay her head on his bare shoulder, and he sighed in relief when her arm slowly crept across his waist. Raven's head lifted slightly, and Dave knew she was staring at the scar on his upper chest. The slice from the motorcycle-club member's knife had trailed down his neck and stopped just above his nipple.

"Who took care of you after this happened?" she asked quietly.

"I did. I checked myself out of the hospital as soon as possible, but not before the lead detective on your case read me the riot act and told me to get the hell out of his city. I went home to Colorado Springs and got back to work. Both at The Pit and at searching the internet for any trace of you."

"I hate that I wasn't there."

Dave chuckled.

She glared at him. "What are you laughing at? Nothing's funny."

"It's a little funny," he countered. "Raven, if you'd been there, I never would've been hurt in the first place, since I got this little memento while searching for *you.*"

She huffed out a breath and put her head back down. "I just don't like to think of you hurting."

Dave sobered immediately. "And I feel the same about you. I'd do anything to turn back the clock and make different decisions on that trip to Vegas. But we can't. We just have to keep moving forward. One day at a time."

She startled slightly and picked her head up once more. "Why'd you say that?"

"Say what?"

"One day at a time."

He shrugged. "It's what I told myself every night when I went to bed. That I had to take each day as it came. One at a time. I couldn't think about next week, or next year, or the next five years without you. I told myself that all I had to do was get through one more day. Anything else seemed too much. Too long."

"That's how I've gotten through everything as well," she confessed. "Every day that I was held captive, I told myself that I just had to hang on for one more day. And when I was living in the barrio, and I was so hungry I was dizzy, and scared of Ruben and everyone else, I held on by thinking that all I had to do was get through the day. That tomorrow would be better."

"I love you," Dave whispered. "Even when we were apart, we were on the same wavelength."

She didn't return the words, but lay her head back down on his chest. Simply feeling her warm breaths against his skin made him feel less jumpy. He truly did have Raven here with him. She was alive. She was a miracle. His miracle.

"Tomorrow after I drop you off to see David, I'm hoping to be able to pick up his passport. It won't be long now until all this is behind us and we're home," he told her, knowing the change in topic was a bit jarring, but he didn't want her to fall asleep before he told her that their time in Peru would hopefully be coming to an end.

They were quiet for a few minutes. Dave thought Raven was asleep when she said, "I dreamed this, you know."

"What?"

"This. Lying with you in bed. You playing with my hair. I never thought it would happen."

"It's real. I'm real."

"I know. Thank you, Dave. Thank you for finding me and loving me."

"Go to sleep, sweetheart. Tomorrow we'll be one day closer to going home and living the rest of our lives in peaceful bliss with our son."

He wanted to apologize once again for it taking so long to find her. For everything she'd gone through, but he kept the words to himself. Deep down, he knew he'd done everything he could to find her, but it still grated that she'd suffered through a hellish ten years.

He felt the happy exhalation on his skin as she sighed. Then she went boneless in his arms as she succumbed to sleep.

Dave didn't sleep. He memorized the feel of his wife in his arms and how her hair looked spread across his shoulder and arm.

Tomorrow would hopefully be the turning point in the limbo they'd been stuck in. He'd pick up the boy's passport, and he and his team would plan the raid on the house David was being held in. Then they'd either be on their way home—or the shit would have hit the fan. He hoped for the former, but knew if the latter happened, the Mountain Mercenaries would take care of their own.

They didn't have the luxury of waiting anymore. He wasn't willing to risk his son's mental well-being and health if del Rio decided to act on whatever perverse plans he had for him.

He fell into an uneasy sleep, knowing tomorrow could change his family's lives forever, one way or another.

Chapter Eleven

"Don't be nervous," Dave told Raven as he pulled over to the side of the road where he usually dropped her off before watching her walk toward the house where David was living.

"I can't help it," she told him, biting her lip. "Every time I come here, I dread walking in and being told he's gone. That del Rio has taken him again."

Dave hated that for his wife. He hated the delay in freeing the boy and getting them all back to the States. "I hope the next time we come to this house, it's to get David and bring him home," he told her honestly.

"Me too," Raven whispered.

"Look at me," Dave ordered gently.

His wife turned her head, and he couldn't help but be awed all over again that he was really sitting next to her. It was still hard to believe, after all this time. "I'm going to get our son home. Where we'll teach him to love LEGOs and to laugh when he leaves his toys all over the house for us to trip over. We'll take him camping . . . show him how to make s'mores. We're going to have a future together. The three of us."

He watched as Raven visibly relaxed. "Okay."

"Okay. Be careful. Don't do or say anything to David or anyone else that might raise any suspicions."

"I won't."

"Did you get enough to eat this morning? Are you going to be all right until tonight when I come back and pick you up?" Dave asked.

Raven's lips twitched. "I had plenty," she told him. "You made me eat that last protein bar, and now I think I might burst."

"You need the calories. Starving you is just one more black mark on del Rio's soul." He held out his hand, and she put hers in his. Dave brought it up to his mouth and kissed her palm. "I love you. This is gonna be over soon."

"Okay," she told him, the emotion easy to see in her eyes. She was overwhelmed and scared, but underneath all that, he saw a belief in him that he hoped he'd be able to live up to.

He watched as she reached over and opened the door. She closed it without another word and walked down the sidewalk toward the small house. Dave had wanted to drop her off closer, so she didn't have to walk as far, but he knew it was safer to stay at least a half mile away so as not to raise any suspicions.

He was still staring at the sidewalk a few moments after Raven had disappeared, thinking about his upcoming appointment at the US embassy to pick up David's passport and the raid his team was planning for that night—

When the glass in the window next to his head suddenly shattered.

Flinching away from the shards, Dave wasn't prepared for two men to reach through the window and physically pull him out. They were strong, and Dave fought like a man possessed. He managed to get a few licks in before one of the men shoved a pistol against his head.

"Stop fighting or I'll blow your brains out right here," the man growled.

Dave froze.

Fuck. He knew he could take these assholes—there were only four of them, compared to the half dozen or more he'd faced in the barrio—but even he couldn't beat a bullet. And he needed to live. For Raven. For his son. He couldn't free them from the grave.

Holding up his hands in surrender, Dave memorized the faces of the assholes surrounding him. He'd make sure they paid. Along with anyone else who stood between him and his family.

"Not so tough now, are you?" one of the men asked, right before something slammed hard into the back of Dave's head.

One second he was glaring at the men and mentally deciding how he was going to kill them, and the next, everything went black.

~

Dave came to in the back of a car, sandwiched between two men, one of whom held a pistol to his head, though he was in no condition to fight, and everyone knew it. His hands were secured behind him, and he had a raging headache. Dave wanted to puke, but managed to keep the bile down.

He stared at the huge compound the car was approaching. Dave recognized it immediately. He'd spent many hours studying the place from satellite photos. The house itself was surrounded by several acres of lush green grass and a ten-foot brick wall.

Once upon a time, Dave had entertained the idea of approaching this place on his own, but his team had convinced him otherwise.

Now it seemed he was going to get his chance to talk one-on-one with the man who had single-handedly tried to ruin his and Raven's lives.

Dave had to assume someone had reported seeing him to del Rio. Or maybe he'd had someone following Raven to keep tabs on her. Either way, he was certain del Rio knew the Mountain Mercenaries were in town—and the man wasn't happy about it. The fact that Dave had been snatched didn't bode well for him.

He tried to review everything he knew about del Rio. With him, money talked. Everything the man did was about a profit. Money was what made his world go 'round. And if money was what it took to get David out of his clutches, then that was what Dave would offer. Given the chance, he'd buy David from the man without a moment's hesitation.

He forced himself not to think about Raven being repeatedly raped somewhere in the large house in front of him. Or gazing out the window at the beautiful lawn and wishing she were somewhere else. It was too painful. As proud of his wife as he was, Dave still had a lot of pent-up anger simmering beneath his skin. Someone would pay for what his wife had been through, and that someone would be del Rio himself. Somehow, someway, the man would pay.

Looking up as the car came to a stop, Dave studied the windows, but they all had the curtains drawn. He had no idea if there were women behind those curtains. Prisoners who were being abused and raped day after day with no hope of rescue. Were there more Americans? More women like Bonita, Carmen, and the others?

He knew it was likely, and the thought was abhorrent, but Dave had to concentrate on the reason why he was there.

Hang in there, he silently begged the captives. *I promise I'm going to send help. You just have to hang on a little bit longer.*

Dave felt guilty about not being able to do anything right this second for the women who might be trapped inside, living a life they never could've dreamed in their worst nightmares. But at the moment, he wasn't even in a position to help himself.

He was dragged out of the car and almost fell to his knees in the driveway. The world spun, and Dave felt a trickle of what he assumed was blood oozing down the back of his head. Whatever he'd been hit with had done some damage, but he was alive.

Not killing him outright was going to be del Rio's downfall.

"How'd you find me?" he asked the men all but dragging him toward the huge house.

"We have many ways," the man holding the gun said. "Del Rio is a god around here. If you thought you and your friends were staying under the radar, you really are stupid Americans. We have eyes and ears everywhere."

Damn. Dave and the others had speculated on more than one occasion about why del Rio hadn't sent his goons after them. They'd remained vigilant, just in case, but the asshole had waited to grab him when he was alone and without backup. It had been a stupid mistake on Dave's part to drop Raven off without one of his team with him.

He was led up the stairs, down two hallways, past at least a dozen doors, all closed, into a large library. There were bookshelves along the right and left walls, and a large window behind the huge desk that sat in the middle of the room. There was nothing on the polished wooden surface. A single wooden straight-backed chair sat in front of the desk, and a guard motioned to it with his gun as another cut the restraints from Dave's wrists.

He sat where he was instructed. It was either sit or fall down, and the last thing he wanted to do was make himself more vulnerable.

As much as Dave hated being in this house, this prison, he wasn't exactly upset that he'd finally get to speak to del Rio.

At least, he *hoped* that was what was about to happen.

He didn't have to wait long to find out.

The door slammed open, making a loud bang as it hit the wall, and Dave jerked in his seat. The movement jarred his already aching head, but he did his best to not show in any way how badly he was hurting.

Three men entered the room. Two dressed in all black, and the third was del Rio himself. It was obvious Dave wasn't going to be able to kill del Rio right then and there. Not outnumbered seven to one. But his time was coming. Even if Dave couldn't be the one to pull the trigger and kill the man, he knew it would be done.

Dave had unearthed a few pictures of del Rio on the internet, but none had managed to capture the evil that seemed to ooze from the man's very being. He wasn't terribly tall, probably around five-eight or -nine. He had brown hair and brown eyes. His skin was dark and wrinkled. Del Rio was said to be in his early fifties, and looking at him, Dave had to agree with that assumption. He wore a pair of jeans, a holster with a pistol around his waist, and a long-sleeve, dark-red button-down shirt, and he walked with a swagger that came from years of arrogance and getting his own way.

He walked around the desk and sat in the chair. One guard stood by the door, and the other settled near the back corner of the desk, near del Rio. The four men who'd dragged Dave up the stairs stayed, all standing around his chair. The pistol was no longer being pointed at Dave's head, but he knew without a doubt that if he made one wrong move, he'd get a bullet in his brain faster than he could lift a hand to protect himself.

With his own hands behind his head, del Rio leaned back as if he didn't have a care in the world. "Who are you, and why are you here?" del Rio asked in English.

Dave hadn't known if the man could understand or speak English, though he'd had a hunch he could. A man didn't come to have as much power as del Rio without knowing how to threaten people in more than one language. He wouldn't be surprised if the asshole knew other languages as well.

It was also a bullshit question. Del Rio knew exactly who he was and why he was there, at least in part.

"I'm here to take back what you stole from me," Dave told him bluntly, figuring the man would appreciate him getting right to the point.

Del Rio shrugged. "Your woman made me a lot of money in the past, but she is of no use to me anymore," he said lazily. "I wasn't concerned that you were fucking her and her friends. But now she's brought trouble . . . and it's time for her to disappear."

That pissed Dave off even more. Raven was more than a means to an end, and he definitely didn't like del Rio's threat. "Then let me go, and we'll leave Peru never to return," Dave told him. "In fact, we were planning on heading out tomorrow, so if you'll just drop me off, I can finish making my plans, and we'll be out of here."

Del Rio chuckled. "I don't think so," he said menacingly. "Especially not when you seem to have plans to take what *doesn't* belong to you."

Dave's eyes narrowed. "The boy is more my son than you'll ever know."

"Here's the thing," del Rio said. "I've got plans for that boy."

"Fuck you and your plans," Dave bit out.

But the other man didn't take offense. He laughed and leaned forward, resting his elbows on the desk in front of him. "But you didn't ask what my plans were."

"I know all about you and your fucking plans," Dave told him.

"I don't think you know as much as you think you do. Do you know about the stash house I own, filled to the brim with bastard children of the whores who work for me? As far as the government knows, it's an orphanage, and I'm an angel for those poor, unwanted children. I help find them homes where they'll be *very* loved for as long as their new families want them."

Dave's face betrayed nothing. He refused to show an ounce of disgust toward the evil man in front of him.

"No response to that, huh?" del Rio asked. "Then how about this—I've decided to keep little David for myself."

At hearing that, Dave couldn't help but flinch slightly.

But del Rio saw, and smiled wider. "I'm going to need a successor someday. Someone to take over for me when I decide to retire. And David, with his striking blue eyes and his adorable dimple, was just too beautiful for me to give up. So I spared him from the life those other brats live. He's gotten the best upbringing money can buy. He'll be educated, and I've even allowed his mom to visit, to teach him English . . . such a handy skill to have in my line of work, don't you think?

"But it's time his coddling is over. He needs to grow up. He's starting to learn that *I'm* in charge. Before too long, I'll introduce him to the joys of sexual pleasure. He'll quickly learn that doing exactly as I say will go better for him than fighting. I haven't had my own plaything in quite a while, and I'm looking forward to grooming him to please me—and *only* me."

Dave felt sick, his stomach roiling violently. Not only was del Rio planning to abuse *his* son, but he would groom him to be as evil as himself.

They'd all known del Rio was evil, that he used and abused both women and children, but this was too much.

Not going to happen. *No fucking way.*

"I see this kind of thing isn't your kink, which is neither here nor there," del Rio continued with a smirk. "For a long time, I simply took what I wanted . . . workers for my compound here, but also children to sell to the more discerning buyer. But I've found it's much easier to snatch women than children. People care more about the little ones. But then I realized that I had my own baby factory right here under my roof! It's been more profitable than you could ever imagine."

"I can pay," Dave told the man. "Whatever you want. For the boy."

"Weren't you listening?" del Rio asked coldly. "I don't want your money. I want the boy. He'll be my plaything, then my successor. I'm going to train him to be even more ruthless than I am. He'll eventually take over my empire, and the del Rio name will be spoken with fear and reverence for decades to come."

"Why?" Dave asked in disgust. "Why do this? There are plenty of women who are actually *willing* to work in the sex trade. The women you keep locked up here have families who love them. They had lives before you so ruthlessly tore them away from everything they know."

"Because I can," del Rio said simply. "Because women are slime. They'll open their legs to anyone as long as it gets them what they want. Money, food, prestige. They're *nothing*. Men are superior in every way, and women need to learn that."

Dave had no response. The man sitting so calmly in front of him was insane. Not only that, but he didn't have a compassionate bone in his body.

"I'm not going to let you take my successor, *my son*, away from me," del Rio finished, lifting his chin.

Dave saw the subtle signal to one of the men standing behind him, but before he could do a damn thing about it, a stun gun was thrust into his side.

Letting out a loud shout, Dave couldn't control his muscles. He fell off the chair onto the floor, and still the man held the device against him. Electrical currents ran through his body, and all Dave could do was convulse on the expensive carpet.

Del Rio stood, the chair he'd been in creaking with his movements, and approached as Dave writhed in pain at his feet. He couldn't defend himself. Couldn't do anything but watch as del Rio said something to the guards. Then, without a backward glance, the most notorious and evil sex trafficker Dave had ever run across turned and left the library, his two bodyguards following without any kind of expression on their faces.

The men who'd grabbed him from his car on the street spoke among themselves, then looked down at him. One pulled out a knife, and Dave shuddered as it gleamed in the bright lights of the room.

Dave closed his eyes as one man pressed the Taser against his body again, rendering him physically unable to protect himself.

The other man pulled Dave's head back, exposing his neck.

Refusing to shut his eyes, Dave glared at the man closest to him, even as he fought against the paralyzing effects of the current flowing through his body.

He thought about Raven. How upset she'd be when he never returned to pick her up.

Del Rio was the devil incarnate. And Dave was just a man. A desperate man who'd wanted to do whatever it took to ease the agony in his woman's eyes . . . but now he'd never get the chance.

~

Dave had no idea what time it was when consciousness returned. He was lying in what he assumed to be the trunk of a car. Lifting a hand, he touched his neck and winced when he felt wetness there.

But he was alive. Whatever had happened while he'd been unconscious hadn't been lethal. Either the men were incompetent, or they planned to torture him further when they reached their destination.

The car slowed, then stopped, and Dave shut his eyes, deciding to gather as much information about his situation as he could before he acted. A stench unlike anything he'd ever smelled before wafted to his nostrils, but he didn't move or otherwise react.

The lid of the trunk lifted, and he listened as two men talked in Spanish. After a couple minutes, Dave felt hands on him. He kept his body limp, making his deadweight difficult to move. The men grunted and swore as they did their best to lift him out of the trunk of the car. He kept his muscles loose and managed to hold back a groan when they finally just pulled him over the lip of the trunk and let gravity do the rest of the work. His head hit the ground hard when he rolled out of the car.

There was more discussion between the men, then they each grabbed hold of one of his ankles and attempted to drag him somewhere. The ground he was being towed over was bumpy and damp. It smelled like a combination of rotting flesh and human feces. But still he didn't move.

With one last grunt from one of the men, they let go of his ankles, and his legs fell limply to the ground once more. Dave was preparing to leap up and fight . . .

But nothing happened.

When it sounded like the men were moving away, Dave risked opening his eyes to a squint to check out his situation.

If the men were going back to the car to get a weapon or something, he'd have to move . . . but he hesitated. He wanted to jump up and attack them, then steal the car, but he felt light-headed and sick, probably from loss of blood and the way they'd pumped him full of electrical current.

As he debated if he had the strength for a sneak attack, Dave watched in disbelief as they started the car and drove away.

They were idiots. Conceited and too confident that they'd killed him, or that he'd eventually die from whatever they'd already done.

They should've made sure they'd finished the job they were assigned.

It was a stupid thought, but Dave knew his Mountain Mercenaries would never have made such a colossal mistake. They weren't killers, as he told them often enough, but if forced to take someone out in their quest to free a captive, they'd make damn sure the job was done.

Groaning, Dave managed to turn onto his side. He brought a hand up to his neck again and applied pressure to the knife wound he found there. Somehow the assholes had managed to fuck up killing him when he was lying helpless on the floor, unable to defend himself. The new slice was perpendicular to the wound he'd received years before. Dave could only imagine what the new scar would do to his already somewhat fearsome appearance, but he could hardly worry about that now. All he could think about was getting the hell out of wherever he was and rescuing his son.

Opening his eyes fully, Dave saw that he'd been tossed in what could only be called a dump. As far as the eye could see, there were mounds of junk and refuse. The stench was horrific, but as long as he was alive, he had a fighting chance. Birds flew overhead, scrounging for whatever they could find to eat, and the sounds of their squawking were loud in the otherwise-quiet atmosphere.

Dave tried to push up to his knees, but the world spun crazily around him. Swearing, he fell flat on his face in the gunk. Rolling to his back, he lay there, trying to get his bearings and strength back.

He had to get to the city. Back to Raven. Had to rescue his son before del Rio could move him or carry out his plan. He also needed to figure out where this "orphanage" was located; the other children didn't deserve what del Rio had planned for them any more than David did.

What had started as a simple trip to find his wife and bring her back home had become more complicated than anything Dave could've imagined.

But it didn't matter. Rescuing women and children was what the Mountain Mercenaries did, and no matter how long it took or how much red tape they had to cut through, del Rio wasn't going to win this battle. David *would* be coming home with him, and del Rio would rue the day he'd fucked with his family.

But first . . .

Dave shut his eyes. First he'd rest a minute and get his strength back. Then he'd get up, find his way back to the city, rescue his son, and get the hell out of Peru.

Chapter Twelve

Mags paced around Gray's room impatiently. It was six in the evening, and Dave hadn't returned to pick her up from meeting with David. She'd walked all the way back to the motel, expecting to find him there . . . expecting Dave to apologize for being detained by his other errands. But there had been no sign of him when she'd arrived.

Gray hadn't even realized Dave was missing until she'd gotten back to the motel and explained he hadn't picked her up.

Zara was in the room with Mags, along with Ro and Ball. The others were in another room, apparently talking over what their next steps were and how to find Dave.

"He told me he was going to get David's passport, and hopefully by tomorrow, we'd be out of here," Mags said. "What happened? Where is he? Is David no longer safe?"

"Don't panic," Ro said in a voice that was way too calm for Mags's peace of mind.

"Don't panic?" she asked, becoming frantic. "How can I not? My husband managed to find me after all this time and by some miracle accepted the fact that I have a child who isn't his. And now he's *missing*. This is bad, Ro. Very bad. Del Rio is literally crazy. If he got his hands on Dave, everyone I love is in danger."

"Dave might not be a soldier, but he's got good instincts," Ball told her. "Even if he found himself in a situation that went sideways, he'll be able to get himself out of it."

"Not if someone shoots him in the head!" Mags exclaimed hysterically.

Ro walked over to her, took her hand, and led her to one of the beds. He sat her down on the mattress and kneeled in front of her. "I know you haven't been around us for all that long, but trust me when I say we're doing all we can to find him and give him backup."

"You know where he is?" Mags asked.

Ro shook his head. "No. But Dave's smart. Hell, he helped us plan hundreds of missions. If he's in trouble, he'll find a way out of it."

She took a deep breath. "So what's the plan in the meantime? Sit around here and just wait for Dave to come back?"

Surprisingly, Ro smiled.

Mags frowned at him.

"Sorry, love, I just . . . I can see why Dave's head over heels for you. You're a cut-to-the-chase kind of person, just like he is. Anyway, the plan is to find Dave, get your son, and get the hell out of this country."

She didn't even crack a smile. "How?"

Ro stood, and then Ball was in front of her. "Meat's getting in touch with our contacts here in the country to get us additional weapons. We have some, but we need more firepower. We'll go to the embassy and see if Dave ever arrived there this morning. If not, we'll get David's passport, along with yours and the other women's as well. The plan is to have our shit ready to go so the second we find Dave and get your son, we can head to the airport. We've chartered a plane, and it's ready to go. We just have to give them a time, and they'll be there to pick us up and take us home."

Mags frowned. "A private jet? Whose?"

"It doesn't matter. The Mountain Mercenaries have a lot of friends back in the States. Friends in high places who are more than willing to loan us a plane if it means putting us in their debt. Meat is doing all he can to find Dave tonight, but even if we don't find him, we want to go in and get David tomorrow. We're done waiting."

She inhaled sharply and felt Zara squeeze her shoulder. "Tomorrow?"

"Yes. We'll go in at dawn, when there will possibly be fewer people around. We can hopefully grab him and go without any shots being fired. But even if there are, we're not going to leave without your son."

"But what about Dave?" she whispered, torn between being thrilled she'd finally have her son and agony over not knowing her husband's fate.

"If we haven't found him by the time we get you and David back here, you, your son, Gabriella, Zara, and half the team will head to the airport with the other women, and you'll fly out of here. The other three of us will stay until we've found Dave."

Mags shook her head. "No, I don't want to leave without him."

"Mags," Zara said tenderly, "you need to get David to Colorado. Del Rio can't touch him there. The longer you stay here, the greater the chance he'll be found and taken again. And Dave would kick our asses if we didn't do everything in our power to get you home, with or without him."

Mags's shoulders slumped. God, what a horrible choice to make. Her son or her husband?

"Mags," Ball said softly, "look at me."

Mags looked up into the man's intense blue eyes. "Dave is one of us. Our team. Hell, he's our leader. He's been there for us countless times. Even without physically being on the missions, he's still *there*. He's bent over backward making sure we have the intel we need and kicking ass when necessary. We aren't leaving without him. I give you my word as a Mountain Mercenary that we'll bring your husband home to you. Okay?"

Mags nodded reluctantly. She didn't like it, but she had to trust that Dave's men knew what they were doing.

"Good. Now, you haven't touched your dinner. You know Dave wouldn't be happy if you didn't eat. So please try to eat something. I don't want your husband to hurt me if he comes back and thinks we didn't take care of you."

That made Mags smile a bit. She turned to smile at Zara as well, then took a deep breath. As Ro handed her a sandwich and a can of soda, she thought to herself, *You'd better not be dead, Dave. Your son and I need you too badly.*

~

Dave felt like death warmed over. The hairs in his nose were probably singed off from the horrific smells coming from the trash piles all around him. He had no idea what time it was, but a glow came from the waning moon, with just a hint of light to indicate the approach of sunrise.

Considering he'd been snatched the previous morning, then dumped while the sun was high in the sky, he knew he'd been passed out for hours.

Every time he turned his head, dull pain shot through him from the cut on his neck. Reaching up a hand, Dave cautiously probed the wound. He didn't have a mirror, but from what he could tell, it seemed pretty shallow, and the bleeding had nearly stopped. The knife was either dull as shit or the guy wielding it was a fucking novice at slitting throats.

His shirt was still damp down the front and sticky from the blood, but he was alive. Del Rio had fucked up. He should've made sure his cronies had killed him.

Dave sat up slowly, testing his equilibrium, and looked around.

His head was pounding, and he felt a bit weak, but figured that was from the blood loss and dehydration. He still had on his clothes and shoes, but nothing was in his pockets, and both the sheath that had been on his ankle and the knife that was in it were gone. Dave was pissed for a moment, until he looked around. He was surrounded by trash, including miles of broken glass, various metal rods . . . he even spied a broken and bent steak knife. He had plenty of weapons to choose from.

Realizing he also still wore his belt, Dave smiled. He'd bought it from a travel website years ago. It had a convenient, hidden zipper pocket on the inside, where he'd stashed a bit of cash, just in case.

Feeling better knowing he wouldn't be unarmed, and all he had to do was walk until he could flag down a taxi, Dave slowly and carefully pushed to his feet. After a few seconds, he took a deep breath and realized he felt pretty damn good for almost being killed . . . again.

He'd been damn lucky, but instead of feeling triumphant that he'd survived, he was getting angrier by the second. He had a wife and child to think about now—and he'd fucked up. He should've been more observant. Should've known del Rio would find out about him and do something to protect what he considered his "investments." He'd put a huge bull's-eye on his son, and possibly Raven too.

He needed to get back into the city and to his team. But more important, he had to get to his son before he was moved or further abused by del Rio.

Thinking about del Rio's plans made the pain in his neck recede. All that was left was a determination to get his son out of the country and home to Colorado, where he'd be safe. He'd make arrangements to take care of del Rio's operation once they were safely out of his reach.

Then Dave and Raven could finally start their life as a family, as they'd always dreamed.

A sound brought him out of his fog of anger. Dave looked in the direction it was coming from and saw a lone headlight coming toward the dump. A motorcycle or scooter.

Smiling, Dave reached down and picked up what probably used to be a pipe from a kitchen sink, as well as the bent knife he'd spotted earlier. He moved as quickly and silently as possible away from where he'd woken up and hid behind a pile of rotting garbage. He no longer even smelled the stench. He was completely focused on the man coming toward the dump.

The man parked the large scooter—and Dave immediately recognized him. It was the guard who'd looked so gleeful when his buddy was shocking him, the one who'd sliced his neck.

Furious, he knew he could easily end this man's life right here and now and not feel an ounce of remorse . . . but he wouldn't. Dave was no killer.

But that didn't mean he couldn't hurt the man the same way he'd hurt *him*.

He shifted his grip on the knife, envisioning exactly what he was about to do. Dave didn't know why the man had returned, possibly to make sure he was dead, but he wasn't going to look a gift horse in the mouth. He had a chance to get some revenge, and hopefully a way out of the trash dump. He also had no idea where the other guard was or if he'd be joining his friend to finish the job they should've done earlier.

The man went straight to the spot where he and his friend had left Dave earlier that afternoon. When he didn't find him, he growled something angrily in Spanish.

Dave quickly snuck up behind him and wrapped an arm around the smaller man's throat before he even realized he wasn't alone.

"Surprise, asshole," Dave hissed, not caring that the man couldn't understand.

The guard struggled in his grip, but Dave wasn't about to let the man get the upper hand. He pressed his knife to the guy's throat and quickly slashed him from ear to ear.

Del Rio's man screamed and thrashed in his grip, making the cut deeper than Dave had planned. He'd just wanted to scare the man, to give him a scar that would forever remind him of the American he should've killed, but hadn't. The man's hands flew to his throat even as

Dave spun him around. Before he could defend himself, Dave planted a hard fist in his face. He went down like a rock.

The man lay unconscious on the same pile of shit and trash that he'd left Dave in earlier. Quickly searching his pockets, Dave took what little money he found, along with the keys to the scooter. Then he stood, spat on the man, and turned his back without a second glance. He wasn't too worried about the guy. If he bled out, he bled out . . . he wasn't his concern. Only his wife and child mattered now.

Dave had no idea where he was, or how in the hell to get back to the motel, but he'd figure it out. The sky was already lightening, and the longer it took him to get back to Raven, and to get to David, the more danger they were all in.

Dave had a bad feeling he'd awoken the beast, and there was a possibility del Rio had already moved his son. The thought made his blood go cold, but it only strengthened his resolve. No one fucked with the leader of the Mountain Mercenaries. No one.

~

Mags was nervous. It was now morning, and there was still no sign of Dave. But it was time for her to go see her son.

Dave's team was planning a morning raid on the house where David was being held. She wasn't thrilled that her son would probably be traumatized by essentially being kidnapped from the home he'd lived in his entire life, but getting him away from del Rio was vital.

Today wasn't one of her scheduled days to visit David. She was going to knock on the door with the ruse that she had been informed by someone in the barrio that del Rio had demanded her presence at the house. When the door was opened for her, the team would storm the house and rescue her son.

They were all stuffed into the remaining minivan, all seven of them, and Black had just finished telling her to act as if nothing was wrong and do whatever she could not to raise any suspicion. The team could probably get into the house even if the door wasn't opened for her, but it would take longer, and del Rio's goons inside could use that time to hurt David.

"Any questions?" Black asked.

She shook her head. "No."

"Okay, just stay calm. You and David will be fine. I swear," he said.

Mags appreciated his reassurance. They were obviously tense and looked dangerous as hell, but she felt safe around them. For a second, she wished she could stay in the van, but then she took a deep breath and squared her shoulders. David would be scared to death if she wasn't there and he was grabbed by strange men. She had to keep him calm.

"I've got this," she said, more to herself than the others, but of course they all heard her anyway.

"Damn straight."

"Of course you do."

"Fuck yeah."

Mags couldn't help but smile at their responses. She liked these men. They were a little rough around the edges, but they obviously loved their girlfriends and wives and weren't afraid to do what had to be done in order to keep those who were more vulnerable safe.

She climbed out of the van and headed the half mile down the street toward the house David lived in. She knew her husband's friends were following her at a safe and discreet distance. It made her feel not so alone and bolstered her courage. She could do this. She *was* doing this. She'd been complacent for far too long. It was time to take her life back, and that of her son while she was at it. Worry for her husband still hammered at the back of her head, but at the moment, she had to concentrate on David. She hated having to choose, but knew he'd also tell her to put David first.

She walked up to the gate at the front of the house and rang the bell, waiting for someone to answer and going over her prepared speech in her head. When nothing happened, Mags frowned and pushed the button once more.

Several minutes later, she was still standing outside the locked gate. No one had answered the ringing of the bell.

Unease bloomed in her belly, and she frantically hit the button again and again. When still no one answered, she peered between the wrought-iron bars of the gate and yelled out in Spanish, "Hello? Is anyone there?"

She saw no movement in the house. No lights were on, and she didn't see any smoke rising from the chimney.

Desperate now, she grabbed hold of the bars and tugged—

To her surprise, the gate moved.

Looking down, Mags realized it wasn't locked. She pushed it open, dread filling her when it swung open with ease.

She took one step toward the house, anxious to see what the hell was going on, but someone grabbed hold of her upper arm.

Panicking, Mags spun around and aimed her fist at approximately where she figured the person's head would be.

Gray caught her fist in the palm of his hand. "Easy, Raven, it's just me."

"Gray! No one's answering," Mags cried. "They should be here!"

"I know. We're on this. Stay calm."

Stay calm? How in the hell could she stay calm? First Dave had disappeared, and now it seemed David was gone as well. Mags did her best to control her mounting panic. Gray nodded to someone behind her, and she barely flinched when she felt someone else take hold of her arm. Two weeks ago she would've freaked if anyone had grabbed her like these men were doing, but she knew her husband trusted them with his life. She wasn't scared of them. At the moment, she was more afraid for her son.

It was Meat at her side now. When she looked back, Gray had disappeared.

"Where'd he go?" she whispered.

"Gray's a ghost," Meat replied, as if they were simply having a normal conversation on a normal day. "Out of all of us, he's got the most uncanny ability to blend in with his surroundings and not be seen. Which is odd, considering how tall he is, but it's true."

He'd pulled her off the street and just inside the gate, so they couldn't be seen by random people walking by. He moved his hand down to her hand and grabbed hold. It should've felt weird, holding hands with a man who wasn't her husband, but at the moment, Mags would take any comfort she could get.

"The others are going to go inside and see what's up," Meat said softly. "If David is there, they'll bring him out to you."

If he was there. She looked up at the large man standing next to her. "Oh God, Meat, he *has* to be there."

"*Shhhhhh*, Raven. Don't borrow trouble." Then he looked down at her. "I swear to you right here and now, if he's been moved, we *will* find him."

Everyone kept telling her that, but she had no idea how they were going to go about it. Thoughts of Zara and how she'd been on her own in Peru from a young age flitted through Mags's head.

As if he could read her mind, Meat said, "He will not have to grow up without his mother. I give you my word."

Without a doubt, the best decision Mags had made in years was rescuing this man when he was lying broken and bleeding in the barrio. She didn't know much about him then; all she knew was that he'd been ambushed and hurt while he and his team were in Lima to rescue children.

She could've ignored what Ruben and his gang were doing outside their hut. She could've told her friends to stay quiet and not get involved. She'd lost her faith in the idea that everything happened for a reason. How could she believe there was a reason for her being kidnapped and held against her will and made to do vile things?

But standing against the wall, watching and waiting for her husband's men to come out of the house, hopefully with her son, made her belief come back stronger than ever before. Yes, she'd lived through hell, but she had a son. She'd always wanted a child, and even though she hadn't gotten him the way she would've wanted, he was still here, and she loved him more than she could've imagined when she dreamed about being a mother. Not only that, but her husband had found her.

And the very man whose life she'd helped save was standing next to her right now, swearing that, if her son was missing, he'd find him. It was almost enough to make her cry.

They watched in silence as the lights flicked on and off in the house. Then the men slowly filed out the front door as if they owned the place.

Mags's breath caught in her throat.

Arrow was the first to reach her and Meat. "It's empty. No one's there."

"No one?" Mags asked.

"No," Arrow told her, his expression filled with sympathy.

Feeling dizzy, Mags closed her eyes. She felt hands land on her shoulders, and her eyes popped open immediately. She didn't like feeling closed in, but she didn't move a muscle.

"They didn't leave that long ago," Arrow said. "There was a cup of tea on the table that was still lukewarm. Whatever del Rio has planned, I'm guessing it takes time. And everything about this empty house feels like it was a rush job, so he's not going to do anything with David right away. We've got time to track del Rio both physically and online. We're gonna find your son."

It seemed that her husband's men were all on the same page. They kept reassuring her they'd find her son and her husband. And she needed to hear it.

Then Meat, still holding her hand, led her out of the courtyard and back toward the van. Mags had no recollection of actually getting into the van or driving back to the motel. She only realized where she was when Zara took her in her arms and hugged her tightly, back in the room where she and Dave had been staying.

Things were a blur after that. The men all gathered in the room, not letting her be alone for even a second. Meat was hunched over his computer, clicking rapidly on the keys, and the others talked quietly in a corner, obviously planning their next steps. Maria, Gabriella, and the other women flitted in and out, fussing over her and trying to reassure her.

It was nearly noon when the door to the room suddenly burst open.

Mags jumped, and three of the guys immediately sprang up and got between the door and where she was sitting in a chair against the wall. Their protective instincts would've reassured her at any other time, but when she heard Black inhale sharply and say, "Dave!" she leapt to her feet.

She pushed her way between the men and stared at her husband in disbelief.

His hair was disheveled, and he smelled absolutely horrendous. But it was the blood coating the front of his shirt that had her gasping in horror.

"Fuck, man, are you all right?" Ball asked.

"Where the hell have you been?" Gray barked.

"Sit down before you fall down," Black added.

But Dave ignored his friends. He only had eyes for Mags.

She held her breath as he stalked toward her. She'd never been afraid of her husband before, but for just a second, the look in his eyes absolutely terrified her. Gone was the funny, gentle man she'd gotten reacquainted with in the last two weeks.

In his place was a warrior. A pissed-off, absolutely furious soldier.

He strode up to her and stood inches away. Mags had to crane her neck to keep eye contact. "David's gone," she whispered to the only man she'd ever loved. "We went to get him out today, but when we got there, the house was empty."

A muscle in Dave's jaw ticked. "Del Rio will regret fucking with my family. I swear to God, he's going to know exactly who ruined his life and why."

Dave's words were flat and cold, yet Mags could see the hate burning in his eyes.

"Okay," she said, wanting to soothe him, but not really knowing how.

Without looking away from her, he said, "Meat, I need you to check del Rio's bank accounts for large deposits. He's got a house filled with kids somewhere that he's passing off as an orphanage. We need to track down any deposits and get our contacts here in Peru to follow the trails. Guarantee they'll lead to rich, high-ranking assholes who've suddenly acquired children they'll claim to have adopted."

"Guessing they aren't doing so out of the goodness of their hearts," Gray muttered.

"No," Dave said flatly. "They bought them from del Rio to live out their perverted sexual fantasies."

Mags gasped. Many already knew del Rio was trafficking children, but the information about the "orphanage" was a whole new level of evil.

"I'm on it," Meat said from somewhere behind them. "Any idea how many?"

"No clue. But I'm guessing it's a pretty damn high number. Girls and boys. We also need to find that so-called orphanage. Prevent any other children from being sold."

Meat nodded, but didn't reply. He was already busy clicking away on his keyboard.

"Things looked chaotic at the house where David was kept," Gray said in a controlled but heated tone. "We're guessing shit happened fast. Probably because of whatever happened with you. What *did* happen?"

"Del Rio panicked," Dave said. "Which isn't like him."

"Yup," Gray agreed.

"I'm guessing he's stashed my son somewhere. Maybe with the other kids . . . at least for the time being. I doubt he'll risk taking David to his compound while the Mountain Mercenaries are still in town." And if possible, Mags saw even more determination in her man's eyes. "We'll head out tonight, as soon as we get any intel about where del Rio's stashed those kids . . . and hopefully David."

The men agreed, and everyone but Meat headed for the door.

"Zara?" Dave asked.

"Yeah?"

"Can you please get in contact with Daniela? I need her to have her ears to the ground about anything having to do with unknown children suddenly showing up in areas where they haven't been before, just in case Meat can't find anything."

"Okay, but Dave? Can she come here to look at you first?" Zara asked.

Mags saw the confusion on her husband's face, and he finally looked away from her to Zara. "Why?"

"You're covered in blood, and I think you're still bleeding," Zara said softly.

"I'm fine," Dave said in a dismissive tone and turned back to Mags.

"But—"

"I'll handle it," Mags said firmly, putting a hand on Dave's biceps. She felt stronger now that her husband was back and she could touch him. It wasn't as if she hadn't believed the others when they said they'd find David, but she knew without a doubt that Dave would turn over every rock and stone to bring him back to her. He'd found *her*; he'd find their son.

"If you're sure," Zara said in a tone that said *she* was anything but. Then she turned and headed for the door.

Mags barely heard the door shutting behind Zara before Dave reached for her hand and intertwined his fingers with hers. He towed her toward the bathroom.

"Dave?" Meat called out before they got there.

"Yeah?"

"What happened, exactly?"

Dave started walking again. "You find me something to go on, and I'll explain it all later when everyone's back."

Apparently that was as much as Dave was willing to tell his friend, because he entered the bathroom, still holding Mags's hand, and shut the door behind him.

He pulled her toward him as he sat on the toilet seat. Then he dropped his hand and leaned forward until his forehead was resting on her belly.

Surprised, Mags didn't immediately react. It wasn't until she felt Dave take a stuttering breath that she asked softly, "Dave?"

"I'm sorry," he whispered.

"About what?"

"I should've seen the guys sneaking up on me. It was a rookie move to let them overtake me after I dropped you off."

Mags could barely breathe. "Del Rio's men?"

"Yeah. He's one cold son of a bitch," Dave said without lifting his head. "I was desperate enough to offer to buy our son from him, but as much as he loves money, he wanted to see me suffer more."

Dave looked up then, and Mags winced as she saw the cut on his neck ooze a bit of blood.

"He's got awful plans for him," her husband said in a voice so furious, she should've been afraid. But because he was reacting to their son being put in danger, she wasn't scared of him. "He wants to raise him to be his replacement. Contaminate our son and turn him into a monster."

Mags inhaled sharply, putting a hand over her mouth. She knew del Rio was evil . . . but she'd had no idea what he was planning for David. It physically hurt to think he had plans to turn her tender, loving son into a stone-cold, heartless bastard.

"But he made a mistake," Dave said.

"What's that?" Mags whispered.

"He fucked with the Mountain Mercenaries. We're gonna find every one of those kids, get them away from him, and ruin his entire organization in the process. And get David out of his clutches. He'll never be like del Rio. *Never.*"

Mags believed every word her husband said. The conviction and confidence were easy to hear in his voice. She was still scared to death because her little boy was out there somewhere, but she believed in her Dave. He'd do whatever he could to bring their son back to her. Seeing him so pissed off, covered in blood and smelling like someone who had literally been dragged through a pile of shit, spewing hatred toward the man who had done his best to ruin her life, and being so confident that he'd go down, made her believe in him even more.

Swallowing hard, she brought her hands to the buttons on Dave's shirt. She slowly began to undo them, one by one.

Before she'd gotten to the last one, Dave caught her hands in his and said, "Go wait out in the room. I'll shower and be out in five minutes."

She shook her head. "No. Let me look at your injury."

"It's fine."

Mags shook her head. "Shut up, Dave. It's *not* fine. You're bleeding all over the fucking place. I'm gonna look at it and make sure your insides aren't about to leak out through your neck. *Then* you can go save our son and kick some ass. All right?"

Amazingly, the hatred and darkness in his eyes flickered, then disappeared altogether. He was back to looking like the gentle and loving husband she'd been getting reacquainted with over the last couple weeks.

"Okay, Raven. You do what you need to do."

"I will," she huffed, then gently pushed the shirt off his shoulders. She'd been up close and personal with his naked chest while she'd slept against him, but for some reason this felt different. His pecs flexed as she stared at him, and Mags forced herself to look at his neck. It was a bloody mess. She reached for one of the washcloths, wincing because she knew she was about to ruin it by staining it with her husband's blood.

"Wait," he said, "let me jump in the shower and wash off the bulk of the blood and stench first." Without waiting for her to answer, he stood, forcing Mags to take a step backward. She watched as he unbuttoned his pants and lowered the zipper. He turned so his back was to her and shoved the material off his body.

Mags held her breath at the sight of absolute perfection displayed in front of her. Dave was a decade older than the last time she'd seen him, but he was still just as fit. He even still had the little dimple at the bottom of his spine that she'd always teased him about. His thighs were large and muscular, and even his ass was still toned.

He leaned over and turned on the water in the shower. He started to step into the tub, still wearing his underwear.

Mags knew he'd done that for her sake. He wouldn't push her to do anything she didn't want to do, including look at his naked body.

But for the first time in years, she wasn't scared of a man. Wasn't terrified to see his cock. Her husband was perfectly proportioned . . . all over.

He was a big man, and if he ever raised his hand to her, he could hurt her badly. He could overpower her and hold her down and do whatever he wanted.

But he wouldn't.

She'd stake not only her life, but her son's life, on that fact.

The certainty rose up within her until she wanted nothing more than to feel Dave's arms around her. To feel him over her, looking down at her tenderly as they made love.

She'd used her precious memories as an escape when she'd been made to do things with other men. And now, she had her beautiful, tender husband back. It had been years since she'd had sex, and a decade since she'd made love. She wasn't ready to jump back into the saddle, so to speak, but for the first time, she realized she wanted the intimacy she'd once had with her husband. She wanted to lie in bed with him for hours and simply explore. Wanted to feel the euphoria that she'd only felt with him. Wanted to show him how much she loved him.

Feeling stronger than she could remember feeling in a very long time, Mags peeled her shirt off over her head. She shoved her pants down her legs and took a deep breath. Leaving on her underwear and bra, she pulled back the curtain and stepped into the shower.

The look on Dave's face was one of disbelief and hope all at the same time. He kept his eyes on her face as he asked, "Are you sure?"

Mags nodded. "I need to make sure you don't bleed to death in here. Give me the soap, and I'll clean your back. You stink." She smiled slightly and held out a hand that only shook a little bit.

Dave put the bar of soap into her hand, then turned away to face the water. He lifted his head and let the water hit his upper chest.

Mags knew the warm water had to hurt the wound on his neck, but he didn't even flinch. She lathered the soap and began to wash her husband. Even this brought back memories. Good ones. Of them laughing and playing together in the shower in Vegas, enjoying the intimacy.

When she was done with his back side, he turned and put his hands behind his head, showing her without words that he wouldn't touch her without permission.

Mags did her best to clean his chest and legs quickly, without letting him know how hard this was for her. But he knew anyway. When she straightened and held out the soap to him, he whispered, "I'm in awe of you, Raven. I always knew you were strong, but I never knew how much until this trip. Will you let me return the favor? I swear you can trust me."

Swallowing hard, Mags nodded. She needed to look at his wound and figure out if he needed stitches, and they both needed to find their son, but at this moment, in their little bubble, she needed to prove to him, and herself, that del Rio hadn't broken her permanently.

As if he could read her mind, Dave said, "Later, when we don't need to be out there looking for our son, I want to do this again. Take my time. Show you how much you mean to me."

Mags swallowed hard and nodded once more.

She turned around and presented her back to Dave, figuring it would be easier if he started there. He quickly soaped her up, his hands kneading her shoulders briefly as he washed her. He knelt down and took each of her feet in his hands and washed them thoroughly. His hands on her calves almost made her knees give out. Then he was standing once again.

She turned to face him.

Ever so gently, Dave soaped up her neck, then each arm. He then knelt down once more and washed the front of her legs. He lathered his hands again and put the bar of soap on a small ledge in the shower. His hands touched her waist, and he gently caressed her belly and sides, making sure not to stray too far north or south. After he was done, he shifted until the water hit her and rinsed away the bubbles.

The washing had been swift and efficient, but still tender and loving. It was a dichotomy, just like he was.

As Mags watched the soap swirl down the drain, it felt somewhat like a new beginning. Out with the old and in with the new. This was her husband. A man she loved with all her heart. A man who'd never stopped looking for her when most people would've assumed she was long since dead. A man who would never stop looking until he found their son and brought him home.

She hadn't seen the angry Mountain Mercenary side of him until he'd come through the door a short while ago, but strangely enough, it didn't scare her; it comforted her. Del Rio was ruthless, and her husband needed to be just as ruthless, or more so, if he was going to keep her and her son safe.

Taking a deep breath, she gently touched Dave's chin. "Look up. Let me see it."

He did as she ordered, another thing that made Mags realize down to the marrow of her bones that she was safe with this man. He was bigger than she was. Stronger. And yet, he was doing what she asked, making himself vulnerable to her. It was a heady feeling.

The wound on his neck didn't look nearly as bad now that he wasn't covered in blood. It was thankfully shallow. She figured a few butterfly bandages would be sufficient to close it up for now. The cut went from right to left, but by the grace of God hadn't been deep enough to cut his jugular or for Dave to bleed out. She touched the edge of the wound with one finger, not even wanting to think about how close he'd come to dying.

Dave's eyes closed, and he asked, "Can I hold you?" He didn't move an inch, didn't crowd her or try to influence her.

Without a word, Mags stepped close to her husband and wrapped her arms around his waist. She laid her head on his chest and held her breath, waiting for the panic to rise up within her at being so close to a man.

Miraculously, she felt nothing but contentment.

Dave's arms slowly wrapped around her waist, and he pulled her even closer. She could feel his hard body against hers, but again, she wasn't afraid or disgusted. Didn't feel even the slightest need to pull away from him. In fact, she wanted to get closer.

For the first time in ten years, Mags felt truly safe. And the spark of hope that had formed while she'd let him wash her flared even higher. She was in his arms and wasn't terrified. Wasn't repulsed. In fact, she felt her nipples harden, as if her body remembered the kind of pleasure only her husband could give it.

How long they stood like that, she wasn't sure, but eventually, Dave pulled back.

"Thank you for that, Raven." He ran a hand lovingly over her hair. "As much as I wish we could stay in here forever, I've got work to do."

She nodded.

"He's not as smart as he thinks he is, sweetheart."

Mags nodded again. What else could she do?

Dave turned off the water and pulled back the shower curtain. He grabbed a towel and handed it to her. Then he held her hand as she carefully climbed out of the tub. Only then did Dave grab a towel for himself. He wrapped it around his waist, then pulled his underwear off from under it, being careful not to expose himself to her. "Wait here. I need to go grab some clothes to change into, and I'll bring you something back."

Mags nodded and shivered when he opened the door and the cool air from the room wafted into the warm, steam-filled bathroom. He was back within seconds, shutting the door behind him.

He turned his back to her and quickly got dressed, while Mags did the same. She wasn't afraid he would turn around and take a peek at her while she was undressed. He was her husband. He'd seen every inch of her, and she wasn't exactly hiding anything from him in the shower. Her white, cotton underthings were practically see-through while wet, but he still gave her the courtesy of keeping his back turned.

After they were dressed, Mags took another look at his neck, shaking her head at how lucky he'd been, so grateful the asshole who'd hurt him had been incompetent. Dave had brought in a first-aid kit they'd bought for Daniela that she hadn't taken back to her clinic yet. She disinfected the cut, then put four butterfly bandages over the wound, pulling the skin together to aid in its healing.

Standing on tiptoe, Mags gently kissed the last bandage before pulling back to stare up at him.

Then, right before her eyes, Dave, her tender and gentle husband, slowly disappeared—and Rex, the badass leader of the Mountain Mercenaries, took his place.

"I need to talk to Meat," he said. "Come on."

Mags followed him out into the room and didn't mind in the least when his focus shifted as he stalked over to where Meat was sitting and asked, "What did you find?"

Mags sat on the bed, pulled her knees up to her chest, and watched as the man she loved did what he apparently did best . . . track down their missing son.

Chapter Thirteen

It was getting late, the sun having long since set. Meat had been working all afternoon and evening on tracking down the house where del Rio had stashed the children, and they were getting close to finding it when the phone rang. Dave blinked in irritation. He was getting more and more anxious to find David before del Rio had time to hide him somewhere they might not find him for years.

Meat clicked the answer button and put it on speaker. "Meat."

"This is Black. I need Raven down in the barrio. Pronto."

"Why?" Dave barked, not wanting Raven anywhere but right where she was, safe beside him in the motel.

"Because she speaks Spanish, and we need a translator," Black said tersely. "Unless Zara is there and can come instead."

"She's still out with Daniela and the others. What's up?" Meat asked.

"When we left earlier, we went and got the passports, then decided to head down to the barrio, just to see if our presence could make someone nervous enough to talk, when we saw that asshole, Ruben. We grabbed him, and he started spouting off. I wasn't sure what he was saying . . . but he said David's name. We're in the hut the women were living in, and I need someone to translate when I interrogate him."

Raven had stood up and was already putting on her shoes.

"Let me talk to her first," Dave told Black. He was well aware of the man's interrogation skills. And while he'd never killed anyone while questioning them as a Mountain Mercenary—at least, Dave didn't think he had—he wasn't exactly Mr. Nice Guy either. He didn't want Raven to have to deal with that kind of violence. He also wasn't thrilled about putting Raven anywhere near Ruben again, even though he needed her Spanish-speaking skills.

"You know I wouldn't ask, but he said your son's name," Black said urgently. "He was smirking, as if he knows something we don't."

"Hang on," Dave said, and quickly explained a little about Black's techniques to his wife.

"I'm going," Raven said, standing up. She looked anxious but determined. "And seriously, I don't mind watching Ruben get the shit beaten out of him. He's had it coming for a long time now."

"If it gets too much, just say the word, and I'll bring you back here."

She nodded.

"I mean it. Black's good at what he does," Dave told her. "Probably a little too good."

"I get it, Dave. But if you think I'm going to get squeamish about Ruben being hurt, you're wrong. If he knows anything about where David is and doesn't want to tell us, I don't care what happens to him."

Dave loved his wife's bravery, but he still didn't want her around the violence he knew Black would dole out to Ruben if necessary. "Fine, but if things get too intense, I'm reserving the right to get you the fuck out of there."

Raven smiled, and Dave held his breath as she reached her hand out to him. In the three weeks since he'd found her, it wasn't often she went out of her way to touch him. But he was as happy as he could be under the current circumstances that they'd reached a turning point after their shower. When her warm hand gently palmed the side of his face, Dave closed his eyes in contentment and satisfaction.

Her voice was low as she spoke. "I wasn't ever going to try to contact you. It tore me up inside, but I thought you were better off without me. I didn't think you'd ever be able to look past what I had to do to survive. I didn't think you'd want to take me back. But more than that, I knew I'd never be able to leave David. Yes, he was conceived in the worst possible way, but I love him. I'd die to protect him. And while I knew you would've been a great father, I didn't think it was fair to ask you to accept a child whose father I couldn't even name. But . . . I realize now . . . I was wrong, and I'm sorry. So damn sorry. If I had just tried to get ahold of you right after del Rio kicked me out, maybe you wouldn't have missed David's first steps, his first words. Or his first smile."

Dave reached up and took hold of Raven's hand. He turned his head and kissed the palm before placing it back on his cheek, with his hand holding it there. "I'd die to protect you and our child," Dave vowed. Her eyes filled with tears, but he continued. "I accept David because of who his mother is. Because you love him. All those years ago when we talked about our hopes and dreams for our children, I realized that I'd do anything to make you a mother. In vitro, a surrogate, adoption . . . it didn't matter. I knew then that you'd make an amazing mom, and the proof is right in front of me. I love you, Raven. I love you because of your strength, your protectiveness, and your ability to keep on going no matter what. I'm in awe of you and all you've overcome. I'll spend the rest of my days doing everything in my power to protect you from the shit life has to offer. And that includes protecting you from the kind of violence the Mountain Mercenaries sometimes have to use to get results. Okay?"

Dave knew his words were rushed and that he'd crazily jumped from one topic to another, but his mind was whirring with emotions. Love for his wife. Relief that he was alive. Hatred for del Rio. And concern for their son. He might've found Raven, but if anything happened to the little boy who she'd given all her love to in the last four and a half years, he'd lose her all over again. And he wasn't willing to let her slip through his fingers. No fucking way.

"Okay," Raven said.

"You ready to go, Meat?" Dave asked louder, not taking his eyes from Raven's.

"Ready," Meat confirmed.

Slowly, so as not to alarm her, Dave leaned forward and gently kissed Raven's forehead. She sighed and looked up at him after he pulled away. It looked like she wanted to say something, but Meat opened the door to the room, and the moment was lost.

Dave took hold of Raven's hand and led them out the door. Ro and Ball were in the hallway waiting for them. Either Black had called them earlier, or Meat had notified them via his computer. The group headed out of the building toward the barrio.

Dave hated that place. Hated thinking about Raven spending even a second living there. It was depressing and dirty. It wasn't safe even for locals, but he was proud of his wife for making the best out of the impossible situation she'd found herself in.

They walked through the entrance in the cinder-block wall and headed for the hut that Raven and the five other women had been living in, six when Zara had been there, and when they entered, Dave wasn't too surprised by what he saw.

Ruben was sitting in a rickety wooden chair, his ankles and wrists restrained by some sort of twine or rope. His head was hanging down, and he had blood coming from his nose and what looked like two black eyes forming. Black had obviously already started making sure Ruben knew who was in charge.

The second Ruben saw Raven, his eyes narrowed, and he began speaking rapidly.

Raven's eyes widened, and she took a step backward, running into Dave. He put a hand on her shoulder to steady her and physically saw her straighten her shoulders.

"What's he saying?" Dave asked.

"Nothing important."

Black walked up to her then and stood so close, Dave felt her press against him as she looked up into his friend's face.

"That's not how this is gonna work," Black said quietly. "You need to tell us exactly what he says. Every word. You can't leave anything out."

"I understand, but all he was saying was shit to rile me up. He said it was about time I got here, that it's not an orgy without a woman to stick his dick into."

Dave stiffened at the crude words. He was glad to see the others in the room get just as pissed when they heard what Ruben had said.

Black turned to face the man in the chair and said, "Yes. Now the fun can begin."

Raven translated, and Dave saw a hint of fear in the bully's eyes.

"What did you say to me when we found you earlier?" Black asked Ruben.

It was a bit awkward having to wait for Raven to translate, but she did so without hesitation, and everyone quickly got used to the stilted back-and-forth.

"Fuck you," Ruben said.

"Nope, that's not what you said. How about some incentive to remember?" Black asked, then didn't give Raven much time to translate before his fist smashed into his nose.

Ruben howled and tried to hunch to protect himself, but he couldn't move much with the ropes binding him.

"Now, let's try this again. What did you say about David?"

"I said you'll never find the fucking brat," Ruben spat, the hate easy to hear in his tone even before Raven translated.

Dave watched Black interrogate Ruben with a somewhat detached eye. He was more concerned about Raven and how she was dealing with the violence happening right in front of her. He kept his hand on her waist, and as the minutes passed, he could feel her tensing up every time Ruben refused to answer, and Black or one of the others dished out a bit of incentive. She was sweating, and she flinched every time one of his men stepped toward their surprisingly stubborn captive.

Ruben was either stupid as fuck, or even more scared of del Rio than he was them. He supposed it didn't really matter, because eventually Black would break him. Would make him tell them everything they wanted to know about David and del Rio.

When Black wandered over to the sparse kitchen supplies in the hut and picked up a knife, Dave said, "Hang on a sec."

Raven had tensed even further, if that was possible, and had started to shake in his arms. Dave turned her until her back was to Ruben. He tilted her chin up and held her head in his hands. She was breathing a bit too fast, and he could see the stress in her eyes. When she reached up and grabbed hold of his wrists, digging her fingernails into his flesh, he wanted to drag her out of the hut and back to the motel and hold her as he'd done in the shower. But they had to get this done. None of them had a choice. *Fucking del Rio.*

"Look at me, Raven," he told her.

"I am," she whispered.

"Concentrate on *me*," he ordered gently. "You can translate without watching what's going on behind you."

She swallowed hard and nodded, the relief easy to see in her eyes.

Dave didn't take his gaze from his wife's as he said, "Okay, continue, Black."

"You seem to be fairly popular with the women around here," Black drawled. "Although I'm guessing that's more because you take what you want instead of wooing anyone. I suggest you tell us what we want to know if you want to keep your cock."

Raven translated loud enough for Ruben to hear, but she didn't take her eyes from Dave.

"That's it," he murmured softly. "You're doing great."

Ruben wailed and spit out a flurry of words. "Get that thing away from me! I'm not telling you shit!"

"The thing about my friend here," Arrow told Ruben, "is that he's not a poker player. Mostly because he can't lie to save his life."

"That knife doesn't look very sharp," Ball said, joining in the taunting. "That fucker won't cut very well. Maybe you should see if you can sharpen it before you cut anything off."

Out of the corner of his eye, Dave saw Black holding up the knife as if trying to decide if he thought it would work or not.

"I think it'll do. Might take longer to cut through flesh, but since a dick doesn't have bone, it'll work."

That seemed to do the trick. Ruben started babbling. "I don't know anything for sure! Only what my friend told me. He lies a lot, so he could've just been trying to look cool or something."

"What'd your friend say?" Black asked in a low tone.

Raven's voice didn't waver as she continued to translate.

"In the barrio where he lives, there was a lot of excitement because del Rio came to visit. He went to the home of an old lady who lives there. He had a kid with him, was dragging him behind him. The kid tried to kick del Rio and run off, but he backhanded him and told him to behave or he'd never see his mother again. He visited with the old woman for a while, then left . . . without the kid. Rumor is, he's paying the woman to watch after the brat, and everyone's pissed off about it."

"Why are they mad?" Ro asked.

"Because del Rio usually talks with a lot of people when he visits, hands out money for information, but this time he didn't. Everyone knows he probably paid the old bitch a lot of money. Money they want."

"What else?" Black asked.

"Nothing, that's it!"

There was a sound of fabric ripping, and Ruben let out a high-pitched scream. Dave knew Black had only cut through the man's pants, but by the way Ruben reacted, anyone listening would've thought he was mortally wounded.

Raven's pupils dilated, and she gripped his wrists harder.

"Easy, sweetheart. He just cut his pants. That's all."

She nodded, and Dave was mesmerized by her stormy, blue eyes. "Hang in there, just a little bit longer. You're doing amazing."

"Ready for more?" Gray asked Raven quietly from beside her.

She nodded, but didn't take her gaze from Dave's.

"We couldn't do this without you," Gray praised. "This isn't easy, but you're doing great."

His friend's words seemed to bolster Raven a bit. He didn't like the situation, but he couldn't have been prouder of Raven if she'd won the Nobel Peace Prize.

"Right," Black said in a menacing tone to Ruben. "So you have a buddy who claims del Rio brought a kid to his barrio. How did you know his name was David? What aren't you telling us?"

"I'm telling you everything!" Ruben wailed.

More rustling sounded behind Raven's back, and Dave could see from his peripheral that Black had cut through Ruben's shirt this time. He held the tip of the knife to one of his nipples and pressed. A bead of blood formed and quickly grew, until it dripped down Ruben's chest.

"Stop! For the love of God, stop! I'll tell you!" Ruben yelled. "My friend went into the old woman's hut, to see what was going on and maybe try to get some money out of her. The kid had a chain around his ankle and was sitting against the wall, crying. He took some money and smacked the old lady around until she told him the kid's name was David, but she didn't know anything else. How long he'd be there or what del Rio wanted with him."

Dave gently caressed Raven's face with his thumbs, wanting to soothe her in any way he could. He hated that she was there listening to Ruben spout his filth. Hated she had to hear about what their son was going through. Wanted to step over to Ruben and fucking kill him. But

Raven needed him right where he was. And if the choice was being there for his wife or exacting revenge, he'd choose Raven every single time.

"The kid asked if my friend knew his mom, Mags. Said she'd be worried about him when she went to visit his house and he wasn't there. Said he was lost, and she'd be looking for him," Ruben went on.

"He's worried about me," Raven whispered after she'd translated the other man's words, tears filling her eyes.

"Of course he is," Dave told her. "He loves you."

"Where's the barrio where your friend lives?" Black asked.

When Ruben didn't answer, Raven tensed in Dave's hold.

"Hang on just a little bit longer," he soothed. "Almost done."

"I asked, where is the barrio where your friend lives?" Black repeated in a deadly tone.

This time there was no noise as Black walked behind Ruben and knelt down. Without a word of warning, he grabbed hold of one of Ruben's hands and, using the dull knife, sliced off the tip of one of the man's pinkie fingers.

The scream that came out of Ruben was piercing in its intensity.

"Stop! Stop! I'll tell you! It's a few kilometers west of here. I can take you to it!" Ruben yelled.

"Just tell us exactly where it is," Ball told him. *"Exactly."*

For the next few minutes, between sobs, Ruben gave explicit instructions on how to get to the barrio where David was supposedly located, and which hut belonged to the old woman. The barrio was larger than the one they were in now, and had double the number of houses, according to Ruben. It backed up to a housing development and was surrounded by a twelve-foot concrete fence, separating the haves from the have-nots.

Dave knew they had what they needed from Ruben. He dropped his hands and reached for Raven's. He'd started toward the door with her when Black stopped him. "Just a second, Dave. I need Raven to translate one more thing for me."

Hating it, Dave stopped and nodded anyway. He knew Raven would protest if he tried to drag her out of the hut. She was selfless and eager to help in any way she could. He couldn't take that away from her, no matter how badly he wanted to wrap her up in cotton and hide her from all the ugliness in the world. She was stronger than that. She proved it every damn day, and he'd be an asshole not to treat her like the warrior she was.

Dave put his arm around his wife's waist, keeping her back to the room.

"You fucked up when you attacked me and my friend Meat," Black told Ruben as Raven translated. "See, my friends and I hate bullies. And that's what you are. You have no problem being tough around those you think are weaker than you, like women, children, and the elderly, but when it comes to standing up like a man, you fold like a baby. Your days of bullying are over, Ruben. You and all your friends. We're gonna make sure, first of all, that you can't force yourself on a woman ever again."

"Don't cut off my dick!" Ruben screeched.

"I won't," Black said calmly, "but I *am* going to make sure it'll be a very long time before you're able to do anything other than piss through it. And don't bother going to the health clinics around here, because I guarantee none will help you. The second thing my friends and I are going to do is make sure del Rio knows what happened here today. How your friend was spouting off and bragging about what he saw—and how you gave us all the info we needed to find the little boy."

"No. No, no!" Ruben yelled. "Please, no. He'll kill me!"

Black shrugged. "Not my problem, is it? Sucks to have someone else making decisions for your life, doesn't it?"

Ball nodded at Dave, letting him know that Black was done talking, and Dave returned the gesture. He quickly led Raven out of the hut—

And stopped in his tracks at the sight that greeted them.

It looked like half the barrio was gathered in the alley outside the hut. For a second, he tensed . . . but then some of the women came forward, talking to Raven. He could see their smiles in the low light of a couple nearby campfires. When he didn't pick up any negative or hostile vibes, and when his wife didn't seem scared, he dropped his arm from around her waist.

She slowly walked through the group, talking quietly. Dave stayed just behind her, ready to protect her if necessary, but he needn't have worried. The crowd that had been listening to what was going on behind the metal door was obviously happy about it.

Meat and Ro were following closely behind Dave, and most of the people, after they'd spoken with Raven, thanked the three of them as well.

Sounds of "*Gracias*" and "*Dios los bendiga*" echoed around them as they headed down the alleyway toward the barrio exit.

"They're saying *Thank you* and *God bless you*," Raven said quietly after they'd left the group behind.

"I figured," Dave said with a small smile. He wanted to stop and hug her. Reassure her that they'd soon have David back with them, but there wasn't time. Now that they had a lead on where their little boy was, he needed to mobilize the Mountain Mercenaries and make a plan.

The men and women listening to the interrogation had seemed pleased, but all it would take was one of them slipping away to inform del Rio of what had happened.

Dave had made a mistake once by not rescuing David the very day he'd learned about him. He wasn't going to fuck up a second time.

"So we can go and get David tonight?" she asked. "Now that we know where he is?"

Dave hurried them toward the barrio's exit and the motel. He glanced at Meat and Ro, then said, "First of all, *we* aren't going anywhere. There's no way I'd take you to that barrio."

"But—"

Dave cut her off. "No. No buts. I know you want to be there, but I swear on my life that I will never do anything ever again to put you in danger. I have a lot of guilt for not watching over you better in Vegas, and you're going to have to put up with my being overly protective. Second of all, you're my wife, not a member of my team. That's a hard line for me. What I do as the leader of the Mountain Mercenaries doesn't touch you. Ever. I realize this makes me sound like an asshole, but I need to know you're safe. I won't be able to function if I'm worried about where you are and if you're okay. I *need* you to stay at the motel while I do this, Raven. If David is there, I'll bring him back to you. I promise."

He watched as Raven struggled between the need to argue to be there for her son and her desire to give him what he needed. He was completely humbled when she took a deep breath and nodded.

"I love you," he whispered.

"I love you too," she returned.

"And to answer your earlier question, we are absolutely going to get our son tonight. I'm not leaving him in that bastard's grasp a second longer than I have to. Meat will stay at the motel with you and make the final arrangements to get the other women to the airport. I'm more than ready to get this done and get home."

"What about the other kids?"

"Meat will continue to do what he can to find them as well. He was close to tracking them down before we left the motel. We won't leave them defenseless. I know it doesn't seem like it, but there are people here in Lima who care about those kids. Meat will get the info they need to get them out and hopefully into the homes of people who will treat them right," Dave told her.

"Good," Raven said softly.

Dave loved how tenderhearted Raven was. She was terrified for her own child, but she still had compassion for the other kids who were still out there, lost and alone. He put his arm around Raven and held her close to his side as they quickly made their way back to the motel.

It was closing in on midnight, but Dave didn't feel the least bit tired. Meat agreed to stay and watch over Raven and wrap up loose ends while the team headed out to hopefully recover David.

Dave knew it would take a bit of time for Gray and the others to get back from the barrio, but as soon as they arrived, they'd head back out to find David. He was taking his son back tonight.

Chapter Fourteen

Dave stood behind five of the six men he trusted with his life, and waited for the signal from Gray to move out.

It hadn't been easy to convince Raven to stay back at the motel with Zara, the other women, and Meat. He hadn't wanted to leave them there alone, in case del Rio knew where they were staying and decided to go after them just to be even more of an asshole.

Daniela had also shown up at the motel to lend her support. Dave liked the feisty doctor. At first he wasn't sure what to think of her. She was a little brusque, and he wasn't sure she liked or approved of any of them. But after getting to know her, and hearing about how her own husband and son had been killed in an uprising in a barrio, he understood where some of her standoffishness came from.

Meat had tracked down two houses that were likely holding the children del Rio claimed to be keeping captive for "adoptions" from clients. The trustworthy Peruvian teams Dave had managed to procure were planning on hitting both houses at the same time that night. He was still searching for the names and addresses of anyone who might've bought a child so the authorities could track them down later.

Now it was time to go and get David. Meat had done some recon about the barrio where David was supposedly being held and realized it was the largest and most crowded of all the local barrios.

There were only ten of them set to enter the barrio—six Mountain Mercenaries and four additional members of an elite division of the Peruvian police force—against what was literally thousands of people living in the barrio. They had no idea how many were working for del Rio, or if the man had already moved David again before they could get there. But hopefully, since they'd left within an hour and a half of finding out where David was being held, he'd still be right where del Rio had left him.

Dave was allowing his men to be the lead, but he refused to stay back at the motel or in the car. He was wearing a radio, as all of them were, and would stay in the background, but he was going to be there no matter what. He *needed* to be there. To put his arms around his son and reassure him that he was all right.

As everyone did radio checks before entering the barrio, Gray slid over to him.

"You okay?"

Dave nodded once.

"All right, we're heading out in two minutes. You know the plan?"

Dave tried not to get irritated at his friend. "Yes, I fucking know the plan. I helped make the damn thing. And I know plans B, C, D, and E too. I get it, I'm an outsider here, but don't forget who planned most of the other ops you've been on. I'm not some Joe Shmoe off the street here." He looked up at Gray and pinned him with an intense gaze. "The bottom line is, if anything goes wrong, I'm taking David and getting the hell out of Dodge."

Gray nodded. "Good. We can take care of any trouble in the barrio. And if del Rio shows up with any kind of firepower, we'll hold him off while you get David out of there. The residents have built a makeshift ladder to get up and over the back wall. You take David and disappear into the neighborhood behind the barrio. I'm hoping del Rio won't show his face at all, but if he does . . . who knows how long he might search for you? We have to assume it would be for a while, because he doesn't like to lose. You two hunker down and lie low. We'll go back to the motel, get the women, and come back to find you. Stay hidden, and don't take any chances. We'll use the tracking device in your radio to get close. No matter what, do *not* go back into the barrio."

"I'm not an idiot," Dave told him. "You know I've pored over the satellite images of this neighborhood. I know exactly where I'm going to go with David to lie low until the coast is clear."

Gray grinned and shook his head. "Sorry. I still have a hard time some days comprehending that you're actually Rex."

Dave relaxed. "I know I don't have the experience you do, but this is personal for me. I'm not going to fuck it up."

"I know you're not," Gray told him. "I trust you."

His words meant the world to Dave. He hadn't realized how much he wanted and needed his men's approval. It was one thing to trust Rex, but another altogether to trust Dave.

They both paused their conversation to listen to the chatter in their earbuds about how the team was ready to set out in one minute.

"I don't know where you found the Peruvian men who are helping us today, but they're pretty fucking badass," Gray said.

"They are," Dave agreed. He'd made connections in practically every country in the world, and he was thankful he'd found some men who hadn't been corrupted by del Rio to help him out. They were going to save countless children from a fate worse than death soon, and in just a few more minutes, they'd help him rescue his own son. Dave would get to meet Raven's child, *their* child, for the first time minutes from now. He was nervous, but calm at the same time.

There were only four Peruvian men with them, but they'd all agreed since this was a scoop and go, and hopefully not a full-scale battle, the ten of them should be adequate for the mission.

After they got the all clear to head into the barrio from four different entrances around the cinder-block wall, and the others dispersed,

Gray said quickly, "We're gonna find him, Dave. Wait until I give you the go-ahead when we get to the old woman's hut. Okay?"

He didn't like it, but Dave nodded anyway. He understood that his men were protecting him. If David was dead, or if the mission went sideways, they didn't want him to have to see his son in that condition, or put him directly in the line of fire in the case of a military firefight.

He and Gray slipped into the barrio and quickly made their way toward the northwest side of the camp, where Ruben had claimed David had been brought. In some ways, this barrio was the same as the one Raven had lived in for years. Trash everywhere, and the smell of campfires permeated the air. But it was the wary and distrustful look in most of the residents' eyes they passed that gave Dave cause for concern.

These were not people who were content to get by with what they had. These were harder, more jaded men, women, and children. No one made a move to stop them as they walked, but it was obvious if something happened, no one would be willing to help, as Raven and her friends had helped Black and Meat a few months ago.

"Target in sight," a voice said in Dave's ear. He looked up and realized Gray had spoken, and they were approaching the end of a row of run-down shacks made out of whatever the residents could get their hands on.

"Approaching from the east," another voice said in his ear.

Dave didn't even bother to look around for the other approaching pairs. Ro and Arrow were stationed by the front wall of the barrio, watching for trouble in whatever form it might arrive and guarding their flank. Black and Ball were each paired with one of their Peruvian counterparts and were converging on the hut, along with the others.

Dave had tunnel vision as he stared at the piece of metal pulled across the opening to the hut. He prayed harder than he'd prayed in his life that David was inside . . . and was all right. He knew from Ruben's interrogation that he'd been knocked around by del Rio, and remembering that made Dave's hands fist. He wanted to kill anyone who dared hurt a little kid. *His* little boy.

"Easy, Dave," Gray said, putting a hand on his shoulder. "Hang on for three more minutes."

Dave nodded and watched as Black and his Peruvian partner walked silently up to the shack. On a count of three, Black pulled the metal back, and the other man burst inside the room.

Ball and three other Peruvians followed close behind them.

There were some loud words spoken in Spanish, but no screams of distress or fright. Dave wasn't sure if that was good news or bad. Within seconds, he heard Black say, "Clear," through the radio, and Dave was moving before he'd even thought about it.

He followed close behind Gray, and they squeezed into the already very crowded one-room hut.

Glancing around the room, Dave saw it was fairly typical as far as living quarters in a barrio went. Dirt floor, tubs used as a sink, dirty dishes, a bucket being used as a bathroom.

As he took in the room in a split second, his gaze stopped on the iron stake in the floor with a chain attached to it. He followed the chain . . .

And inhaled sharply when he saw a pair of small blue eyes staring at him from behind a large box.

He knew about the chain from Ruben's interrogation, but seeing it firsthand, and knowing it was *his* child attached to that chain, made him almost lose his mind.

Keeping his temper in check by the skin of his teeth, Dave strode over to the stake in the floor and, using brute strength, pulled it up and out of the hard-packed dirt. His muscles strained, but within seconds, the chain slipped off the bottom of the stake and fell to the ground with a loud clang.

He dropped the stake and turned to the child. To his surprise, instead of having to coax the boy out from behind the box, the child was already standing next to it. He had messy, dark hair and a bruise on one cheek. He was wearing shorts and a T-shirt and was covered in dirt. And Dave had never seen anything more beautiful in his life.

Then the boy shocked the shit out of Dave, and everyone else in the room, by holding up his arms and shouting, *"Papá!"*

Instinctively, Dave took a step forward and reached down to pick up the little boy. "David?" he asked.

The child smiled, even though it was a little unsure. "Where's *Mamá*? Did you find her too?"

"He speaks English," Black said in surprise.

"Raven said she'd taught him," Dave heard Gray explain.

"Yeah, but I thought he probably just knew a few words here and there," Black replied.

Dave tuned them out, all his focus on the boy in his arms.

"Your mom's safe. We're going to take you to her now. Are you all right? Do you hurt anywhere?" Dave asked.

David shook his head. "No, *Papá*. I'm okay now that you're here."

"How do you know who I am?" Dave asked, as Black came forward with a pair of bolt cutters to cut the shackle off the little boy's leg.

"*Mamá* told me what you look like. The second I saw you, I knew. She said we were lost and that you were looking for us and that one day you'd find us. I was scared when del Rio came and took me from my home because I didn't know how you'd find me. But you did!"

Dave wanted to cry. Wanted to sit down in the dirt right then and there and bawl like a baby. Raven had talked about him to her son. Had told him what he looked like and reassured him that he was looking for them.

She'd had no reason to believe she'd ever see him again, and she certainly had no idea if he'd accept David because of how he'd come to be born, and yet she'd still told her son that he was his *papá*. The intensity of his emotions was almost too much to overcome.

He examined the little boy and couldn't get over how much he looked like his mom. From his blue eyes to his black hair, he was a mini Raven. He looked healthy enough, although a bit too skinny for Dave's liking. He wanted to put him down and run his hands over his little body to make sure he wasn't hurt anywhere, but he literally couldn't bear to let go of him for even the few minutes it would take to examine him.

Black finally got the shackle cut off David's ankle, and Dave felt the boy's little legs wrap around his waist and squeeze. His arms came up around his neck, and he held on tight. Almost desperately. Dave wrapped both his arms around the precious child and held him even closer to his chest. He might not have been there for the boy's first four and a half years, but he'd damn well be there for the next fifty.

David's eyes widened as he moved his little hands to one of his *papá's* biceps and squeezed.

"They *are* as big as the trees in my yard!" he exclaimed.

Dave heard one of his friends chuckle, but couldn't take his eyes off the precious bundle. It was hard to believe he was standing there holding Raven's child. There were no thoughts of the plan, just utter awe. Raven had given birth to a baby who was currently in his arms. Nothing could've prepared him for the level of emotion he felt at this moment.

Then, they heard Ro say urgently through their radios, "Bloody hell. There are three SUVs approaching the front of the barrio, fast."

"Fuck," Gray muttered.

Dave turned his head and saw the local team of men talking with the older woman who'd been in the hut when they'd entered. She was gesturing with her hands, her eyes wide with terror.

"Fuck me," Arrow said through the radio. "It's del Rio," he informed everyone. "Someone must've tipped him off that we're here. He's wearing a fucking suit when it's a million degrees and walking around like he's a goddamn king or something."

Everyone in the hut knew their time had run out.

"How many men are with him?" Gray asked Ro and Arrow.

"At least a dozen. And they're spreading out. You guys aren't going to be able to come out the way you went in. Move to Plan B," Ro ordered.

Without another word to the woman who'd most likely had no choice but to harbor his son, Dave turned and left the hut with David in his arms. He knew the Peruvian team would make sure the woman was safe in case del Rio wanted to take revenge on her for allowing David to be taken away.

He was well aware of the progress of del Rio and his men as they made their way toward the hut, because of the blow-by-blow he was receiving through the radio in his ear. The men weren't moving in any huge hurry. It was clear they thought Dave had no chance of escaping the barrio with David. Cocky bastards. Most of the residents had disappeared into their shacks, not wanting the attention of del Rio or his men.

"Here's what's going to happen next," Dave told little David. "I need you to hold on to me as tightly as you can. No matter what happens, do *not* let go. Understand?"

"Yes, *Papá*. Are we going to see *Mamá*?"

"Yes," Dave told him. "But del Rio is here, and we need to stay away from him."

At the mention of del Rio, David's face paled, and his arms tightened almost painfully around the back of Dave's neck. He said almost desperately, "Is he gonna take me?"

"No," Dave immediately reassured him as he wound his way through the nearby shacks. He was headed for the wall on the back side, where he and David could hopefully disappear into the night.

"But he said if I run away, he would kill *Mamá*."

"He's not going to touch one hair on your mom's head. I promise," Dave told him. It was a bullshit threat, since David had been chained to the floor. Del Rio was just asserting his control over the little boy and continuing to scare him.

"But he said I belonged to him. That I have to do everything he tells me to, otherwise I'll never see her again." His little voice quivered. "Maybe I should just stay."

Dave's heart nearly broke, but at the same time he was so incredibly proud. David was selfless and willing to do whatever it took to keep his mom safe. "We aren't staying here, and your mom is safe," he reassured the boy, picking up his pace. "I give you my word. Remember, all you have to do is hold on to me. Okay? Intertwine your fingers together behind my neck. Good, just like that. Can you hold on if I don't have my arms around you?" Dave asked.

When David nodded, Dave tested him, holding his arms out to his sides in airplane fashion. David tightened his legs around his waist, and his arms locked, keeping him right where he was against his side.

"Good job," Dave praised, wrapping his arm around the little boy once more. "You're really strong."

David gave him a small smile, and a flush appeared on his little cheeks. God, had no one other than Raven ever complimented him?

But Dave knew the answer to that, and he vowed right then and there to make sure David knew how amazing he was.

"If you guys aren't on the move, you need to get gone," Arrow warned through the radio.

"We're moving, closing in on the back wall," Dave said into the radio. Then he addressed his son once more. "David, the men who were in the shack with me are my friends. *Your* friends. If something happens, and we get separated, you trust them and no one else. Understand?"

David nodded.

"Their names are Ball, Gray, and Black. I know, they're funny names, but they'll help you if necessary."

"Do they know my *mamá*?"

"Yes. And our other friend, Meat, is with her now, making sure she's safe. Arrow and Ro, two more friends, are also waiting nearby. You aren't alone anymore, champ. Got it?"

"Champ?"

Dave couldn't help but grin. "Yeah, it's a nickname. Is it okay?"

David nodded enthusiastically. "*Mamá* said you call her Raven, even though her name is Margaret. And *Grandpapá* and *Grandmamá* call her Magpie. I've never had a nickname!"

"You do now, champ," Dave told him as his gaze swept the unnaturally dark and silent barrio around them. "It's time to keep quiet and hang on now. No matter what."

"Okay, *Papá*," David whispered.

Every time he heard that name come out of his son's mouth, Dave fell more and more in love, and it made him even more determined to get him and Raven out of Peru.

Hyperalert and still listening to the progress del Rio and his men were making toward the hut from the reports he was getting through his headset, Dave made a beeline for the crude stairway the residents had built into the back corner of the barrio, so they could easily go up and over the cinder-block wall separating them from the nicer neighborhood on the other side.

He saw Ball and Gray approach after he was on top of the wall, and they immediately began to dismantle the staircase. He hoped it wouldn't take long, since it was constructed of boxes, pallets, and whatever other trash the residents had been able to scavenge, but the pile was immense.

The top of the wall was only about two feet wide, but Dave had no problem keeping his balance. He might be a big man, but he was agile—and he was carrying the most precious thing in his life. There was a twenty-foot drop-off on the other side, because of the hill the barrio was built on, but two hundred feet down the wall was a large slope that butted up to it, taking the twenty feet down to only eight. Walking along the top was the most dangerous part of the plan. They were exposed, and there was nowhere to hide. The other men had a plan to make their way to his location and fan out around them, but if del Rio wanted to pull out a gun and shoot, they'd be sitting ducks.

But Dave was fairly certain the man wouldn't do that. He was conceited, and killing him quickly wouldn't be satisfying enough. Dave had a feeling the second del Rio realized who he was, and that he'd survived only to outmaneuver him, he would crave some one-on-one retribution.

He was also betting the asshole wouldn't want to damage his investment . . . David. He had a lot of plans for the boy, and it wasn't likely he'd order his men to shoot either of them.

At least, Dave was counting on that.

He started walking, reaching the halfway point to his destination when del Rio's men spotted him and ran toward him with their weapons drawn. Dave had time to tell his men that he'd been spotted and to get their asses to his location to mitigate the threat when del Rio called out.

"Stop right there, or I'll order my men to shoot!"

Eyeing how much farther he had to go, Dave knew he could make it to where he needed to be with five or six quick steps. But there was no way he was going to risk David getting shot. He needed the cover of his team so he could make it the last fifteen feet or so to relative safety.

He turned to face the man who'd made his life a living hell for the last ten years.

Del Rio looked up at him in absolute fury. "You!" he exclaimed.

"Me," Dave confirmed, squinting at the light shining in his eyes that someone was using to spotlight him on the wall.

"I told my man to make sure you were dead. I should've known when he didn't return that he'd failed," del Rio said in disgust.

"I'm not dead," Dave told him flatly.

In an instant, the anger disappeared from his tone, and the arrogance returned. "No matter. You aren't going to get away with my boy," del Rio said as he tugged on his suit jacket and absently brushed dirt off the front.

"Like hell I'm not," Dave called out. He heard his men through the radio telling him they'd be there in twenty seconds. Just enough time to tell del Rio what he thought of him before he could get out of there with his son. David was holding him with a firm grip and had his head buried in his neck.

Tightening one arm around the boy's waist, Dave didn't give del Rio time to say anything else.

"I'd planned to give you a quick and easy death. There's no way I'm going to let you live to continue to ruin the lives of women and children as if they're nothing but dirt under your shoe. But now, I'm going to make sure you suffer endless pain before you die. For every woman you forced into a life she didn't want. For every child who lost their mother, and for every kid you stole from their family and forced to do things no sane person would allow, you'll pay."

Del Rio laughed. "And how do you propose to do that?" he asked. "You're the one surrounded with no way out. You have no idea how much power I hold in this country. I own the government, the military, the police. Even the people in this shithole work for me! There's nowhere you can go and nowhere you can hide. Just give me the boy, and I'll make sure *your* death is quick."

"That's what's wrong with people like you. You think you're invincible. News flash, *Roberto*, you're not."

Dave saw that the use of his first name pissed him off. Del Rio loved being known by his surname. Loved the fear it struck in the hearts of his countrymen.

Ten seconds.

"I'm going to kill you," del Rio growled. "Then I'm going to find your woman, bring her back to my home, and offer her up for free to anyone who wants a go. Maybe I'll bring her to the barrios and allow anyone and everyone to take their shot without giving a fucking sol in return! You've fucked not only *her*, but anyone she associates with as well. They'll *all* pay for your interference!"

Dave didn't rise to the bait, but he felt David trembling against him and was relieved this conversation was almost done. His men would converge on del Rio and his goons, and in seconds, all hell was going to break loose. "The problem with being on top is that you have a hell of a long way to fall." He mock-saluted the man on the ground beneath him. "So long, Roberto. I won't ever see you again, but you'll constantly be looking over your shoulder. Karma is a bitch—and she's coming for you."

The second the last words were out of his mouth, he heard his Mountain Mercenaries yelling from what sounded like every direction. Telling the men to put down their weapons. The light that had been pointed at Dave disappeared as del Rio's men were suddenly busy protecting themselves, plunging him back into darkness.

Dave turned his attention back to the wall, striding confidently and quickly toward his target destination. He heard del Rio yelling orders at his men, but all Dave's attention was on his footing and getting off the wall. "Ready, champ?" he asked his son as he moved into position. He sat on the edge of the wall facing away from the barrio, his feet dangling off the other side.

"I've got you, son. Do you trust me?" Dave asked when the boy didn't respond. He tightened his arm around David and held him tightly against his body.

"Sí."

"Good. Close your eyes, and hang on."

He waited until David's little eyes clenched shut and he tightened his legs and arms around him once more. Then Dave pushed off the wall and jumped.

The landing hurt a bit, but Dave bent his knees and absorbed most of the impact with his legs. He stumbled and had to use his other hand for balance when he began to fall, but caught himself. No way was he going to fall over with his son in his arms. It would scare the boy to death and could possibly hurt him in the process. Dave would sooner die than do anything that would hurt his son after everything he'd been through.

He was up and running down the hill as soon as he'd gained his balance, not daring to look behind him. He heard more shouting from the direction of the barrio and in his earpiece, but he didn't stop or slow down, tuning out the voices. It was obvious they hadn't guessed he would jump off the other side of the wall. Del Rio was conceited enough to believe that Dave would have to simply surrender.

Not happening.

Having studied satellite pictures of the area until he knew them by heart, Dave knew exactly where he was going and where he would hide. Del Rio was arrogant. He wouldn't give up easily, but the Mountain Mercenaries would keep him and his men busy until Dave could disappear with David and hide until morning.

He knew his team was good, but the barrio was unfamiliar territory, even if they'd studied surveillance photos. Del Rio and his men were much more comfortable there. It was likely del Rio would be able to escape, but Dave wasn't concerned. As he'd told the man, he'd get his own one day. Dave would make sure of it.

He hated that Raven would be frantic with worry when he didn't immediately return with their son. The next few hours would be uncomfortable, but his team would come pick them up as soon as they could, and they'd be on their way back to the United States, so it would all be worth it.

The voices of his men now crackled in his earpiece, and the farther he got from the wall, the more static there was. The radios were made for short ranges. They'd all known there was the possibility of losing touch, so Dave wasn't concerned. The plan was set, and his men could take care of themselves.

"He was really mad," the little boy whispered after they'd headed away from the barrio wall and into the neighborhood.

Dave didn't slow as he quickly made his way toward the first street. The houses were close together, and the tallest were only two stories. There were hundreds of houses in the neighborhood, and while it was nicer than the barrio, it was still poor. An upscale neighborhood would be harder to hide in. Del Rio would come looking for him, especially after Dave had gotten the best of him and insulted and threatened the man. He couldn't let that slide, not when several of his men had overheard. He'd look weak.

But Dave didn't give a shit. Let del Rio look for him. He wouldn't find him.

His team and the Peruvians would kill del Rio, if given the chance, and if they failed, Dave suspected his men would be pissed. But what they didn't know was that del Rio would still pay . . . eventually. He hoped the man would spend some time wondering when and where payback would occur. He wanted him to become paranoid and more concerned about his own safety than putting together plots to sell children and kidnap more women.

But if that didn't happen, and del Rio shrugged off his threats, karma would still happen one day. Dave would make sure of it.

"He *was* mad," Dave told his son, "but he's not going to find us. We're going to hide, then we're going to get your mom and go home."

David's head came up off his shoulder as he stared at him. "Promise?"

"Promise," Dave said immediately.

"Del Rio said if I left, he'd kill *Mamá*," David reminded him fearfully.

Dave was furious at the mental torture del Rio had inflicted on this precious little boy. Knowing this was important and that he needed to address it right this second, Dave dashed between two houses and crouched down. David put his feet down and stood, biting his lower lip uncertainly.

Dave put his hands on David's shoulders and looked him in the eyes as he spoke. "Del Rio is a bad man, champ. He's mean and a bully. He doesn't care if he hurts other people. I have no doubt that he was telling you the truth, that he meant what he said. But he can't hurt your mom if he can't find her. And trust me when I say he's never going to find her. Or you. Today was the last time you'll have to see that man, and the last time he'll ever see you. He won't be able to hurt either one of you because we'll be gone."

"But he said there was nowhere I could hide!" David argued.

Frowning, Dave asked, "What else did he tell you? What other mean things did he say that hurt your feelings? I want to hear all of it so I can reassure you that he was wrong."

It took a second, but then David began speaking. "When I asked if I could go to school, he said it would be a waste of money because I was stupid. He told me I was ugly and my eyes were a funny color. I had to do everything he told me since I was dumb and wouldn't be able to work and make money on my own. I cried in front of him once, because he hit me and it hurt, and he called me a crybaby."

David's head dropped, and he looked at the ground as he quietly admitted the next thing. "*Mamá* said that you were looking for us, but I didn't think you'd find us in time. When I had to sit in del Rio's friend's lap without my clothes, he told me that soon, the man would be my new friend and would take me home with him, and if I didn't do whatever he told me to, if I didn't let him touch me, that he'd kill my *mamá*." He looked up at Dave then. "Will your friends make me do that?"

Dave wanted to turn back the clock twenty minutes and order Gray to put a bullet through del Rio's brain the second he spotted him, and damn the consequences. Whether he'd planned to keep David himself or sell him to some other sick pedophile, the outcome would have been the same.

He took a deep breath and shook his head. "No, champ. Never. No one is allowed to touch you without your permission. *No one.* Understand?"

The little boy didn't look convinced.

"Your *mamá* is fine. She's safe. I give you my word as your *papá.*"

David looked like he wanted to believe him so badly.

Dave knew they had to continue on their way. He picked up his son and started walking once more. "I know this is hard to understand, but just know that del Rio is a bad man. He uses his words to get other people to do what he wants. He uses his fists to hurt people too, but if you're told something often enough, over and over, you can start to believe it." He looked at his son. "You aren't stupid, champ. In fact, you're one of the smartest little boys I've ever met."

David didn't say anything.

"You know two languages. I can't speak or understand Spanish, and you can. In fact, none of my friends you met today understand Spanish, so you're already smarter in that way than we are."

"Really?" David asked.

"Really," Dave reassured him. "And you sure don't talk like any four-year-old I've ever met. You also didn't run away when you saw me and my friends. You knew who I was, even though we'd never met."

"*Mamá* told me what you looked like."

"Right, and you remembered. That's smart." Dave continued his praise as he walked quickly through the streets of the neighborhood, looking for the building he'd scoped out on the satellite images.

He felt David nod, then bring a hand up to the wound on Dave's throat. "You have a boo-boo."

It would take a bit for Dave to get used to the way his son rapidly changed subjects, and he realized he couldn't wait to know everything about the boy in his arms. He had a lot of catching up to do. Four and a half years' worth. "I do," he told him.

"It looks like it hurts."

Dave shrugged. "There's pain, and then there's pain."

David looked understandably confused.

"Sometimes getting a splinter, or blister, or scraping your knee doesn't hurt nearly as bad as a hurt that comes from your heart," Dave said. "When your mom got . . . lost . . . my heart hurt. I was so sad that I didn't care about eating, or sleeping, or if I cut myself while chopping vegetables for dinner. The pain in my heart from your mom being lost was much worse than any pain of the flesh."

David nodded sagely. "Like when *Mamá* had to leave when our day was over. I didn't like that. Everyone was mean and yelled at me. I had to stay in my room and only got a bit of rice to eat. Then *Mamá* would come again, and I'd be happy for a little while." His finger gently traced the wound on Dave's neck once more. "But . . . you're okay, right? You won't lose *Mamá* and me again, will you?"

"No. You and your mom will never be lost again. And I'm going to be fine. Thank you for being concerned about me."

David nodded and leaned forward to rest his head on his *papá*'s chest once more.

Dave's heart felt like it was going to burst. He understood now better than ever why Raven hadn't tried to contact him. He'd told her that he understood, but he hadn't really. Now, holding David in his arms and feeling the way he completely trusted him, and how he was solely responsible for the little guy's well-being, Dave knew he'd do whatever it took to keep him safe. And if he was feeling that after knowing him for such a short time, he also knew Raven felt it a hundred times more deeply.

His love for both his wife and the little boy snuggled in his arms was almost overwhelming. He'd do anything to protect them both. *Anything.*

After walking for another ten minutes, Dave started to get worried. He'd begun to hear shouting and vehicles in the distance, and he knew he needed to find his hidey-hole, pronto.

Just when he thought he'd gotten lost, or the satellite images had been wrong, Dave turned a corner and saw what he'd been looking for.

He'd reached the outer edges of the neighborhood, and the houses were a bit more run-down. They were nothing like those in the barrio they'd just left, but it was obvious the owners didn't have the means, or the desire, to care for them in the way the other houses had been. Looking around to make sure no one was nearby, Dave jogged across the lawn to one of the houses in the middle of a long row. There were no fences between the yards, and he slipped around the back side.

Smiling when he saw what he was looking for, Dave said, "Okay, champ, I'm going to need you to hold on to me really tightly. I need both hands and won't be able to hold you."

David's eyes widened. "You're going to go up there?"

"Yup," Dave told him, eyeing the tree growing close to the house. "Have you ever climbed a tree before?"

David shook his head. "No. I wasn't allowed to. And the only time I went outside was when *Mamá* was there."

"I'm glad I get to share your first tree climb with you, then," Dave said. "Think you can hold on to me?"

"Sí."

"All right. If you feel yourself slipping, just let me know, and we'll stop and readjust."

Dave didn't hesitate. He reached up, grabbed the lowest branch of the tree, and began climbing. He was a big man, and the tree was a little scrawnier than it had looked on the satellite pictures, but within minutes, he was inching out on one of the larger branches toward the roof of the nearby house.

David was like a little monkey, holding on to him as if he'd been born to it.

When he was far enough out, Dave took a deep breath and jumped. He landed exactly where he'd been aiming, although his balance was off with the extra weight of his son on his chest. He began to fall, but he bent his knees and twisted until he landed on his back instead of on top of David.

Closing his eyes in relief, he heard a quiet giggle.

Looking up, Dave saw his son straddling his chest, laughing. "That was fun!" he said in excitement.

More relieved than he could say that the little boy wasn't scared out of his mind, Dave returned his smile. "It was, huh?"

"Uh-huh . . . can we do it again?"

"I'm old, champ. I need to rest for a bit. Is that okay?"

David nodded.

Wrapping his arm around the boy, Dave sat up and scooted toward the middle of the roof.

One of the reasons he'd picked this house was because of the tree and easy access to the flat roof. The other reason was because of the amount of stuff the owners had stashed up there. Boxes, metal containers, a large air conditioner, and a tarp covering something. Dave knew they could be on the roof for a few hours, although he hoped his team would get there a lot sooner. The tarp, along with the other junk, would give them a place to hide from del Rio and his goons if it became necessary.

Keeping hold of his son, Dave was relieved that there was room for them to hide among the boxes under the tarp without having to move anything. He scooted backward until he rested against a box and smiled at the little boy.

"Papá?"

"Yes, son?"

"I'm hungry."

Dave smiled again, happy he could do something about that. He reached into one of the pockets of his pants and pulled out a protein bar. "It's not terribly exciting, but I've got a few of these that will tide us over until we can get out of here and get something more filling."

David stared at the bar suspiciously. "What is it?"

"A protein bar. It's good, I promise."

The little boy's nose wrinkled, but when it was unwrapped and the smell of chocolate hit him, his eyes widened, and he jerked his gaze up to Dave's. "Chocolate?"

"Yeah, and peanut butter. You're not allergic to peanuts, are you?"

But David wasn't listening. His eyes had dropped down to stare at the bar as if he was scared of it.

"What's wrong?" Dave asked.

"For me?" David asked.

"Yeah, champ. For you."

He looked up into Dave's eyes once more. "I'm not allowed candy."

Dave's heart squeezed tightly, but he forced himself to stay calm. "It's not candy, champ. I mean, it's got chocolate in it, but that's for energy and calories. Besides, the rules you had to follow when you were staying at del Rio's house no longer apply. We'll make new rules. Go on, take it," he urged.

But the little boy didn't reach for the food.

Dave broke off a small piece of the protein bar and held it out. "Here you go, son. I promise it's okay."

Ever so slowly, David reached out for the small bite of protein bar. He brought it up to his nose and smelled it. Then his little tongue came out, and he licked the granola and chocolate gingerly. His eyes lit up, and he stuffed the bite into his mouth. He chewed for a really long time, as if trying to get every single bit of taste out of the food before he finally swallowed.

"Like it?" Dave asked.

David nodded. He didn't reach for the rest of the protein bar, but eyed it hungrily.

For the next few minutes, Dave broke off piece after piece and handed it to his son. Watching how eagerly he ate, and the amount of pleasure he got out of the simple treat, was both touching and heartbreaking at the same time.

When the protein bar was gone, David smiled and looked at him. "That was the best thing I've ever eaten."

"Have you ever had chocolate and peanut butter before?" Dave asked.

The little boy nodded. "Once. *Mamá* snuck in a piece of candy for me at Christmas one year. I wasn't allowed to have candy or presents for Christmas, but *Mamá* said Santa found her and dropped off the candy for me. It was smushed, but when we were outside, we were able to eat it without anyone seeing. It was really good."

This boy was killing him. And with every word out of his mouth, Dave was reminded of how much his wife and son had suffered, and what they'd lost. But somehow, they'd made it through almost five years and come out the other side compassionate and loving. They were a miracle. His miracles.

"I've got a couple more of those protein bars that we can eat later if we get hungry," he said in a voice choked with emotion. He cleared his throat and said, "When we get to Colorado in the United States, what do you want to eat for your first meal in your new home?"

The boy's eyes got big. "You mean I can choose?"

"Yes, David, you can have whatever you want."

He looked excited for a second, then looked down hesitantly.

Dave put a finger under his chin and urged him to look back up. When he did, Dave asked, "What's wrong? It's okay, you can be honest with me. I won't be upset at anything you tell me."

"Will *Mamá* get to eat with us too? I don't want to eat in front of her if she can't eat too. She acts like she doesn't care, but I hear her stomach making hungry noises, and it makes me sad."

The sacrifices Raven had made for her son made Dave's heart just about burst. "Your mom will never again go hungry. She can eat when she wants and what she wants. And that goes for you, too, champ."

"We can eat together?" David asked.

"Yes. In fact, we'll eat together as a family as much as possible. There might be some nights I won't be able to be home to eat dinner with the two of you, but I promise right here and now to do my best to be there as often as possible."

David's eyes lit up. "I love you, *Papá*."

His chest actually hurt at hearing his son's words. "And I love you, champ. Now, what do you want to eat when we get back together with your mom?"

David turned big, blue eyes to Dave. "*Arroz con pollo.* And *Mamá's* favorite is *pollo empanada*."

He chuckled. "Can you translate that for me, champ? Remember, I don't speak Spanish."

"Rice with chicken for me, and chicken . . ." His brow furrowed. "I don't know what *empanada* is in English."

"I'll figure it out," Dave assured him.

Just then, they heard a car driving down the road. It was moving very slowly, and they could both hear men talking loudly in Spanish.

David's eyes got wide, and he reached up and put his little finger across Dave's lips.

Nodding, Dave gripped his son's hand in his and kissed the palm reassuringly. He wasn't surprised del Rio's men were looking for them. He'd expected it. But that was why he'd chosen this house. Looking at it from the road, there didn't seem to be any way to get to the roof. The tree they'd climbed wasn't much taller than the house, and no one would think that a man as big as Dave would be able to use it to get to the roof.

The SUV continued on its way, but Dave knew the threat wasn't gone. They needed to be patient and stay put. Eventually del Rio's men would get called off after assuming he'd escaped.

Whispering, he praised his son. "Good job on staying quiet, champ."

When David flushed and looked away from him, Dave once again vowed to praise the boy as much as possible. He'd had way too much hate directed at him in his short life. He needed to know he was capable and smart, because he was.

They made small talk for a while, then David asked, "When we get home . . . do you think . . . can I go to school?"

Dave nodded. "Of course, champ. Why wouldn't you?"

He shrugged his small shoulders. "Because I'm stupid. And no one wants to be my friend."

Hating del Rio more with every word out of his son's mouth, Dave said, "We've already been over this, champ. You aren't stupid. Not at all. And why wouldn't anyone want to be your friend?"

"Because I'm a bastard."

Dave flinched at hearing the crude word come out of the innocent child's mouth.

"What does *bastard* mean, *Papá*?"

Controlling his fury at the mental damage del Rio had inflicted, Dave wished Raven was there. She'd know exactly what to say to reassure their son. He was winging it and felt completely out of his league at that moment. "I'm guessing you're going to have too many friends to count, champ," Dave reassured him. "You're a good boy. Friendly. Considerate and smart. Why wouldn't someone want to be your friend?"

Dave knew he had to be careful explaining. David wasn't even five years old yet, but he'd heard the word and, because he was *smart*, knew it was some kind of insult. The last thing he wanted was his son thinking he was less than anyone else. "And *bastard* is a mean word that bullies use to try to make someone else feel bad."

"But what is it?" David asked, not letting it go.

Dave thought fast and decided to tell the truth . . . sort of. "A bastard is someone whose mom and dad aren't married when they're born. And since your mom and I *were* married when you were born, you aren't one."

The relief on David's face would've brought Dave to his knees if he was standing.

"So I'm not a bastard?"

"No, son, you aren't. You're David Justice, son of Margaret and Dave Justice."

His eyes widened. "Your name is Dave?"

"Actually, it's David. But all my friends call me Dave."

"We have the same name!" David exclaimed.

Dave nodded, smiling as his son's eyes filled with pride. He hugged the small child to him and asked, "Did you get any sleep before we showed up to rescue you?"

David shook his head. "I was scared. The old woman wouldn't talk to me. I was hungry too."

Lying down, Dave settled his son on his chest until they were both comfortable. "You don't have to be scared now, son. I'm here, and I'll make sure you're safe. Close your eyes, and take a nap. When you wake up, you can have another protein bar."

"I'm not tired, *Papá*," David said, then yawned huge.

Smiling, Dave said, "All right, champ. You just lie there with your eyes closed, and I'll tell you stories, then, okay?"

"Okay."

Then, lying on top of a random person's roof in the middle of Lima, while the most vile man on earth hunted them down, Dave held his son while he told him stories of what his new life was going to be like in Colorado. Even after small snores sounded from little David's mouth, he kept talking, reassuring his son that he was smart and loved, and that he'd never be hurt again if he could help it.

Dave wasn't tired in the least. He was wired. He worried about Raven and what she was thinking since he hadn't returned. He knew his friends would take care of her and reassure her that he and David were both fine. But he also knew that she wouldn't rest until she saw her baby for herself. Saw that he was free of del Rio once and for all.

Whispering, he said, "Hang on, sweetheart. Just a little bit longer. Hang on."

Chapter Fifteen

"What do you mean, they aren't here?" Mags asked semihysterically when everyone returned to the motel. Everyone but her husband and child.

"Don't panic," Gray ordered. "They're fine."

"But they aren't here!" she practically yelled. "And you said that del Rio was there? Oh my God, did he get to David before you got there? Did Dave go off to find him?"

"No. Take a deep breath, Raven," Arrow ordered as he took her hands in his and gently guided her to the edge of the bed she'd been sharing with Dave.

"Everything went according to plan," Arrow told her.

"Which plan? A, B, C, or D?" Mags asked snarkily. As soon as the words were out of her mouth, she regretted them. She was being a bitch to the very men who'd entered the country to rescue her.

But amazingly, Arrow and the others simply laughed.

"She's definitely Dave's wife," Ball said with a chuckle.

"Plan B," Arrow told her. "We found David right where Ruben said he'd be—"

"And he was all right?" Mags asked, interrupting.

"He was fine. He was chained to the floor, but other than a few bruises, he was unhurt."

Mags sighed in relief. "Then what?"

"Then plan B was put into action because del Rio showed up at the barrio," Ro said.

Mags tensed, but forced herself to stay calm. None of the men around her were freaking out, so that had to mean David was all right. At least, that was what she told herself.

Ball picked up the story from there. "We knew from the satellite photos that the residents had built a shortcut out of the barrio along the back wall. Dave went up on the wall with David, and we tore down the access to it before del Rio and his men arrived. By the time they realized what Dave was up to, it was too late for them to get to them. He and del Rio had some words while we all got into place to give them cover, and Dave disappeared over the wall. They're both hiding until we can get there to pick them up and get to the airport."

"We're leaving?" Mags asked.

"Fuck yeah, we're leaving," Meat added. "We've been here long enough, don't you think?"

Mags nodded. She was scared to death that her husband and son were somewhere out in the city being hunted by del Rio and his men. "So what now?"

"Now we make sure you and the others are ready to go," Arrow said. "You, Zara, and Gabriella should say your goodbyes to Daniela, Bonita, Carmen, Maria, and Teresa."

"We're leaving them?" Zara asked from next to Meat.

"No," Meat reassured her. "We're taking the women to the airport tonight. As soon as possible. We got their passports today and arranged for tickets on red-eye flights to their respective countries. They'll be met on the other side by friends or family. You and Gabriella and Mags will go to the airport with me and Black as well, and board the plane that's waiting for us. The others will go pick up Dave and David and meet us there."

Mags wanted to protest. Wanted to insist that she go with the others to pick up her son, but she kept her mouth shut. They'd already done so much for her, and the last thing she wanted was to do something that might mess up her son's rescue. Screw up their chance to get out of Peru once and for all. She was as close as she'd ever been to going home, and she was petrified something would happen and she'd end up back at del Rio's compound.

"What about del Rio?" Zara asked. "Did you guys take care of him today?"

Gray shook his head. "No. He managed to escape the barrio with a few of his guards. We assume he's looking for Dave right this second."

"Why didn't you kill him?" Zara asked.

Before any of the others could say anything, Mags spoke. "Because they aren't like him."

Zara frowned. "But he needs to die," she insisted. "He's ruined so many lives. I don't understand."

Meat kissed the top of Zara's head. "Honestly? We all wanted to, but Dave told us if it didn't happen, not to spend time tracking him down. He promised he'd get what's coming to him. Dave has something planned. I don't know what. But whatever it is, del Rio won't be an issue for much longer."

"Rex knows people," Gray said quietly. "Now that I know Rex is actually a bartender, it's hard to believe." He grinned. "But we've been working with him for a long time, and we've always been amazed at the connections he has. If anyone can make sure del Rio gets what's coming to him, it's Rex."

It was difficult for Mags to believe, as well, that her mild-mannered husband was the kind of man the Mountain Mercenaries had gotten to know as this Rex person. But then again, he'd always been stubborn and charismatic. If anyone could amass a secret network of very powerful and dangerous allies, all in the hunt for her, it would be him.

"Can you talk to him right now?" she asked.

Meat shook his head. "Our radios are only good for communicating within short distances. But we're tracking him." He went to his laptop and opened it, bringing it over so Mags could view it. "See? That blinking blue dot is Dave. He's safe, hunkered down right where we planned."

Mags stared at the screen, at the blue dot Meat indicated. It wasn't moving. Dave was on the outside edge of a large neighborhood that backed up to the barrio where Ruben had claimed her son was being held. She took a deep breath and nodded. Dave had proved time and time again that he could take care of himself, and she trusted he'd take care of their son as well.

Her life had changed so much in such a short time, she was still reeling somewhat. But one thing remained the same—her love for and trust in her husband. She'd almost forgotten how stubborn he could be. But in the last two weeks, he'd found her, processed the fact that she'd been raped and impregnated by a stranger, and accepted with open arms the baby she'd had as a result. He'd somehow gotten past the shields she'd erected as a coping mechanism and had made her feel safe being touched by him. Sleeping next to him. Even being mostly naked with him in the shower after he'd been hurt.

In short, he'd performed a miracle. Made her think that maybe, just maybe, with him by her side, she'd be able to return to the States and not be a complete basket case.

Out of everyone in the world, she trusted him and him alone to keep her son safe and to bring him back to her.

"Okay, then. We've got a lot of work to do in a short amount of time if we're all going to get out of here as soon as possible."

She saw the admiration in the men's eyes, and it helped her get control of herself even more. It was going to be hard to say goodbye to the other women, but knowing they could keep in touch, and that they were finally going to be safe from del Rio, made the sorrow not quite as painful.

And Gabriella being able to come with her made her very happy. Not only for her friend, but for herself as well. It wouldn't be easy to acclimate back to a normal life, but with Zara, Gabriella, and Dave, and of course, David, it would be easier than if she were on her own.

After most of the men left the room, Zara came up to her and asked, "Are you okay?"

Surprisingly, Mags felt pretty good. She was worried about David and Dave, but knew deep down they were okay. Dave wouldn't let anything happen to their son. "I'm good."

"Are you excited about going home?"

Mags nodded. "Yes. And scared to death."

"I was too," Zara shared. "But I'll be there to help you. You'll have Dave too. Your son will keep you busy, what with shopping for him and enrolling him in school. Except I'm sure once the others find out about him, you and Dave will have to beg them to stop buying stuff for your son."

"You haven't talked much about them," Mags said. "I'm sure I'm quite a bit older than all of them. Do you think . . . Will they like me?"

"Oh my God," Zara exclaimed, "they already *love* you! See, the thing is, they've all been through their own kinds of hell, and they think the world of Dave. So you don't have to worry at all about them accepting you. They're good people, Mags. Swear."

Mags sighed. "I'm really nervous about seeing my parents," she admitted.

Zara reached out and grabbed Mags's hand and squeezed. "From what Meat has told me, he's been keeping them informed about what's been going on here. That Dave found you and that you're alive and well. He also told them about their grandson. They're over-the-moon excited, but they're nervous too. Just take it one day at a time. Okay?"

"They know about David?" Mags asked, shocked.

Zara nodded. "I gave Meat hell about that. It wasn't his place to tell them. I'm sorry."

"No, it's okay. I mean, I'm surprised, but kinda relieved too. I wasn't sure how they'd react . . . you know, because of the circumstances of his birth."

"He's a miracle," Zara said quietly. "They know that, just as Dave does. I'm the worst person to talk to you about this, since I was a virgin when I met Meat, but I can pretty much guarantee no one thinks any less of you or your son because of how he was conceived. I'm in awe of you, Mags. You were there for me when I didn't have anyone else. You've been my mom and my friend, and that's all I think about when I see you. What you've been through just makes you a warrior woman, not someone to be pitied or looked down on. Anyone who thinks differently can fuck off."

Mags got teary eyed as her friend spoke, but at her last comment, she chuckled. "Thanks, Zed," she said softly, using the nickname Zara had used when she'd pretended to be a boy for her own safety in the barrio.

"Come on. You've only been in the motel about a week, but I think you have more stuff than I came with. We also need to make sure Daniela is good. The purchase of her new clinic is progressing quickly. Let's get the suitcase the guys got you, and we'll see how much we can fit." She squeezed her hand and headed for the closet.

Mags nodded. Zara was right. They had a lot of stuff to do, and things would be very emotional when they left the other women. She would prefer to have Dave here with her, telling her everything would be fine, but he was busy protecting their son. So she had to pull up her big-girl panties and get on with things here.

Closing her eyes and saying a quick prayer for her family's safety, Mags turned and followed Zara to the closet.

~

"Tell me another story, *Papá*?" David asked.

Dave had no idea how much time had passed, but it was still dark outside. David had slept for a while, and then he'd woken up and eaten another protein bar with as much enthusiasm as he had earlier. It was very warm under the tarp, even without the sun shining overhead yet, but Dave wasn't going to risk leaving. Not until his team came to get him. He hadn't heard del Rio or his soldiers recently, but that didn't mean they weren't out there waiting and watching.

"What kind of story?" Dave asked.

"The story of how you met *Mamá*," David said without hesitation.

Surprised by the request, Dave wasn't sure where to start.

Luckily, his son helped him out. "You bought a building, and *Mamá* came to look at it," David hinted.

Chuckling, Dave realized that the little boy had already heard the story of their first meeting from Raven. Probably several times, if he wasn't mistaken. "Right, your mom came out to make sure my new building was safe for people to be in it."

"She was nervous because you were big enough to lift cars and beat up bad guys!" David added enthusiastically.

Dave nodded. "Yup. But the thing was, the second I saw your mom, I knew I wanted her to feel safe around me. I didn't want to make her scared of me. She was wearing a pair of tan pants and a pretty dark-blue top that made her eyes even more blue. Her hair was blowing in the breeze, and she looked like a fairy princess to me."

David's eyes were huge in his face, and he was listening with bated breath to every word Dave said. The little boy had only heard Raven's side of things for years, and Dave wanted to make sure he understood exactly how much Raven had bowled him over that day.

"She nervously bit her lip when she looked at me, and I could see her hands shaking. And I hated that. I don't mind if some people are scared of my size, but the last person I wanted to scare was your mom. I made sure to keep my distance from her so as not to scare her even more. She had to walk around the building, and I forced myself to stay right by the door so she wouldn't be nervous with me following her. I didn't want to, though. I wanted to stay right by her side and make sure no one else could get near enough to hurt her. Not that there was anyone around that would, but I wanted to be sure."

"She was glad," David said. "She was scared of you."

"I know, and that hurt me here," Dave said, putting a hand over his heart. "I didn't want her to be scared of me. I wanted her to like me as much as I liked her. When she was done looking at the outside of the building, she had to come inside and look at that too. She laughed at something I said, and I swear, champ, I fell in love with her right then and there."

"Really?"

"Yes, really. Her blue eyes sparkled when she laughed, and I couldn't help but want to see her smile every day for the rest of my life."

"*Mamá* said you were funny," David informed him.

"I don't know about that. All I know is that at least an hour went by while we talked, and then she had to go. I asked her if she might want to go out to eat with me later."

"And she said yes!" David said, clapping his hands. "And you had fish, and she had a steak!"

"That's right. We did. Here's the thing, champ, one day you're going to meet the person that you know you want to spend the rest of your life with. The one you want to have a family with, and who you would give up everything you own for, if only to make them happy. There should be a spark, something about this person that makes you feel like, if you don't get to see or talk to them every day, your life won't be complete. That's how I felt about your mom when I first saw her. And on that first date, in that restaurant, I knew if she didn't marry me, I wouldn't be complete. She completes me, your mom. I would never hurt her. Not ever. We might fight and yell, but I have never and will never put my hands on her in anger. How could I do that to the woman who is like the other half of my soul?"

Dave hoped to start undoing any damage del Rio might've caused in his son by desensitizing him to violence and devaluing women. He didn't know if it was working, but David was watching him with a rapt gaze that seemed piercing in its intensity. "How'd you lose *Mamá*?"

The question was painful, but Dave made an unspoken promise to himself and to his son right then and there never to lie to him. "You know what? I'm still not sure how I lost her. But I do know that it was painful. Every day she was gone was more painful than the last. I didn't know where she was or if she was hurt. I didn't know if anyone was feeding her or making her feel unsafe. I missed her, champ. Every day, I missed her more and more. My heart felt empty without her. I looked everywhere for her. I got all my friends together to help me. It took a long time, way too long, but I finally found her. And you know what?"

"What?"

"I found you too. You were a surprise, one of the best surprises of my life."

"I was?"

"Yeah, champ. Because me and your mom talked a lot about wanting to have a baby. We wanted a son or daughter to love and to complete our family. But she got lost before we could do that."

David studied him, and Dave could see his little mind whirling. "I know you're not my real *papá*," he said after a long moment. "Del Rio said *Mamá* didn't know who my real father was, and that he didn't want anything to do with me."

Dave put his finger under the boy's chin and gently forced him to look him in the eyes. "*I'm* your real *papá*," he said firmly. "I love you, and I love your *mamá*. That's what makes a family. Love. Del Rio doesn't know what he's talking about. He's mean and a bully, remember? His goal in life is to make other people sad. Would I be here if you weren't my son? If I wasn't your real *papá*?"

He could tell the boy was confused, but eventually he shook his head.

Dave lowered his head until his forehead rested against David's. "Finding you and your mom is a miracle, son. I haven't been happy since the day I lost your mom, and now that I've found her *and* you? I'm twice as happy. We're going to go to Colorado and live happily ever after. You're going to go to school and get even smarter than you are now. You'll have a ton of friends and grow up to do amazing things. I just know it."

"And you'll always be my *papá*? Even when I'm bad? You won't send me back?"

"No, David. You aren't ever coming back here, not unless you want to. You're my son. *Mine.* I'm not leaving you or your mom. Ever. And you can't be bad. It's not possible. You might make some decisions that aren't the right ones, and you might mess up, but that doesn't make you bad. Understand?"

David nodded.

Feeling as if he needed to lighten the mood, Dave pulled back and said, "So . . . your mom said that she's been teaching you numbers. Want to show me what you've learned?"

David smiled so big, Dave swore the air around them brightened. "Yes!"

"All right then, champ. What's one plus one?"

David held up his hands and showed one finger on each. "Two!"

Dave widened his eyes and exclaimed, "Wow, you *are* smart, just like your mom said." The smile on his son's face got even bigger, if that was possible. And Dave swore he'd spend the rest of his life doing everything in his power to keep that smile on his kid's face.

~

An hour or so later, Dave had moved him and David out from under the tarp. His team would be coming soon, and he wanted to be prepared. They lay on their backs, side by side, and gazed up at the stars.

"I don't know much about the constellations," Dave apologized to his son, "so I can't point them out, but I can tell you one thing I know for sure."

"What?" David asked.

"The stars saved my life."

"Really? How?" the little boy asked in awe.

"I was really sad about your mom being lost and that I couldn't find her. I just knew she was scared somewhere, and I couldn't be there to help her. It was the most painful thing I'd ever experienced in my life. I went to my bar, the one where I met your mom, and climbed onto the roof. It's flat, a lot like the one we're on right now. I lay down and stared up at the stars, like we are now. I was missing your mom a lot, and I asked her to show me a sign that she was still alive. That she was okay. And you know what happened?"

"No. What?" David asked in a hushed tone.

"A shooting star. That's what. The brightest one I've ever seen. It shot across the sky right above me. I realized then that your mom could've been looking up at the exact same stars as me at that very moment. That she might've been thinking of me, and that's why I saw that shooting star."

"Wow," David breathed.

"Yup. So from then on out, I went outside and looked up at the stars as much as I could. It comforted me to know that wherever your mom was, she was looking at the same stars. It made me feel closer to her."

"*Mamá* wasn't allowed to stay with me when it got dark, but she told me once that if I got scared, to look out my window at the stars, and that means she was thinking about me. That the stars sparkling was her winking at me and looking over me," David told his dad.

Dave took a deep breath and closed his eyes to try to control his emotions. Eventually, he opened his eyes and turned his head to look at his son. "When we get home, the three of us are going to lie in our yard, look up at the stars, and rejoice in the fact that we found each other. Okay?"

"Okay. *Papá*?"

"Yes, champ?"

"I'm ready to go now."

Dave chuckled. "I know. Me too. We have to wait just a little bit longer. My friends, *our* friends, will be here soon to get us."

"Will *Mamá* be there too?"

"No. But she'll be at the airport, ready to meet us. Are you excited about flying in an airplane?" Dave asked, wanting to take the boy's mind off missing his mom. He'd been exceptionally good all night. Not scared of the darkness and not complaining at all when he was bored. He was easily entertained, and so smart for his age. Raven had done an amazing job raising him so far.

"Yes!" David said, a touch too loud.

"*Shhhh*, keep your voice down, champ," Dave warned him.

"Sorry, *Papá*. Yes, I'm very excited!"

Checking his watch, Dave saw they only had an hour or so to go until it was time for them to be picked up. Getting off the roof would require the help of his men. They'd be down and off fast, without anyone knowing they'd been there in the first place. He was anxious to get to check in with the team. He assumed everything had gone according to plan back in the barrio and that no one had been hurt, but he simply didn't know.

Turning his attention to his son, Dave did his best to contain his adrenaline. After ten long years, it was almost time to take his wife home. He couldn't wait.

Chapter Sixteen

The sound of the radio crackling in his ear was one of the best sounds Dave had ever heard. He was more than ready to get the hell off this roof and out of Peru. David was sound asleep on his chest. It was shortly before dawn, and there was very little noise in the neighborhood around them, and very few lights on as well.

Sitting up slowly so as not to disturb the boy, Dave pressed on the radio in his ear, activating the hands-free connection.

"Rex, if you're out there, your queen requests the honor of your presence."

Dave wanted to laugh. But if his men had brought Raven with them to pick him up, he was gonna be pissed.

"If my queen is here, someone's fired," he replied softly.

Laughter greeted him. "Of course she's not, although she begged. You and the prince ready to go?"

"Yes."

"Be there in five. Out."

Dave recognized Ball's voice and relaxed a fraction. Out of all his team, Ball was the best driver. If the shit hit the fan, he knew without a doubt that Ball would be able to get them to the airport quickly and safely.

Very slowly, Dave stood, amazed that David didn't even stir. He was either the world's heaviest sleeper, or he was exhausted from the excitement and stress of everything that had happened. Dave assumed it was probably a little bit of both. He couldn't wait to learn more about his son. To get to know his quirks. Was he a morning person? Would he talk their ears off over breakfast, or would he be fuzzy headed and quiet until he really got going? What would be his favorite subject in school? Would he be athletic or more academic?

But first things first. They had to get out of Peru safely.

Clutching the deadweight of his son against his body, Dave walked silently over to the side of the house. Getting down off the roof would be easier than getting up, because the plan was for Ball to drive the minivan through the yard right up to the side of the house. Dave would hand his son down to Gray, since he was the tallest of the Mountain Mercenaries, who would be standing on the roof of the vehicle.

He heard his team counting down the minutes until they arrived, tensing when he heard Ball swear.

"What's wrong?"

"We've got company," Ball said tersely. "Apparently del Rio's men are more stubborn than we thought. They're still casing the neighborhood. We're going to have to make this pickup quick."

"Or they've got a lot of bloody incentive," Ro said. "I'm guessing del Rio said if they came back to the compound without Dave or the kid, they'd not live to see another day."

Dave gently shook the sleeping boy awake. "David? You need to wake up."

One second David was dead to the world, and the next he was wide awake and alert. "What's wrong, *Papá*?" he asked, the fright easy to hear in his voice.

"Are you ready to go to the airport to see *Mamá*?" Dave asked.

David nodded enthusiastically.

Dave quickly explained the situation as best he could to the little boy. "You're going to have to be brave for just a little longer. My friends, the ones you've already met, are going to pull up in about a minute and a half. They're going to park right down there." Dave pointed to the spot below the edge of the roof they were standing on. "Gray, our really tall friend, is going to get on top of the car and help you down. Can you be brave for that?"

David bit his lip and looked concerned. "Are you coming too?"

"Of course, champ. I'll be right behind you. But it's too far for me to jump with you in my arms. I'm going to have to lower you down over the edge of the roof. But Gray will be right there. You'll be fine. I promise."

"Okay, *Papá*. I can do it."

"Good boy," Dave praised. "But we're going to have to do it very fast because del Rio's men don't want you to go back to your mom. We hid out here on this roof in the hopes they'd give up looking for us. Do you understand?"

David nodded solemnly, and Dave hated that the little boy understood all too well what the consequences would be if they were caught. "We're going to be fine," he told him firmly. "Do you believe me?"

It took a second, but David's chin finally dipped once.

Bending, Dave put his son's feet on the ground and crouched to look him in the eye. "I haven't found you and your mom after all this time to lose you again. I swear, son, that soon you'll be reunited with your mom, and we'll all be on our way back to the United States."

Father and son stared at each other for a long moment until finally Dave whispered, "Okay, *Papá*."

"Twenty seconds out," Ball said in Dave's ear.

"You ready, champ? Our friends are comin', and they're comin' fast."

"Ready," David said, although his little voice quivered a bit.

Dave was furious at del Rio. How dare he cause his son so much fear! How dare he feel as if he had the right to kidnap whoever he wanted for his despicable plans. Hatred rose within Dave, but he pushed it back. There was no room for anything in his mind other than the mission at hand. He had to control himself. David and Raven were counting on him.

Time slowed as Dave waited for his team to arrive. He saw the minivan at the same time he heard Ball say he was almost there through the radio in his ear. He got down on his knees and scooted closer to the edge of the roof. "Give me your hands, champ. Feel free to keep your eyes closed if you want. This is going to happen very fast. You won't have time to be scared."

"I trust you, *Papá*," David said.

Once again, Dave's heart felt as if it was going to burst with pride and love for this small human. He'd known him less than twenty-four hours, and had known *about* him for only around two weeks, but already he was his whole world.

Dave watched as Ball barely slowed down as he barreled toward the house. He slammed on the brakes and skidded to a halt inches from the side of the building. Even as Dave took David's hands in his and began to lower him over the edge of the roof, Gray had leapt out of the van and was climbing on top of it.

"Ready, champ?" Dave asked when Gray was in place to catch the little boy.

David looked up into his eyes and nodded. "I'm not scared, *Papá*. You wouldn't do anything to hurt me."

Fuck . . . This kid.

Dave leaned his head a bit to the side and met Gray's eyes. "Ready?"

"I've got 'im, boss."

Dave didn't hesitate or count down. He simply let go of David's hands, and in two seconds, he was in Gray's arms. It had been the longest two seconds of Dave's life. He hated losing touch with his son for even the small amount of time it took for him to throw his legs over the side of the roof and lower himself down, hanging from his arms. The second he heard Gray say, "Clear," he let go and landed on top of the minivan himself.

Gray had already climbed off with David and was getting back into the vehicle. Hearing the squeal of tires, Dave knew they had no time to spare. They'd been spotted by one of del Rio's roving bands of men.

He jumped off the roof and threw himself into the minivan. Ro slammed the door behind him, and Ball was moving before Dave got his balance. He turned and reached for David, and Gray immediately handed him over.

Putting one arm around his son and bracing the other on the front passenger seat, Dave sent up a silent prayer of thanks that the extraction had gone so well. Of course, they weren't out of the woods yet.

"Can you lose him?" Arrow asked Ball from the seat next to him.

"Piece of cake," Ball muttered as he flicked off the headlights and pressed on the gas.

How the hell the man could see anything in the poorly lit neighborhood, Dave didn't know, but he wasn't worried. Ball had proven himself time and time again when it came to eluding bad guys. The minivan they were in wasn't exactly the fastest or most maneuverable vehicle, but Ball would find a way to lose their tail and get them to the airport safely.

David's eyes were huge in his face as he stared at the other men.

"Hey, little man," Ro said. "It's good to see you again."

"You good?" Gray asked the seemingly shell-shocked little boy.

Looking up at Dave, who nodded encouragingly at him, David nodded. "I'm good, Mr. Gray."

"You remember my name?" Gray asked in surprise.

David nodded. "I don't see Mr. Meat, though."

"He's going to meet us at the airport. He's making sure your mom is safe until we get there to be with her. I told you about the other men here, they're our friends too. They aren't like del Rio or *his* friends. They won't hurt you. Not ever. If you're ever scared or unsure, you can go to one of them, and they'll help you and get in touch with me or your mom. Okay?"

David nodded.

"Good. This is Ro. He'll be easy to remember because he's the one with the funny accent. And that's Arrow, and Ball is the one driving."

"Hang on," Ball said in a firm but calm tone as he took a corner on what felt like two wheels. Dave tightened his hold on his son as the minivan shot forward after making the turn.

"Everyone get to the airport all right?" Dave asked Gray.

The other man nodded. "Yeah. The women all left with no issues whatsoever. Gabriella and Zara cried buckets of tears and promised to stay in touch."

"And Raven?" Dave asked.

"Solid as a rock," Gray told him, the pride easy to hear in his voice. "She was sad, but because she went through what they did, she was more happy than upset that they were leaving. Zara told them they were finally free and to never look back. To take one day at a time."

David nodded. That sounded like his Raven.

"And Daniela?"

"She's safe at the clinic and has already promised to do whatever she can for any children that are found. She's working with the men from the Peruvian teams. After del Rio's escape from the barrio, they immediately raided two of the houses where he'd stashed some kids. The team and Daniela will work together to find the children's families, or new homes. They'll continue looking for any buyers of other kids, using whatever intel Meat can provide."

"Good. Sounds like things have gone according to plan."

Ro cleared his throat, and Dave turned to him. "They haven't?"

Everyone shifted in their seats as Ball took another sharp turn. He was driving way faster than was safe, but no one said a word as he did his best to evade their tail.

"Meat got in touch. He said it's a good thing the plane arrived in the commercial section of the airport. One of the contacts he's been talking to at the airport said there are police officers crawling all over the international terminal, looking for a group of Americans who don't have the proper paperwork to leave the country. Rumor has it that a couple is trying to kidnap a Peruvian child."

"Fuck," Dave swore—then sighed. "David, you didn't hear me say that. It's a bad word, and your mom would *not* be happy if you started saying words like that. She'd be very disappointed."

Amazingly, David giggled. "Okay, *Papá*, I won't tell."

"Thanks, champ, I appreciate it." Then, turning back to Ro, Dave asked, "So what's the plan?"

"Ball's gonna drop us off, and we're going to meet one of the thousand-and-one contacts you seem to have, and we'll be escorted to the plane where everyone else is already waiting. Then we're getting the bloody hell out of here," Ro said succinctly.

"How *do* you know so many people, anyway?" Arrow asked.

"Left turn!" Ball called out.

Everyone braced as Dave said, "I've spent the last ten years making friends in high places. Every time the Mountain Mercenaries completed a mission, I made more and more connections with powerful people. I've called in a lot of markers in the last two weeks, that's for sure."

"Right. I'm grateful for each and every one of your contacts. There's no way we would've been able to get all those passports without them," Arrow said.

"Or rescue all those kids," Gray added.

"Or get this private plane down here and ready to go," Arrow finished.

"If something goes wrong at the airport, take David and get out of there," Dave said, ignoring his team's praise. He'd done what had to be done, and even if he'd owe the men who'd helped him rescue his family for the rest of his life, he wouldn't regret it.

"We aren't leaving you behind," Ball said as he wrenched the steering wheel sharply to the right. "All we gotta do is lose this car tailing us, and we're home free."

Dave knew that wasn't exactly true. He could read between Ro's words. Del Rio had mobilized his army and would do whatever it took to prevent him from leaving the country with David and Raven. He'd sacrifice himself if that was what it took to make sure they were able to escape the hell they'd been living.

As if he could read his mind, Gray said, "Don't even think about it, Dave. We're all getting on that plane. Don't do anything stupid. Your wife needs you. Not to mention this little guy."

The minivan surged forward as Ball pulled onto one of the highways around Lima. "We're going to be cutting things really close here in a second," he said as he gunned the engine. "This guy is proving to be a bit stubborn. But don't worry, I'm gonna lose him in just a minute or two."

Dave sat back in the seat and held David to him a little bit closer. He trusted Ball with his life, and his son's, but he didn't trust the other drivers around them. Luckily, the highway was fairly empty since it was still so early. But that also meant that whoever was following them could more easily follow.

No one said a word as Ball weaved in and out of the light traffic.

They were about to pass an exit when, at the last second, Ball swerved and cut off a truck to take the off-ramp. He laughed after a few seconds and said, "So long, sucker!"

"Lost him?" Arrow asked.

"For now," Ball confirmed.

"How in the bloody hell do you know where we are?" Ro asked.

"I studied maps of the area," Ball said without pause. "You think I'd risk messing up this entire mission by getting lost?"

Ro chuckled, "No, but there's always a first time."

"Not with me. I'm a road savant," Ball bragged. "I never get lost."

David's head was on a swivel, turning from one man to the other as they spoke.

Fifteen minutes later, Ball was pulling into the commercial side of Lima's international airport across town. He was doing the speed limit and not driving like a crazy man, as he'd been just minutes earlier.

"You've got about five minutes after you drop us off to park this thing somewhere and get your ass inside," Gray told Ball.

The team had discussed leaving the van right at the curb when they arrived at the airport, but decided it would bring more attention to them than they wanted.

"I know. I've got it. I'll be there."

Dave looked at his son. "Okay, champ. We're almost there. Can you be brave for just a little bit longer?"

The little boy nodded. "I'm not scared, *Papá*."

"Good. Your mom is going to be so happy to see you!" Dave enthused.

The second Ball stopped the minivan, Gray had the door open, and they all walked quickly, but not too fast, toward the entrance.

A man stepped forward as soon as they entered the building.

"Mr. Justice?"

"Who wants to know?" Arrow asked, putting himself between Dave and the man.

"A friend of Rex's," the man said.

Everyone relaxed a fraction, and Dave stepped forward. "Thank you for your assistance."

The man nodded and said, "We must hurry. The plane is ready to go, but there's a storm brewing, and it'd be best if you were gone before it arrives."

Understanding the man's not-so-cryptic meaning, Dave nodded. He leaned over and picked up David once more, knowing he could move faster if he carried him.

The group started walking through the terminal, and the man who had met them at the door asked, "You have your passports?"

Gray answered. "Yes, everything is in order. We've got one more member of our group coming. He's parking the car."

Lifting a cell phone to his ear, the man nodded and punched a button to call someone. He said a few words, then hung up. "He'll be met at the door and escorted to the plane."

Dave wasn't surprised when they didn't even have to go through any kind of security. His connections knew the importance of staying under the radar, and they'd obviously already greased whatever wheels needed to be greased in order to make their departure as smooth as possible.

Their escort stopped by a door and opened it. Dave could see a medium-size private plane waiting about a hundred yards out on the tarmac. The engine was on, and the steps were lowered.

Sighing in relief, but not completely comfortable yet—he wouldn't be until they were in the air—he turned to the man and held out his hand.

They shook hands, and Dave said, "Tell your boss I owe him."

The man shook his head. "He said you'd say that, and he asked me to tell you that you're even now."

Dave smiled. "How's his daughter doing?"

"Good. Things were rough there for a while, but because you found her so quickly and got her home, she's going to be all right."

Dave knew his friends were listening with great interest, but he simply dipped his chin and said, "Good. That's great."

"Have a good flight," the man said, then turned to head back into the terminal.

Dave didn't look back as he headed for the plane. It was as if he could feel Raven's eyes on him. He knew she was probably freaked out and worried as all hell.

He felt like he had tunnel vision as he walked toward the plane. He reached the stairs and took them two at a time, blinking as he adjusted his vision from the rapidly lightening tarmac to the bright interior of the plane.

He heard Raven's cry of excitement and relief, then she was there.

She threw herself into him, wrapping her arms around both him and her son at the same time.

"Mamá!" David exclaimed happily.

Raven didn't pick her head up, but kept it pressed against Dave's shoulder as she gripped on to both of them tightly.

Knowing his team had to get onto the plane behind him, Dave walked her backward until they were farther down the aisle. He kissed her temple and said softly, "We're here. We're good."

He felt Raven nod against him and take a deep breath. When she lifted her head, there were tears in her eyes, but she smiled up at him. "Hi."

"Hi, beautiful. We're okay."

Then she turned to her son. "Hey, buddy."

"*Mamá!* Look! It's *Papá*! He found us!"

"I see that," Raven said.

"Del Rio took me to a really small house with an old lady. She wasn't mean, but she wasn't very nice either. Then *Papá* showed up with Mr. Gray and Mr. Black and some other friends and rescued me! We climbed up on a really high wall, and *Papá* made del Rio mad. We jumped off the wall and walked and walked and walked. Then we climbed a tree and slept on the roof of someone's house! Under a *tarp*! It was fun. *Papá* and I looked up at the stars, and he told me stories. Then he dropped me off the roof, and we were in a car zooming here and zooming there. Mr. Ball was driving, and Daddy said a bad word. Now we're here, and we're going to the United States!" David's words were all jumbled together as he did his best to recount everything that had happened to him in the last several hours.

"Wow, that all sounds very exciting. Were you scared?" Raven asked.

David shook his head. "At first. But when *Papá* got there, he told me that he wouldn't hurt me and I'd get to see you soon and we could eat together and all live in the same house!"

Raven nodded and took a deep breath before resting her forehead against Dave's chest once more.

He knew she was doing her best to keep her composure, and while he didn't like the fact that she was crying, he did like the fact that they were happy tears.

"I'm here!" Ball said as he entered the plane. "We need to get the hell out of here. *Now.*"

The two flight attendants shut the door as Dave urged Raven to sit in a row with David. He leaned down and kissed the tops of both their heads. "I'll be right back. Tighten your seat belts."

"Is everything all right?" Raven asked, her voice quivering.

Dave nodded. "Of course."

He turned to walk away, and Raven caught his hand. He looked down at her, and his heart turned over in his chest. He could hardly believe this wasn't a dream. That he'd finally found her, and they were going home. He squeezed her hand, then turned toward the front of the plane and the cockpit.

He nodded at Zara and Gabriella as he passed them and pushed through his team—who were all ignoring the poor flight attendants telling them they needed to be seated—to get to the door of the cockpit.

He stuck his head inside and said, "I'm Dave Justice. And while I'm very glad to see you, I'm hoping like hell you aren't intimidated easily, because I have a feeling the shit's about to hit the fan."

The man on the left nodded his head. He was probably in his fifties or so. "I'm Captain Mark Brown. That's my copilot, Porter Hilliard. We both flew over a hundred missions in the Gulf War. We know what your story is, sir, and you can count on us. Your wife and child have been through enough. It's time you all got home."

Dave nodded at both men, as glad as he could be that he had two combat veterans at the helm.

Mark lifted a hand and pressed the radio headset at his ear—and every muscle in his body tensed. He whipped the headset off and began flicking switches and pushing buttons. "You should probably go sit down and buckle up. This is most likely gonna be a rough takeoff."

Seeing lights from the corner of his eye, Dave looked over at one of the windows—and saw a police vehicle heading their way with its lights whirling.

"Shit," he muttered. Then, turning back to the pilot, he asked, "Can we take off if we haven't been given clearance?"

"Fuck yeah, we can," Porter said to Dave's right. He turned and told Meat, who was standing right behind him, "Things are about to get dicey. Go tell the women to hold on, and everyone else needs to strap in as well."

"Will do." Meat turned to go. "What about you?" he asked Dave.

"I'll be there in a second," Dave told him.

He nodded, then hurried to relay the information to the others. Before he could leave, Dave stopped him by putting a hand on his shoulder. "Meat?"

"Yeah?"

"Thanks for looking after Raven for me and getting her and the others to the plane."

Meat nodded. "Of course." Then he turned and headed for the rows of seats.

Dave saw Raven's concerned face as she leaned out into the aisle of the plane, watching him. He gave her a quick chin lift, then turned back to the cockpit.

They were now barreling down one of the access roads to the runway. He couldn't see behind him, and asked, "Are they following us?"

Mark chuckled. "Never thought I'd see the day when a police car was chasing a fucking plane, trying to pull it over. But don't worry, we're not stopping. After everything I've heard you and your wife have been through, they'll have to do more than flash a few lights to get me to stop."

"What about clearance? What are they saying on the radio?" Dave asked as he looked to Porter, who was still wearing a headset.

"They're not happy, sir, but it's really too bad that I can't understand them very well with their accented English." He winked. "They gave us approval earlier, and as far as I'm concerned, they're just making sure we're good to go."

Dave winced. These men were putting their careers on the line for him and his team. He wouldn't forget it. Yes, they were there because he'd cashed in some huge favors that were owed to him, but if they were able to get this plane off the ground and out of Peruvian airspace, he would be forever in their debt.

He stood behind the men, barely breathing as the captain pushed the yoke forward. The turn at the end of the road to get to the runway was sharp, and he heard Gabriella swear in Spanish from behind him. He'd heard enough Spanish swearing since his time in Peru to recognize her expression for what it was. He still didn't move to strap himself in. He couldn't. He was too tense. Ready for something awful to happen to prevent them from taking off. If del Rio's flunkies were smart, they would've gotten in *front* of the plane, not chased it from behind.

With that very thought in mind, he saw police lights speeding toward the runway from their right.

Time was almost up. If the vehicles made it onto the runway before they'd taken off, they wouldn't make it.

"Yipee-ki-yay, motherfuckers," Mark mumbled as he leaned forward, revving the plane's engines to full throttle.

"Flight three-two-seven taking off," Porter said into the radio.

Dave held on to the back of the pilots' seats until his fingers turned white. He kept his eyes on the quickly approaching police cars. They weren't slowing down, and if they didn't stop, they were all going to die in a fireball of massive proportions.

"Come on, come on," Mark muttered as the plane shook and shuddered, picking up more and more speed as it careened down the runway.

There were at least three police cars bearing down on them from the right, and who knew how many more behind the plane. Dave also saw two military Humvees behind the police cars. Del Rio had called out the cavalry for sure.

He knew if they were stopped and taken into custody, he'd never see his wife or child again, and his team, the men he'd grown to love and respect as brothers, would spend years locked away in a Peruvian prison as del Rio's connections made sure their cases never went to court. Zara and Gabriella would also probably become prisoners of del Rio as well.

And Dave himself would be tortured to within an inch of his life and probably forced to watch his wife be assaulted day after day, until they both went crazy from pain and helplessness.

"Get us out of here, and I'll personally pay you each a million-dollar bonus," Dave told the pilots.

"Fuck you," Mark said between clenched teeth. "Did you not hear me say that I knew what your story was and I'm gonna get you home?"

The plane shook even harder as the pilot pushed it to its limit.

Dave held his breath and couldn't take his eyes from the spinning lights coming at them, faster and faster. The plane and the cars were playing a game of chicken. A game that would end with them all being killed if someone didn't flinch.

Luckily for them, the police car in the lead finally flinched.

The driver slammed on the brakes just before the car sped onto the runway, right in front of the plane.

The wheels left the ground, and Dave saw the men from the cars leap out and raise their rifles, aiming for the plane.

It was too late. They were in the air.

But were they safe?

"Dave?" a voice asked from behind him.

Flinching as a hand touched his back, Dave spun around to see Raven standing there. Her face was pale, and she was shaking. Without a word, Dave wrapped his arms around her and pulled her into him, turning to face the front once more. Looking over his shoulder, he saw David was sitting with Gray, who was pointing out the window, keeping the boy distracted from the rough takeoff.

Stumbling a bit because of the steep angle of the plane, Dave braced his legs and used one hand to grab hold of the doorway to the cockpit.

"Will they shoot us down?" Raven asked shakily.

Dave opened his mouth to respond, but Porter got there first.

"No, ma'am. They wouldn't dare."

Dave wasn't sure he completely agreed with the copilot, but he didn't contradict him. He couldn't relax, though. Not until they were well above missile range and out of Peru once and for all.

Raven didn't pull away. Didn't try to get him to come sit with her. She simply rested her head against his chest and hung on.

He had no idea how much time had passed, but the flight attendants began walking down the aisle, asking what everyone wanted to drink, so he knew he'd been standing there, staring out the front windshield, for quite a while.

It wasn't until Mark, who had put his headset back on, said, "Ten-four. Flight three-two-seven entering Ecuadorian airspace," that Dave felt his knees go weak.

He closed his eyes and slowly felt himself sinking to the floor. Raven held on to him the entire way and, once he was down, straddled his legs and wrapped herself around him.

David must've been watching, because he ran forward and snuggled into both of them.

It was then, and only then, with his wife and son in his arms, that Dave lost it.

He cried for the decade they'd lost. He cried for the pain and suffering Raven had endured. He cried that he hadn't been there to help protect David and wasn't there for his birth.

But most of all, he cried because he'd done it. He'd found Raven. Everyone had said she was gone and he should get on with his life. But he hadn't been able to. His life had stopped the day Raven was taken from him, and he could finally get on with it.

They could both begin living again.

Chapter Seventeen

Hours later, after the plane had landed at the Colorado Springs Airport, Mags was nervous. Dave and the others had reassured her that there would be no press there when they landed. No one knew about her and her ordeal. As far as the airport was concerned, they were just a normal private plane landing. They would disembark onto the tarmac and walk into the terminal like any other travelers.

She'd been so relieved to see David and her husband enter the plane. She'd been worried sick, and even though Meat and Black had reassured her over and over that things were going according to plan and they were fine, she hadn't relaxed until she'd seen them with her own two eyes.

After the grueling takeoff, which Dave had told her about once they'd been in the air for over two hours, the flight had been uneventful. David had been so excited about his first plane ride and had spent most of it with his nose glued to the window. There was so much he had to learn about the world, and now she could get him into school, and give him everything else he'd been deprived of for the first four and a half years of his life.

Mags had no idea what she was going to do with herself, but Dave had reassured her that she didn't have to do anything. She could spend as much time reacclimating to life in the US as she needed. She and Zara had talked a little bit about how difficult it had been for her to feel comfortable doing even the easiest tasks, like grocery shopping, and it made Mags feel a little better knowing she would have both Zara and Gabriella to lean on.

Seeing her husband break down nearly crushed her heart. Dave had always been the strong one. A "man's man." So seeing him cry as if he would never stop had been heartbreaking and touching at the same time. Somehow she knew he was letting out all the emotions he hadn't let himself feel for the last decade. She still felt a little numb herself, but knew she'd have her moments in the near future as well.

But sitting in his lap, with her son under one arm and holding Dave with the other, Mags was exactly where she wanted to be. Dave wouldn't hurt her. Ever. He would protect her and David with his life. She had no idea if she could ever be a "real" wife to him again, but she decided in that moment to do everything in her power to try. She'd go to counseling, talk with other sex-trafficking survivors, and do her best not to give del Rio one more second of power over her.

Dave held back as the others got off the plane and headed for the terminal. He shook both pilots' hands and said, "You'll both be hearing from my accountant very soon."

The pilot scowled and said, "I'll be happy to receive an invitation to your kid's birthday party or his graduation, but if you send me anything else, I'm gonna be pissed."

"Same," the copilot said. "We've been over this. We were doin' our job, and I have to say, it was a hell of a lot of fun playing chicken with those assholes. The only thanks I need is these two standing right here, smilin' like they are." He nodded at Mags and David.

"Fine. But if you ever need *anything*, call," Dave said.

"Will do."

"Of course."

And with that, the two men headed out to do their checks of the plane.

Dave turned her toward him and put his hands on her shoulders. Just days ago, that might have freaked her out, but after what had happened after takeoff, she saw her husband in a new light.

"I need to tell you before you get in there . . . your parents are here."

Mags stared up at him in disbelief. She shook her head. "No . . . I . . . I'm not sure about this."

"Sweetheart, trust me. They've been just as devastated as I've been. This is gonna be fine."

She couldn't help but worry. She knew her parents had already learned about her son, but that didn't make the upcoming meeting any easier. It had been a long time since she'd seen her parents, and while she wanted to be the daughter they knew and loved, she'd changed a lot.

"It'll be okay," Dave repeated, reading her mind, leaning forward and resting his forehead against hers. "They couldn't be happier about David. They're excited to meet him, but more than that, they just need to see you for themselves. I warned them that right after we landed probably wasn't the best time, but you know your dad, he wasn't going to wait a second longer to see you."

Mags was scared. She knew she had to do this. Hell, she *wanted* to see her parents. Had worried about them for years, wondering if they were all right, if they were even alive. Hearing that they were still alive and doing very well had been such a relief. But seeing them now? Right this second?

"Come on," Dave said, reaching for David. "They're probably freaking out since the others are already inside."

Mags let him take their son and relaxed a bit when he took her hand in his. She looked up at him. "You'll be there the whole time?"

"Right by your side. And if anyone says anything negative, which I don't think will happen, we're out of there."

"Okay."

"Okay."

She squeezed his hand, then walked down the narrow stairway and waited for him at the bottom. When he got to her side, he grabbed hold of her hand once more and said, "Raven?"

"Yeah?"

"Everyone else is gonna be there too."

She huffed out a laugh and shook her head. "Care to elaborate on who 'everyone' is?"

"Allye, and her and Gray's son, Darby. Chloe, Harlow, Everly, and Morgan, and her and Arrow's daughter, Calinda."

"Is that all?"

Dave shrugged. "Barbara Ellis, the owner of the dance studio Allye works at, Nina Scofield and her mom, Noah, one of the bartenders at The Pit. Maybe Carrie, Julia Sue, Melinda, Ann, Lauren, and Bethany. Wouldn't be surprised if Loretta Royster and Edward showed up as well. Oh, and of course, Elise, Everly's sister."

Mags couldn't help but shake her head again in exasperation. "Seriously? Am I supposed to know who all those people are?"

"No," Dave told her as he brought her hand up to his mouth and kissed the back. "Just warning you that there will be a crowd. I kinda left town pretty fast when I found out that Zara knew you."

"So they're here for you," Mags said softly. "Because they admire and care about you."

"I suppose," Dave admitted. "If it bothers you, let me know, and I'll get you and your parents out of there so you can talk with more privacy."

Mags shook her head. She was touched that so many people were coming out to support her husband. Yes, they were probably glad she was all right, but they didn't know her. They knew Dave. He was important to them, and they wanted to make sure he knew how happy they were for him. For *them*. How could she get upset about that?

Dave held open the door for her when they got to the building, and she took a deep breath. She'd dreamed about this moment for ten long years and could hardly believe it was actually happening.

They walked up a flight of stairs, and Dave held open one more door. They entered the small airport, and Raven had to smile at how big David's eyes were. He was soaking in everything silently and with the beautiful wonder of a child. She couldn't wait to bring him to the Colorado Springs zoo. And the Children's Museum of Denver. And an aquarium. There were so many things he'd been deprived of in his first five years, and she couldn't wait to make it all up to him.

Dave had told her on the plane that he thought David was gifted. He thought he was extremely smart for a kid his age. Didn't even sound like a four-and-a-half-year-old. Mags pretty much already knew that . . . and had worried about it in the past. David had no trouble learning both English and Spanish and was saying words around ten months old. He'd soaked up everything she'd taught him about numbers, colors, and anything else she could think of to entertain him on their days together. She'd been proud, but also worried about what that would mean for him in Peru.

Any thoughts about her son flew from her head as soon as she saw the large group of people waiting for them on the other side of security. Walking slowly, she was suddenly nervous, and she almost asked Dave to get her out through a back door so she didn't have to deal with the welcoming party.

But then she caught a glimpse of a gray-haired woman in the crowd. She was standing next to a tall, older man. He had his arm around her shoulders, and they were staring at Mags as if she were a ghost. Tears coursed down the woman's face, and she looked both devastated and elated at the same time.

And just like that, her reticence faded away.

"Mom?" she whispered.

Pulling away from Dave, she walked faster, her eyes glued to her mother. Tears formed without her noticing, and she broke out into a jog as she got closer and closer. Her mom stepped away from her dad and held out her arms.

Mags ran straight into them. "Mom!" she sobbed as the familiar lavender scent of her mother surrounded her, just as her arms did.

They were both crying, and Mags couldn't stop. She was really here. In her mother's arms. She hadn't died while Mags was gone. In fact, she seemed stronger somehow. Mags felt like the weak one.

Her mom pulled back and put her hands on Mags's cheeks. They were about the same height, and as Mags stared into her mother's eyes, she realized how much they looked alike. "I love you, Mom," she whispered.

"Let me just look at you," Justine Crawford cried as she held her daughter's head in her hands.

"Stop hogging her," John Crawford complained as he nudged his wife gently with his hip.

Mags laughed and looked up at her dad, and saw that he had tears in his eyes as well. She hugged him tightly, inhaling his familiar scent of smoke. He only smoked when he was stressed, and she supposed he'd probably been very stressed recently. Her mom hated the habit and gave him hell every time she caught him.

"Hey, Magpie," he said softly as he hugged her.

"Hi, Dad," she returned, closing her eyes in contentment when she heard the nickname her dad had always used for her.

Seeing them still together made Mags smile. She'd always known they had a good relationship, and after everything she'd been through, she wanted that kind of marriage as well. Unable to help herself, she looked behind her for Dave.

The second their eyes met, he came forward. He'd been standing nearby, ready to interfere if needed, just as he'd promised he would.

"Mom, Dad, I'd like you to meet my son, David."

"Oh my word," Justine said under her breath. "He looks exactly like you."

Dave walked up, shook her dad's hand, and turned David to face them. "Champ, this is your grandmama and grandpapa."

His eyes were wide. He looked at them, then at his mom, then back at Dave. "Really?"

"Really," Dave reassured him.

David squirmed in his arms, and Dave leaned over to put him down. David ran right up to Justine and put his arms around her waist. He rested his head on her belly and said, "I've always wanted a grandmama!"

Mags saw her mom cry fresh tears at her son's embrace. Then David let go and moved to stand in front of her dad. He looked up at him and smiled. "Hi! I'm David."

"Hi, David. Did you have a good flight?"

It was the right thing to ask.

David nodded happily. "Yes! I've never been in a plane. I could almost reach out and touch the clouds! And the mountains looked so tiny, and we flew over the ocean! And I got to eat pretzels, and Mr. Meat even brought me some *arroz con pollo* to eat, and *Mamá* had her favorite, *pollo empanada*. *Papá* and our friends all ate hamburgers. And when we landed, the plane was going so fast. Zoooooom!" He made a swooshing motion with his hand to demonstrate exactly how fast he thought they'd been going.

Mags watched as her dad crouched down in front of him. "Yeah? *That* fast?"

David nodded. Then he tilted his head and looked at his new grandpapa closely. "*Mamá* got lost. Then she had me, and *Papá* found us."

"Yes, he did. And I can never thank him enough for that," her dad said, his voice breaking.

Then, as if David had just needed to say the words out loud to his new grandparents and have them verified, he nodded and turned back to Dave.

Her husband leaned down and picked him back up.

"Someday I'm gonna have arms like tree trunks, just like my *papá*," David declared loud enough for everyone around them to hear.

Everyone chuckled, and Mags leaned into Dave, putting her arm around his waist. She looked around at all the people smiling at her and relaxed. She'd imagined what this would feel like so many times, but had no idea how soul-deep amazing it would actually be.

She was finally home. And nothing had ever felt better.

~

That night, after going to Gray and Allye's house for an impromptu welcome-home party, and after David fell asleep on the way to the apartment in the new car seat Meat had purchased, and after Raven and David had inspected his apartment from top to bottom, and after they'd all piled into the king-size bed in the master bedroom, Dave watched his wife and son sleep.

For the first time in ten years, he felt as if he could finally breathe. He knew where his wife was. She was right here. Next to him. She wasn't a victim. No way. She was a survivor. She'd gone through experiences that had broken others. She'd been battered and beaten and stomped into the dirt time and time again. But she'd risen each and every time, stronger and more determined to survive anything and everything del Rio and his followers had thrown at her.

Not wanting to leave them for even a second, but knowing he had one more thing to do before he could finally let go of the rage and hatred he had in his heart for the man who'd taken what didn't belong to him, what he had *no right* to take, Dave silently slipped out of bed, careful not to jostle either his wife or son.

He picked up an untraceable satellite phone he'd received from one of his contacts in the FBI and padded out of his bedroom. He walked over to the balcony and opened the sliding glass door. He could see Pikes Peak from his apartment, and usually the view soothed him. He couldn't see it in the night sky, but even if he could, he wouldn't have paid it any attention tonight.

He dialed a number he'd committed to memory a year or so ago and held the phone up to his ear.

"Silverstone Towing. How can I help you?"

"This is Rex. I have a job for you."

"Rex! We haven't heard from you in a while. Everything all right?"

"I found my wife," Dave told the man on the other end of the line.

"Seriously? That's fucking awesome!" The man paused, then asked, "Assuming this job has to do with that?"

"You'd assume right. Job's in Peru. Lima, to be exact. That going to be a problem?" Dave asked.

"You know it's not. Send over the details. We'll take a look and see what we can do."

"'Preciate it. And . . . I need you to make it hurt."

The other man's voice dropped. "Raven's gonna be all right?"

"Eventually. But I need him to pay."

"Done."

"I owe you," Dave told the man on the other end of the phone.

"Nope. This one's on the house. Payback for all the times you've helped those who couldn't help themselves."

"Thanks."

"If you're ever in the Indianapolis area . . . and need a tow . . . we wouldn't mind if you stopped by the shop."

Dave chuckled. "Will do. Thanks."

"Happy for ya, Rex. Seriously. We'll take care of this. You just go live your life the way you haven't been able to for the last ten years. All right?"

"I will. Bye."

"Bye."

Dave clicked off the phone and sighed. He felt not even a hint of guilt. In fact, his shoulders felt ten times lighter after making the call. He went back into his apartment and locked the sliding glass door behind him. Then he slipped into his bedroom and smiled at seeing his family still sleeping soundly. He climbed under the sheet and snuggled up against his wife's back. She didn't move, which showed exactly how tiring the last few days had been.

He closed his eyes and fell into a deep sleep. The kind he hadn't had for at least three thousand, six hundred and fifty days.

Epilogue

Two Months after Returning Home

Dave was on the couch watching the late-night news with Raven. David was asleep in his room. Both of them had been to the doctor for complete checkups. They both had some vitamin deficiencies, and Raven would have to see a doctor regularly for a while, at least, but that wasn't unexpected. They'd seen a dentist and an eye doctor too, and Dave had taken both to the mall, when Raven was ready, to do some much-needed shopping for necessities. David had been wide eyed at seeing the array of stores, and he'd almost cried when Dave had bought him a bagful of brand-new clothes, something he'd never had in his entire life.

David had also started kindergarten, and he was loving every second of it. Dave was so proud of the boy. David had been nervous and scared on his first day, not sure if anyone would like him, but since then, he'd been outgoing and popular with the other children. In fact, on the weekends, he was sad when he didn't get to see his friends.

They'd had a long talk with the teacher, who'd agreed that, intellectually, David was way ahead of his peers. She suggested they test his IQ so they knew exactly what they'd be working with. She also volunteered to work closely with David to make sure he was being challenged. Everyone agreed he'd be better off staying where he was and not being pushed into a higher grade just yet. He needed to connect with children his age and learn how to be social with others.

Gabriella was flourishing in her new country. She lived in the apartment with them for a while, and they'd moved her into her own place nearby just a couple weeks ago. She'd enrolled in an English as a Second Language class and was learning amazingly fast. During the day, she was either in class or working with Harlow. The two women had hit it off immediately, and Gabriella was becoming an excellent chef. In the evenings, she usually came over to visit with Raven and David.

And Raven had begun to accompany Dave to The Pit. At first she'd been extremely nervous, even with the subdued crowd that came in during the day. Men still made her skittish, and every time Dave thought about why, he had to control his rage.

Strangely enough, however, when she worked with him behind the bar, she seemed to be okay. They'd figured that since he was with her, and because the bar was between her and everyone else, it gave her a bubble of protection that her psyche needed.

Dave loved having her near. Loved working side by side with her. It was literally a dream come true, for both of them. So during the day, they tended bar, and in the afternoon, they picked up David together and spent the evenings laughing and relearning how to be husband and wife, as well as a family.

Every night, they both read to David, then tucked him in and sat next to each other on the couch. It had become their new tradition. Sometimes they watched TV. Sometimes they talked. Other times they read books. But no matter what they did, they did it together, touching. They would hold hands, or Raven would lean up against him, or put her legs in his lap as she used the arm of the couch as a pillow.

Dave relished these times. In the past, he'd sat on that couch and stared off into space, torturing himself by wondering what his wife was doing right that second. Wondering if he'd ever get a chance to tell her how very much she meant to him.

They were still living in Dave's apartment, but they'd been talking with a real estate agent and scouring the listings to see if they could find either a home on a few acres, or land they could buy to build a modest house, where they could live out the rest of their lives peacefully.

Dave was lost in his head, thinking about one of the homes they'd seen online earlier, when Raven gasped. Tensing, he was immediately on alert.

Raven gripped his forearm tightly, but her eyes were glued to the television screen. Dave's eyes whipped forward to see what had alarmed his wife. The news anchor was sitting behind a desk on the set—and a picture of none other than Roberto del Rio was superimposed over her left shoulder.

"The man known as del Rio was found dead today in his sprawling compound in Lima, Peru. Details are sketchy, but based on crime-scene photos, an inside source has suggested homicide, due to the gruesome nature of the scene. Del Rio has long been suspected of being the head of a massive sex-trafficking operation, and when police raided the compound, evidence of child pornography was found, along with dozens of young women from all over Central and South America as well as countries around the globe. Sources speculate that del Rio may have been targeted by rival criminal factions.

"Lima has long struggled with corruption throughout its police, military, and government agencies, and along with the women and pornography, guns, drugs, and lists of names were also found inside the home. The lists are alleged to be those del Rio was extorting, and perhaps others whom he was paying to turn a blind eye to his operation. Our source says it will take months, if not years, to sort through the mess, and that hundreds of people will most likely lose their jobs as a result of the corruption. Thousands of cases in the Peruvian courts will also have to be reexamined. Hundreds of innocent victims could be released from Peruvian prisons, once the extent of the corruption is uncovered.

"Experts warn in the coming months, there will be a power struggle in Lima among those who may want to take up where del Rio left off. We'll bring you more information as it comes in on this constantly updating situation in Peru. Tom, what's the weather going to be like tomorrow?"

Raven pulled back and turned to stare at Dave. "Oh my God . . . is it true? Is he really dead? Are we really free?"

Dave pulled his wife against his side, thankful that she no longer flinched when he moved too fast or when he hugged her. "If it's on the news, it's got to be true," he told her.

"I can't believe it. I . . . intellectually, I knew I was safe here. I mean, he's all the way down there in Peru, and I'm here, but a part of me couldn't relax. He got to me when I was in Vegas. I wasn't sure if he was so pissed we got away that he wouldn't send someone to grab me and David again. But . . . if it's really true . . . we can truly relax! You don't think someone else would come up here to get revenge, do you?" she asked, her voice quivering just a bit.

"No way, sweetheart. As the lady on the news said, everyone is going to be way too busy trying to cover their asses or to rise to the top of the pile to worry about you. Or me. Or David." He kissed her temple. "And you're right. We're free. Free to live our lives the way we should've been doing for the last ten years. To be happy. To watch our son grow and thrive. To hang out with our friends and laugh about the silliest things."

He was ready to console Raven if she cried, but he shouldn't have been surprised when she sat up next to him with a radiant smile. Not a tear in sight. "I know it's wrong to celebrate the death of another human being, but I don't care. Do we have any ice cream left, or did David eat it all tonight?"

Dave smiled back. "I may or may not have hidden a pint in the back of the freezer so he wouldn't find it and beg to have 'one more scoop.'"

Raven laughed, the sound so carefree. "You know our son well."

Dave's heart felt as if it was going to burst. "Yes, I do," he agreed. Then he stood and pulled Raven to her feet next to him. He wrapped his arm around her waist, and they walked to the kitchen together. He pulled out the pint of double chocolate chunk with caramel swirl, his wife's current favorite, while she got two spoons. They headed out to the balcony, and Dave pulled her onto his lap.

They were both lost in their own thoughts as they took turns dipping into the ice cream container and gazing up at the stars.

"Thank you for not giving up trying to find me," Raven said after a long moment.

"Thank *you* for not giving up," Dave retorted.

Later, after they'd finished the ice cream, they headed to the master bedroom and, as they had every night for the last two months, got ready for bed, then snuggled together under the covers.

"Dave?"

"Yeah, sweetheart?"

"I'm not ready right now, but . . . one night, I'm gonna want you to make love to me."

Once again, Dave felt as if his heart was gonna bust out of his chest. He was so proud of his wife. She was the bravest and strongest person he'd ever met in his life.

He didn't want to belittle her bravery by telling her he didn't need sex. So he simply said, "All right, love."

~

Three Months after Returning Home

Dave sat at a table in the back room of The Pit and looked at the men of Mountain Mercenaries. They'd asked if they could meet with him, and of course he'd agreed. He enjoyed sitting here with them rather than talking to them on the phone anonymously, as he'd done before they'd found out he was their handler, Rex.

Like the no-nonsense man he was, Gray cleared his throat and got to the point. "We've been discussing it for a while, and we'd like to see if you'd consider having the Mountain Mercenaries only take on domestic cases from this point forward."

The request was blunt, and not entirely unexpected.

Dave knew his team extremely well. He'd been observing and leading them for years now. He'd sensed a change in their priorities, starting when Gray had first met Allye. He hadn't been entirely pleased with the change, worried that it would hinder a rescue mission for his wife, if he ever found her. But after seeing for himself how dangerous things could be in overseas missions, he'd changed his mind.

It wasn't as if he didn't know his men faced danger on every mission, but it was more than bullets and putting their lives on the line. It was dealing with language barriers, corruption, and even the threat of being thrown into some murky foreign prison with the key thrown away.

And they all had families to worry about now. Women and children who were counting on them and who loved them. The entire team had taken off the three months since they'd returned from Peru, and Dave had seen the difference it made in his men. They'd been more relaxed. Laughed more. Were less stressed.

Black had informed everyone that Harlow was pregnant, and both Meat and Arrow had gotten married. Calinda and Darby were growing like weeds, and at least once a day, one or more of the group stopped into The Pit to say hello to Raven and to talk.

Looking around at his men, Dave said, "Maybe it's time to retire the Mountain Mercenaries."

As if planned, all six men emphatically disagreed.

"No!"

"That's not what I meant!"

"Absolutely not!"

"We can't disband!"

"What the fuck?"

"That's not what we want!"

They all chuckled at their simultaneous outbursts. Ro leaned forward and spoke for the group. "We don't want to stop doing what we're doing. There are still thousands of women and children out there who need our help. It's just that the overseas missions take us away from our own families for long amounts of time. And they're more unpredictable. We don't want to quit, just change our focus. But if that doesn't work for you, we're still not quitting. We'll just ask for more time between missions."

"Done," Dave said without hesitation. "I'll concentrate on finding those in the US who've gone missing."

"Just like that?" Ball asked.

"Just like that," Dave confirmed.

"But what if we find information about someone like Morgan, who's been taken outside the US and needs rescuing?" Meat asked.

"Then I'll pass the info along to one of my connections," Dave said, leaning back in his chair and crossing his arms.

"One of your connections," Arrow echoed.

"Yup," Dave agreed.

"How many teams are you running?" Black asked.

"Just this one," Dave reassured his friends. "But I know of other groups similar to ours out there. Not to mention my connections with the FBI, CIA, police chiefs, and heads of various Mafia and mob organizations that don't deal in human trafficking."

Gray simply shook his head. "I knew you were connected, but we still don't know the half of it, do we?"

Dave didn't even crack a smile. "No."

"Fair enough," Gray said. "So, it's settled, then."

"Yup."

"That was way easier than I thought it was gonna be," Ball admitted. "You're normally a stubborn son of a bitch, Rex."

At that, Dave did smile. "Thanks."

"Wasn't a compliment," Ball muttered. Then he pulled an envelope out of his pocket and threw it on the table toward Dave.

"What's that?" Dave asked.

"You're stubborn," Ball said. "But we're more so. You're taking that—and we won't take no for an answer."

Leaning forward, Dave picked up the envelope and pulled out the papers that were inside. It took a minute for what he was looking at to register, but when it did, his head jerked up, and he stared at his team in shock.

"It's forty acres of land up near Monument. You're directly responsible for us meeting our women and for helping hundreds of others. This world would be a worse place without you in it. We know you've been looking for a place to settle with your family, and this land is perfect. It's secluded, but not so far out that there isn't phone and internet service or an infrastructure in place for water, electricity, and septic. The view from the north end of the property is unparalleled because there's a bluff that overlooks a mountain valley below. You can build as big or as small a house as you want. But what you *can't* do is refuse our gift."

Dave didn't know what to say. He didn't feel like he'd done anything special. After all, he'd formed the Mountain Mercenaries for extremely selfish reasons. He'd been looking for his wife, and had found other women and children along the way. But looking around at the men he trusted with his life—and more important, trusted with the lives of his wife and child—he nodded and simply said, "Thank you."

~

Seven Months after Returning Home

Mags stood on the bluff of their property and looked up at her husband. The wind was gently blowing, and, at the moment, there was nothing but the sound of birds singing all around them. They were alone—well . . . almost alone—something that didn't happen often anymore.

Dave stood in front of her, his hands gripping hers as they faced each other.

When Dave had asked her to remarry him when they'd been in Peru, Mags had said yes. They could've had a big ceremony in front of their family and friends, but when Dave had suggested this, a simple but meaningful exchange of new vows with just the two of them, she'd jumped at the chance.

They'd both been in hell. A different kind of hell, but hell, nevertheless. And somehow reaffirming their vows with just the two of them seemed right.

All their family and friends were waiting for them back at The Pit. Gabriella and Harlow had made all the food, and there would be upward of fifty people there to help them celebrate. But for now, they just had eyes for each other.

"Margaret Crawford Justice, you are the love of my life. You are the reason my heart beats, and you give me the courage to get out of bed every day and face the world. I'm in awe of you and am prouder than I know how to put into words of your fortitude and strength. You're a warrior through and through," Dave said as he stared into her eyes. The wind blew her hair into her face, but before she could lift a hand to brush it away, Dave's hand was there. Mags shivered as his fingertips brushed against the sensitive skin of her ear.

"The only thing that kept me going when you were gone was the promise of one day being able to look into your beautiful blue eyes again. I give you my solemn vow right here and now that I'll always be there for you. I will never cheat. Never raise my hand to you or our son. I'll bend over backward to give you what you want and need. I'll love you for all the days of my life and even beyond that. You hold my heart and soul in your hands, Raven, and I wouldn't want it any other way."

Mags got lost in Dave's deep, brown eyes as he spoke. She swore she could see the love shining out of them. It was fanciful and silly, but she'd never forgotten how expressive his eyes were. How in the hell she'd gotten so lucky, she had no idea.

"The only thing that kept *me* going was thoughts of you," Mags said as she started her vows. She hadn't planned anything to say, wanting her words to come from the heart and to fit the moment. "I wanted to give up. Wanted to find a way to take my own life, but I couldn't do it. I knew you were looking for me. *Knew* you'd do whatever it took to find me . . . and you did. I didn't try to contact you when I had the chance, not because I didn't think you'd love me, but because I didn't think I was worthy of your love anymore. But it took less than two weeks after you found me to change my way of thinking, and to regret not finding a way to let you know I was alive, and to ask you to come get me and David.

"Love heals all wounds, and while I'll never forget what happened to me, your love has helped me take one day at a time, and to enjoy and live in the moment every day since. I love you, David Justice. I'll never cheat on you, and I'll stand by your side in support every day for the rest of our lives. Thank you for finding me. Thank you for not giving up. But most of all, thank you for loving me."

Dave moved his other hand up and cupped her head in his hands, slowly leaning forward and brushing his lips against hers. Then he did it again and again . . . until Mags was so turned on, and frustrated with how gentle he was being, that she thrust a hand into the hair at the back of his head and growled against him.

Her sudden passion surprised her. Mags loved her husband, but she'd worried that her libido had been suppressed forever. To find that she suddenly wanted Dave with a bone-deep need was surprising . . . and a huge relief.

She felt his lips curl up in a smile, but he didn't deepen the kiss.

He'd been so careful about not pushing himself on her. Not doing anything that might bring her demons to the surface. So Raven took control, showing him what she wanted. What she needed.

Thrusting her tongue into his mouth, she gave him the kind of kiss she hadn't had in years.

He moaned, and she felt his erection against her belly. But for the first time in a very long time, Mags wasn't turned off. Wasn't scared of a man's arousal.

Feeling giddy that her body was reacting the way it always had around Dave before she was taken, she gave herself over to him. Her husband.

How long they kissed on top of the bluff, Mags didn't know. But a loud backfire sounded in the near distance, and she pulled away, laughing.

"So much for our romantic renewal-of-vows ceremony," Dave said in disgust.

Mags wrapped her arms around him and lay her head on his chest. "The faster they build our house, the faster we can move in," she reminded him.

The construction crew was there working on building their dream house. Dave had wanted to give them the day off so they'd have the property to themselves when they said their vows, but Raven had disagreed, saying that every day they weren't working was one more day they wouldn't be able to move in. He'd agreed reluctantly.

"I love you, Dave. You mean everything to me."

"The words seem so . . . flimsy . . . compared to what I feel for you," Dave returned.

Raven smiled up at him—and flushed in mortification when her stomach chose that moment to growl. Loudly.

It was Dave's turn to chuckle. "Looks like I need to feed my girl," he said. "Come on. I'm sure David is driving everyone crazy with his impatience to dig into that cake."

As they walked away from the bluff toward Dave's car, Mags said, "Whose fault is it that he's got a massive sweet tooth?"

"Mine," Dave admitted immediately and without shame.

All Mags could do was shake her head. Deep down, she didn't care if Dave spoiled their son. He was trying to make up for his first four and a half years of his life when he was denied just about everything—food, love, friends.

Dave held open the door for her and waited until she was settled in the passenger seat before heading around to the other side. Before he started the engine, he leaned over and put his fingers on Raven's chin. He turned her head and kissed her gently. "Love you, Raven."

"Love you too."

As they drove toward The Pit and the huge-ass party that awaited them, Mags marveled once again over how lucky she was to have this man by her side. He was patient and loving and completely devoted to her. He wasn't without his faults, but it was hard to care much about them when he was so amazing in so many ways.

Soon, she'd gather up the courage to physically prove how much she cared. At one point, she truly hadn't thought she'd ever be able to share her body with a man again. Slowly but surely, Dave was resurrecting her desire, and she couldn't wait for the day she was able to make love with her husband . . . and purge the past once and for all.

~

One Year after Returning Home

Dave couldn't believe the house was finally built. They were finally moved in.

He hadn't minded living in an apartment for so many years, didn't care about much of anything other than finding his wife. But now that he'd had Raven back for a year, and had the privilege of seeing their son blossom into a well-adjusted and happy child, he couldn't imagine ever living in such a small, cramped space again.

Their house was a collaboration of both his and Raven's visions. Glass windows lined one side of the house, letting them see the beauty of the land at any time of day or night. They'd built an extra-large deck, and even had a small gazebo built out on the bluff.

The entire Mountain Mercenaries crew and their women had chipped in to help move their furniture, and they'd had an impromptu barbecue afterward, and Dave couldn't remember a time when he'd been this happy and content.

David had fallen asleep almost the second his head hit the pillow. He was excited to be sleeping in his room, and although Dave knew Raven was a little sad that he seemed to be growing so independent, she was pleased that he didn't seem scared in the least to be in a new room in a new house.

Raven had gone upstairs about ten minutes earlier while Dave finished putting the last of the dirty dishes into the dishwasher. Now he headed up the stairs toward their room, eager to hold his wife and to spend the first night in their new house with her in his arms.

He opened the door to the beautiful, huge master bedroom he'd designed with his wife in mind—and froze at the sight that greeted him.

Raven was standing next to their bed wearing a skimpy, white negligee.

When she saw him, she smiled. "It's about time you got up here," she teased. "I thought you were never going to finish up down there."

Dave didn't know what to say. He'd always found his wife attractive, but what he loved most about her was who she was as a person. Though he couldn't deny, seeing her standing there in nothing more than a scrap of lace turned him on.

"Raven?" he said hesitatingly, not wanting to misinterpret her intentions.

"It's time. I'm ready," she told him.

Dave walked slowly toward her and stopped two feet away, giving her space. "Ready for what?" he asked, wanting her to tell him exactly what her expectations were.

"Ready to make love to my husband. Ready to put my past behind me once and for all."

"Are you sure?" Dave whispered.

"One hundred percent. I'm not saying that this is going to be easy, or that I won't have any bad moments, but I have no doubts whatsoever that you'll be careful with me and won't push for more than I can give."

"Fuck no, I won't," Dave muttered. Then he slowly reached for the hem of his shirt and raised it over his head. He loved the lustful look in Raven's eyes. He'd dreamed about this moment, and it was so much more than he could've imagined. He stripped off his pants and socks, leaving his boxer briefs on for the moment. With how turned on he was, they didn't leave anything to the imagination, but Raven didn't even hesitate. She closed the distance between them and plastered herself against him.

~

Mags was nervous, but not about what her husband might do. She was unsure about her own reactions. She wanted this. Needed to make love with her husband. But even though she was one hundred percent in, she wasn't sure how her body might unconsciously react.

As she wrapped her arms around Dave and felt his erection against her belly, she wasn't the least bit repulsed. She inhaled deeply, and the scent of her husband filled her nostrils. He didn't smell anything like the others. Didn't feel anything like them either. He was big. Surrounding her and making her feel safe.

"Are you sure?" Dave whispered in her ear.

In response, Mags pulled back, slipped her hands under his boxer briefs, and palmed his ass. The muscles there clenched, and she smiled as she playfully dug her fingernails into the sensitive skin of his backside. "I'm sure," she told him, then moved her hands to his hips and slowly eased his underwear down until he was standing in front of her as naked as the day he was born.

She stepped back, keeping one hand on his biceps as she examined him. Good Lord, he was gorgeous. He might be in his late forties, but he looked better than she ever remembered him looking a decade ago. His thighs bulged with muscles, and while he didn't have a six-pack stomach, he certainly wasn't fat. He had a smattering of chest hair that she loved running her fingers through when they lay in bed together.

But it was his cock that she couldn't take her eyes off now.

He was a big man, all over. That hadn't changed in the last decade. It had been a long time since she'd enjoyed sex, but seeing him standing before her in all his naked glory reminded her of how he'd always made sure she came first. How gentle he'd always been. How she'd loved it when she could make him lose control. They'd enjoyed experimenting in bed and had made love in just about every conceivable position. She wanted that back. Needed it.

"Look at me, sweetheart," Dave said.

Realizing she'd been staring at his cock, she lifted her chin and met his gaze.

He was smiling down at her in amusement. "As much as I'm glad you aren't freaking out at seeing me naked, if we're going to do this, I'm going to need you to talk to me. I need to know where your head is every step of the way. If I touch you in a way that you can't handle, you have to tell me. Don't be a martyr. I can't do this if I think for one second you're uncomfortable but don't want to tell me."

"I will."

"I mean it, Raven. I already know you're a fucking warrior. You don't have to be one when you're in bed with me. You don't like something, you tell me. All right?"

And that right there was reason four thousand and sixty-seven why she was head over heels in love with her husband. "All right."

"Good." Then Dave slipped around her and lay down on the bed. He put his hands behind his head, and Mags could see the lust in his eyes. His cock wasn't completely hard, but was impressive even at half-mast.

She walked around to the end of the bed, climbed onto the mattress, and crawled toward him on her hands and knees. She watched as his dick twitched, and she grinned. She didn't stop until she was straddling his stomach.

The white teddy she'd put on had been a confidence booster. She'd come a long way from the skinny, malnourished woman she'd been a year ago. She'd put on weight in all the right places and had curves again. She felt sexy.

She reached for one of the straps and pulled it off her shoulder and down her arm. She did the same with the other one and let the nightie fall to her waist.

Dave's pupils dilated, and he licked his lips.

Mags had decided, while she'd been waiting for her husband to come upstairs, to take control of their lovemaking. She knew if she let Dave have his way, he'd take his time and do everything in his power to make it all about her. He'd be gentle, and while she wouldn't mind that, it wasn't what she wanted for this first time. She needed to take back everything that had been stolen from her, and at the top of that list was asking for what she wanted.

No, *demanding* it.

Reaching between her legs, she unsnapped the teddy and bunched the material around her stomach. She crawled forward on her knees until her pussy was over his mouth. "Make me come," she ordered.

Without a second's hesitation, Dave lifted his head and licked her from top to bottom.

They both groaned.

He took his time relearning her. Licking gently and nuzzling her folds. Every now and then his tongue would flick over her clit.

Loving his attention, but deciding he was taking too long, she reached for his hands, which were still under his head, and brought them to her sides. "Hold me," she told him.

His fingers dug into the sensitive skin at her hips, and she arched her back, letting him take some of her weight. But he still wasn't giving her what she wanted. She looked down her body and saw his eyes were open and staring up at her face, as if trying to read her state of mind.

She smiled.

"Lick my clit, Dave. Make me come. Please. I need it. It's been too long."

That was all he needed to hear. His fingers dug into her flesh, and he closed his eyes as he concentrated all his attention on her clit. His mouth formed a suction, and his tongue flicked at her as if it was a mini vibrator.

"Oh yeah, that's it. Right there! More . . . oh God, I'm going to come!"

Her orgasm rose hard and fast, and Mags hadn't been prepared for it. She undulated against her husband's face, but he kept hold of her and never lost contact with her clit. Her whole body shook as the orgasm overwhelmed her.

It felt so good.

So good.

It was freeing. She hadn't felt this way in a very long time.

Mags felt as if her bones were jelly. She rolled off Dave to the side, but made sure to pull him with her when she fell. He cautiously propped himself up on one elbow next to her and used his free hand to brush her hair off her face and out of her eyes.

"Make love to me," Mags begged as she gazed up at him.

"Are you sure? I'm perfectly happy to just hold you in my arms as we fall asleep," Dave said.

"I'm sure," Mags told him. "I need you now more than ever."

"You want to be on top?"

She loved how sensitive he was, but she shook her head. "No. I want you on top."

"It's not going to bring back bad memories?" Dave asked.

Mags shook her head again. "No. I want to look up at you as you take me. I want to hold on to your arms and wrap my legs around your waist. I know who's in my bed, Dave. You are. And you'd never hurt me. You'd never do anything I didn't want to do."

"Damn straight," he said as he eased himself over her and held himself there for a moment, as if giving her a chance to change her mind.

But Mags didn't feel even one second of panic. This was Dave. Her husband.

He used a hand to fit his now rock-hard cock to her opening, and then he paused once again. She knew how difficult this had to be for him, but he didn't let on that he was in any kind of erotic pain in the least.

Mags lifted her hips toward him, feeling the head of his cock slip farther inside. Dave's nostrils flared, but he held himself in check and slowly pushed inside her.

It was a little painful, as it had been a long time since she'd made love. They both let out the breaths they'd been holding when his hips met hers, and he was all the way in.

"Fuck, I love you," Dave whispered.

"I love you too," Mags told him.

"Are you good?" he asked.

She nodded. "I forgot how this felt. How good *you* felt."

"I never forgot, not for one second," Dave told her as he lifted his hips, then gently pushed back inside her. He did that a few times, making sure she was really all right.

"Faster," Mags urged.

To Dave's credit, he didn't ask if she was sure; he simply sped up his movements.

He was still holding back, though, Mags could tell.

She brought one of her hands down between their bodies and flicked her clit, making her hips jerk against him.

His steady rhythm faltered for a moment, and she smiled. Moving her hand lower, she caressed his length as he pulled out of her body, using her index finger to swirl around his balls on each downstroke.

"Damn, sweetheart. If you keep doing that, I'm not going to last."

"Who said you had to?" she asked.

"I want to make this good for you," he said between clenched teeth.

"You are. It is. And I want it to be good for *you*," she countered.

"It's never been better," Dave told her as he came up on his hands and stopped holding back.

Mags flicked her clit as he fucked her, and just when she was on the verge of a second climax, Dave stiffened over her and thrust as far as he could go. His whole body shook, even his arms, as he emptied himself inside her.

Mags was a little disappointed that she hadn't quite reached orgasm, but she should've known better than to think they were done.

Keeping himself inside her, Dave raised himself higher and stared down at her. "Keep going," he ordered. "Make yourself come."

She didn't need him to say it twice. She stared up at him as she masturbated. It felt even more intimate with him staring into her eyes. Her hips bucked up, and he slipped out of her with the movement. She moaned in disappointment, but didn't stop touching herself. Dave shifted until he was resting on only one hand and the other caressed her side, then he gently eased a finger inside her soaking-wet sheath.

He still didn't take his eyes from hers. "That's it, Raven. Fuck my finger."

And she did. His finger wasn't as thick or as long as his cock, but it felt amazing to have something inside her as she clenched and bore down on him, and her climax inched closer and closer to the surface.

He didn't try to take over, didn't push her hand out of the way, assuming he knew her body better than she did.

Within seconds, she lifted her hips up and flew over the edge. Mags closed her eyes, and her head tilted backward as she arched her back and came. She grabbed onto his biceps once more, grounding herself as the world turned inside out.

The material of the teddy dug into her waist, but she didn't even feel it. Dave's finger slipped out of her body slowly, and he lay on his side, taking her with him until she was lying next to him with her head on his shoulder. She threw one leg over his, and he palmed her ass as he held her to him.

When she could breathe again, she tilted her head back and looked up at him.

He was staring down at her with a look of love so intense, it would've scared her if she wasn't sure she had the same look on her own face.

"I feel like it's my birthday, anniversary, and Christmas all at the same time," he whispered.

"Me too."

Several minutes went by when they were both lost in their thoughts. Then Dave said, "Thank you."

"I think that's my line," she quipped.

"No, I mean it. Thank you for being so brave. I was prepared to go the rest of my life without making love with you again. I don't know how or where you've found the strength to do that after what you've been through, but I'm more thankful than I can say that you have the inner fortitude to power through. And I'm not saying that I'm thankful you had sex with me, I'm saying that I'm glad for *you* that you've been able to say 'Fuck you' to each and every one of those assholes who hurt you and not let them get you down. Does that make sense?"

It did. Every word. And Mags was pretty damn proud of herself too. "Yeah," she whispered. "It does."

Then Dave kissed her temple and climbed out of bed. He stood next to it and held out his hand. "Shower with me? Maybe without our clothes on this time?"

She grinned at his reference to that time in Lima, when he'd been hurt and smelled horrendous after spending time in one of the many dumps around the city. She reached out, took hold of his hand, and let him help her out of bed. She stood still as he pushed the teddy down over her hips, and shivered as his warm breath wafted over her chest, making her nipples harden.

Dave pretended he hadn't noticed her reaction, but of course he did. They walked into the huge master bathroom he'd spent way more money than she'd thought reasonable on, even though she was secretly as giddy as a teenager before her first date about how it had turned out.

As he leaned over to turn on the water, Mags couldn't help but ogle his ass. She was one lucky woman.

~

Seven Years after Returning Home

"This is absolute insanity," Allye Martin said to the rest of the women sitting on Dave and Raven's back porch.

"But we wouldn't have it any other way," Morgan said with a laugh.

The seven women agreed and smiled as they watched all the children, and their men, running around the backyard. They'd just finished the scavenger hunt that David had set up for everyone. He'd spent the last two days writing out the notes and hiding them all over their property.

Mags couldn't be prouder of their son. He was almost twelve and loved hanging out with Darby, Calinda, and all the younger children of their friends. They all thought of each other as cousins and saw each other all the time.

Harlow had two children, Chloe one, Everly had a set of twins plus one more, and Zara and Meat had decided not to have children, and instead had a menagerie of pets at home.

Peals of laughter rang out in the yard as the men played tag with the kids. David stood off to one side with Everly's youngest in his arms.

In some ways, Peru seemed a lifetime away for Mags, and in others, it seemed as if it were yesterday. But the women sitting around her now had turned out to be her saving grace. They'd laughed together and cried. They'd each been through their own traumatic experiences, and it felt great to be able to thumb their noses at the people who'd tried to take them down. They were all living amazing lives despite what had been done to them.

"David looks good," Zara observed. "He's not going to be very tall, though, is he?" she said with a laugh.

Mags shook her head. "Unfortunately, no. He's never going to have 'arms as big as tree trunks,' as he once said he wanted either." They all chuckled.

"But he's still a hell of a basketball player," Morgan observed.

"Well, he's a good shooter, but when the other kids grow taller than him, he's going to have a hard time getting around them," Mags said with a shrug.

"He's a good kid," Harlow said quietly.

Mags looked over at the other woman, trying to read her. "He is."

"No, I mean, he's a *really* good kid," Harlow said again. "The other day, he came over to help me and Gabby with the food we were preparing for the shelter, and he didn't complain at all about having to spend the whole afternoon with us. And when we got to the shelter, he immediately went over and started playing with the kids. I'm just saying, he might've had a rough start, but you and Dave are doing everything right with him. You should be extremely proud of him."

Mags's heart felt as if it was going to burst out of her chest. She *was* proud of her son. "Thanks. I'm sure we'll have some issues when he gets into his teenage years, but he's not only smart and athletic, he's empathetic too. I'm not sure if that comes from a part of him remembering how things used to be or what, but I'm thankful."

"Have you told him about Lima?" Chloe asked.

Mags shook her head. "Not yet. I will, when he's ready. He's asked to see pictures of him as a baby, and I had to tell him I didn't have any, not because I didn't care about him enough to take them, but because we were so poor when he was a baby, I couldn't afford it. That seemed to appease him for now, but I know he'll continue to have questions."

"I have no doubt you and Dave will figure out how to tell him about his past in a way he'll understand," Everly said confidently.

"I hope so," Mags said.

"Our men needed this," Harlow said after a minute went by.

Mags nodded. They did. They'd all gotten back from a mission a few days earlier that had been really rough. They'd raided a house in New York that had been rumored to have several women and teenagers being kept there against their will. The rumors had been right. They'd rescued eight women, all between the ages of fourteen and nineteen. Four were missing children from the States, and the other four were from Canada, Italy, and Mexico. They were all addicted to meth and being forced to pimp themselves out in order to get the drugs their bodies craved.

It was horrific, even more so because half the women didn't want to be rescued. They were all being cared for in various rehab facilities, and in the process of being reunited with their worried and very thankful families.

The Mountain Mercenaries had been instrumental in saving the lives of more than two hundred women and children over the last seven years, since they'd concentrated on missions in the continental United States. They'd even been given commendations by the president.

But if anyone saw any of the men on the street, they wouldn't see them as the larger-than-life saviors that they were. They'd see men devoted to their wives and families.

Calinda came running up to the porch panting, saying, "I'm thirsty, Mom. Can I please have something to drink?"

"So polite," Morgan murmured. Then louder, she said to her daughter, "Of course. Maybe this is a good time for a snack break anyway."

Calinda turned to the yard and, at the top of her lungs, screamed, "Cookie time!"

Everyone stopped in their tracks and ran toward the porch en masse.

Mags stood and laughed, just as the other women did as well.

Dave came up beside her and wrapped an arm around her waist, leaning down to nuzzle her neck.

"Ew! You're all sweaty!" she complained, trying to push him away even as she laughed.

"That just means I'll have to shower later," Dave whispered in her ear. "And if I get you smelly too, you'll have to join me."

Mags rolled her eyes. But secretly she loved that her husband was still as into her now as he had been before she'd been taken.

He held out an arm for his son, and Mags's heart twisted when David snuggled into his father's side. She knew the time was coming when he wouldn't want hugs from them anymore, so she tried to cherish each and every one they got.

"Hey, champ?" Dave said.

"Yeah, *Papá*?" David said, turning to look up at his dad.

"You stink."

David just laughed. "Yup. That's because it's hard work corralling all the kids and crawling around in the dirt helping them look for clues in the scavenger hunt. Would you rather I be inside reading or doing math problems? You're always telling me to go outside and find something to do."

Dave chuckled. "True. I was just pointing it out because your mom told me I smelled, and I didn't want to be alone in my smelliness."

"Dork," David said with a shake of his head.

Mags knew she was smiling huge. It was true, their son loved learning. He read anything and everything he could get his hands on, and adored logic puzzles and watching people solve math problems on YouTube. He wasn't much of a TV watcher, which she was thankful for.

They walked into the house, and the noise level inside was off the charts. But looking around at their amazing friends, and hearing the happiness and comradery, she couldn't help but feel content.

~

Ten Years after Returning Home

Dave lay on the blanket on the bluff between his wife and son as they all stared up into the star-filled sky. Every month or so they'd do this. Come outside after it got dark and simply soak in the goodness of the outdoors and enjoy being together.

David was getting older and busier. He was on the basketball team. Though he wasn't a starter and didn't get much court time, he swore he still enjoyed it. He wasn't very tall, only around five-nine, but the coach loved having him on the team because he was currently twenty-seven and 0 when it came to free throws. He was an excellent shot and was their main man when it came to penalty shots.

He was also on the robotics team and in the debate club. He was one of those rare kids who was friends with the popular crowd as well as the nerds and geeks. David didn't care how much money someone had or what their status was at school. He was nice to everyone and didn't discriminate or talk behind anyone's back. He was the first one to stand up for girls when they were picked on or treated like crap by others.

Dave was as proud as he could be of that. He didn't care about his kid's athletic ability, and didn't really even care much about his grades, other than he wanted him to at least pass his classes. What he did care about was the fact that David was compassionate and had learned how to treat women by watching his dad and "uncles."

David was also beginning to date, much to Raven's dismay. He knew she wanted her baby boy to stay young forever, but it was inevitable that their son would be quite the catch. The girls in his school knew he was a good guy, and that if they went out with him, they'd be treated right. Dave couldn't ask for anything more.

With how busy David was, and because he had only a couple years left in high school, Dave knew their time of hanging out, camping, and hiking, would soon be coming to an end. Lying around on their property staring up at the stars would become just another fond memory. It saddened him, but Dave knew it was all a part of his son growing up.

"I remember doing this with you back in Peru," David said suddenly, startling Dave out of his thoughts.

"You do?" he asked in surprise. "You were only four and a half."

"I know. But I do," David insisted. "We were hiding on a roof from the bad guys who were looking for us. We lay next to each other, just like we're doing now, and looked up at the stars. They weren't nearly as bright in the city as they are out here, but I was still in awe at the sight of them. You told me that you didn't know anything about what the stars were called, but you told me the stars had saved your life."

Dave blinked in surprise. He'd forgotten what he'd talked about on that roof with David all those years ago. But as soon as his son mentioned it, it came back to him as if it were yesterday. "Yeah. I told you that when your mom was lost, I'd look up at the stars and imagine her doing the same thing wherever she was. And the thought that we were looking at the same stars comforted me."

"And you saw a shooting star," David continued. "You said that you thought it was a sign that Mamá *was* out there, looking at the same stars right that second."

Dave heard Raven inhale sharply, and he reached for her hand, but didn't take his eyes from the multitude of brilliant lights above him. "That's right."

"I remember you said that when we got home, the three of us would do this. What we're doing now. Lie on the ground and look up at the stars. Together. I just . . . I just wanted to let you know that I remembered that conversation, and I'm happy to be here right this second. Lying here with you guys and looking up at the stars together."

Dave could hear Raven sniffling, and he squeezed her hand. "Me too, champ. Me too. And remember, no matter where you go in your life, no matter where you might live or what you might be doing, when you look up at the stars, your mom and I are thinking about you, and are so very proud of you."

He felt his fourteen-year-old son brush his hand against his own, and Dave took hold of it and held on tight.

They lay like that, all three hand in hand, and gazed up at the stars for a long time. Thankful for what they had and for each other.

Life wasn't always easy. In fact, all three of them knew for a fact that life could be a son of a bitch. But it was the people you surrounded yourself with that made it better. And Dave knew they had the most amazing people in their lives, and that made all the difference.

~

Fifteen Years after Returning Home

"Who's the letter from?" Dave asked as Raven came back into the house after getting the mail. She'd ripped open the envelope on the way back to the house and had her head bent reading as she walked.

He knew it could be from any number of people. Daniela, Teresa, Bonita, Carmen, Maria, or even their son, who was off at college. For some reason, they all loved writing actual letters back and forth, rather than communicating via faster and more efficient emails. It was a weird quirk, but he couldn't deny he loved watching his wife's face light up when a letter came in the mail for her.

"Maria," Raven said, not looking up. "She had her baby. They're both doing well. She says she wants to come up and visit in a few months."

"That's great, sweetheart. It'll be good to see her again. How many kids is this for her now?" Dave asked.

"That was her fifth."

Dave whistled low.

That got Raven's attention. She looked at him for a long moment, then padded over to where he was sitting on the couch. "Are you sorry we didn't have any other kids?"

Dave immediately shook his head. "No. I love David with all my heart. But I'm also selfish, and I'm glad I didn't have to share you with anyone else."

She rolled her eyes and shook her head at him.

Dave pulled her down onto his lap and rested his chin on her shoulder as she brought the letter back up to continue reading. He couldn't understand a word of it, as it was written in Spanish, but he knew it was full of happy news, since his wife was chuckling under her breath as she read. When she was done, she folded the letter and put it back into the envelope. He knew she'd immediately write back that evening so as not to make Maria wait for her response.

"The guy I'm considering selling The Pit to is coming over to check the place out later. Want to come with me to show him around?"

"Of course. Are you sure you want to sell?" Raven asked, turning in his arms.

"Yes. I'm ready to relax and not have to worry about ordering stock and dealing with assholes anymore. I'm not getting any younger, you know."

Raven scoffed. “Even at almost sixty, you can still overpower just about anyone. Especially drunk assholes who get a little too handsy and disrespectful.”

That was true, but now that the Mountain Mercenaries had retired as an active team, he wanted to enjoy his twilight years with Raven. He hoped they still had decades left together, but the last thing he wanted was to regret spending so much time working if something happened to either one of them. They both knew how short life could be, and he didn’t want to waste one second of it.

Money wasn’t an issue. Between his investments and the sale of The Pit, he and Raven wouldn’t have to worry about money. They could simply enjoy life.

“I know, but I’m ready to have nothing better to do than sit on our back porch, sipping coffee and enjoying your company.”

Raven laughed. “As if that’s all you’re going to do once you sell the bar. I know you, Dave. You’ll find some project or another to get involved in. You have to be busy. You have to help others.”

“Then we’ll find others to help together,” he said simply.

Raven nodded. She curled her arm around his shoulders and rested her forehead against the side of his head. “Together. I like that.”

“Always,” Dave told her. He looked at his watch. “I think we might have time to . . . shower, before we have to go meet the buyer.”

Raven shook her head and rolled her eyes. “But I’m not dirty.”

“I can get you dirty,” Dave told her with a straight face.

“You think you can keep up with me, old man?” Raven asked as she jumped off his lap and headed for the stairs.

Grinning, Dave gave her a head start before jogging to catch up. He heard her giggle from the stairs above him and, for the eight-millionth time since he’d found her in Peru, said a silent prayer of gratitude that she was here with him, healthy and whole, before he ran up the stairs after her.

~

Twenty Years after Returning Home

Dave felt Raven's fingernails dig into his forearm as they sat in the bleachers at the University of Denver and watched their son stand up to give the commencement address.

Everyone had come out for the occasion: Gray and Allye, Ro and Chloe, Arrow and Morgan, Black and Harlow, Ball and Everly, and Meat and Zara. Gabriella was also there with her husband and two young kids.

Dave had tried to give them all an out, saying that graduation ceremonies weren't exactly the most exciting things to sit through, and that they'd meet them all back at The Pit—now under new management, but still owned by Dave—but they'd said there was no way they were going to miss hearing David give his speech.

David was one of the smartest people Dave had ever met, and he didn't think that just because he was his son. Today, he was celebrating earning his applied quantitative finance master of science degree. He'd already been hired by a mutual-fund company based in Denver as a financial engineer. He'd had more than a dozen job offers, but he'd chosen a job that was close to Colorado Springs and his family. David had always remained close to Raven, and Dave loved watching their bond continue to grow deeper with every day that passed.

"He looks so good," Raven whispered. "I'm so freaking happy for him."

Dave squeezed his wife with the arm he'd wrapped around her, and he turned his attention to his son up on the platform in front of the crowd.

"Good afternoon. Provost, deans, family and friends, and of course, fellow graduates. Thank you for giving me the honor of speaking with you at our graduation today. We've been through a lot of late nights, gallons of coffee, and stressful meetings with our thesis advisers. But we made it. We're here!

"And let me tell you . . . it's literally a miracle that I'm standing in front of you today. I have a story to tell you, one that I've never publicly talked about. It's more about my mother than it is about me, though.

"I was born in Lima, Peru, in a locked compound where my mother was held captive. She'd been kidnapped from Las Vegas, and forced into the human-trafficking trade. Day after day, she was abused, but when she found out she was pregnant with me, she begged her captor to allow her to keep her baby.

"He allowed it, but when the time came, she was locked in a room by herself to give birth. Then she was thrown out, separated from her baby, and with no money, she was forced to find a place to live and forage for whatever food she could scrounge. But every Monday, Wednesday, and Friday, she walked ten miles to come see me. You see, the man who'd imprisoned her had decided to keep me for his own depraved reasons."

David paused when the audience gasped.

"That's right. My future was set on the day I was born. There was no need to educate me because all I was good for was making money for a sick, twisted, evil man. But . . . obviously that didn't happen, because I'm standing in front of you today.

"My mother taught me English. She taught me math and my colors. She taught me the meaning of human decency.

"When I was four and a half, and hours away from being separated from my *mamá* forever, my father appeared like the larger-than-life hero I'd always thought he was after hearing stories about him all my life. I wasn't even five years old, but I remember lying on the roof of a building in Lima, as the bad guys did their best to find us, looking up at the stars with my *papá* . . . and being happy. I was too young to understand what had almost happened to me, but not too young to know that the man who'd carried me away from the bad guys would keep me safe.

"My mother and father are my heroes. They never laughed at me when I wanted to stay up late watching YouTube videos of people solving math problems. They encouraged me to be a good person and to keep mean and judgmental comments to myself.

"What's my point? First . . . human decency. Have it. Every time I turn on the TV, I see stories of people being robbed, shot, and hurt by others. Then I log on to my social media account and see people ripping into others, complaining about their lives, and generally being mean or miserable, simply because they feel as if it's their right to be so. There's nothing wrong with having an opinion, but you don't always have to share it. The next time you pass someone begging on the street, maybe stop and talk to them. If you see someone using food stamps in the grocery store, if you've got the money, maybe offer to pay for their meal, give them a break. Don't judge others until you've walked a mile in their shoes.

"And second, I don't think anyone who might've seen the kid I was in Peru would've thought I'd be standing here in front of you today. But *everyone* has the potential to succeed if they're only given the chance. Don't judge someone for the clothes they wear, the color of their skin, or how much money they have.

"And *Mamá*? Thank you. Thank you for not giving up. For loving me enough to get through one day. Then the next. Then the next. Thank you for seeing the potential in me and loving me despite the circumstances of how I came to be. Thank you for bringing *Papá* into my life. For giving me a man I can look up to. Someday, I hope to be half the man he is. And thank you for showing me what a healthy, loving relationship looks like. It's laughing, crying, fighting, but at the end of the day, it's about enjoying every single moment of life with someone at your side.

"Today, we've earned our degrees, but just holding a piece of paper doesn't make us smarter or better than someone who hasn't had the resources and opportunities to do the same. As you go forth into your lives, remember to be decent human beings. Live every day as if it's your last, and appreciate those around you. Thank you."

The crowd immediately erupted into thunderous applause, and Dave stood alongside his wife. He was immensely proud of his son and felt a little teary eyed at hearing his words. Turning to Raven, he saw tears coursing down her cheeks.

Leaning down, he said into her ear, "You okay?"

Still crying, she looked up at him and said, "I'm more than okay."

Dave used his thumb to wipe the wetness off one of her cheeks. "You sure?"

She beamed. "These are happy and proud tears. I love you."

"Love you too."

They turned and watched their son shake the hands of every person on the platform. Then, as he made his way back to his seat, he was stopped by just about everyone he passed with a fist bump, a handshake, or a thump on the back.

Dave beamed with pride as his son sat back in his seat. He was an exceptional young man, and Dave was proud to call him his son. He just knew David was going to make a positive difference in the world.

~

That night, after arriving home from a celebratory dinner, and after sitting on their back deck talking about the beautiful ceremony they'd attended that day and how proud they were of their son and all he'd accomplished, Dave and Raven eventually moved inside to the couch.

Once upon a time, Mags might've been embarrassed about David telling her story to an auditorium full of people, but she'd long since decided that she didn't have anything to be ashamed of. If her story could help even one other person who might have been in a similar situation, it would be worth it.

She and Dave had sat him down when he was a senior in high school and told him the entire story of his life before he'd turned five. How he'd been conceived, how they didn't know who his biological father was, and what he'd lived through in that small house that belonged to del Rio. They even told him what the evil man had planned for him, how Dave had arrived in the nick of time to save him from that life, and how he'd gotten them both out of Peru and back to Colorado Springs, where they'd made a new life.

David hadn't said much. Had just listened intently. But when the entire story was out, he'd taken his mom in his arms and told her he loved her and was proud of her for all that she'd endured. He'd thanked her for taking such good care of him and said as far as he was concerned, from now and forevermore, Dave was his father, he had no desire to ever step foot back in Peru, and he certainly had no intention of ever wanting to find the rapist who had gotten his mother pregnant. It had been a tough conversation, but David had taken it like the mature young man he was.

Mags hadn't expected him to open up about his past in his speech today, but she couldn't have been prouder of the amazingly smart and compassionate man he'd become.

Feeling content and mellow, she snuggled into Dave after he sat down next to her. Being with her husband and having his arms around her was one of the places she felt the safest.

As they sat there, each lost in their thoughts about all that had happened that day, Mags couldn't stop herself from asking something she'd wondered about off and on for the last twenty years.

"Dave?"

"Yeah, sweetheart?"

"You killed del Rio . . . didn't you?"

He looked surprised at the question, but as soon as the shock showed in his eyes, he wiped his face clean of all emotion. "Why would you ask that? You know I didn't leave your side after we came home.

I think it was around three years before I was able to spend even one night away from you and David."

"I know you didn't do it yourself, but you arranged it . . . right? It's okay," she hurried to say. "I'm not upset about it. I just . . . I need to know."

Dave pulled her closer, and Mags went willingly. She curled her hand around his belly and rested her head on his shoulder. They might be in their sixties, but she and her husband still enjoyed pleasing each other in bed, and she would never get tired of snuggling with him.

"I didn't kill him . . . but I know the team of men who did. I called in a favor. It was one they were happy to take on."

"Did he . . . did he suffer?" Mags held her breath as she waited for his answer.

"Yes, Raven, he did. I'm not going to tell you the specifics, because you've lived with enough shit in your head because of that man, but rest assured that he knew exactly who sent the men who killed him, and why he died the way he did."

Mags let out the breath she'd been holding. "Good. I'm glad. I love you, Dave," she whispered. "I don't know what I did to deserve you, but I do know one thing."

"What's that?" he asked.

"I'd go through everything that happened to me all over again if it meant I'd end up right here with you now."

"Raven," Dave whispered, but he didn't say anything else.

"Thank you, *Rex*. Thank you for making sure no one else suffered as I did. You're my hero."

"No," Dave protested. "You're *my* hero. I've never met a stronger or more amazing woman in all my life."

Mags leaned up and kissed Dave's jaw, then rested her head back on his shoulder. Wanting to lighten the moment, and feeling settled inside for some reason, now that she knew Dave had had a hand in killing her tormentor, she said, "David did good today, didn't he?"

"Hell yeah, he did," Dave said with a smile. "Are you watching this?" he asked, gesturing to the television with his chin.

"Not really, why?"

"I thought we might head upstairs."

Mags smiled. "Oh yeah? Got something you want to show me?"

"Oh yeah. It's something I know you'll love too," Dave told her, moving her hand from his belly down between his legs.

"You're a dirty old man," Mags teased as she felt him harden beneath her palm.

"And you're a dirty old woman," he returned. "*My* dirty old woman."

Grinning huge, Mags stood and held out her hand. "Well, then, let's just head upstairs and see what trouble we can get into."

As they walked hand in hand up the stairs to their master bedroom, Mags kept her eyes on her husband's ass, and smiled. She'd been through hell, there was no denying it, and she'd chosen not to be a victim, but a survivor. And people might not believe her, but she'd been happier over the last twenty years than she'd been in her entire life. And it was all because of the protective alpha man holding her hand and practically dragging her to bed.

"Love you, Dave."

He stopped just inside their bedroom and turned. He wrapped his arms around her waist and pulled her close so they were plastered together. "I love you, too, Raven. You'll never know how much."

She smiled because she *did* know.

Without another word, Dave pulled her toward the bed, and as her husband laid her down on the mattress, Mags knew she was the luckiest woman in the world.

Author's Note

Thank you all for reading my Mountain Mercenaries series! When I started writing *Defending Allye*, I wasn't sure what Rex's story might be. But the more I wrote, the more excited I became to get to the final book. Both Rex and Raven have been through hell, but I love that I was able to give them the happily ever after they deserve.

You may be curious about the other "team" Rex knows . . . the one he called to take care of del Rio. You'll get to know all about them in my new, upcoming series! The men of Silverstone Towing are dedicated to ridding the world of evil—no matter what it takes.

I appreciate each and every one of my readers. Thank you for picking up my stories. And remember to always be kind.

About the Author

Photo © 2015 A&C Photography

Susan Stoker is a *New York Times*, *USA Today*, and *Wall Street Journal* bestselling author whose series include Mountain Mercenaries, Badge of Honor: Texas Heroes, SEAL of Protection, Ace Security, Delta Team Two, and Delta Force Heroes. Married to a retired Army noncommissioned officer, Stoker has lived all over the country—from Missouri and California to Colorado and Texas—and currently lives under the big skies of Tennessee. A true believer in happily ever after, Stoker enjoys writing novels in which romance turns to love. To learn more about the author and her work, visit her website, www.stokeraces.com.

Connect with Susan Online

Susan's Facebook Profile and Page

www.facebook.com/authorsstoker

www.facebook.com/authorsusanstoker

Follow Susan on Twitter

www.twitter.com/Susan_Stoker

Find Susan's Books on Goodreads

www.goodreads.com/SusanStoker

Email

Susan@StokerAces.com

Website

www.StokerAces.com

Newsletter Sign-Up

http://www.stokeraces.com/contact-1.html